MARINA HEMINGWAY
A NOVEL

The story—follows Dan Fletcher, who left a lucrative job in the Las Vegas gambling industry with a vision of finding a native girl on a South Pacific island. His journey is cut short at his first port, a mere 90 miles from Florida, when he falls for an exotic Cuban beauty. From cigar smuggling to tracking down a despicable villain, Dan finds himself, seemingly against all odds, in his quest for romance and revenge.

At the heart of the novel—is Lily Lopez, whom we first meet when Dan encounters her in a Cuban discotheque. Lily turns Dan head-over-heels, but she dreams of finding a rich Italian and living in Italy. Tragically, she learns too late the perils of looking for greener pastures.

Cuba—is the setting for this partly true novel that takes a look at Fidel Castro's oppressive management of ten million people and emphasizes the shortcomings of the communist management of a beautiful island.

Dick Barrymore—is a detailed storyteller and a thrilling, inventive narrator. Sometimes his writing is contemplative and easygoing – but a lot of it is also too wildly TRUE! Sometimes the details carry the narrative along so fast the reader has no idea where the story is headed and can't wait for the next chapter.

MARINA HEMINGWAY

Dick Barrymore

Note for Librarians: a cataloguing record for this book that includes Dewey Decimal Classification and
US Library of Congress numbers is available from the Library and Archives of Canada. The complete
cataloguing record can be obtained from their online database at:
www.collectionscanada.ca/amicus/index-e.html
ISBN 1-4120-3756-5
Printed in Victoria, BC, Canada

TRAFFORD

Offices in Canada, USA, Ireland, UK and Spain
This book was published *on-demand* in cooperation with Trafford Publishing. On-demand publishing is
a unique process and service of making a book available for retail sale to the public taking advantage of
on-demand manufacturing and Internet marketing. On-demand publishing includes promotions, retail
sales, manufacturing, order fulfilment, accounting and collecting royalties on behalf of the author.
Book sales for North America and international:
Trafford Publishing, 6E–2333 Government St.,
Victoria, BC v8t 4p4 CANADA
phone 250 383 6864 (toll-free 1 888 232 4444)
fax 250 383 6804; email to orders@trafford.com
Book sales in Europe:
Trafford Publishing (uk) Ltd., Enterprise House, Wistaston Road Business Centre,
Wistaston Road, Crewe, Cheshire cw2 7rp UNITED KINGDOM
phone 01270 251 396 (local rate 0845 230 9601)
facsimile 01270 254 983; orders.uk@trafford.com
Order online at:
www.trafford.com/robots/04-1584.html

10 9 8 7 6 5 4 3 2 1

ACKNOWLEDGMENTS

I would like to thank my friends who suffered through early manuscripts and offered encouragement. Special thanks to Bill Mirams, Ron Funk, Wayne Schafer, Jerry Simon, Jim Houston, Harry Leonard, Paul Allen, and my Cabo Pulmo neighbors: Earl and Ridge Rickers, Danny Weinstein, Parke and Sheila Johnston, and Cremin Huxley.

I would also like to thank my Cuban connection, Martha, who painstakingly edited the historical facts and translated the novel into Spanish.

My appreciation to William Greenleaf for walking me through the many rewrites and the manuscript's much-needed final edit.

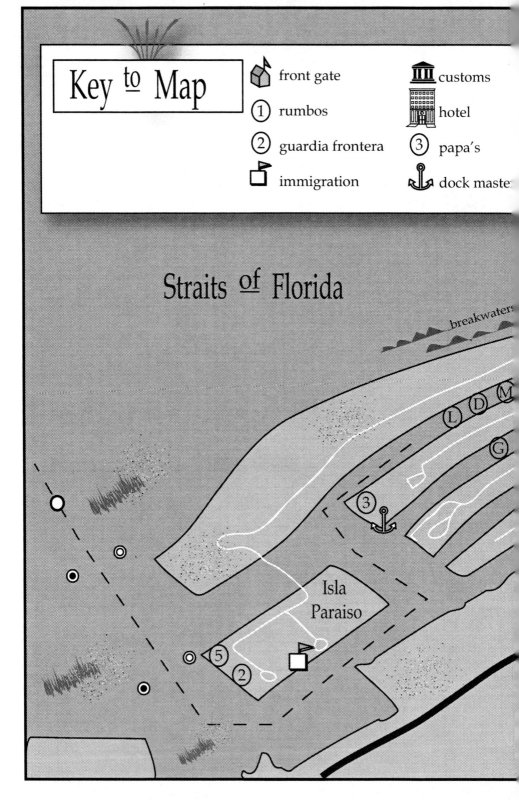

Key to Map

- front gate
- ① rumbos
- ② guardia frontera
- immigration
- customs
- hotel
- ③ papa's
- dock master

Straits of Florida

breakwaters

L D M

G

③ ⚓

Isla
Paraiso

⑤

②

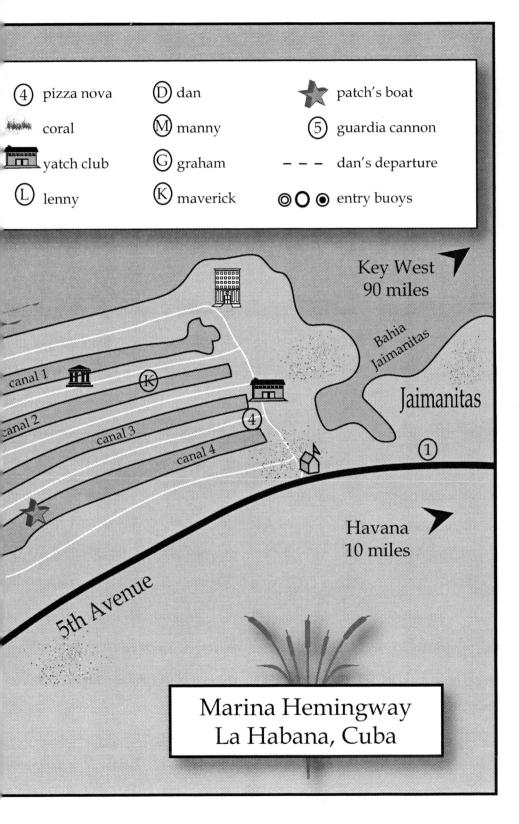

4 pizza nova
coral
yatch club
L lenny
D dan
M manny
G graham
K maverick
patch's boat
5 guardia cannon
- - - dan's departure
◎ ○ ◉ entry buoys

Key West
90 miles

Bahia Jaimanitas

Jaimanitas

canal 1
canal 2
canal 3
canal 4

K

4

1

5th Avenue

Havana
10 miles

Marina Hemingway
La Habana, Cuba

PROLOGUE

THE STRAITS OF FLORIDA – 2000

T he slapping of the tiny chop against the tubes of the Zodiac was the only sound Dan Fletcher heard as he lay on the undulating floor of his nine-foot inflatable dinghy. He stared up at the blue sky, dotted with puffy white clouds, then sat up to scan the horizon, half hoping to see a boat.

If he hadn't been afloat in the middle of the ocean without food or water, he mused, it would be a perfect day for fishing. Five or six birds were dipping into the sea a few hundred yards away, picking up scraps of bait – a sure sign of game fish feeding. *Drag a green and white feather through that area at eight knots*, he thought, *and I'd have me a nice Dorado.*

The sea conditions were unusual for this time of year: calm, with just a slight breeze blowing out of the west. He estimated his position to be about halfway between Cuba and Florida on the ninety-mile rhumb line between Hemingway Marina and Key West. He wore tennis shoes, a pair of blue shorts, and a stained white shirt. He was thankful for his sunglasses and his red baseball cap with *Mighty Mouse* emblazoned on it in white letters, the latter a gift from Miles Clinton, a fishing buddy from his days of chasing the fast-swimming yellow-fin tuna off the southern tip of Baja California.

Those were the good old days of launching a fifteen-foot Boston Whaler off the beach at dawn and heading out at full throttle over the glassy clear waters of the Sea of Cortez, the most fish-infested body of water in the Western Hemisphere. His salivary glands tried to moisten his dry mouth as he remembered dipping thin raw tuna slices into soy sauce, hot *wasabi* horseradish racing through his sinuses. He could almost taste the cool white Zinfandel as it chased the day's catch down his throat.

He smiled as he caught himself fading off into dreamland. He was helplessly facing a life or death situation – and he was thinking about eating tuna.

What a dilemma, he thought. *How the hell did I manage to get myself stuck out here, halfway between Florida and Cuba, floating around in a rubber boat? Maybe I should have stayed and taken my chances with the Cubans.*

The Cubans had taken a dim view of his unscheduled departure from Hemingway Marina, but waiting to clear the port authorities, customs, immigration, and the Cuban Coast Guard would have meant sticking around and taking a chance on getting his head blown off by Pencil-thin and his sidekick Fat-face. If it hadn't been for Big Mac risking his own neck with his Cuban intelligence pals and telling him to get the hell out of Cuba, he most likely would have been found dead in his bunk. As it was, he had lost his forty-foot sloop after the Cuban Coast Guard lobbed a lucky shot from their ancient cannon at the marina and hit the bow at the water line.

After plugging the hole with pillows and working the manual bilge pump, he had managed to nurse the sinking vessel through the black night into international waters until it finally went down at daybreak. There had not been much time to assemble a survival kit, but he had managed to grab a gallon of water and the bag of money and throw them into the dinghy before abandoning ship.

He looked at the bag of money lying on the wet floor of the dinghy and wondered if he would soon be willing to trade the two hundred thousand dollars inside it for a few sandwiches and a fifty-five gallon drum of cold water.

He estimated that the Gulf Stream would carry him east and into the shipping lanes. The current would eventually turn northeast and run parallel to the Florida coastline, where it would come within ten or fifteen miles of land. But that would be at least a hundred, maybe two hundred miles. Even with the current running at two or three knots, he was looking at four or five days of drifting.

A feeling of despair came over him as he recalled the stories of Cubans who had found themselves in similar situations while trying to escape Fidel Castro's oppressive regime. Thousands of those escapees had never reached the land of freedom. Literally cooked in the sun, they had died at sea from dehydration and its precursor seasickness, their empty rubber boats, inner tubes, and makeshift rafts eventually found washed up on Florida beaches. What made him think that he would be one of the lucky floaters to be picked up by a passing freighter? Did he really think he would be awoken one morning by the bump of his raft as it gently nudged a white-sand beach on one of the Keys?

A smile crossed his face as he visualized himself stepping out of the dinghy and ordering a beer and a burger at the palm-thatched beach bar. Why not? *Life has been good to me, he thought, and I'm not going to end it out here floating around in this stupid raft.*

He took another long look at the horizon, still hoping to see a boat. He had a flare gun, a smoke bomb, and a white T-shirt tied to an oar. If a ship came by, he'd damn well get their attention. Meanwhile, he'd rest and conserve his sweat by keeping covered.

Actually, he was quite comfortable. It was a nice day to bob around on the water and ponder where it had all gone wrong. He had been so happy and full of adventure when he had left Key West a year ago and set sail for Havana, the first port on his world cruise.

CHAPTER
1

Dan Fletcher sat at the helm and watched the bow slip through the troughs of a deep blue sea. If he had ever had any doubts about his actions over the last six months, they were gone now. He was on the adventure of his life, on his way to a crystal-clear cove lined with coco palms. He envisioned an outrigger canoe coming toward the boat. A topless Polynesian girl wearing a necklace of flowers was smiling and paddling slowly toward him.

Under white clouds and a blue sky, Dan arrived at Cuba's Hemingway Marina, a relatively easy overnight sail from Key West. After too many years as a dealer and pit·boss in Las Vegas, Dan had sold everything he owned to pursue his lifelong dream of sailing to the South Pacific. He had purchased a forty-foot sloop in Florida and hired Eugene Kopt, a sixty-year-old professional sailboat captain, to drill him on ocean sailing. A romantic at heart, Dan saw himself as Tyrone Power in the old movie *Son of Fury*. He would escape from England on a square-rigger sailing vessel to a tropical island, find a treasure in pearls, and marry the beautiful native girl played by Gene Tierney.

After taking on water and fuel in Florida, Dan had left the United States with a hopeful heart to begin his world cruise. His first stop was the forbidden communist island of Cuba.

When he reached the marina's white entrance marker, he started the fifty-horsepower diesel auxiliary and brought the boat into the wind. He flipped on the autopilot and furled the Genoa from the cockpit. After securing the mainsheet, he went forward, lowered the sail, and raised the yellow quarantine flag. He returned to the cockpit, took the boat off autopilot, and turned back toward the marina channel.

He pressed the transmit button on his handheld VHF radio. "Hemingway Marina, this is the vessel *Pass Line*. I am entering the marina and have the channel markers in sight."

The reply came back in excellent English. "*Pass Line*, this is the dock master. Welcome to Marina Hemingway. Proceed straight ahead until you pass the *Guardia Frontera*, then turn left and tie up at the customs dock. Do you copy, *Pass Line?*"

"Roger, Hemingway. Pass Line is proceeding past the *Guardia Frontera* to Customs."

He released the button on the radio and said aloud to no one, "Right. Just where the hell is the *Guardia Frontera?*"

He continued straight ahead, keeping to the center between the red and green pilings that stuck ten feet out of the water a half-mile ahead. He noticed that the channel was extremely narrow, with shallow coral reefs showing their ugly teeth as the sea rose and fell on the brown barriers. There was a breeze out of the east, forcing him to crab the boat to stay in the center of the channel.

It was his first foreign port, and Cuba was about as foreign as a place could get. More than one sailor in Florida had told him that the penalty for Americans going to Cuba could cost him his boat. Sailors willing to take the risk often received a letter from the U.S. Treasury Department demanding big fines and threatening prison time. No one could recall a case where a tourist had been criminally prosecuted, but there were stories about stiff fines levied against sailors who had tried to get back into Florida with a few boxes of Cuban cigars.

Dan was not worried about being arrested or fined because he was not planning to take his boat back to the United States. Cuba was the first stop on a cruise that he thought might just take the rest of his life. He was fifty-five, retired, and in no hurry.

He was barely moving as he approached the nearest dock and brought the boat to rest alongside the concrete quay.

A middle-aged man wearing a white coat approached. "Hello, Captain. I am Doctor Francisco Serrano. May I come aboard?"

Dan nodded and waved his right arm. "Of course. Please do."

The mild manner of the man put Dan immediately at ease. He watched the doctor open a briefcase and take out a pair of white shoe covers that he put on before stepping onto the boat.

"Is it possible to go below?" the doctor asked.

"Sure," Dan said, "but it's a hundred and ten degrees down there."

The doctor just smiled and disappeared down the companionway.

Dan followed with a shrug. Evidently business was not done on deck.

Once below and seated at the table, the doctor produced a list of foods that could not be brought into the country. "Do you have any chicken, eggs, or fruit?"

Readily compliant, Dan got up and produced a dozen large grade-A eggs from the refrigerator.

The doctor shook his head. "Eggs are forbidden," he said politely before quickly adding, "If you were to put on a pot of water and start boiling them, you would not be required to give up the eggs."

"You mean hardboiled eggs are okay?"

The doctor nodded. "Cuba has no salmonella – and doesn't want any."

Dan watched the doctor take out a small can of aerosol spray and make his way forward with a slight hiss from the can, leaving a smell that momentarily relieved the boat of its normal moldy odor.

Before leaving, the doctor asked if Dan could make a small donation. "Perhaps a ballpoint pen?"

Dan gave him a pen and wondered if the rest of the landing process was going to be as easy. *Where are the storm troopers with machine guns who are going to stand me up against the wall and interrogate me?* he wondered. *After all, this is Cuba, Fidel Castro, and the red commie bastards that America is at war with.*

Next aboard was the immigration agent, who looked briefly at Dan's U.S. passport and issued a thirty-day tourist permit.

Customs checked the boat for drugs and firearms and made a note of electronic equipment, cautioning Dan to make sure he had all items listed on board when he left the island.

Pass Line was then cleared to proceed to Berth No. 36 on the first canal. When the boat was secured, Dan walked to the bow and stood in the pulpit with one hand on the forestay. He looked to the west at billowing afternoon clouds and inhaled the smell of the ocean that drifted in with the breeze out of the east.

"Well, here I am. I did it – my first stop."

It had been just two hours since he had sailed into Marina Hemingway, and he was comfortably secured at a dockside slip complete with 110 volts of electricity and fresh water. The doubts he had brought with him from Florida were gone. The boat had sailed well, and he had felt confident during his first crossing. *After all*, he surmised, *a trip around the world is just a bunch of short trips like the one I just made.*

He was a mere ninety miles from Florida, but he felt like he was already halfway around the globe.

CHAPTER

2

Dan Fletcher was born in Los Angeles and grew up in the sprawling San Fernando Valley when it was still a dry, dusty suburb of L.A. From the day he was old enough to hitchhike, he spent weekends and summers at Malibu, where he learned to surf.

In high school, Dan liked to wear his blond hair long, sometimes tied back against his forehead with a blue band that matched the color of his eyes. One of his female friends once told him that his straight jaw line, high cheekbones, and strong nose made him look like a museum statue. His classmates started calling him *Vike*, short for Viking.

By the time he finished high school, he was a lean, six-foot-one athlete who excelled in track, football, and swimming. He finished first in the league in freestyle – and near the bottom of his class in academics. It was just as well – Fletcher's idea of freedom and adventure did not include the mundane regimentation of a higher education.

The day after graduation, Dan joined the U.S. Navy and applied for the tough UDT corps, precursor of the now famous SEALS. He finished first in his class and earned the right to pick his next station. He chose Hawaii and spent the rest of his four-year enlistment at Pearl Harbor. His summers at Malibu gave him good basic surfing skills, and he soon melded into Oahu's North Shore surfing community. Instead of roaming Honolulu's cheap bars with his Navy buddies, Dan spent his free time camping in an old panel truck at Sunset Beach, where he became one of the island's better big wave riders.

On one of the nights he did go to town with his shipmates, a big Samoan broke a beer bottle over the back of his head as he took on two Hawaiians in a sleazy Hotel Street bar. He finished the fight, but it took sixty-six stitches to close the cuts on the back of his head.

Fletcher's barroom brawl brought the coach of the Navy boxing team to see him, and Dan soon found himself studying the fine art of pugilism. Between the rigorous UDT maintenance training, his weekend surfing, and the workouts in the gym, he was in the best condition of his life. He managed to hold his own in the Pearl Harbor Wednesday night fights and was promoted to chief third class because of his efforts. But Dan lacked the killer instinct to take boxing any further than just a good conditioning sport.

Fletcher's athletic activities left him little time to pal around with his shipmates, who spent their evenings in Honolulu. They were constantly goading Fletcher into giving up just one surfing trip in order to spend a couple of nights having some fun.

"You guys must be sick," he told them as he recalled his last trip to town. "Why would anybody in his right mind keep hanging around Hotel Street?"

"Because that's where the girls are, and that's where sailors hang out – that's why."

"That's stupid," Dan answered. "Because that's also where the locals hang out looking for sailors to beat up." He rubbed the back of his head. "And I got the scars to prove it. Besides, the island is loaded with nice girls who never heard of Hotel Street."

"That's the trouble with you, Fletcher. You're looking for a nice girl."

It was true. Dan was a romantic. He planned to see the world after his tour in the Navy. He vowed to see the South Pacific. Maybe hire on as crew on one of the big sailboats that left Honolulu for Tahiti. Instead, he found himself living and working in Las Vegas after his discharge.

Dan was home in California living with his parents and adjusting to civilian life when he got an offer he could not refuse. His uncle Andrew had driven across the desert from Las Vegas in his new Cadillac convertible for a weekend visit and offered to take Dan back with him to see the sights of the bustling gambling Mecca.

Once in Las Vegas, Dan was blown away by the action of the city, where casinos with no windows or clocks took the bettor's money twenty-four hours a day.

Andrew was a chef at Bernard's Saddle Club in downtown Las Vegas and arranged for comp tickets to most of the best shows on the Strip. After a week of nonstop entertainment, Dan decided to stay.

His uncle put him up in the spare bedroom and got him a job bussing dishes at the club. Dan was a personable young man and well liked by the staff. It took only three weeks before he was moved from the dining room to the one-arm-bandit area, where he cleaned ashtrays, carried out trash, and collected coins from the slots, carting the heavy sacks to the counting room.

When his boss recommended him for dealer's school and offered to pay the tuition, he jumped at the chance, learning to deal 21, poker, and baccarat. The toughest was craps, a fast game with different bets and changing odds. Dan was fascinated with the action and learned fast.

He breezed through the school and went to work for Bernard. He loved the job, and after three years at the Saddle Club, he moved up to the Strip and began working at Wilbur Clark's Desert Inn. Dan Fletcher was under an apple tree, and the apples were getting ripe. The Vegas boom was on, and he

•

was established as an experienced dealer. He was making $55,000 a year and living in a new apartment complex, complete with a swimming pool that was usually filled with bikini-clad change girls and cocktail waitresses. He dressed in casual desert clothes and drove a Mustang convertible.

Life was good – until he started to gamble.

His addiction began the night he made $22,000 shooting craps at the Sands. He told himself it was just for the thrill of it. After that, he was hooked and could hardly wait to get off work and hit the tables at the hotels on the Strip.

Within two weeks of his big win, Dan had lost the $22,000 plus everything in his savings account. Living in Las Vegas with a gambling habit meant having a ticket on the fast train to poverty.

Fortunately for Dan, a tall blond cocktail waitress saved him. Her name was Nancy, but her girlfriends called her Bambi. She turned men's heads, and the girls often told her that with a body like hers, she could be making a thousand a night as a dancer in a strip bar.

Nancy talked Dan into joining Gamblers Anonymous, and with both of them working, the family account began to grow. The marriage lasted four years.

Once a year he took his thirty-day vacation and went to Baja, where he camped at his favorite surf spot, ate lobster, speared fish, and rode waves. And on his last trip there, as he sat on the sand after a great day of overhead surf and wondered where his life was going, he decided to make some changes.

He had been in Las Vegas for thirty years and had worked his way up to pit boss at the prestigious Hilton Hotel. It was a great job, but other than his annual trips to Mexico, there was no adventure, no spontaneity. He couldn't help wondering what had happened to the dream of sailing into the palm-lined harbor and meeting the beautiful native girl. Where was his island and Gene Tierney? Life was slipping by, and it was time for a change.

When he got home from his trip, he gathered up his financial records and headed down the street to his favorite coffee shop, an out-of-the-way all-nighter called Foxie's. He took his normal booth in the back, just as Emma plopped the empty cup down.

"You know where it is, Danny boy." Emma had worked at Foxie's since Dan had first started coming in sixteen years ago.

"Thanks, Emma."

He always sat in the back, a half step from the fresh brew. He preferred pouring his own, and he and Emma had come to an agreement long ago. Dan filled the cup, sat back down, and began spreading his papers out on the table.

An hour later, he leaned back and studied the figures. The gambling business had been good to him. He made good money at the Hilton, lived comfortably, and put as much as he could into investments. He avoided having money lying around for fear of slipping back into his old gambling habit.

He had started building his savings by putting away ten thousand a year into a mutual fund retirement program and had increased the amount gradually. Other than the small payments he paid on the house mortgage, his expenses were minimal, and investing in the market seemed to satisfy his urge to gamble on the tables. By letting it ride on the downside, he had watched his stocks weather several storms, including a couple of market crashes. He wondered if his ex-wife was as well off after leaving him – a departure that had come out of the blue, with a goodbye note waiting for him on the kitchen table after another nightshift.

He worked the calculator until he found what he was looking for. If he quit his job, sold the house, and walked out today, he could live comfortably after investing in an offshore money market. He found it hard to believe that a $40,000 house could be worth a half million dollars a quarter of a century after buying it. That was what a similar place down the street had sold for three months ago.

Without planning it, Dan Fletcher had lived the American dream: he had taken a job, bought house, made payments, saved – and waited. He had been playing craps with life by betting he would live long enough to spend his savings. Now it was time to cash in his chips and leave with his winnings. He had watched too many gamblers at the tables let it ride. They always walked away broke. He doubted if riding the market would leave him broke, but he was over fifty and into the sixth decade of his life. He had about ten, maybe twenty years of quality time left. It was time for a change. It was time to go looking for the native girl on the island.

He gave the Hilton his two weeks' notice the next morning and put his house up for sale. And he bought every boating magazine he could find and started shopping. His plan was simple. He would buy a plane ticket to Florida, the boating capital of the world, and look for a sailboat. A few months of cruising around the Keys, and he'd be ready to take off for the Caribbean and Central America, then through the Panama Canal to the South Pacific.

Finding a boat in Florida had not been a problem; there were hundreds on the market. In the end, he selected a sturdy French-built Gib'Sea and equipped the forty-foot sloop for a world cruise. He named the boat after the best bet on the craps table: *Pass Line*.

He was thankful for the weekends of sailing on a fellow worker's Cal-40 in regattas off Newport Beach – at least he knew the bow from the stern. And navigation was not a problem; he had had plenty of that in the Navy. But solo cruising was not something to be taken lightly. Dan hired Eugene Kopf, a sixty-year-old professional sailboat captain, to drill him on ocean sailing.

Kopf took his assignment seriously but also kept his sense of humor. More than once he dragged Dan out of bed at 3:00 a.m. during a downpour and made him take *Pass Line* out into the Gulf Stream, where he carefully watched him manage the boat by himself in heavy seas.

Dan's first solo voyage was from Fort Lauderdale to Key West, a 230-mile, two-day shakedown cruise to his jumping-off point into the Caribbean.

CHAPTER

3

D an studied the layout of the marina on the map he'd received at the port captain's office. According to the literature, Hemingway Marina was known as one of the best hurricane ports in the Caribbean. There were four well-protected channels about a hundred feet wide and a half-mile long. Boats were tied up along the concrete quay, allowing mariners easy access to their vessels.

It took the rest of the day to tidy up the boat and settle in for a lengthy stay. The final touch was setting up the direct TV satellite antennae dish.

He poured himself a rum and Coke and tuned in to the world news station. He hated CNN like an addict hated his addiction. Bad news was reported twenty-four hours a day, every day of the year. It was always the same: theft, rape, and murder, with a war thrown in once in a while for good measure.

But he couldn't help himself. He felt as though he would be missing something if he didn't catch the breaking news, whether that meant learning of another ethical misstep amongst the Kennedy clan or watching footage of protestors as they burned down their neighborhood, complete with close-ups of kids climbing through broken store windows with television sets on their shoulders.

He knew he was hooked on the news station, and had spent more than a few moments wondering why he and millions of other people felt it necessary to tune into the all-news station instead of a PBS broadcast of the New York Philharmonic performing Tchaikovsky. Yet here he was, glued to the set, making sure he was up-to-date on world politics, the windstorm in Chicago, and the box office success of a new Arnold Schwarzenegger film.

It was a major flaw in his character. He laughed to himself as he remembered coming home from Mexico years earlier only to find out he had missed a whole war after the Falkland Islands conflict began and ended during his vacation.

I'm sick, he thought. *Here I am on the first leg of a world adventure, and I'm sitting down here in this cave, drinking alone, glued to a television screen. Fuck it! I'm changing this life. Right now.*

He reached over and turned off the set, feeling a twinge as he realized he was missing the results of the president's weekly popularity poll. He slipped in a CD of famous tenors, turned up the volume, and took his drink up on deck.

Up above, he found the horizon on fire. The setting sun, hiding behind a row of low cumulus, fired red spikes skyward into a mural of high stratus. A dull red glow radiated off the sea and bathed the marina in pink pastels. Pavarotti was halfway through *Che Gelida Manina* as Dan sipped his drink and took in the panorama, thinking, *What could be better than this?*

The answer came in a quiet feminine voice from the quay behind him. "*Hola.*"

Dan snapped his head around and looked up into the face of an adorable young woman dressed in shorts and a halter-top. "*Hola* yourself. Do you speak any English?"

"*Si.* I have brother who live in Miami. Where you from?"

"*Estados Unidos.*"

God, he thought, *she can't be more than eighteen.*

She smiled, and a mouthful of white ivories stretched across her face as she climbed aboard.

He stood up and moved to the companionway. "How about a drink?"

She nodded and sat on a cockpit cushion.

Dan hurried below to get a glass. He reached down into the refrigerator and grabbed a cold Coke. When he turned around, he was surprised to see her standing behind him.

She looked around the interior. "*Que lindo.* It is a beautiful boat."

"Thank you. And you are a beautiful girl." She was about five-four, with a short brown pageboy haircut that barely covered her small ears. "How old are you?"

She moved forward to accept the rum and Coke and looked up into Dan's eyes. "Nineteen." She kept eye contact as she took a sip from the glass. "Do you have a girlfriend?"

Before he could answer, she turned away and walked slowly to the front of the cabin, letting one of her small hands drag casually along the dinette.

She peaked into the V-berth, opened the door to the head, took a seemingly uninterested look, and moved her gaze back to Dan, who was studying her slow-motion movements.

He was frozen. There had not been a sensation in his groin like the one that was pulsating down there now since high school. He was alone with a cute little teenager that stood before him on pale thin legs, accentuated by a pair of white shorts barely shrouding a perfect bubble butt. And she was asking if he had a girlfriend.

When he tried to speak, it came out a hoarse whisper. "No," he rasped. "No girlfriend. I just arrived a few hours ago."

She smiled as she moved toward him. She set the glass down as she passed the table, moved closer until her head was almost touching his chest, and said in a teasing voice, "Do you want one?"

Dan Fletcher was speechless. In his wildest dreams, he had never imagined a situation like this. *I can't believe this,* he thought. *She's young enough to be my daughter.*

He did not answer. Instead, he took her face in his hands, bent down, and kissed her full-unpainted lips.

Her tongue darted into his open mouth as her hands unbuttoned his Levis, pulled his pants down to his knees, and took a firm hold of his hard manhood. She looked down, then back to his flushed face, and said, "Ah, a beeg one."

Then, without letting go, she moved backward toward the V-berth.

Dan obediently stumbled forward with his pants down around the knees. *If this is the way men seduce women here, I love this country.*

He lay in a sweaty state of exhaustion with his eyes closed. He was afraid to open them, for fear he would wake up and find it had only been a dream. He knew he didn't have to ask, "Was it good for you?" Shit, no one could move – and scream – like that without having a climax.

She lifted her head from his chest and said, "*Mi amor,* will you get me a Coke, or some juice, with ice?"

Her request was his command. He made his way to the refrigerator and pulled out a carton of mango juice, along with his only tray of ice from the tiny freezer compartment.

By the time he had broken out the cubes and poured the juice into a plastic tumbler, she was beside him, fully dressed and looking at her watch.

"Oh my God," she said, "Look at the time." She downed the cool drink. "I have to go."

She reached up and pulled his head down, guiding his lips to hers, then scampered up the companionway.

"Hey, wait a minute!" he called. "When will I see you again?"

She was already on the cement dock, putting on her shoes. "Tonight. Meet me at Papa's Disco. Eleven thirty." She spoke without looking up, then disappeared into the night.

Dan went below and sat on the settee, wondering what had just happened. He had just made passionate love with a teenage goddess and failed to even get her name.

His wonderment turned to anger a few minutes later, when he put his pants on and found that his money clip that held more than a hundred dollars was missing.

•

13

Later that night, Dan walked down to the end of the dock to Papa's
Disco. Fifty girls wearing everything from evening gowns to spandex leotards
lined the entrance. Every pair of eyes was on him as he walked the gauntlet
of women, and he felt like a piece of raw meat at feeding time in the big cat
exhibit at the San Diego Zoo.

He scanned the lineup, looking for the tart who had stolen his money.
He wanted to find her and give her a couple of raps on the noggin with his
knuckles.

No such luck. She was too clever to show up here. She was good at what
she did. Good at sex, and good at the stealing part. She had asked for the juice
and the ice to give herself enough time to go through his pockets, get dressed,
and head for the dock before he could put his pants back on.

There was a five-dollar cover charge at Papa's, but boat owners got in free.
Two of the more aggressive girls approached Dan and asked if he would take
them in with him. Why not? he reasoned. If every single guy took in two girls,
it would be a two-to-one ratio in there and the opposite of any club he had
ever been in.

He slipped the girls five apiece and walked into the disco. He was surprised to find out he was wrong about the ratio. The place was packed, with
four girls for each guy.

Dan immediately liked Papa's, an outdoor cement pad at the end of the
dock with water on two sides. Palm-thatched roofs covered the bar, two dance
floors, and a kitchen that served barbecue chicken.

The place was teeming with people, some of whom were seated behind
white plastic tables. Most of the girls were dancing with each other while their
men chatted at the bar. There was movement everywhere. The night was alive
with loud music that drowned out most of the bar conversation.

"What a place," Dan said to himself as he took in the popular marina
nightspot. He could feel the cool breeze drifting in off the Florida Straits as
he watched the dancers move on the floor – perfect for cooling hot sweaty
bodies on humid tropical nights.

The disc jockey dropped the needle onto a fast salsa number, and twenty
single girls hit the dance floor, gyrating their torsos wildly and over-revving
the imaginary rpm meter in Dan's head.

He made his way to the far side of the oval bar, carefully avoiding eye
contact with a dozen lascivious females, and took a seat on one of the fixed
cement stools to order a rum and Coke.

Behind him, six attractive girls were crowded around a six-foot-high
glass-enclosed claw machine. For a dollar bill, a person got two chances to
position the three-fingered crane over small stuffed toys. Once positioned, the

release button dropped the claw. With precision positioning and a little luck, the claw lifted the stuffed animal and dropped it into the recovery chute.

One look, and Dan wondered who the lucky guy was that had that franchise. *What a scam. Deposit a dollar, and with some skill you might win two stuffed toys worth ten cents apiece.* Dan smiled. Success would be to own a string of bunny machines in Cuban discos. It made him wonder. Here was a communist country where Castro owned everything and Cubans made the equivalent of seven dollars a month. How could a bunch of teenagers spend dollar after dollar on a toy vending machine?

Across the bar sat a cutie with seven small animals lined in front of her as she sipped a *cubalibre*. This disco was a microcosm of conflicting systems: communism and capitalism. It was a state-owned establishment with booze, music, women, dancing, and profit.

He hadn't taken the first sip of his drink when a *chica* came up behind him and asked for a dollar for the *Maquina de muñecos*.

Dan's bar stool was closest to the action, and after several requests for dollars and cigarettes, he changed a twenty into ones and ordered a pack of Marlboros and a propane lighter. He set the bait on the bar, and his evening of entertainment began to take shape. He was soon the center of attention, handing out dollar bills for the bunny machine and lighting borrowed cigarettes from his open pack. He sat back and smiled at the enthusiasm exhibited by the girls cheering for each other as they tried to grab the stuffed animals.

He was down to the last dollar on the bar when she appeared. She came from nowhere and tapped Dan on the shoulder. When he turned around and looked into her eyes, he lost his breath.

Pretty or beautiful did not begin to describe her. She had dazzling green eyes with a slight oriental slant, long silky black hair that cascaded halfway down her back, and a full Whitney Houston mouth. She couldn't have been more than twenty. Dan Fletcher was in love.

She reached over his shoulder, picked up the pack of Marlboros, and asked, "Still passing these out?"

Dan nodded and reached for the lighter as she pulled out one of the smokes. She took a deep draw and blew the smoke out away from him. Then she took the last dollar, looked into his confused eyes, and gently pulled him off the stool and over to the glass machine.

After inserting the bill, she placed her hand on the control bar and asked, "What's your name?"

"Dan," he stammered. "What's yours?"

"They call me Lily."

He stood there, paralyzed. "Did anyone ever tell you that you look like Gene Tierney?"

"I don't know who Gene Tierney is, but I'm sure he is a very handsome man."

He started to explain, but words failed him. He just looked at her.

"Well, Dan, would you like to guide me in, or should I guide you in?" She laughed as his jaw dropped. "The machine, Dan, the *muñecos.* Tell me when I have it lined up."

His head was buzzing as he studied the arrangement of the toys in the glass case and motioned her to move the stick a hair to the right.

She pressed the release button, and the claw dropped onto a miniature pink bunny. The three prongs closed on one leg and the head, then slowly lifted the little rabbit and dropped it into the recovery chute.

"One down, one to go," she said as she kissed the little toy.

On the second try, Dan moved to the other side of the glass and once again motioned the claw into a winning position. Their five-minute relationship produced two stuffed toys.

She held the animals to her chest and said, "Thanks." Then she smiled and added, "I live in Baracoa."

When Dan didn't reply, she turned and disappeared into the crowd.

Why didn't I say something? he fumed. *I let the love of my life just walk away. I must be going nuts.*

Dan wandered into the crowd, hoping to catch another glimpse of her. As he picked his way through the dance floor, he spied her in the corner dancing to a hot salsa number with a girlfriend. Chills ran from his feet up through his body.

She wore a black satin dress that stopped just above the knee and was held up by one thin shoulder strap. If she was wearing underwear, there was no visible sign of it. A long thin neck lifted her to a statuesque height. He estimated her at five-nine or ten. She had long legs with slender thighs and no sign of saddle britches. Her breasts were too small to make her a candidate for a centerfold, but shape and placement made up for any lack in size.

When the music stopped, she moved off the floor with the grace of a black panther stalking its prey.

He wondered (A) if it was possible for a body like that to be filled with passion and (B) what it was going to take for him to experience that passion.

Dan envisioned the scene: his head between her thighs, her head thrown back in ecstasy, with her hands messaging her nipples, then crushing the pillow to her face to drown out her cries.

He came back to reality and quickly rearranged the bulge in his pants by pulling the erection straight up inside his Levis and covering the protruding head with his tropical shirt.

Two girls at the bar noticed the awkward maneuver and gave a good laugh.

He spent the rest of the night looking for Lily, but she disappeared before he could get a telephone number or even her address. He walked back to the boat determined to fulfill his fantasy.

CHAPTER

4

Dan left the marina on foot and walked two blocks to Rumbos, the local watering hole. Two weeks had passed since he met the mysterious Lily, and he was hoping to run into her at the little outdoor bar in Jaimanitas, which sold ice cream bars, fried chicken, cheap bottles of rum, and expensive sixty-cent cans of cola. The adjoining vine-covered disco, the closest bar to the marina and a good place for sailors to meet women, sold mixed drinks and played loud salsa music on a tape deck.

Dan approached the small opening in the seven-foot-high iron fence that surrounded the outdoor establishment just as his boat neighbor Lenny pulled up on his dilapidated Honda scooter.

"Hi, Dan."

Dan noticed that Lenny was dressed in his girl-hunting attire. Brown suede shoes peeked out from under straight-legged khaki Dockers, the latter held up by a white canvas belt. A white silk shirt with bloused sleeves topped the outfit. He looked like a yachtsman with money to burn in the clubs of Havana, but nothing could have been further from the truth. Lenny Kowalski, a wiry 53-year-old Polish immigrant who had moved to Canada in the early 50s, was a retired steel worker living on a thousand-dollar-a-month pension.

He had spent ten years building his current home, a crude 36-foot cutter made of ferro-cement that had lumps on its dirty white hull to prove it. The two-inch-thick concrete boat was so tough that Lenny claimed he once dropped dynamite over the side to blow away some of the coral reef he was stuck on.

When Lenny exited the front gate of Hemingway Marina, he became Leonardo, a dashing gentlemen that God had given to the beautiful women of Cuba

Lenny wanted to find a woman. Not just any woman. He wanted to fall in love with a young beautiful Cuban and live happily ever after – on his thousand a month.

Lenny prowled the cheap neighborhood bars late at night, searching for his future wife. The girls at Rumbos had him pegged as another middle-aged tourist looking for sex.

"How're you doin' tonight, Lenny?"

"Leo, Dan. Leo."

"Yeah, I forgot. Let's go in. I'll buy you a drink."

As they made their way through the crowd of people sitting around white plastic tables stained brown from years of spilt beer and rum, Dan scanned every face, hoping to see Lily. Later, he would make his way around to see if any of the girls knew about her. Where did she go at night? Who did she hang out with?

"The locals are out early," Lenny commented.

One of the girls in the crowd yelled, "*Hola*, Leonardo. You buy me a *cubalibre* tonight?"

"*Si, chica. Mas tarde.*"

The girl laughed, knowing there would be no rum and Coke from Leonardo later. The locals knew him as *Tacaño*, Spanish for cheap. Lenny's idea of helping a girl's family buy food was fifty cents at the end of a romantic evening.

"Let's go into the disco, Dan, and see if there's any new talent from out of town."

When they were seated, Leo played the part of tour guide. "Rumbos has a constant turnover of women who come from the eastern part of the island. They come here from towns like Holguin, Camaguey, and Las Tunas, looking for a good time, maybe meet a tourist who will buy them ice cream and *cubalibres*."

"Kind of like us, eh, Lenny? Oops – Leonardo," Dan said, rolling the *r* and lending a *th* sound to the *d* so that the word came out *Lee-o-narrr-tho*.

"Yeah, except the rich guys take them to the disco for a night of dancing. They think it's like the States. Wine 'em and dine 'em and hope to get laid. It's not that complicated here, Dan. A normal date with a *chica* usually ends in bed, and Cuban women are not shy about asking for some cash on their way out the door."

Lenny waved an arm at the crowd. "All these ladies enjoy rum, dancing, and sex – and not necessarily in that order."

Rumbos' house band struck up a lively salsa beat, enticing bodies, with or without partners, to step out onto the beer-stained cement dance floor. Many of the *chicas* danced with each other or just moved alone, keeping time with the music.

Lenny talked Dan into buying a bottle of three-year-old Havana Club for $3.50 and a six-pack of Coke for five dollars. The bartender brought a bucket of ice and a half dozen plastic cups.

"We got six lines in the water," Lenny said as he arranged the bait on the table. "I bet we get a hookup within five minutes.

"You know, Dan, I been thinkin'. I'd like to take a shot at settling down with just one girl. I'm getting tired of the one-night stands. Sometimes I wake up in the morning wondering what the hell I've been doing. Like the night I took twins back to my place because I couldn't decide which one was more beautiful: the blonde or the brunette. God, they were heavenly. I gave each of them ten dollars when they left the boat at five-thirty in the morning after pleading with them to stay. But they said their mother would not let them stay out later than six a.m. I never saw either of them again. Where did they go? Were they out for just one adventure? Did their parents discover the twenty dollars and give them hell? Was it so much money that they retired from nightlife? Who knows? It's Cuba."

Lenny went on, recalling the night two lesbians came to the boat and produced a variety of toys that included a vibrator and two giant dildos. He was pretty drunk for that one.

He poured himself a half-cup of Dan's rum and splashed in a little cola. "*Salud*," he said, eyeing several girls at the next table. "What's up, Dan? You still looking for that gal you met at Papa's?"

"Well, yeah. I'd like to run into her again." He tried to act nonchalant. "Her name is Lily. You haven't seen her around, have you?" Dan regretted asking the question as soon as he asked it. For all he knew, Lenny was about to launch into some raunchy story about having a wild night with Lily.

"I think she was in here last week. A real beauty. Long black hair. Kind of an oriental look in the eyes?"

Dan's heart skipped a beat. "That's her. Does she hang out here?"

"Don't know. First time I ever saw her in here, and she came in and left alone. I think she was looking for someone."

Lenny seemed more interested in the three *chicas* approaching the table. "Forget Lily, Dan. Concentrate on what's right in front of you. Look what's coming."

He motioned the trio to sit down and began pouring drinks.

Dan didn't say anything. If he made up his mind to take a woman back to the boat, it would be as easy as ordering a beer, but like his previous evenings, he held out hope of spotting Lily.

He hated the thought of being compared with single men who came to Cuba looking for sex and love – in that order. Sex was no problem for a guy like him. In his brief stay in Cuba, he had learned already that if a man wanted to meet a woman, he only needed to stand still for five minutes in a Havana nightclub. Very few *chicas* spoke English, but they could home in on a North American from across a smoke-filled bar like a SCUD missile attacking a radar site in the Middle East. Eye contact for more than two seconds resulted in the sexy young lady sauntering across the room and speaking her four practiced words of English: "Where are you from?"

A reply of "*Estados Unidos*" brought a wide smile and some Spanish expression like "*Que bueno.*" Adding "Hollywood, California" sealed the deal.

An American with a fat wallet who came to Cuba looking for love usually lost his wallet without finding any love, but donating to the economy of the working class carried a special satisfaction.

For the *chicas*, it was a way of escaping the mundane Castro system of shared boredom. Unlike many people in rich First World countries, Dan was not quick to call it prostitution. He sided with Cuba's attitude of leaving pious principals to the rest of the world. He was happy to find a place where sex with a stranger carried a lesser degree of guilt than having a coffee date in the States with a new acquaintance. He saw Cuba as one of the world's few countries where social structure and religion had not ruined one of man's most basic and pleasurable emotions.

Under the Castro dictatorship, Cubans didn't have much, but it didn't keep them from enjoying life. A young, attractive Cuban woman had two choices: sing, dance, and make love with some poverty-stricken Cuban, or go out and do it with a man who would buy her a fine meal in a fancy restaurant and pay her way into a disco where she could dance all night. Afterward, she could make love on clean sheets in a private room with a hot shower and TV. Later, the guy might slip a twenty-dollar bill into her hand after taking her home in a taxi. If she did that twice a week, she could quench young hormones, have fun, and take home more in seven days than her father brought home in five months as a government worker.

On one of his first visits to a disco, Dan was approached by a young girl and asked if he would give her some money. When he told her that only prostitutes asked for money, she was not in the least offended. She went on and said that she never went with a man she didn't like and that she did not charge for sex, she simply accepted donations for a new blouse or a pair of shoes, if offered. On some occasions, she said, if her date did not offer, there was no harm in asking if he could come up with a little money to buy her a gift, was there?

"But you just came up and asked me for money."

"This is different. You look like a nice guy, and I really need a new pair of *chooze.*"

Up until then, Dan had met three basic types of women in Cuba: those who never asked for money, those who sometimes asked for something at the end of the evening, and those who took a more direct route. The latter made their deals up front, minus any bullshit. They were high-fashion hookers who hung out at the expensive clubs, dressed in evening gowns, and wouldn't get close to a tourist without setting a price. The local *chicas* who appeared at Rumbos around ten o'clock in the evening fell into all three categories.

Lenny was in deep conversation with a cute little blonde who had just arrived from out of town and who was happy to be in the presence of what she thought was a rich yachtsman.

Dan poured himself another drink and noticed that the bottle was empty. He knew he had been in another of his melancholy moods and had drunk too much. He was aware of a body next to him, too close. When he looked to his right, he was staring into the eyes of a not-so-pretty woman who would not qualify as a *chica*. She was about thirty and overweight, with kinky, greasy hair, and a missing front tooth. Leaning on the palms of her hands with her elbows resting on the wet table, she looked to Dan like a giant vulture waiting for something to die. He knew he was drunk because he had never seen a vulture up close.

"Len, I mean, Leonardo," Dan said, the words seemingly too thick to push out, "I've had it. See you later."

When he rose from the table, the plastic chair tumbled back and hit the floor. *Yep*, he thought, *I'm drunk*. He said goodbye and made his way out of the bar and headed back to the boat.

Lenny watched Dan stagger out, then ordered two more Cokes and a bucket of ice. When the waiter left the table, Lenny pulled a small plastic tube from inside his shirt, removed the restraining clip, and squeezed the rubber hot water bottle inside his left armpit. Cheap Cuban rum ran from the tube and filled the plastic cups. The *chicas* squealed with delight. The bartenders were not fooled by Lenny's clandestine activities, but said nothing. Hey, it was Cuba. Everybody had a scam.

Lenny had three women with him at the table, but he was concentrating on the new girl from Holguin named Ella. She was small, blond, shy, and very pretty. By 2:00 a.m., Lenny was in love and suggested she accompany him back to the marina to see his yacht. Ella wanted to know how she would get home.

Lenny, ever the gentleman, told her, "On my scooter, *mi amor*. I have a motor scooter."

Once back at Lenny's boat, they disappeared into the cement sloop and didn't come out for three days.

CHAPTER
5

Graham Wellington came out of the tiny shower and yelled at the body wrapped in covers. "Hey, Maria. It's ten-thirty – time to go home."

It was a cardinal sin to send a lovely female home while he was sporting a woody, but abstaining from morning mattress gymnastics would give him more energy later. He had a date that night with a stunning blonde he had met at the Cuban Expo the night before last.

Graham was walking proof that the male sex drive doesn't end with middle age. He was seventy years old with a well-defined muscular body. His baldhead, gray mustache, and wrinkled face were the only indicators that he was over forty.

There was a light tap on the fiberglass cabin top.

Graham looked out the porthole and saw Dan Fletcher standing on the quay. "Hurry up, Maria," he hollered as he climbed up into the cockpit. "I got company."

He had taken a liking to Dan. He enjoyed his humor and carefree attitude. "Hi, Dan, jump aboard."

Maria wiped the sleep from her eyes and fluffed up her short pageboy haircut. She bumped her head as she made her way out of the aft cabin. She quickly slipped into her skin-tight spandex slacks, pulled on a blouse, and reached for her shoes.

"Put 'em on after you get off the boat," Graham warned. "You'll end up in the canal."

Maria, he knew, had no intention of putting on her new shoes and adding mileage on the soles just to get home. She smiled at Dan as she came topside carrying the red-spiked heels.

Graham handed her a twenty for cab fare, knowing it would only cost four.

She kissed her finger and pressed it to his lips. A faint smile crossed her mouth as she turned and climbed out.

The two men watched as she sauntered down the sidewalk carrying her evening shoes in both hands.

"It still amazes me the way Cuban women handle the morning after," Graham muttered as he threw Dan a cockpit cushion. "Never a sign of guilt, just minor irritation at being rousted out of bed so early. She'll probably go

•

23

home and sleep for another eight hours. How 'bout you? Still chasing that black-haired beauty? What's her name? Lily?"

"Yeah," Dan replied nonchalantly, "I connected with her that first night at Papa's but haven't seen her since."

Graham was moving back down the stairs into the boat. "Hang on a minute. I'll get us some coffee. I got a new pot almost ready."

The aroma of the freshly ground Cuban coffee beans drifted up out of the cabin of the 38-foot *Benateau*.

Graham had been entertaining the night before, but his boat was never anything but spotless. After running his own charter business for forty years, he kept things shipshape at all times.

The former sea captain could tell Dan enjoyed hearing him expound on his sailing experiences, not to mention his favorite topic: women.

Born in Sussex, England, Graham earned a degree in literature at Oxford before he was twenty-two. He came from a long line of Wellingtons and was expected to follow in his father's footsteps as a professor at the local university. Instead, he took a job on a tramp steamer out of Liverpool and never looked back. The sea was where he wanted to be.

At the age of twenty-eight, he bought his own sailboat, single-handed the 42-foot ketch to the West Indies, and started his own charter company. Thirty years later, wealthy clients were paying sixty thousand dollars a week to book his 135-foot luxury motor-sailor.

Graham ran a tight ship. He stocked it with the best French wines, Argentinian beef, Russian caviar, and a crew of attractive women.

"I used hundreds of women crewmembers over the years," he had told Dan during a conversation at the bar. "There were three qualifications for applicants: young, good looking, and they had to agree to do exactly what the captain said." He smiled and added, "Every woman who ever crewed for me knew the job included sleeping at least once with the captain."

Graham was a wiry, leather-skinned connoisseur of fine wines and good Cuban cigars. After selling his big yacht, he retired at age sixty-six and banked the cash in his offshore savings account. He had purchased a new 38-foot sloop four years ago and parked it in the Hemingway Marina.

When Dan asked him, "Why Cuba?" Graham looked him in the eye and gave a one-word answer: "Women." He then added, "This island, Dan, is the only place I've been where the Church and *Cosmopolitan* magazine have not messed up man's number one physical need: fucking. And I refuse to call it by any other name, except in mixed company, when I am pretending to be someone I am not. I usually call a spade a spade and a fuck a fuck."

Graham came up from the galley carrying a flowered oriental ceramic coffee pot and two matching cups. There was no cream or sugar. As he had said on numerous occasions, "I like my coffee to be like my women: strong and black."

When they were settled, Graham continued to expound on his favorite subject. "It's not unusual for a healthy young Cuban woman to sleep fifteen hours a day. Take Maria, the one who just left. She didn't say, 'Goodbye,' or 'Will you call me?' Not even, 'When will I see you again?' Nothing. For her, it was just another night on the town with good food, dancing, and sex. To a Cuban woman, sex is like a late night cup of coffee, except it feels better."

While they were talking, a small group of sailors hurried by on the dock. One stopped and said, "Hey, Graham, there's a lot of commotion over in the entry channel. Looks like the whole Cuban navy has some old schooner surrounded."

Graham grabbed his jacket and stepped out onto the pier.

Dan ran to his boat and grabbed his high-powered binoculars. Excitement ran through his veins as he jumped back onto the pier and joined Graham, who was headed toward the coast guard building.

A sixty-five-foot wooden-hulled derelict of an era long gone by was limping into the Hemingway Marina at a thirty-degree list. Dan wondered if it was an abandoned vessel being swept in by the incoming tide and whether or not it was going to go aground and obstruct the narrow channel.

On closer inspection with his binoculars, he noticed a cadaver strapped to the helm. The scarecrow-like figure seemed to move on its own volition as the groaning schooner, sails down, creaked along on a sputtering auxiliary engine in its desperate attempt to enter the marina.

A *Guardia Frontera* patrol boat, two salvage boats, one customs launch, and three Zodiacs were powering out to prevent the battered relic from blocking the channel.

A rail-thin, deeply sunburned, medium-height Ichabod Crane surprised officials by wrestling the tired schooner through the red and green channel markers and into the calm waters of the marina.

The dock master assigned the new arrival to a vacant slip three spots down from Dan Fletcher.

When the old schooner came chugging down the canal, Dan went to give a hand with the mooring lines. He was taken aback when he got a closer look at the man at the helm. The little man's head was topped with frizzy gray porcupine-like spikes. His eyes appeared enormous, magnified by coke-bottle lenses encased in black plastic frames, the bridge of which was held together by a band-aid perched on his protruding beak-like nose, a nose that seemed to be modeled after a Boy Scout can opener. His thin parched lips spread almost to his oversized hair-encrusted ears. Thin sticks-for-legs protruded down and out of baggy, salt-encrusted, dirty brown Bermuda shorts.

Dan gabbed a line thrown in his direction and mumbled, "My God, this guy's a mess."

When the boat was secured, the captain waved feeble thanks and disappeared into the bowels of the old boat.

CHAPTER

6

Two days later, concerned about his new neighbor's health, Dan rapped gently on his deck.

A head covered with a black skullcap poked out of the companionway. The man peered at Dan though heavy lenses and said, "Yes?"

"Hi, I'm Dan Fletcher, your neighbor. I helped you tie up a few days ago, and, uh, I was just a little worried about you. Is everything okay?"

"Yes, thank you." He suddenly perked up as though he had just remembered where he was. "I'm Manny Glickman. I came in from Key West by myself. I was at sea for five days and nights without sleep. Please come aboard and have a drink."

Dan went below and was surprised to see a tidy cabin.

Manny produced a bottle of local rum and said, "Welcome to *Mud Runner*. Make yourself at home."

When Dan inquired about the unusual name of the schooner, Manny said, "I thought *Sea Goddess* was a little too common. I wanted a name that no one else had, so I changed it to *Mud Runner*. I thought it was appropriate because I had some navigational problems when I was learning to sail her." He smiled a sheepish grin at Dan. "I went aground a few times, five to be exact including times in the mud flats in Biscayne Bay."

Hey, the guy's got a sense of humor.

"But I made it to Cuba. You know, Dan, I hear this is a pretty backward country. An experienced guy like me could make a fortune here."

Experienced in what? Dan asked himself. *This guy took five days to find a seven-hundred-mile-long island that lies less than a hundred miles from Florida.*

The skinny little man who was sprawled on the settee across from him was like most sailors he'd met in the marina who went to sea alone: he suffered from verbal diarrhea. The symptoms only appeared when a listener was cornered, and Dan was cornered.

He sat for an hour, sipped Manny's rum, and listened to *The Tales of Glickman*. He didn't mind. It was a story right out of a dime novel and a hell of a lot better than watching CNN.

Manny Glickman had grown up in Brooklyn. He was the only son of a Jewish immigrant who worked long hours to make his meat market a profitable neighborhood establishment. Manny hated meat.

27

When he graduated from high school, he told his father where to stick the family meat and went over the bridge to Manhattan, taking a job in the rag business pushing racks of clothes through the streets. He lived in a small room and paid five dollars a week to a cousin who made a living selling fruit.

Manny was single, medium height, and skinny. He walked with a limp even though he had never been in an accident, swinging his feet out to the side in a half circle before putting them down in front of him. Doctors told him there was nothing wrong with him even though his bulbous knees were a constant source of pain. Cruel acquaintances told him he had the appearance of a man whose lower body had been run over by a bulldozer. Besides his lower body problems, he had wire for hair, wore thick glasses, and talked in a high-pitched, irritating voice.

He dated once in a while, but nothing ever came from the evenings where all he could think of to talk about were ways to make lots of money.

Lady luck smiled on Manny when he was forty-seven. His grandmother died and left him a $150,000 life insurance policy. He waved the policy at his father as he left the funeral parlor. He had not spoken to the old man for thirty-five years.

With the surprise windfall and the realization he was approaching the half-century mark, Manny decided to take a chance at another lifestyle. He felt there was still time if he had the guts to cut the tight cord that held him in New York. He lacked many things, but he had guts.

He packed one suitcase of light clothing and took a bus to Miami to look for a boat.

He found one sitting in the DEA impound yard in Miami that was up for auction. The opening bid, the closing bid, and the only bid was made by Manny. It seemed nobody wanted a rundown, aging, sixty-five-foot wooden boat that had been sitting out of the water in a vacant lot for two years. The wooden hull was so dry sunlight streamed into the hull through shrunken planks.

Manny bought the boat for a mere two thousand dollars. It took him three months to re-caulk the seams and slap on a new coat of paint. When he launched his new floating palace, it took another two weeks of pumping the bilges before the wood swelled enough so it would float on its own.

The boat had been used to run marijuana from Colombia to the Bahamas until the U.S. Coast Guard boarded the schooner at the Cay Sal Banks near the Old Bahama Channel. The three Panamanian crewmembers swore they had no idea the boat was loaded with two hundred bales of dope. The owner who hired them in Colon told them it was cotton. It was obvious to the Coast Guard that the Panamanians had been sampling the cotton. The lower deck of the once-classic vessel reeked of burnt cannabis. The crew was last seen out on bail in Miami before disappearing.

Manny learned to be a resourceful mariner. He scoured the salvage yards on both sides of Florida and refitted the boat with a surprising array of usable sails, winches, sheets, and hardware. The result was an old boat, but a passable schooner with classic lines. The sun-bleached railings showed an occasional streak of red peeking through the wood's grain, giving testament that the bright work had once been varnished.

The sails had more patches than ol' Jeter's inner tube in *Tobacco Road*, but they were able to move the boat along in light air.

Shit, Dan thought as he left Manny's boat, *that guy's story would make a good movie – with Dustin Hoffman playing the lead.*

He could see the opening of the film: an aerial shot of a clean white boat sailing into the marina with the narrator saying, "Here's Manny Glickman, another sailor entering into the Cuban holding tank of wayward mariners and failed entrepreneurs, lately of New York City, Miami, Key West, and all points of modern day pirates, commonly referred to as confidence men without destination or abode."

Dan smiled and climbed aboard his boat. He showered and dressed in his evening attire of clean pressed jeans, white tennis shoes, and a light-blue long-sleeved dress shirt. Tonight he would try the disco on the top floor of the Havana Libre Hotel. *One night*, he told himself, *she would appear. Lily whatever-her-last-name-is can't hide forever.*

CHAPTER
7

Dan spent three more weeks searching every disco in Havana for Lily until he finally gave up, exhausted.

It was another two weeks before he accidentally ran into her at a small party at a fellow boater's nearby apartment that the boater shared with his girlfriend, Ana.

Dan was sitting on a ragged couch with sagging cushions and watching a video of a Christopher Reeve *Superman* movie when Lily walked in alone. She was wearing jeans, sneakers, and a T-shirt with Woody Woodpecker silk-screened on the front.

Dan jumped to his feet. "Hi. Remember me?"

Lily beamed and said. "Sure. Dan. The guy from Papa's."

Ana moved in and said, "Lily Lopez, meet Dan Fletcher."

Dan's head began spinning. "I know. We're old friends."

Lily smiled and waited until Ana moved away. "If we are such old friends, why haven't I seen you since that night at Papa's?"

"Because you vanished before I could find out how to get hold of you. I've been looking everywhere. Are you the kind of girl that takes the bunny and runs?" *God*, he thought, *she looks stunning, even in jeans.*

Lily laughed as she walked past Dan and slapped him on the butt. "I like you," she said.

Dan followed her to the kitchen, where she opened the refrigerator and grabbed a can of beer. He placed both hands on her shoulders and turned her until she was facing him. "Did you know I have been scouring every disco in Havana for weeks looking for you?"

"Is that something like cleaning a frying pan – scouring a disco?"

She's teasing me, he thought. "Its tougher, especially if you're scouring for just one person."

"Did you find that person?"

"Yes, tonight."

"And what made you look so hard, Dan Fletcher? You must have seen hundreds of beautiful *chicas* along the way."

He wanted to say, "Once in awhile, a woman comes along and knocks a guy for a loop, and you are that woman." Instead, he said, "Let's just say there is something about you that strikes a chord in me, and I'd really like to get to know you better." *Shit, that sounds stupid. I'm blowing it.*

She did not answer. Instead, she studied his face, her eyes darting from his lips to his eyes, then up to his hairline and back to his eyes, as if looking deep into his soul.

Dan returned her eye contact and felt his heart racing. The conversation had come to a sudden halt, and it would be difficult to continue in Ana's close quarters. The rest of the party had quieted down, aware that something was taking place between Dan and Lily.

He wanted to get out of there to be alone with her. "Can we go some-place? How about Papa's?"

"Sure, I'd like that."

They slipped out of the party without saying anything and walked back toward the marina. Dan's heart was pounding as they made their way down the dark narrow streets that eventually put them on Fifth Avenue, two blocks from the marina entrance.

As they walked, Dan took her hand.

She gave it a squeeze and began talking. "I live in Baracoa, just six miles from here. I live with my mother, my sister, her husband, and two nieces." She paused, as though she was wondering if she should continue. Then she said, "I'm twenty years old. Does that bother you?"

"Not if fifty-five doesn't bother you."

She smiled. "Americans are hung up on age. For Cubans, age is never a factor."

He hardly knew this girl, but he could feel himself falling into a space he had never known. "Do you have dreams of going to America? I heard all Cuban girls want to go to America."

"Italy. My friend went to Italy with a tourist she met here. She lives in a villa. Her husband has lots of money, and she sends five hundred dollars a month to her family here in Cuba. I'm sure America is nice, but I want to live in Italy."

The thought of living with Lily in Las Vegas did not appeal to him either. She was too young and beautiful to be accepted as the wife of a fifty-five-year-old man in mainstream America. His friends would be hitting on her, and their wives would hate her. Besides, he was not going back to the States. Italy was also out of the question. Happiness for Dan would be sailing away with Lily and setting up house in a grass shack on some remote island.

Once at the disco, they took seats at the bar.

Dan laid a hundred dollar bill out and said, "Here. You pay for the drinks and hand out the dollars for the bunny machine. You're in charge."

•

31

Dan watched as Lily bought drinks for her friends, played the *muñeco* machine, and danced.

Boy, could she dance. When they played a fast salsa, it was as though someone had wound up a doll and set it on the dance floor going full speed.

He was amused by the way she divvied up his money. She shared her newly found fortune with every friend who came along. She seemed to know everyone.

At 3:30 a.m., after drinking more rum in one night than he could remember, he popped the closer question. "Would you like to continue this evening back on my boat?"

"Sure, why not?" Lily paid the bill and handed Dan the remainder of the hundred.

They walked down the quay hand in hand and climbed aboard *Pass Line*.

Lily was pleased. "Oh, Dan, what a beautiful boat."

Dan opened the hatch and climbed down the companionway.

Lily followed.

Once below, she seemed completely at ease. It was he who felt awkward. At his age, he should have been the experienced one. Instead, he felt like he was in high school on his first date. She was so young, so beautiful, so perfect, and so in control.

She sat down then blurted out, "I can't sleep with you, Dan."

He was more than disappointed, but he tried not to show it. He responded nonchalantly, "Okay. No problem."

He wanted to ask why, but he was suddenly afraid of what the answer might be. Maybe she was married. If that were the case, then why was she here alone with him on his boat at four in the morning? He held out hope that it was something simple, like the wrong time of the month.

Dan lifted the lid on the refrigerator and rummaged through a jumble of food and several cans of soda. "Would you like a drink? I have rum and Coke."

"Sure, but we need to talk."

They sat at the dinette across from each other.

She extended her hand across the table and took his. "You must be wondering what I am doing here, alone with you on your boat." She gave a hint of a smile. "I really don't know myself. The first time we met, you seemed so nice. Not like other men, who look at a girl like she is nothing more than a quick screw. I was impressed and a little amused. Then when I saw you at the party tonight, something stirred inside me."

She released Dan's hand, exhaled, and sat back. "But it can't happen, Dan. I have my mind set on something that I see very clearly, and it does not include a footloose sailor and a boat. It would not be fair to either of us if we became involved in a romantic situation."

If she was attempting to turn Dan off, it was not working. Evidently, she was not some easy pick-up who would jump into bed with anybody. She had principles and self-esteem. This woman was going to be a challenge.

Dan slumped and grinned. "Hell, Lily, I thought there was something seriously wrong with you, like AIDS or a terminal illness. You are as normal as can be. Don't worry about me. I have my own dreams and plans. Cuba is just my first stop on a world cruise. You are one of the most beautiful women I have ever laid eyes on, and I really like you as a person. Let's be friends and enjoy each other's company. Sex is not important," he lied.

She thought a moment and said, "I'd like that, Dan. Let's be friends." She glanced at the clock. "Walk me back to Papa's, and I'll take a taxi home. And please don't try to visit me in Baracoa. It doesn't look good to the neighbors. I know where you are, and I'll be seeing you."

He put Lily into a taxi and began formulating a plan as he walked slowly back to the boat. He had found the girl he was looking for; now he would win her love and change her mind about living in Italy. He had it all figured out. Together they would sail away to the South Pacific and set up house in a palm-thatched bungalow.

•

CHAPTER

8

The next day Dan walked up the quay to Papa's, looking for a cold beer and some lunch. It was a typical hot tropical day, and Dan could feel the sweat running down his forehead. He knew he had wet spots in his armpits big enough to star in the "before" part of a deodorant commercial.

He took a seat in the almost empty disco that doubled as a restaurant during the day and ordered a pork lunch and a can of Huatuey. The place carried Heineken, Corona, and several Cuban beers, but he had just read the story of Hautuey in the guidebook and decided on the beer that bore his name. Hautuey was the Cuban Indian chief who had refused the Spanish demand that all Cuban Indians become Catholics.

When Huatuey was given the choice of embracing Catholicism and going to heaven, or being killed and going to hell, the little chief asked, "Where do the Spaniards go when they die?"

"They go to heaven, of course."

Huatuey thought a moment and replied, "Okay, I'll take death. I'd rather go to hell."

They killed him.

Dan looked down at the plate of pork, rice, and shredded cabbage garnished with a tiny slice of lime and wondered why it was so hard to get a decent meal in Cuba. He remembered seeing restaurant signs in the States advertising "authentic Cuban cuisine." What method of preparing rice and pork could be called Cuban?

Last week a waiter had talked him into ordering what he said was "the best beef on the island." He could have used a pair of Vice-Grips to help him chew the beef, which could have doubled as shoe leather. And the chicken he'd eaten so far was only passable. "How can a guy screw up chicken?" he asked himself. On the other hand, where would a Cuban chef find the incentive to make a chicken leg taste like Colonel Sanders' chicken when he was making the same wage as the guy who cleaned the floors?

Dan was also surprised to discover the lack of fresh fish. With the exception of an expensive government lobster tail, there was seldom seafood listed on the menu. How could an island in the Caribbean with more than three thousand miles of coastline exist without a fishing industry?

It was not hard to answer that question. To catch fish, there had to be fishermen with boats. Any Cuban fisherman who could freely leave land in a boat would most likely be halfway to Florida by the time his communist party boss wondered why another boat in his fleet had failed to return to port with the day's catch. "What a tragedy. Now Jose is missing, and on such a calm day."

The pork steak was okay. It was just that Dan was tired of eating pork.

He made a mental note to get directions to a good *paladar*. Fidel Castro had recently authorized restaurants to be operated in private homes but had limited each eatery to minimum seating, insuring that the capitalist establishments did not earn too much. *Paladar police* made frequent inspections, and stiff fines were handed out to owners who had more than twelve chairs.

While Dan was eating, a tough-looking heavyset man sat down at the next table and ordered a beer. The big guy was wearing a stars-and-stripes headband that partially covered a thin coating of greasy black hair. A bushy mustache hid the upper lip of a full mouth, and an oversized tank top partly concealed a cheap-looking necklace of beads that hung over a hairy chest that bore traces of white talcum powder. He wore green camouflaged Army fatigue pants that were bloused over huge muddy G.I. brogans.

Dan sized him up as a cross between Thomas Gomez in the Bogart film *Key Largo* and John Wayne from *The Green Berets*.

The big guy looked over at Dan and asked, "Are you by any chance an American?"

Dan nodded. "Yes, and I assume you are, too."

"Yeah, how'd you know?"

"Lucky guess," Dan said as he extended a hand. "Dan Fletcher."

The stranger said, "Maverick's the name."

Dan shook his fat hand and wondered if it was his real name.

Maverick moved to the empty chair at Dan's table. "I live in the marina. You got a boat here?"

"Yeah," Dan said. "It's forty-foot sloop in the first canal named *Pass Line*."

"Oh, yeah, I've seen it. How long you plan on staying?"

"I haven't decided yet. Is your name really Maverick?"

"Naw. My real name was Arland Bodanus. Never liked Arland. I was pretty big in school, and the guys called me Spike. Later, I legally changed it to Maverick. Sounds better."

Dan didn't respond, so the big guy continued. "My mother and father were Rumanian gypsies. Came to the United States in the twenties. My ol' man ended up making a good living manufacturing and selling metal garbage cans in Boston."

He paused for a moment and appeared to study Dan.

Dan answered the stare and said, "How about another beer?" He had the whole afternoon, and for a few beers he figured to get a sailor's tale or two.

The drinks arrived and Maverick launched into the story of his life.

"I spent three years in the Army as a Green Beret. You know, Vietnam."

Now we're getting into the deep bullshit, Dan thought. He was well aware of the type of soldier a person had to be to spend time in the Green Berets, and Maverick didn't fit the bill. The guy carried at least seventy-five extra pounds on what looked to be a six-foot frame, and his arms were too flabby. Dan doubted they would have lifted his chin up to the bar during the difficult Green Beret physical test that required twenty chin-ups, for starters. It was not likely that twenty years would change a fine-tuned athlete into what now sat before him. Dan summed him up as a soldier of fortune wannabe.

"Stop by my boat in the marina sometime," Maverick said. "It's in the second canal – a ketch called *Pipe Dream.*"

Good name, Dan thought.

"Bought the boat from a Florida insurance adjuster after Hurricane Hugo lifted it off its moorings and left it high and dry in a motel parking lot a half mile from the harbor," he bragged. "I made a quick deal with the insurance adjuster, who was swamped with claims resulting from the billion-dollar storm. I got it for a thousand bucks."

He took a big swig from the beer bottle and spilled most of it down his chin as he laughed. "It was for the salvage rights, but the boat was hardly damaged. I sold the radar, the radios, the life raft, and navigational electronics for five thousand. By the time I got the boat back into the water after a few repairs, I had a grand total of just over five thousand in the whole thing. It's a fifty-eight-foot ketch. I could go around the world in it."

"Hell of a bargain," Dan said.

Dan ordered more beer and wondered how much of Maverick's story was true and how much of it was just another sailor's tale. For all he knew, Maverick could just as easily be an escaped rapist from Omaha named Percy.

Maverick pulled two long cigars from his shirt pocket and offered one to Dan. "Here, try a good Esplendido. A man can't live in Cuba without smoking an occasional cigar."

Dan took the cigar and bit the end off as Maverick produced a mini blowtorch. Dan rolled the end of the tobacco in the flame before drawing several puffs of smoke.

"Looks like you know how to smoke a cigar."

Dan took a few puffs and replied, "Smoked a few in Vegas. I used to work in a casino there. Once in a while, one of the big rollers would hand me a Cuban."

Maverick leaned over and fingered the beads that hung around his neck. "You know what this necklace represents?" He moved closer and whispered, "*Macumba.*"

Here it comes, Dan thought. *This guy's selling beads.*

Maverick leaned back and resumed a normal voice. "*Macumba,* Dan. I am a high priest in the ancient religion known as *Santeria,* or *Macumba* to many. It originated in Africa and came to Cuba by way of Haiti."

Dan was getting the picture. *He's a voodoo freak. Next he'll pull out a doll and stick pins it.*

Maverick then told the strange story of his acceptance into the cult.

"My girlfriend is the one who got me started. Cubans can be very superstitious, you know. Anyway, she set up a deal to have my fortune read by a high priest of the *Santeria.*"

A wandering band of musicians approached the table, but Maverick waved them off before they could start playing. "I hate these guys," he said with a sneer. "They waltz up when you're talking, make lots of noise, and get pissed off if you don't tip 'em.

"Anyway, as I was saying, this old wrinkled black man, and I mean *black* – skin the color of ebony – opens a leather bag of bones and throws 'em out on the sand. Then he starts telling me details about my life that nobody knew but me.

And probably his girlfriend, Dan surmised.

"The arrangement of the bones also revealed a message the old man had witnessed only one other time in his one hundred and sixteen years as a priest."

Dan's gut was starting to quake. He was going to break up if he couldn't collect himself. He held up his hand to stop the storyteller and called to the waiter, "*Otro vez, por favor.*"

The waiter went for more beer as Dan recovered and looked back at Maverick, who was still in mid-sentence.

"You know what them bones said, Dan? They said I had the special gift of priesthood, that I was ready for the initiation."

Dan was a born skeptic. He wondered how much all this had cost Maverick. Cubans were experts at separating gullible Americans from their money, but this scam was the best he'd heard.

"It was the most intense experience of my life. I met the old man at the top of a small hill in the woods outside of Havana at midnight during the full moon."

His face took on a sincere expression, and the veins bulged in his neck. "I was stripped naked and whipped with a live chicken until the bird was dead–"

The mental picture caused Dan to choke. Beer gushed from his nose as he rose from the table and made his way toward the men's room. Inside, he broke out laughing. *God, this is good. I've got to hold it in. This guy's serious.* He splashed cold water on his face and dried off with toilet paper before returning to the table.

"Sorry. Had some beer go down the wrong way."

Maverick didn't miss a beat. "Then I deposited a bag of my own shit into a hole of a nearby dead tree, and the priest placed these around my neck." He pulled down his baggy tank top and exposed a long multi-colored beaded necklace resting on a mat of chest hair. "Then he told me I was a *Santeria* priest with voodoo powers. It was at that very moment, Dan, that I could actually feel the power running through my body."

"How much did all this cost?" Dan asked.

"Just nine hundred dollars, but that included the necklace. It identifies me to other *Santeros* as a high priest in good standing."

Dan was starting to laugh again but bit his lip to keep it from coming out. The beads looked like children's costume jewelry from K-Mart, but the story was too good not to hear the ending.

Maverick went on. "My friends in the marina had their doubts all right, but I took care of that by blessing one of the fishing boats during the Hemingway Wahoo Fishing Tournament. They laughed when I waved my necklace around the forty-foot *Hatteras*, but that boat landed the most fish and won the tournament."

"Hell of a story," Dan said. *This guy has really convinced himself he has the power of seeing the future and casting spells of good and evil.*

"I take maintenance sessions from the old black man every so often, just to keep my power at full strength."

Dan was impressed with the Cuban ingenuity behind the whole thing. Maverick not only paid a bundle for the religious ceremony, but they were also collecting regular fees to tune up the magic beads. What the hell, Dan figured. It wasn't hurting anybody, and he'd seen other religions that did plenty more harm to their believers.

He didn't know what to say when Maverick looked hard at him for a word of confidence. The best Dan could come up with was, "Interesting. Very interesting."

Then Maverick changed the subject. "Hey, if you're not doing anything tomorrow, come with me. I'm going downtown to buy some cigars. You might want a couple of boxes for yourself."

By now, Dan's cigar had burned past the halfway point, and he found himself savoring every puff. Why not have a few on the boat to go with a glass of good Cuban rum?

"Sure. Stop by the boat. I'll go with you."

CHAPTER
9

Julio sat on the dock of the produce center sipping a small cup of strong ink-black coffee. As he prepared for another day of receiving and shipping tomatoes and potatoes, he read the letter again. It was from his longtime friend Marcus, now in Miami. He read it at least once a week. Marcus and another friend, Carlos, had escaped from Cuba on windsurfers.

Julio liked to read the part where they had lowered their sails into the water as soon as they had seen the lights of Key West. They ate sandwiches and drank bottled water from their backpacks as they bobbed up and down in twelve-foot seas. And they laughed at the ease with which they had slipped out of Cuba.

They had launched their long competition slalom boards off the same beach in Jaimanitas where they had practiced every day for two months, sailing in and out through the surf. On the day of their escape, they sailed the same course until the sun spread its afternoon glare across the water. Then they altered course on a seaward tack, and by the time anyone noticed they had not arrived back at the beach by dark, they were effortlessly skipping along at twenty knots toward Florida, suspended from the booms in their harnesses and laughing at the wind. They had watched weather reports, estimated the winds and the seas, and selected the right sail size for the occasion. They had sailed so fast they had to sit for several hours next to a lighted buoy in the Key West entrance while they waited for sunrise.

Julio liked the next part best. When they had been sure they could find their way into the confusing Key West harbor, they had sailed downwind through the outgoing fishing boats that hardly took notice of a couple of Sunday windsurfers heading down the channel. For them, there would be no landing on a deserted, mosquito-infested island, where they would have to wait until they were found. They cruised right past the Coast Guard station, waved at the sailors on deck of the moored patrol cutter, and dropped their sails at the end of the Texaco gas dock in Key West Bite. By stepping onto U.S. soil, they were automatically guaranteed asylum in America.

Julio read the letter over and over. He imagined himself strolling down the streets of Key West or Miami, free to choose what he wanted to do and when he wanted to do it. All he would ask for was the right to work hard, earn a decent wage, and not have to worry about being arrested for doing nothing. But Julio could not windsurf and had no opportunity to learn. He didn't even know how to sail a boat like the guy who had stolen the Hobie Cat from Marina Hemingway one night and slipped by the *Guardia Frontera*. He had made it to a small sandbar in the Marquesas but almost died of thirst waiting to be found.

How about Pino Pedroso? Julio thought to himself. Now that was one hell of a gutsy guy.

The name always brought smiles to Cubans who knew the story. Pino had installed a one-cylinder Perkins diesel engine into the back of a 1948 Buick sedan. After wedging empty watertight cans into the empty engine compartment and trunk to give the car buoyancy, he welded the seams and transported the car on a flatbed truck in broad daylight to *Playa del Este*, where he commandeered some bathers to roll the car off the truck and into the water. Then Pino climbed into the front seat through a hatch in the roof and simply drove the Buick to Florida.

The story got even better when Pino landed his Buick in the front yard of Senator Strom Thurmond's summer beach house, where a party was going on. The senator was so impressed with Pino's story he had his photo taken with him and arranged to have the Buick installed in a Key West museum.

But Julio didn't have an amphibious Buick or the tools to make one. Besides, next time the police would be on guard. The Florida papers had made a big deal of it and razzed the stupid police for letting Pino get away so easily. No, Julio would save and buy his way out on a big, safe boat. Maybe even the *Guagua 400*, the fast cigarette boat that arrived at 4:00 a.m. on dark, moonless nights and went back to Florida at more than sixty miles an hour. The fare for one of the seven spaces was an astronomical eight thousand dollars, payable in advance. But it was assured the American speedboat could outrun the old Soviet-made Griffin patrol boat.

At the produce center, Julio kept his head down and worked hard. He was a strong twenty-eight-year-old mulatto, built like a bear with a thick solid torso and short, powerful arms. He hoisted three crates of tomatoes while each of his coworkers could carry only one.

Julio had been a produce supervisor in the Playa distribution center for a little more than sixteen months and managed the busy facility that cleared forty to sixty trucks a week, trucks that came directly from farms as far away as Pinar del Rio at the west end of the Island to Holguin, four hundred miles to the east. The farmers had been paid by the State, so when Julio shorted the incoming trucks, he was not stealing from the farmers, even though that would not be so bad, he'd thought many times. The farmers, with their rundown houses, tattered clothes, and dirty children, were by far the richest of all Cuban workers. They owned their own land, received a stipend from the government for seed and pesticides, and were allowed to sell their crops to government agencies, private restaurants, and the general public. They kept a low profile and dealt in cash that was later added to the stash buried in the backyard.

Julio had saved enough money for such a journey but recent developments had changed his plans. After telling his mother he was eventually going to leave the country, she became hysterical. Only after promising his mother he would take his fourteen-year-old brother, Manuel, with him did she acquiesce to the escape. "And no rubber inner tubes, Julio. You get a good, big boat, and you take care of him when you get to Florida," his mother demanded.

Julio was disappointed. Now he would have to earn twice as much to make the trip to Florida, but he loved his little brother and it would be a selfish move to leave him behind. He would be over thirty years old before he could get sixteen thousand dollars, plus the extra money he and Manuel would need to get started in the United States. He would just have to work harder and spend less money on luxuries.

His mother's house, where he and Manuel lived, had been fixed up with Julio's extra earnings. On the outside, the old house looked like the others on the block. Inside, the walls had bright new coats of white paint. A twenty-one-inch color television was connected to a hidden satellite receiver on the roof. There was an electric hot water heater connected to the showerhead, and a rare wooden seat adorned the white porcelain toilet.

Julio first began raising his standard of living while working at the Havana Club Rum Factory. His coworkers taught him that he could earn extra pesos by selling rum concentrate on the street after work. He left the job every afternoon with three liters of the valuable fluid concealed in the handlebars and frame tubing of his bicycle.

Julio did not consider himself a thief. Everyone in Cuba lower than *The Bearded One* earned extra dollars on street sales of everything from lobster tails to pantyhose.

No one that Julio knew really believed that Cubans could actually survive on the seven-dollar monthly wage that the socialist system paid workers.

Besides, Marxism taught that everything belonged to the State and that the workers *were* the State. If that were true, there was nothing wrong with stealing things.

Secretaries took pencils, paper, erasers, typewriters, computer parts, and even toilet paper from the bathrooms when and if there was any. Janitors took the toilet seats and in some cases the toilets. Doors disappeared, and sacks of cement left construction sites, along with truckloads of sand and gravel during the night.

Two out of five cases of chickens delivered to a government restaurant went out the backdoor. Even the bones of eaten pork chops were traded on the street for a pair of shoes lifted from a shoe store.

Cubans could trade, sell, or buy almost anything on the street. The State turned a blind eye toward most of the black market thefts, with a few exceptions. Drugs and guns were illegal, and their traders punished by long prison terms and even death.

Julio was proud of his contributions to the family's high standard of living. The counterfeit access card to the television alone had cost two hundred and fifty dollars, but the system allowed him to watch a hundred channels that included uncensored news and the latest American movies with alternate Spanish audio for his mother and brother. Julio preferred to watch the movies in English to improve his language skills, which he would need when he got to Florida.

He was jolted back to reality when he heard the hissing of the big semi's brakes. It was 8:00 a.m., and the garlic truck was backing into the dock. The parking area was suddenly alive with people coming out of dark doorways across the street. Rusty pre-revolutionary American cars and Russian Ladas moved in for loading.

Two hours later, the semi was empty, and the dock area was quiet. The hundreds of buyers had disappeared as suddenly as they had made their appearance.

Customers on foot left with bags stuffed with garlic, and cars and trucks were loaded for rendezvous with owners of private restaurants.

Julio walked into the tiny room just off the dock that served as an office. He locked the door behind him, set the sack of pesos on the rickety wooden table, and poured a cup of black coffee from the pot on the hot plate. He pulled out the cheap white plastic chair and wondered just how many more coffee spills it would take to connect the stains and turn it into a brown plastic chair.

Fifteen minutes later, he leaned back and admired the neatly stacked piles of pesos. *Not a bad day so far,* he thought. Eight thousand pesos in just two hours, with tomatoes and bananas still to come.

With thirty percent going to the head of the municipality, ten percent to the local police, and ten percent to the dockworkers, he had enough pesos to buy about two hundred and forty U.S. dollars on the black market. He would add the money to his growing stash in the one-gallon tomato can buried in his backyard. But even with the money he would earn from garlic and other produce, he was still looking at two more years before he and Manuel could make their escape. By then, with the *Guardia Frontera* and the U.S. Coast Guard tightening security, there may not be a *Guagua 400.*

•

If it were just himself, he would find a way. But he had promised his mother he would take his brother – and not risk his life in the process.

He sat looking at the piles of pesos, and a feeling of despair flooded his body as he thought of two more years of stealing, when the only thing he wanted was an honest job in a country where he was free to make his own choices.

CHAPTER
10

Maverick showed up at the boat with a private taxi he often hired for twenty-five dollars a day. The '47 Studebaker had seen better days, and it was certainly not a candidate for *Antique Car* magazine. The new canary-yellow paintjob looked as though some amateur body-and-fender man had pounded out fifty years of dents with the wrong side of a ball-peen hammer. It accentuated the lumps and gave it the appearance of a shiny yellow bag of marbles on wheels. The headliner and door panels were long gone, and the seats had a few springs sticking up. But Cuban ingenuity had kept the relic running well into its fifth decade. Dan was preparing to ride around Cuba in an American car powered by a British diesel engine, a Russian transmission, and a Rumanian differential.

Maverick told the driver to take them to Old Havana. It was a pleasant thirty-minute ride down tree-lined Fifth Avenue.

As they passed the expensive mansions with manicured lawns that lined both sides of the street, Maverick said, "They were once owned by wealthy Cubans who fled the country after Castro came into power in 1959."

The old Studebaker belched diesel smoke as it barreled toward the center of Old Havana along the *Malecon*, Havana's seaside drive that protected the city from the harsh waves that rolled in from the Florida Straits. Today, the waves crashed into the coral seawall and sent plumes of saltwater across the road. The driver turned on the wipers and adjusted the volume on the stereo so his clients could share in his new CD recording by The Buena Vista Social Club.

The south side of the boulevard was lined with weathered concrete buildings that appeared to be decomposing from years of exposure to the ever-present salt air.

Dan made a mental note to apply for a Sherwin Williams paint distributorship if Cuba ever opened its doors to capitalism. After forty years of neglect, every building in Havana looked in need of a paintjob. The city's only color seemed to come from the laundry hanging on wrought iron balconies or stretched across black, windowless holes.

The taxi rounded the last curve along the sea and turned into the harbor area.

Maverick said, "I guess Havana Harbor was once full of oysters and sea life. Look back there." He pointed across the bay, where black puffs of smoke rose like columns in the sky. "The oil refinery has been dumping crude oil directly into the south end of the harbor for years. The Castro government says it has been trying to clean up the pollution. Last month Fidel went on television and said, 'My plan is working. Just look at all the Cubans now fishing in the bay.'"

Maverick grunted. "I don't think the water is any cleaner. It's just that the people are hungrier."

Dan was dressed in a bright tropical shirt, shorts, and sneakers, and his sunglasses peeked out from under his baseball cap.

Maverick wore his baggy fatigue pants, a white sleeveless T-shirt, and his colorful headband that announced he was an American.

Dan followed as they wandered the streets of old Havana. Maverick seemed to be looking for someone, but said nothing. Dan snapped a few pictures of dirty stucco buildings, relics of once classic Spanish architecture.

They passed street vendors who sold books about Castro's triumphant revolution and Spanish versions of Hemingway novels. Artists displayed photographs of Che Guevara, woodcarvings, seashells, handmade wood humidors, black coral jewelry, and original oil paintings of everything from vintage American cars to naked native maidens.

A female beggar holding a dirty child with one arm encased in a plaster cast held out her hand as they passed. Dan reached into his pocket and handed her a dollar.

Maverick laughed. "She's been working this section of Havana for years holding different kids."

Dan spotted a fat black woman sitting on an old stone bench and smoking a huge cigar. She wore a white Caribbean dress topped with a bright red bandana. *What a shot*, he thought. He got her attention, and she struck a pose with the cigar, held between her fingers close to her mouth, pointing upward. He framed the shot and pressed the shutter button.

"*Gracias.*"

"*Gracias* nothing. That'll cost you five bucks."

He gave her three and told her to get a sign if she wanted to charge.

Maverick watched and smiled, as if to say, "Tourist!"

Dan kept up the pace as they passed through Park Central but paused near a group of Cubans in the midst of a hot debate.

Dan could not understand the rapid Spanish and assumed that he was witnessing a controversial political debate. Two of the older men were nose-to-nose, shouting at each other. Several other men had formed a circle around the two and were shouting encouraging remarks to the combatants in the center of the ring. It was obvious to Dan that some punches were about to be thrown, and he wondered where the police were. There were uniformed men on every corner of the park, but none of them took notice of the heated altercation.

"What's going on, Maverick? I thought political opinions were not allowed, especially in public."

By now Maverick was playing the know-it-all tour guide role to the hilt. He pretended to listen intently then proclaimed, "Today they are arguing about who was better: Joe Louis or Rocky Marciano." He laughed and added, "Last week it was probably Babe Ruth and Joe DiMaggio. Don't worry. They never throw blows."

Dan followed Maverick down the crowded tourist aisles as he pretended to study some of the items. It wasn't long before a young boy, about twelve, approached Maverick. They spoke for a few minutes until the boy turned and quickly left the tent city, walking down one of the narrow streets that exited the big square.

Maverick motioned to Dan, and they followed thirty yards behind the youngster, who stopped occasionally and looked back. Dan kept several paces behind Maverick until the sidewalk widened and he could catch up.

"Act like a tourist," Maverick said. "Don't make it look like we're following the kid. If you spot a cop, act nonchalant and start looking around at the architecture."

Dan looked up and saw nothing but old beige colored cement buildings in dire need of repair. Drab wash hung from the balconies.

The boy glanced over his shoulder as he disappeared into the dark entrance of a six-floor walk-up.

When they turned into the doorway, Dan felt a small pang of apprehension. He was carrying several hundred dollars in cash and suddenly found himself following some kid up a dark stairway in the toughest part of town. The setting was a mugger's paradise.

He could not see the kid, but he could hear the footsteps going up the stairs. Maverick did not seem concerned and puffed along without looking up. Dan's senses were on full alert. He took the stairs slowly, one at a time. He was in no hurry to turn a narrow corner and walk into a situation that might cost him his life. In the event someone said, "Your money or your life," Dan was ready to fork over the roll of one-dollar bills he always carried in one pocket. He had learned to keep a low profile and felt relatively safe walking around Cuba. His thirty-dollar Timex was hardly worth the eight-year jail sentence given to thieves who stole from tourists.

Actually, Dan felt safer in Havana carrying cash than he did walking down a street in Pasadena or downtown Boston wearing a gold Rolex. The

Cubans could steal the laces out of a tourist's shoes if he stood in one place long enough, but violent crime with knives and guns, or even strong-arm muggings, were rare. Cuban justice was swift and severe. Unlike in America, murderers, burglars, and drug dealers didn't walk the streets while out on bail.

Maverick, he could tell, had no such worries. He sported his Rolex and 18-karat-gold chains openly. In the taxi, he had bragged about carrying a deadly razor-sharp knife concealed in his belt buckle, plus he hid under his shirt a giant Army-issue commando bowie knife, complete with special hooks to scale chain link fences. He had seen that one in a *Soldier of Fortune* magazine, he said, and had to have it.

Maverick was waiting on the fifth floor, but the kid they had been following was nowhere in sight.

Then a small window in the nearest door opened, and a dark face looked out. Moments later, Dan heard the bolt slide, and the door opened. A small man with a bushy mustache studied the long, empty corridor before motioning them in, just like in the old movies about prohibition-era speakeasies. Dan felt like saying, "Joe sent me."

The whole scenario was right out of a drug deal going down, where kilos of cocaine were being purchased. Dan studied the situation and wondered, *Where's the sleazy guy tasting white powder from a plastic bag with a wetted fingertip?*

A second Cuban, equally as tiny, came out of another room carrying a cardboard carton. He opened it and laid out the goods.

Maverick shook his head. "Forget it. How about Esplendidos? Got any?"

The Cuban just stood there. When he spoke, it was as though he realized he was about to lose a great deal of money. "Sorry, *Señor*," he said in a soft voice. "The Romeo and Julietas are the only big cigars I have been able to get for two weeks."

Maverick was confused. "Whataya mean? Everybody's got Esplendidos."

"Sorry, *Señor*. It's the same everywhere. The factories are running at thirty percent capacity because of the tobacco shortage. The hurricane that hit Pinar del Rio wiped out all of the wrapper leaves. I can get little cigars, Monte 3s and 4s, and plenty of Petit Coronas, but for anything longer than Coronas—" He held both hands palms up in a gesture of apology. "There is no tobacco. It may be next year until we have long class-A cigars again. These four boxes are the last of the big ones."

Maverick opened one of the boxes, took out a cutter, and snipped the end off one of the cigars. He lit it up, took a couple of short draws, and rolled the smoke around in his mouth. "Draws okay. How much for these?"

"Forty dollars." He paused before adding, "Each box."

47

"Impossible," said Maverick. "The highest we can go is twenty. They're only Romeo and Julieta Churchills. Maybe thirty a box for some Esplendidos, but we can only go twenty for these."

They bought two boxes each, settling for a hundred dollars.

Dan counted out fifty dollars from the money he carried in his shoe and gave it to the smiling Cuban, who said, "I have really good cigars. My brother works in the factory."

"Sure," said Maverick, "and your sister's a virgin."

"No, *Señor*, but she is very beautiful. You want I get her?"

Maverick and Dan left the apartment with the four boxes of Churchills and made their way down the stairs and out onto the street. It was Dan Fletcher's first experience buying black market cigars.

"If we'd been caught, the Cubans would have been arrested," Maverick stated. "But now that we've left the apartment, we can walk back to the taxi area without worry. A Cuban can be stopped and searched at any time, but police are instructed not to hassle the tourists."

"Shit," Maverick added as they walked. "I wanted to get you some Esplendidos, but those Churchills you bought are good. Some say better."

Dan was impressed. True, Maverick was an overweight slob who made up stories about fighting with the Green Berets, but he had another side to him. He obviously knew Cuba and cigars. And today's buying experience had been one hell of an adventure.

Once in the taxi, Maverick said, "Well, you got yourself a couple boxes of good smokes. You know what those sell for in the States?" He looked at Dan and smiled. "As much as a thousand dollars a box."

They rode in silence for a while before Maverick said, "A guy could make a lot of money taking a few hundred boxes of those things back to the States."

"Yeah, I guess so." Dan had a feeling that Maverick had had ulterior motives for taking him on the black market shopping spree.

CHAPTER
11

Dan decided to walk over to Graham's for some conversation late one afternoon. As he passed the forty-two-foot cruiser *Hatchback*, he saw Lester Madson sitting on a white plastic chair on the raised after-deck and drinking a cocktail with his feet up on the stainless railing. Lester was a forty-five-year-old Canadian who had kept his boat in Hemingway Marina for the past three years. He had just flown back from Cancun after a three-day jaunt so he could renew his Cuban tourist permit. Roundtrip to Cancun was one hundred and ninety dollars, and many of the permanent boat owners made good use of the trip by buying food and boat parts not available in Cuba. When he returned, Lester found his boat had been ransacked.

"Hi, Lester. Can I come aboard?"

"Sure, Dan. You hear? I got ripped off."

"Yeah, that's what I heard. Any news on who might have done it?" Dan figured he already knew the answer to his question.

"Oh, they'll catch 'em all right. It just depends on your definition of catch."

Lester was not a happy camper, and his words dripped with sarcasm. "I had the whole secret police force down here. You should have seen it. Six plain-clothes detectives and two forensic specialists in full-length white coats. One had a fingerprint dusting kit, and the other had a bright white light going over the whole boat looking for hidden clues. It was right out of a Charlie Chan movie. There were more detectives here than on the O.J. Simpson case. Sorry, Dan. Want a drink?"

"Sure, why not?" He took a chair as Lester went below for another glass.

Lester came back up and was hardly out of the companionway when he continued. "It took a while to figure out how they broke in. Pedro was the only guy with the combination to the lock.

"You know Pedro, Dan. He'd never steal anything. Hell, when I first hired him, I set little traps. You know, like a bunch of bills where he could have slipped out one or two without it being noticed. I even used to count the bars of soap. I finally gave up. I know it sounds stupid, but I trust Pedro."

"It's not stupid. What did they get away with?"

.

"Enough stuff to make me really pissed off. My TV satellite receiver, two drills, my jigsaw, fins, two wetsuits, the printer for my computer, my fishing filet knives, and the slide-in control unit for my stereo CD sound system."

"Probably an inside job, Lester."

It was no secret that many of the marina guards who were supposed to watch the boats were doing the stealing.

"It makes no sense, Dan, that somebody could walk up to a boat forty yards from the security station and drill holes in a window that faces the guards, then rummage around for an hour or so and exit through the same window with bags full of stolen items, then stroll out the main gate in full view of the security guards."

Dan was warned by Graham never to trust the marina's rent-a-cop security system. Their job was to keep track of the foreigners and make daily reports on every person living aboard a boat. They were probably looking for CIA agents disguised as sailors. As if a CIA agent would risk sailing across the Florida Straits, heaving his guts out, when he could take a one-hour plane ride from Nassau and enter Cuba with the same tourist permit as a boater.

Lester was getting worked up now. "You know who the number one suspect is?" He didn't wait for Dan to answer. "Me. That's right: me. Can you fucking believe it? I spent three hours down at their little security shack on Canal Four this morning going over my story about where I was during the time the theft took place. Jesus Christ, my passport and my tourist permit show that I was out of the county."

Lester was really wound up. "They say I took the stuff and sold it, then reported the theft so customs would take the things off my entry manifest. That's the last time I'm going to report something stolen from my boat. Fuck 'em, Dan. Fuck 'em."

"Maybe that's just what they want, Lester."

Dan knew the downside of protesting too much about Cuban justice. "Look, Lester, I know you're upset about this thing, but shit happens. If you make a big deal out of it, the *Guardia Frontera* comes to your boat one day and says, 'You are not wanted here. Please pay your dockage fees. You have twenty-four hours to leave the marina.' And if you don't have enough ready cash to pay your bill, they escort you to the airport, put you on a flight to Nassau, and confiscate your boat."

Lester looked defeated. He knew Dan was right. It did no good to complain. "Yeah, I hear you." He changed the subject and asked, "How about you, Dan? You were supposed to be on your way to the South Pacific. You've been here for months. What keeps you on this island?"

"A girl, Lester. What else?"

Dan left Lester and continued on to Graham's, wondering why Lester had not learned in three years what he had found out in a few months.

He found Graham in his usual position, sitting in the cockpit smoking a cigar and sipping brandy. Graham seldom missed a good sunset, and the clouds on the western horizon promised another vivid afternoon show by announcing the ending of another blue-sky day with a purple and red exit.

"Hi, Dan. Come aboard."

Mariners who did not wait for a formal invitation received a cold reception from this seasoned sailor. But with Dan, he was quick to offer a cigar and two fingers of *Courvoisier* in a spotless snifter.

Dan recognized Graham as a dogmatic old salt who seemed to know exactly what he wanted out of the rest of his life. He was a strong seventy and enjoyed sex at least five times a week, more if he could get it. Graham was a good listener but always ready to interject strong opinions.

He started with his usual, "Well, Dan, how goes the battle?"

"I just talked to Lester. Someone robbed his boat, and a special detective force is looking into it."

Graham chuckled and said, "Lester's never going to find out who stole his stuff because the police won't arrest one of their own. The thieves have a higher rank in the system than the detectives."

"What's wrong with these guys, Graham? Lester gets ripped off and they're tightening security by making it impossible to get girls into the marina. I don't get it."

"It's easy, Dan. The security guards steal stuff and blame it on the *chicas*. Even *Iliana*, the girl who cleaned my boat for two years, isn't allowed past the front gate anymore. And they pulled *Pilar's* card yesterday, and the word is, 'No women in the marina unless they're married.'"

"Why do they do it, Graham? This attitude of keeping the Cuban women away from the tourists is insane, and it's killing tourism."

It was also killing Dan. He had high hopes of winning Lily and moving her onto the boat.

"Don't worry, Dan. It'll all change. They'll weed out the undesirables, and the girls will get their passes back. You have to remember where you are. This is a communist country. Control over the people is number one, even if it means taking a cut in tourist revenue."

Dan lit the cigar, took a couple of puffs, and said, "I heard that Castro passed a regulation that prohibits Cuban women from even being seen with a foreigner. How did a stupid law like that ever come about?"

"Well, Dan, you can thank your CNN for that."

"What's CNN got to do with it?"

"When the Soviet Union collapsed and stopped financing Cuba, Castro survived by opening the island to tourism. The tourists took home tales of exotic women, and when CNN did a piece on single men going to Cuba just for hookers, Fidel went ballistic and put his brother's ex-wife in charge of the problem. Her solution was to hire more police and instruct them to arrest any unmarried Cuban woman seen with a tourist."

Dan watched the brandy as he swirled it in the snifter and contemplated Graham's statements.

"In Cuba you are presumed guilty until proven guilty. Bring on the tourists with their dollars, but not at the risk of exploiting the female population." Then Graham added, "If you know your Cuban history, you'll remember that before the revolution Cuba had a reputation of being a whorehouse for America."

Dan thought a moment and said, "I guess that's my problem, Graham. I don't know much about Cuba other than they almost blew up the world with missiles during Kennedy's days."

Graham perked up and said, "That's pure unadulterated bullshit, Dan. The United States and the Soviet Union played much bigger roles than Cuba in that fiasco. That's the trouble with you Americans. You epitomize the saying, 'A little knowledge is a dangerous thing.' Americans don't know much about what is going on in the rest of the world, and most of you think Cuba is a rock somewhere down by Puerto Rico."

Dan was used to Graham's dogmatic personality and took no offense.

Graham took several puffs on his Monte Cristo before saying, "Sorry, Dan, but it does help if you know the history of this island in order to understand some of the actions of the present government. Think about it. Cuba has been dominated by either Spain or the United States since Columbus arrived in 1492." He thought a minute and said, "You interested in a history lesson?"

"Go ahead," Dan said. "I can always stand a little education, and I am interested in Cuba."

"You have to promise not to interrupt." He refilled his glass, passed the brandy over to Dan, and lit a new cigar.

"I'll start at the beginning. Columbus discovered Cuba in 1492 and claimed it for Spain. The Spaniards then killed most of the hundred thousand Indian inhabitants in the name of religion before they realized they had done away with the workers, forcing them to import slaves from Africa.

"By the mid 1800s, Cuba was rich with sugar, tobacco, and fruit, but the wealth from the crops went back to Spain, and that led to the first of Cuba's many conflicts. By 1878, more than 135,000 people had died in different Cuban revolutions.

"In 1895 another revolution was getting underway, with Cuba fighting Spain again. The United States was well aware of Cuba's sugar treasure, and they had more than fifty million dollars invested in the island. So the politicians in Washington came up with a plan to help Cuba win the war. They sent a ship to Havana to supposedly protect U.S. citizens living on the island."

Graham looked at the red colors in the sky and said. "Look at that. I never get tired of sunsets.

"The ship was the *USS Maine*. When it exploded in Havana Harbor, the U.S. called it an act of war and sent troops to fight the Spaniards. You probably remember Teddy Roosevelt and the charge up San Juan Hill. Anyway, Spain lost and exchanged one dominating power for another.

"Many historians say the U.S. blew up its own ship. It has never been proven, but it served the purpose. Cuba spent the first six decades of the 20th century militarily and economically controlled by the United States – until Fidel Castro's revolution. America has practiced just two policies regarding Cuba for the last one hundred years. The first sixty years they exploited it, and for the last forty years they have been trying to destroy it."

It was getting dark, but Graham was on a roll.

"In 1953, Fidel began the revolution against the Batista government by storming the Moncada barracks in Santiago de Cuba with one hundred and fifty fellow rebels. Most of the rebels were killed, but Castro survived and was sent to prison. However, after mounting pressure from the citizens, the Cuban congress passed an amnesty bill, and Batista signed it. Castro and his fellow rebels were freed after serving seventeen months of a fifteen-year sentence. Fidel was self-exiled to Mexico, where he began making plans to continue the revolution.

"Fidel and eighty-one revolutionaries returned to Cuba in December of 1956 aboard an old wooden boat to continue the fight. A storm hit them in the gulf, and they arrived two days late on the wrong beach, where Batista's forces met them.

"They lost the boat, weapons, and provisions, but Castro and his tiny army made their way into the rugged Sierra Maestra on Cuba's south coast, where they began a guerrilla war against Batista. They raided villages and made their way back to their secluded camps with captured guns and villagers who wanted to join the revolution. They took the island, and in January of '59 Castro and his army rode into Havana as Batista fled to the Dominican Republic."

"This is interesting," Dan said. "I like it. Keep going."

"Okay. You asked for it. Castro began making big changes in Cuba. First, he nationalized all estates over one thousand acres, a move that directly affected U.S. holdings. Then he closed the mafia's casinos and reduced the rates charged by American-owned electric and phone companies. A half million Cubans suspected full-blown socialist reform and fled to Florida.

"When Castro began nationalizing big American companies, the real pissing contest between America and Fidel began. Your government, Dan, the good ol' U.S. of A., couldn't stand having a Cuban government that would no longer do as Uncle Sam dictated. Just because Castro prevailed in a revolution didn't mean he could defy the big guy next door.

"The United States government decided to bring Castro to his knees with economic pressure. They began by refusing to sell more oil to Cuba. Castro responded by buying oil from the Soviet Union. That was a blow to America's ego, so they pressured Texaco, Shell, and Standard Oil to stop refining the crude oil the Soviets were bringing in. Fidel responded by nationalizing the refineries.

"Now the U.S. was really getting pissed off. So they removed all the American refinery technicians. Cuba got technicians from Mexico. The little pissing match really heated up when the U.S. refused to buy Cuba's seven hundred thousand tons of annual sugar. Fidel got just as pissed off and nationalized the American-owned sugar refineries."

Graham held up a finger to make his point. "Then he started selling the annual sugar crop to the Soviet Union. Before it was over, Castro nationalized eight hundred million dollars of U.S. interests that included everything from the telephone company to the American-owned cigar industry."

Graham sounded like a college professor on a podium lecturing to a thousand students. Dan was impressed with his delivery and his memory for dates and details. Graham obviously knew his stuff.

"You following all this, Dan?"

"Yeah, I'm hooked. Go ahead." Dan was all ears. His host had a way of condensing history into a tight, easily understood package.

"When John Kennedy became president, he inherited a war Eisenhower began the year before when he had ordered the CIA to train Cuban exiles in Guatemala. The plan was to launch an invasion of Cuba in April of 1961, with the United States providing air cover for the fifteen hundred invading troops. Kennedy cancelled the flights at the last minute, and the invasion became a one-sided affair. Three hundred mercenaries were killed. The remaining twelve hundred were captured and later ransomed to the U.S. for fifty-three million dollars worth of food and medicine. History remembers it as the Bay of Pigs. The U.S. was so embarrassed that they declared a full trade embargo on Cuba.

"Until the embargo, everything from bicycles to chocolate bars came from the United States. But in just two years, Washington's Cold War policies had pushed Cuba into a position where it began relying on the Soviet Union for almost everything.

"Then came the big one – the one where all countries sat up and took real notice. It was the closest the world has come to a full-blown nuclear war. History remembers this one as the Cuban Missile Crisis."

Graham was finally getting to the part that was familiar to Dan.

"Castro was aware that the United States was planning another invasion, so when the Soviets offered to donate a few nuclear missiles, Castro agreed. Fidel thought a couple of ICBMs aimed at Miami would be a good deterrent, but Khrushchev had bigger ambitions.

"The Soviets began installing nuclear missiles in Cuba that were capable of hitting every major city in the U.S. with the exception of Seattle. When a U.S. spy plane discovered the missiles, Kennedy ordered a naval blockade and threatened to open fire on any Soviet ship not stopping and allowing the U.S. Navy to inspect its cargo.

"The discovery of tactical nuclear weapons in Cuba was a grave Cold War crisis, and it put the world on the edge of an unprecedented nuclear catastrophe. Kennedy's military advisors wanted to solve the problem with a full-scale invasion of the island, a decision that would have led to holocaust.

"Castro kept trying to convince Khrushchev to fire the Russian missiles at America. In the end, cool heads prevailed. In return for removing the missiles from Cuba, Kennedy agreed to take his missiles out of Turkey and guarantee that America would never invade Cuba.

"Between 1963 and 1990, Cubans enjoyed a decent way of life as the Soviets financed the country with billions of dollars a year in the form of military subsidies and petroleum. The U.S. continued harassing Cuba on all fronts. In addition to the economic embargo, there were sixteen U.S. plots to assassinate Castro. They tried poisoning his cigars, poisoning a chocolate milkshake at his favorite lunch counter, planting an explosive seashell on the beach where he went swimming, and even contaminating his wetsuit with a lethal agent that would cause serious illness. The U.S. also tried a more direct route by offering the mafia one hundred and fifty thousand dollars to assassinate Fidel.

"Cuba was doing well until 1990, when the Soviet Union collapsed and left Cuba to fend for itself. Cuba went into tough times until 1995, when Castro opened the island to tourism and foreign investment. He had finally turned to the thing he had spent his life fighting: capitalism. Canada, Spain, and Italy jumped at the chance to invest in the island. Above all, Cuba was located just ninety miles from the richest country in the world that would someday send over millions of tourists.

"Think about it, Dan. By the time the United States gives up trying to break Cuba with its absurd embargo, every beach on the island will be owned by companies from every country but America. Americans will be spending millions of dollars a year staying in resorts that send the dollars back to Spain, Canada, Italy, and all points east. Talk about a trade deficit. In retrospect, it seems Washington made huge mistakes by trying to change the political state of affairs in Cuba. Who knows what would have happened if the United States had not interfered?

"On the Cuban side of the equation, Castro won the hearts of the Cubans, then let them down. Keeping a revolution going became more important than taking care of his people, even though the war had been won. History will probably remember him as a man with a lot of good ideas who made many improvements for Cuba, a man who controlled the island, but at the expense of the people. Christ," Graham said, "I'm beginning to sound like I'm standing on a soapbox."

"That's okay," Dan answered out of the darkness.

"The other side of it is that Cuba is the only country in the world where you can exist without working, and you won't see people dying from starvation, beggars on the street, or homeless people living in cardboard boxes."

Graham summed it up. "Cuba is the last of man's ideal that everybody can get along by giving everybody nothing. It's a society of shared misery.

"There you have it, Dan: the history of Cuba. Take it or leave it, but if I were you, I'd be careful about repeating it to anyone you don't know well. Fidel does not look kindly on anyone who speaks against him. Therefore, please don't quote me on anything I said. Anyway, it's just an opinion."

The sun had disappeared and the colored sky had faded into darkness. The only light in the cockpit was the small glow of the cigars. Graham sipped on his drink while Dan sat in the silence and digested the history lesson.

Graham broke the silence. "How goes it with the girl?"

"Lily? I'm stuck on her, Graham. I can't get her out of my head. I'm hopelessly in love."

"So what's the problem? Why are you alone so much?"

"That's just it. She says she likes me, but her goals and mine are so different she won't even sleep with me. Says she doesn't want to get involved. If it were up to me, I'd put her in a sack and sail the hell out of here."

"That has been done before, Dan. There are ways."

Dan slumped in his seat and thought about hiding her on the boat and paying off one of the customs guys to look the other way. "Yeah, I know there's a way, but I'm not sure she'd go with me if she had the chance. Living on a sailboat doesn't fit in with her dream." His voice rose a few decibels as he added, "She sees herself with some young fucking Italian, with bushy brown hair, a mustache, and ten pounds of gold hanging from his neck. She wants to live in the big city – in Italy."

.

"Hey," Graham said, "relax, Dan. I know all about Cuban women and their desire to live in Italy, or Spain, or America – anywhere where the streets are paved with gold and there's a shopping mall."

CHAPTER
12

Lily was still asleep as Dan eased out of bed. She had shown up unexpectedly the evening before, and they had wandered over to the pizza restaurant in the marina for dinner and a few games of 8-ball in the adjoining poolroom. Later, they had sat in the cockpit and watched the stars, making small talk about their pasts. It had been a beautiful evening, and Dan had sensed a need in Lily, as though she wanted someone she could trust. As a result, Dan had fought the urge to seduce her as they spent the night cuddled in the forward berth. She would have to be the one to make that first move.

He gazed down at her before heading to the galley. It amazed him how she looked as stunning in the morning as she did after preparing for an evening on the town. No blotched makeup or runny mascara. Lily looked good gyrating on a dance floor, stuffing her mouth with pizza, lining up a cue ball, or lying asleep under a bundle of covers. She was beautiful.

He carefully closed the door to the berth and made his way to the galley. He stopped and pressed the CD player button. Moments later he was singing along to Jimmy Buffet's "Margaritaville." He ground a full cup of Cuban coffee beans before carefully placing the dark grounds into the French press.

He had the feeling Lily was finally coming around. She seemed more at ease, and he was confident that she cared for him. Maybe she was even falling in love. If and when that happened, part of his dream would be fulfilled. If Lily made a commitment, he would figure out how to get her out of Cuba. He knew there was no way he could live in a communist country.

He poured boiling water onto the coffee and waited four minutes before slowly pushing down the plunger. The worn-out screen only separated eighty percent of the grounds from the mud-like fluid, but a small strainer took out the remaining twenty percent as he poured himself a full cup.

"None of that miniature cup crap you get in restaurants," he said to himself. Dan liked a full eight ounces of coffee in a cup. He enjoyed the flavor of espresso, but he felt they never served enough of it.

Of course, anything was better than the coffee he had drunk while surfing in Baja, where they served it unassembled: a paper cup of lukewarm water, a jar of instant Nescafe, and a tiny plastic spoon.

Dan switched on the TV and watched CNN to make sure the U.S. had not gotten itself into another war, then checked the weather channel to make sure an early seasonal hurricane was not threatening.

There was a rap on the boat, and when he looked out, he saw Maverick standing on the quay holding a box of cigars.

He slid back the hatch.

"Permission to come aboard, Captain?" Maverick asked.

"Sure, Maverick. Come on down."

Maverick made his way down the stairs and plopped his two hundred and fifty pounds onto the settee. Dan heard it groan.

"I brought you a present." Maverick placed the box he'd been carrying on the table and said, "Esplendidos." He opened the box. There was a neat row of seven-inch-long cigars with gold bands. "These are Cohiba Esplendidos, Cuba's finest. They cost three hundred and eighty-three dollars a box in any government shop here in Havana. There are twenty-five cigars in a box. In one of New York's private clubs, they sell one of these cigars for fifty bucks, making this box worth twelve hundred and fifty dollars. We can buy 'em for twenty-five and sell 'em for five hundred to a guy in Florida who'll sell the same boxes to the clubs for six or seven hundred."

Dan's antennae went up. "What do you mean *we?*"

"You and me, Dan. It's a real scam. Foolproof and almost legal."

Dan was just a little confused. What was this guy doing here cutting him in on such a good deal, and what was the "almost" in the legal part? He looked at his visitor, who was waiting for a reply.

"Well, thanks a lot, but what makes you think I would be interested? And just how legal is this scheme?"

"I'll answer both questions at once," Maverick replied. "The legal part is almost perfect. If we get caught, it's a slap on the wrist and we lose the cigars. And if you weren't interested just a little, you wouldn't have asked about the legal part."

Maverick studied Dan before continuing. "I know what you're thinking. Why does he need me? Okay, I'll be honest with you. I can't sail the cigars back to Florida because I got busted the last time. Five perfect trips, then my auxiliary went out, and I had to take a chance going into Key West. Some dock guy turned me in. I lost the cargo and got my wrists slapped. It cost me five grand in legal fees."

Dan was amused. "Assuming I would be interested, what's the deal?"

Maverick moved from his position to the dinette across from Dan. "I know what sells in the States. I'll do the buying. All you have to do is put up some front money, sail away with five hundred boxes and deliver them to my contact in Florida." There was excitement in his voice. "We split fifty-fifty."

Maverick pulled one of the cigars out of the box, bit the end off, and fired up the butane lighter. He rolled the end of the cigar through the flame a few times before drawing on it. When the cigar was well lit, he looked at the end as he let the smoke out of his mouth. "Draws good, burns even. It's a good box. Right off the street."

He took a few more puffs and looked at the ceiling. "Try one, Dan. Savor the flavor of the world's most expensive smoke."

Dan lit a cigar, still pondering Maverick's business deal. "Where exactly do these street cigars come from?"

"With luck, they actually come from the factory."

Maverick leaned back and made himself comfortable. "Pour us a couple glasses of the seven-year you have over there, and I'll give you a little more information about Cuban cigars."

Dan did as he was told and set two half-filled tumblers of Anejo on the table.

Maverick picked up a glass and studied the dark fluid like a wine connoisseur preparing to taste a vintage Bordeaux. "Good dark rum without ice or cola. That's the way to enjoy a good cigar."

Then he looked at Dan and said, "Let's start at the beginning. Cuba has the best soil, the best climate, and the best tobacco seed for making the world's finest cigars. The plants grow fast, several months, and after cutting the leaves, they're dried for six to eight months before being shipped to the factory. Don't let the trademarks on the boxes fool you. The same factories roll for many different brands. Take the El Laguito factory, for instance. It's one of the oldest, built in 1942. They produce five of the top brands, plus a bunch of lesser-known brands.

"The thing is, they get all the tobacco at the same time. So why is one cigar three times the cost of another? It begins with the hand selection of the leaf. The best go for the Cohibas, second best quality to Romeo and Julieta, the third is for Hoyo de Monterrey, and so on."

Dan had never heard Maverick speak so eloquently. He seemed to know his subject, and he was obviously in love with Cuban cigars.

"To ensure the quality, cigar rollers go to school for nine months before they are allowed to roll the finished commercial product. The making of a cigar begins with a small bunch of filler leaves that are rolled with a binder leaf and left in a wood press to give the cigar its shape. Once out of the press it is cut to size and rolled with a wrapper leaf. The last step is gluing on the tiny end. That's the part you cut off before smoking. The cigars are then separated by color, banded, and boxed.

"The entire process is done by hand." He let that sink in before adding. "There are no machines used in the making of a good Cuban cigar."

Maverick seemed to be in a trance while he talked. "There are about five hundred rollers working in Havana's biggest factory. They produce more than a hundred thousand cigars a day and earn twelve million dollars a year for Fidel. The workers are paid the normal communist salary, about seven bucks a month, but they get an additional fifty U.S. dollars if they roll fast and produce good quality. Another bonus is that they get to take home a few cigars – three a day, to be exact.

"So figure it out at three cigars a day, eighteen a week. And by slipping a few extras into their pocket, they have a full box of twenty-five every week. Multiply that by five hundred rollers times five factories and it means there are about ten thousand boxes a month that can be sold on the street.

"If a worker has his nephew or cousin selling boxes for thirty a pop, the guy in the factory earns another fifty dollars a month. Two million tourists a year come to this island, and every one of them wants to take home a couple boxes of cigars."

Dan did not have to use a calculator. He took Maverick's word for it.

"Gathering up five hundred boxes is not that easy. But don't worry, Dan. That's my job. Putting up the front money and getting the boxes into the States is where you come in.

"I usually take five or six hundred boxes a trip. They are light, small, and easy to hide on a boat if you know what you're doing. Customs' dogs are trained to smell drugs, not tobacco."

Dan cringed at the word *customs*, and it suddenly brought to mind that he might be getting involved in something that could cost him his boat, or worse, his freedom.

He heard Maverick saying, "Even so, it isn't like drug smuggling. It's just a little more than a token punishment for smuggling cigars."

That was the part that worried Dan. "What do you mean by token punishment?"

Maverick waved the question off. "Not to worry. I have a lawyer who can get you out for five grand. Of course, you could lose your boat."

Dan made rapid calculations. If they bought the cigars for twenty-five a box and sold them for five hundred, they would be making close to two hundred fifty thousand dollars on one trip on a twelve thousand, five hundred dollar investment. Several trips like that, and he'd have enough to make the small change he had been thinking about with his plan to get Lily out of Cuba and to a villa on an island that had a mall.

Maverick was blowing perfect smoke rings as he waited for Dan's answer.

Dan head himself say, "I'll think it over." But he had made his decision. He was going to try his hand at cigar smuggling.

•

CHAPTER
13

Dan answered the knocking on the hull and discovered Manny Glickman standing on the quay.

"Hi, Dan. Wonder if you would come over to my boat and take a look at some things I bought."

"Sure, Manny, I'll be over in a few minutes." Dan didn't like playing the role of a know-it-all-guy just because he had been in the marina a little longer than Glickman, but Manny seemed like such a lost soul. If Dan guessed right, he wanted to talk about cigars. Every sailor who came into the marina wanted to take a few boxes back and pay for the trip.

When he got to Manny's boat and went below, his suspicions were confirmed. Manny had purchased fifty boxes of cigars from a black market street vendor for two thousand dollars.

He produced a sample of his new purchase for Dan's inspection and opened a classic box of Cohiba Esplendidos, proudly announcing, "Store price is three hundred eighty-three dollars a box. I got fifty boxes for forty bucks each."

The word had gotten around that Dan was keeping company with Maverick and had learned a lot about Cuban tobacco – a fact that was far from the truth. But after his indoctrination by Maverick, he felt he did know a little more than the average guy that came to Cuba for the first time.

"Not bad, Manny." Dan noticed that the cigars were all the same color and the right size and the bands looked even. "How about the others, Manny?" He didn't tell Glickman he had paid ten dollars a box too much.

"I don't want to open 'em," Manny said as he carefully slid the opened box back into one of his galley cabinets. "They're sealed with Habanos bands and Cuban tax stamps. Makes 'em authentic. When I get them back to the States, I can sell 'em for five hundred bucks a box. I know a guy in New York who owns a club, and he's ready to buy."

"Manny!" Dan looked at him hard. "The guy gave you the seals and stamps, didn't he? You put them on yourself, didn't you? You checked each box, didn't you?" Before Dan had finished, he was afraid he already knew the answers. His new friend had obviously failed Cigar Smuggling 101 in school.

"No, the guy said he spent a lot of time getting them on just right. It's not easy, you know."

"Yes it is, Manny. You buy the box with the seals and stamps inside. You put them on yourself." He felt like he was teaching a kid how to tie his shoes. "Get some of the other boxes, Manny. We'd better take a look inside."

"You mean break the seals?" Manny was standing with his back to the door that went back to the compartment where he kept his cargo. "The boxes were sealed at the factory by the guy's uncle."

Dan thought of just walking away. What the hell did he care if Manny Glickman, a New York dress salesman, got his legs broken for selling Tampax for five hundred a box to some mafia restaurant owner? But the sight of the bony legs sticking down out of Manny's baggy Bermuda shorts softened him. He knew Manny's lower extremities could not take much more punishment, especially from a baseball bat.

"Get the rest of them, Manny," he commanded.

Manny reluctantly brought in another box.

Dan cut the seal and opened the lid. "Well, it's not filled with Tampax, Lenny, but it's close. It looks like they were rolled by blind chimpanzees that didn't know the difference between tobacco and banana leaves."

Manny froze for a tenth of a second before he scrambled back into the master bedroom and began tearing open the remaining boxes. "That son of a bitch!" Manny was furious as he kept tearing open more boxes. "He fucked me. Look at this shit. It's all crap. That cocksucker sold me counterfeit cigars."

Dan wasn't sure if he should disappear or wait for Manny to cool off. The hustler had been out-hustled. He stopped himself from replying. It was not a good time to tell Manny that counterfeit cigars never looked as bad as those, and you could at least smoke a bad counterfeit Cuban cigar.

He left Manny to his swearing and walked the two hundred feet back up the canal to *Pass Line.*

Where do they come from? he thought. *A guy like Manny Glickman belongs in New York selling suits. Yet here he is, a disaster waiting to happen. He's dangerous for the rest of us honest smugglers.*

He flopped down on the settee and poured himself a shot of seven-year-old Havana Club before saying out loud, "Quit trying to be a good guy, Dan. Stay away from Glickman. The guy is dangerous."

CHAPTER
14

Whenever Lily went home to see her family, Dan wandered the marina and visited with the other boaters. On one of his nightly sojourns, he discovered the Hemingway International Yacht Club, located one block from the Fifth Avenue entrance to the marina at the end of Number Three Canal. The small two-story clubhouse had several offices on the top floor and a small bar on the ground floor that sold watered-down rum drinks, T-shirts, belts, and baseball caps to sailors who wanted to prove that they had been to Cuba.

Dan sat deep in a plush leather armchair next to Maverick and nursed his drink. A couple of sailors were at the bar having one too many, while CNN was blaring the latest news.

The club's commodore, a short fifty-year-old man named Nestor Montana, came through the main entrance and waved to Maverick quickly. He continued through the dim room and up the stairs to his office.

"The guy's a prick," Maverick said gruffly, nodding after Nestor. "He was appointed to his position as a reward for years of dedication to the communist party. He knows nothing about boating. He thinks the toilets on ships are located on the poop deck."

Dan smiled, enjoying the alcohol's relaxing effects and refusing to let Maverick's negative attitude get him down.

Dan had paid the three-hundred-dollar lifetime membership fee to the club and enjoyed a thirty-five-percent discount on his dockage fees as a result. With his new plan to stay six months, he figured he would save one hundred and twenty dollars a month. Three weeks after he joined, the discount was lowered to fifteen percent, with a ten percent gratuity added to the marina services.

After paying monthly dues of thirty dollars, Dan figured the membership resulted in a net loss of two dollars and forty-nine cents a month. "What the hell," he had said to himself at the time. "It's Cuba. A small price to pay for membership in such a prestigious organization."

"Can you beat it?" Maverick continued. "Nestor's first rule was to prohibit Cuban women in the clubhouse. That's why you hardly ever see any boaters in here. The two guys at the bar haven't yet made it out of the marina to the local places where the girls hang out. But his biggest blunder is scheduling the St. Petersburg to Cuba Sailing Regatta on the same weekend as the Hemingway

Marlin Fishing Tournament. I can see it now. A thousand sailors and fisherman fighting over everything from slips to showers."

Dan had been told that the club-sponsored sailing regattas and other activities were supposed to make a membership worthwhile. He let Maverick's complaint go without commenting on it.

Two weeks before Christmas, a religious holiday celebrated for the first time in Cuba since the revolution, Commodore Montana sent his office staff out to distribute to the captains of each sailboat flyers announcing a Christmas regatta.

The big news was that Montana had arranged it so Cuban girls could crew on the boats, enabling them to leave the island and sail the ten-mile course to Havana Harbor and back. For the first time in their lives, they would be able to leave Cuban soil on a pleasure yacht.

Dan, who was not fond of sailing races and compared them to watching grass grow, was not intrigued, but for some reason he let Manny talk him into crewing aboard his old schooner.

"You'll love it, Dan. Graham's going and bringing Pilar. I'm taking Rita, and you can take Lily. Just give me her I.D. number, and away we go. Jeez, Dan, it's a chance to get out of the marina with the girls. You know – nice sunny day, cruising down to Havana and taking in the skyline from a couple miles out, drinking beer and having some sandwiches. It's just ten miles down and ten back. *Mud Runner's* an old boat, but I talked the race committee into giving me a big handicap."

"Handicap? A minute ago you said this was a fun race. Why do you need a handicap?"

Something inside Dan said to forget the stupid race. Most of the sailboats in the marina had been sitting there for ages. He doubted that more than half of the entries would make it to the checkout dock at customs. But the carrot being held in front of him was the thought of a Sunday boat ride with Lily. If she liked sailing, it might convince her to join him on his long cruise. She could meet him in another country, maybe Grenada. Cubans could get flights to Grenada without visas. Like Manny said, a couple of beers and a sandwich while watching Old Havana drift by.

"Okay, Manny. Lily and I will go with you. But if by any chance the wind comes up and it starts to get rough, it's back to the marina, okay? It's a pleasure cruise, not a race." He knew if it got rough, the girls would get seasick.

Most of Dan's sailboat racing experience had been limited to weekends on a friend's CAL-40 in Southern California. Most of those regattas had been light air, drifting parties from Newport Beach, to Ensenada, Mexico, during the annual *Cinco de Mayo* race. The starts had been exciting and colorful as

·

three hundred boats jockeyed for position. After that, it was a slow 120-mile downwind race that required few sail changes and minimum navigation skills. "Go out of the harbor, turn left, and follow the beer cans to Ensenada," had been the race committee's advice to first-time participants.

Dan had less than a little confidence in Manny's old boat, but this was not going to be the America's Cup trials, just a Sunday boat ride, an easy sail down to Havana with a couple of tacks back to the marina. It was Dan's idea of a sailboat race. It would be a smooth-water, sun-tanning, beer-dinking, grab-ass cruise with three beautiful women.

It all seemed simple enough, but doubts about Manny lingered in the back of his mind. The guy had earned the reputation as the marina's resident disaster. By the time he had been there three weeks, he had managed to get his dinghy stolen by forgetting to lock it up with a chain, ran his bicycle and himself into the canal, had eight hundred dollars in cash stolen after inviting a young lady to spend the night, and set his boat on fire while trying to light his rail-mounted barbecue with gasoline. Trouble seemed to follow Manny Glickman.

Unfortunately, Dan was his closest neighbor, and Manny had adopted him as his best friend, so it was Dan that Manny turned to whenever he had a problem. Manny was so helpless it was hard not to like him.

On the morning of the race, Manny returned from the club with the weather report. "Nice day," he said. "Mild wind, six to ten knots."

Graham, the more practical of the group, sized up the situation, looked at Dan, and said, "This is a big tub for just two guys. I doubt we can count on Manny if anything goes wrong."

"Yeah," Dan said, "the girls are really excited, but I just found out Lily can't swim. Let's make sure we keep this thing a no-brainer. Why don't you take the helm, Graham? You've got the most experience."

"Okay, you take the foredeck, and Manny can pretend he's the captain and handle the sheets. We're not going to make any sail changes, so it should be pretty simple."

"Okay. Captain Manny," Dan announced to the world, "to the Morro Castle and back. Please don't heel the boat and spill the beer.

"This will be nice," he said to Graham as they were preparing to cast off. "An easy cruise."

"Yeah, let's hope so." Graham was at the helm moving the big wheel around. He yelled down to Manny, who was putting beer into the refrigerator. "Hey, Manny, check the cables on the helm. It's stiff as hell."

Manny hardly took notice. "It's okay, Graham. It has always been like that."

"Well, check it anyway, please."

"Yeah, sure."

Captain Manny's idea of the race seemed to differ from Dan's. Dan was out for a Sunday cruise with his sweetheart, but he was concerned that Manny was taking it a little too seriously.

When Dan had arrived at the boat that morning, Manny had already piled up a huge mound of boating stuff on the grass beside the dock. He had removed all the extra lines, anchors, chain, heavy sails, the dinghy and the outboard, and his heavy extra batteries. "Too much weight," he had said. "Borrowed a lightweight one-ounce nylon Genoa and a pretty green sail in a sock that goes between the masts."

"It's called a staysail, Manny, and I don't think we'll need it. We haven't got enough people to manage it if the wind comes up."

"Maybe, but with a good crew and the right wind this heavy boat will cruise right by the lighter boats bouncing along in the chop."

Dan knew Manny's boat was doubtful to finish under sail, let alone win the race. But Captain Manny had lobbied hard at the skippers' meeting, and the race committee had given the lumbering *Mud Runner* a generous handicap. Manny seemed confident of capturing a trophy with what he referred to as his racing machine.

The start was a surprise. Graham showed great skill and maneuvered the heavy boat through a series of tacks to cross the line just as the flag was raised and the starting horn sounded.

The first leg of the race was downwind to the Morro Castle buoy at the entrance to the deep Havana Harbor.

Mud Runner was actually out in front of the fleet for a time, and Manny was ecstatic. "Great job at the start, you guys. We're winning."

Everyone was happy, drinking beer and eating sandwiches. Manny's girlfriend Rita was playing her guitar. Lily and Pilar were sprawled out on cushions enjoying the sun as the island drifted by on the right, while the rest of the fleet drifted by on the left.

"This is the first time in my whole life I have ever been on a boat," Lily said as she reached for one of the sandwiches. "I love it."

Thirty minutes later, *Mud Runner* saw the last of the fleet pass by. Manny's boat was even slower than Dan and Graham had imagined. Even with a big handicap, Manny stood little chance of earning a trophy.

Just as well, thought Dan. *Now that we're last, we can sit back and enjoy the trip.*

Dan was concerned about the black clouds building on the horizon behind the boat. Manny's weather report gave all aboard little reason to be concerned, but now Dan was skeptical about the accuracy of the report and doubted that Manny had read it right.

Dan mentioned the weather to Graham, who said, "I don't like it either. We're sailing way too close to land. Let's change course and get some sea room. If the wind changes, we're going to have a lee shore."

"Change course?" Manny was up instantly, looking toward the Morro Castle about four miles dead ahead. "If we head out, we'll lose all that distance to the mark."

Graham gave Dan a glance then addressed Manny in a serious tone. "A lee shore is a sailor's nightmare, Manny. When a boat sails close to land, a lot of things can happen, all of them bad."

Manny was adamant. "We're only a couple miles from the mark. I'm the captain, and I say hold your course, helmsman." Manny sounded like Captain Horatio Hornblower ordering his vessel into high seas combat.

Graham shrugged and said, "Might be a good idea to fire up that old diesel. It didn't sound that good when we were motoring out. Give it a check." Graham continued glancing back at the approaching weather.

Dan studied the direction of the boat. Their present course would take the boat within a quarter mile of land, where the island jutted seaward at the *Malecon*. He could see the hotels along the seawall now appearing dangerously close.

"You're right, Graham. Take it out a little."

By the time Graham had the Havana Harbor buoy in sight, the rest of the fleet had turned the corner and was headed back to the marina.

The classy eighty-foot racing sloop *Mara* was well ahead, followed by the rest of the Hemingway regulars. As *Mara* went by in the opposite direction, Dan could see her ten-member crew in matching red T-shirts sitting on the windward rail. "Now that's a sailboat," he muttered.

The wind changed as *Mud Runner* finally rounded the downwind mark. It was now out of the west and freshening by the minute.

Graham set a tack out to sea, and within twenty minutes the wind had risen to near gale force, whipping the sea into a foaming froth.

Dan glanced at his watch and noted the time. It was four-thirty in the afternoon. He would recall this moment later because it was the time when everything started to go wrong. Forty-knot winds were driving stinging rain against bare skin as Graham fought to keep the lumbering vessel pinching to weather, but making little headway toward the marina. The boat was on a port tack heading out to sea – away from Havana, but also away from the marina. The wind was getting stronger, and the patched sails were becoming more suspect with each gust.

Lily came up halfway out of the cabin. She was green in the face and obviously seasick. "Why is there so much water in the cabin?" she groaned before disappearing again.

Dan took a quick look below and came back up to report to Graham. "One of the ports in the forward cabin is frozen in the open position, and we've been taking on a lot of water. I crammed a pillow in the hole, but there's three inches of water above the floorboards. I managed to start the bilge pumps. But without the engine to charge the batteries, the pumps are going to suck the batteries dry. Get Manny to start the engine, and let's call it quits."

"Manny!" Graham yelled above the wind, "this is a lost cause. Start the auxiliary. This boat is barely capable of going anywhere, especially into this wind. We are going to motor back to the marina."

"If we start the engine," Manny yelled through the pelting rain, "we'll be disqualified."

Dan was starting to lose his temper. "Who gives a shit, Manny? We're dead last. And the way we're headed, we'll have to go to Florida before we can tack back. We got a bilge full of water, and we need the pumps. Start the fuckin' auxiliary."

Manny reluctantly went below and started grinding on the starter. Ten minutes later, the engine had still not come to life, and the batteries gave a last groan before going completely dead.

Graham was careful not to venture too far out into the Gulf Stream, so the port tack only resulted in a half-mile gain toward the marina. It was tough sailing, and everyone was cold. The wind and rain chilled their exposed bodies.

"Manny!" Graham yelled. "Where's your fowl weather gear?"

"Don't have any," came the reply.

Then the clew of the borrowed lightweight Genoa blew out.

Dan struggled onto the foredeck and took down the unruly headsail while the bow rose then fell, burying him in warm seawater. Each time the bow went up, he pulled sail. As the boat fell, he had to let go and grab the rails with both hands to keep from being washed overboard. He finally managed to secure the sail and make his way back to the cockpit, where Graham was wrestling with the helm.

The farther out into the gulf *Mud Runner* went, the farther the current carried the boat from the marina. The blue water of the gulf had turned black. White wavy lines danced between the waves that were being flattened by the strong wind. It reminded Dan of the picture he'd seen in a heavy weather sailing book that described extreme conditions. Under the picture the caption read, "You should not be out in this kind of weather."

Graham struggled at the helm before finally getting the boat headed back toward the island.

"There's something wrong with the steering, Dan. I could hardly bring the boat through the wind. Take a look below, and see if you can see anything."

Dan came up a few minutes later. "The cables jumped the pulleys and are grinding up into the wood floor supports. The friction is affecting your steering. The cables are getting looser and starting to fray. If they jump the main steering drum, we're really in trouble."

"Manny, where's the emergency rudder tiller?" Graham yelled. He knew the answer before it came.

"There isn't one."

"Great! Just fucking great!" Graham howled. "We are on an east tack, and if those cables jam, we'll slam right into Havana. Let's get on the handheld radio and make contact with the marina, just in case we need help."

"The radio batteries are dead," Manny said nonchalantly.

The boat was now making even less time to weather. It was getting late, and everything that could go wrong was going wrong. Even if they managed to make the eight miles to the marina, negotiating the narrow channel into the harbor at night with a following sea would be treacherous.

But the immediate problem was just as bad: they had no idea how far they were from land. Manny had a GPS, but its batteries were also dead. It was getting dark, and the low clouds and driving rain made visibility less than a quarter mile.

Dan was a strong swimmer, but for the first time in his life he realized he might drown at sea. Even though it would be just a short swim to shore, there would be huge surf pounding the twenty-foot high coral wall. Anyone in the water would not have a chance.

He formed an emergency plan in his mind. *If we're going to hit the rocks, I'll go over the side with Lily and drag her seaward. The crashing boat will bring the authorities, and hopefully we'll be spotted drifting offshore.*

Manny stood halfway down the companionway, holding on for dear life as he watched Graham wrestle with the wheel.

"This is it, Manny. We've got to make one more tack out of here and get away from the land, wherever it might be. When we get a little sea room, I'm going to jibe this tub back to Havana Harbor."

"What? You can't do that!" Manny screamed. "We're not permitted to go into the harbor. They'll take my boat." He puffed up his skinny chest and in a firm voice said, "I am the captain, and I say head for the finish line."

Dan grabbed Manny and shouted into his face, "Listen, you little fuck, we have a situation here, and Graham and I don't give a shit about the finish line or even your boat! We're talking survival! Call it mutiny if you want. We're heading to a safe harbor then dropping the anchor."

Manny just stood and stammered, "But ... but ... we don't have an anchor. I left it on the dock."

The wind was now out of the northwest, and they found themselves in a dangerous lee shore situation, with the wind pushing the boat toward land. Dan was leaning forward as if the extra distance would allow him to see through the rain. Suddenly, the low clouds lifted for a moment, and he could see lights. "Jesus Christ, it's one of the hotels!"

Through a momentary clearing, they saw the fifteen-story Cohiba Hotel rising out of the mist. Huge waves crashed over the coral wall and splashed cars driving on the busy street.

Graham began spinning the wheel. "Ready about. Manny, get the main sheet. Dan, go forward and put your back to the jib and backwind it. With this fucked steering, it's going to be a bitch making this tack."

Graham turned the wheel hand over hand as the cables burned farther into the beams, and the boat came into the wind two hundred meters from the pounding surf. Dan put his back into the jib and breathed a sigh of relief as the schooner heeled over and changed directions to a port tack out to sea and away from the breakwater.

Mud Runner was once again headed out to sea and away from immediate danger. But without the Genoa and with the steering cables continuing to fray, the heavy boat was out of balance and difficult for Graham to control. Suddenly the boat righted as it turned straight into the wind and stopped.

Almost too nonchalantly, Graham yelled, "Hey Dan, look!"

Dan got a sick feeling in his stomach as he watched Graham grab the wheel and spin it. The wheel kept spinning as the boat sat facing the oncoming gale.

"The steering must have come off the rudder drum," Graham yelled above the wind. "We've lost steerage. Great! Just fucking great! The steering is out, and we have no emergency tiller, no engine, no radios, dead batteries, and not even an anchor, if we're lucky enough to sail into some calm water. We've got a boat with shitty sails that won't sail to windward, a dangerous lee shore, and a stupid owner who still thinks he can win a trophy."

Dan went below, took a look, and came back on deck. Graham was sitting now, dejectedly looking at the worthless, spinning wheel.

"Cold as it is up here, Graham, you don't want to go below. It looks like a scene out of a slave ship movie. The girls are down there in a cabin half-filled with sea water and vomit."

Suddenly, Manny came topside carrying an emergency flare and fired it into the mainsail. It burned a hole in the canvas before the flare landed on the deck, spinning around like a Fourth of July pinwheel before going out.

Dan was cracking up at Manny's attempt to set the boat on fire and said, "Maybe we'll get lucky and get run over by a freighter and end it all." He paused, then added in a serious tone, "We're fucked, Graham, unless we can get the steering fixed."

He looked at Graham and saw a cold, exhausted sailor who had been wrestling the stiff helm since ten that morning.

He went below and returned with a wool shirt he had found in Manny's locker. "Here, put this on. I'm going down to take a look at the cables."

He made his way back to the master stateroom and started tearing the bunk apart to get at the cables and the rudder drum.

Two hours later, he emerged with blood still dripping from the ends of his fingers after wrestling with the frayed steel cables.

"The cables are back on the drum, but I don't know how long they'll stay there."

The wind had died to about fifteen knots, and Graham was standing on deck staring at a white light in the near distance.

"See that light, Dan? It's the marina entrance. We've been drifting in this direction since you went below. The wind has shifted, and we've been getting a little help from the current. It just might be enough to let us jibe and run downwind into the channel."

Graham had found new energy and had taken charge. "Drop the main and the staysail. We'll run in on the jib. Be ready to drop the sail as soon as we pass the last marker." He paused then turned toward the cabin. "Manny, get up here."

Manny had been curled up in one of the forward bunks for the last two hours. When he came up on deck, Graham explained the situation to him.

"Manny, we've lucked out to a certain degree. We've drifted to within about a half-mile of the marina entrance. It's that white light over there. The cables are working, but it's touch and go. We think we can jibe the boat and head into the marina. The wind is down, but the seas are still breaking in the channel.

"There are reefs on both sides of the channel, but with a little luck we can we can catch a wave and sail right into the calm water. But if we broach, or if the steering cables don't hold, your boat's going to be on the reef. If that happens, we're going to have a problem getting everybody to shore."

Manny seemed confused. "The boat might go on the reef?"

Graham answered, "It's either the reef here or the reef farther up the coast later tonight, Manny. It's your boat and your call." Graham was asking permission from the boat's owner, but Dan knew they were going into the marina with or without Glickman's okay.

The friendly red-and-green-lighted buoys were plainly visible, and less than a half-mile farther was the customs dock.

"It looks so close," Manny mumbled. "I guess we better do it."

Dan was worried about Lily. "Do you have any life preservers?"

"There's one under the forward bunk."

"One? That's it? Shit."

He went below and spoke to the seasick girls. "We're at the marina, but we may have a rough landing. Get up on deck and hold on. If we have to go into the water, everybody stick together."

He rushed forward and came back moments later with a life vest that looked like it had been used on the Titanic. After fumbling with it, he managed to put it on Lily.

"Go into the water?" Lily said, her voice cracking. "We might go into the water?"

It was pitch black out there, and Dan could tell she was deathly afraid of water. He cinched up the straps and told her not to worry and stay close.

When he got back up on deck, Graham had already jibed the boat and was carefully easing her downwind. They passed the outer buoy, moving well but not fast enough for Graham. He told Dan he wanted as much speed as possible to surf the breakers up ahead.

As he thought about the frayed steering cables, Dan held his breath. The boat moved slowly down the channel, and the roaring surf meant that with one mistake now, the coral reef would claim another victim.

Mud Runner's stern was suddenly lifted up by a wave as Graham fought to keep the boat on course. Then the lumbering schooner accelerated as it surfed momentarily down the wave before the bow lifted and the heavy vessel settled back into the water. The wave had passed, and they were still in the center of the channel.

Graham had an iron grip on the wheel. "So far so good," he said as he prepared for the next wave that was getting ready to break on the stern.

They had surfed past the red and green channel markers. The marina was just up ahead, and they could hear the music drifting out over the marina from Papa's Disco.

Another wave, bigger than the last one, hit the stern and lifted the boat. This time there was a loud bang.

Dan looked at Graham. He had that sick look on his face one gets when all the options in an emergency situation have been played out. The wheel was slowly spinning again, controlling nothing.

"Shit. We're so close."

The boat had no steering, but the following sea and wind was moving the boat at four knots straight ahead.

"Hey," Manny said, "look! We're heading right for the customs dock. We're going to make it to the dock."

"Make it is right!" Dan yelled. "We're going to hit the fucking thing. We can't turn, and we can't stop. Drop the jib. Grab the girls and hang on!"

The dolphin striker on the bow took the blow and snapped like a toothpick as *Mud Runner* hit the concrete dock head on.

The next swell picked up the boat and slammed it down as Dan jumped off onto the dock with the thought of fending off. When he saw the eight-foot-long bowsprit rise into the air over his head, he jumped back aboard the out-of-control boat. The bow crashed onto the concrete as the stern swung downwind. The boat was bouncing along down the dock, rising and smashing against the concrete.

Customs officials, responding to the cries from the women, came running along the dock to offer assistance as Manny threw a line from the bow. One of the men on shore caught it and secured it to a palm tree as the waves lifted the boat up and smashed it onto the dock.

Graham threw another line from the stern, and the men on the dock managed to control the bucking twenty-ton boat long enough for Dan and Graham to offload the women. They finally wrestled the boat around the corner to gentler water and secured it for the night.

Dan stood alongside the boat with Lily, who was soaking wet and shivering. Dan was thankful that everybody was safe and on dry land. Manny's boat had taken a few hits from the concrete dock, but that was a lot better than having it out there on the reef grinding holes in the hull all night. A few bangs against the dock was a small price to pay, considering they could all be out there in the dark swimming for their lives. They were on solid ground, and he really didn't care whether Manny's boat sank right there at the dock or not.

Graham had called a taxi to take them around to the other side of the marina and back to their boats. The driver didn't comment when the four wet bodies climbed into his cab.

They arrived back at their boats at ten-thirty, thirteen hours after they had left for an easy afternoon sail.

Dan made some tea and splashed a shot of rum into the cup before handing the brew to Lily. "Well, *mi amor*, how do you like sailing?"

Lily took her time. After a few sips from the cup, she said, "It was fun, Dan. Real fucking fun. Do me a favor. Next time, *include me out!*"

Dan smiled as he recognized her humor. "It's not always like that, sweetheart. That was not normal."

But Dan knew there would be little hope now of convincing Lily to join him on his world cruise.

He vowed to stay away from sailing regattas, and Montana's club events in particular. He also vowed to stay clear of old, beat up boats – and Manny Glickman, the walking disaster.

After all his experiences in Vegas and his awareness of hustlers trying to take the gaming business, he'd been sucker-punched by the skinny little Manny, who had talked him into sailing his broken-down pile of junk. It was another lesson delivered by the sea gods that would stay with him the rest of his life, a life that might have been cut short if those steering cables had broken on that tack they had made when they saw the lighted windows of the Cohiba Hotel.

It took three days to locate five boats feared lost in the storm. *Fair Maiden* managed to drop anchor in a small cove and bounced the night away just a few yards from passing traffic on the *Malecon*. One race entrant broke a rudder, but the resourceful captain managed to jury rig a whisker pole to a cabinet door, and by lashing it to the side of his boat, he made it into the marina just after dark. Another boat made it into Havana Harbor, where it was immediately impounded. It bumped around in rough water alongside a Russian tanker for four days before port authorities released the vessel. Many boats had made it back to the marina before the weather deteriorated. Others had no trouble sailing back after the wind came up. To a real sailor with a well-maintained boat, it was just another race that started under calm conditions and ended up as an exciting blow.

One twenty-eight-foot sloop single-handed by an experienced sailor blew the mainsail then lost its engine. With no sail or power, and with waves breaking in the narrow channel, he called the race committee and requested assistance.

The call came into the clubhouse bar well after dark as the other crews were slamming down shooters. Commodore Montana took the distress call on the radio behind the bar.

"Hemingway, Hemingway. This is *Red Robin*. I am a mile west of the channel entrance buoy. I have no engine and a blown mainsail. I need assistance. Over."

"*Red Robin*," came the reply. "This is Commodore Montana. The weather is bad. It is very dangerous out there. I repeat. It is very dangerous. You must come in immediately." Montana switched off the radio and returned to the party.

Red Robin finally managed to get the engine running and limped in at two in the morning, but the sixty-foot ketch, Maria, was not so fortunate. After sitting three miles offshore all night, she went aground early the next morning trying to negotiate the marina entrance in heavy seas.

The Hemingway Marina Christmas Regatta probably didn't rank up there with the famed Fastnet or Sydney-Hobart sailing disasters, but for Dan Fletcher and Lily Lopez, the race would be remembered as a near-death experience.

CHAPTER
15

"We're all set for your first run, Dan."

Maverick was standing on the quay, announcing to the world in a loud voice that Dan was getting ready to illegally take cigars out of the marina.

"Not so loud, Maverick. There's no need to advertise it. Come aboard."

Maverick was dressed in his uniform of the day. He wore pressed army fatigue pants and an oversized olive drab tank top. His stars and stripes flag covered his head, and the remains of a fat cigar, barely long enough to clear the mustache, protruded from one side of his mouth.

As soon as they were in the cabin, Maverick sat down and reached for the rum bottle. "I told you I had connections. We don't need those street guys. I called my friend Julio. He can get us everything we want, and at five bucks a box cheaper."

He tilted the bottle up and took a swig without taking the cigar stub out of his mouth. Dan made a mental note to mark the bottle and put it out only when Maverick showed up.

"That's the good news," Maverick said. "The bad news is it's time to cough up the twelve-five I need to make the buy."

"So it's zero hour, eh? How long before we get the cigars, and how much time do I have to get ready?"

"Better figure a couple of weeks. Don't worry: you'll have plenty of time to get ready and find a good window in the weather pattern." He moved toward the stairs. "I'll wait topside so you can go to your bank."

When Maverick was out of sight, Dan pulled the Makita screw gun from the tool locker and began disassembling the floorboards below the chart table.

Five minutes later, he was on deck handing Maverick a plastic bag. "There's a hundred and twenty-five one hundred dollar bills in there. Don't lose it."

Maverick stuffed the money behind the fly in his pants, pulled his grungy undershirt over the bulge, and said, "See you later."

Dan watched as Maverick walked off. He wondered if he was doing the right thing. His Las Vegas training helped put it into perspective. It was a twelve thousand, five hundred dollar bet with a chance at a hundred thousand dollar return. *Not bad odds. I hope I have a winning hand.*

CHAPTER
16

Julio moved quietly through the darkness in his backyard, tightly clutching the $12,500 Maverick had given him to buy five hundred boxes of cigars. He went to his hands and knees and felt the ground for the small twig that indicated where his stash was buried. He scraped several inches of dirt away and lifted the plastic lid of the one-gallon container.

Even though there was little chance of being seen, he worked fast; withdrawing the waterproof bag and adding Maverick's money to the eight thousand dollars he had saved in the sixteen months he had been dock supervisor at the produce center.

Julio was as excited as he could ever remember. The events of the day had moved his escape from Cuba right up to tomorrow night. It must have been the hand of God that brought him the opportunity of a lifetime.

Frankie Alvarez had come to him today with the most wonderful news. The *Guagua 400* would land tomorrow morning at East Beach with two open seats. The high-speed cigarette boat would take him and his brother to Florida in a matter of hours. A miracle had put a ten-year-old boy and his father off at the last minute when the child had been stricken with appendicitis. The second act of God was Maverick handing him the $12,500 that very afternoon – enough for he and Manuel to buy the remaining two seats, with four thousand dollars left over to get started in Florida. He had to pay Frankie five hundred to broker the deal, but it was worth it. Without Frankie, he had no way of knowing when or where the speedboat would land.

He put the money in the small nap sack and went inside to make sure Manuel was getting ready. Their mother was sitting on the small bed sobbing. Her only two boys were leaving forever. They spoke in soft voices.

"Don't worry, Mama," Julio said as he knelt down next to her, "I will get a good job, and Manuel will go to school and work at night. We are going to make enough money to send for you, then we will all be together in America."

As he spoke, he knew his words were not true. Once he was listed as missing at work, the police would come to the house and question his mother, who would have to tell them the truth. There would be little chance of his mother immigrating to Florida at the request of two sons who had left on the *Guagua*.

Frankie would be coming for them at midnight for the drive to East Beach. Julio made sure Manuel packed a warm jacket, a hat, sunglasses, two ham and cheese sandwiches, and a one-gallon plastic bottle of water. The trip should take just a few hours, but more than one Cuban had died in the Florida Straits from exposure and thirst when something had gone wrong.

While trying to calm his mother during the last-minute check, Julio thought about Maverick and what he might think when Julio and his money turned up missing. But it was not as though he was stealing the money; it was just a loan until he could repay it. In Florida, he could make as much as five hundred dollars a week as a construction worker. With that kind of money, he would be able to pay back the money to Maverick in no time. Besides, what could Maverick do? Go to the police?

Julio held his brother's hand tightly as they crouched in the darkness. Frankie Alvarez had gathered the seven passengers and brought them to the grove of coco palms fifty meters from the water. A single bulb atop a lone rusty pole cast dim light on the long white sandy beach. They had been quietly huddled there for two hours, waiting for the sound of the patrol boat. Julio had not had a chance to study the other passengers, but he knew from talking to Frankie that he and Manuel would be accompanied by three young men in their twenties, a middle-aged woman, and man about fifty years old.

Julio checked his watch. It was three-thirty and just a half-hour before the punctual cigarette boat was due to arrive. Every Cuban in Havana knew about the *Guagua 400*, but only a select few knew exactly when and where it would land. It could be anywhere along the north coast, from Varadero to Casilda.

Much of the coastline west of Havana was protected by shallow coral reefs. Night landings with any type of boat through these narrow entrances bordered on suicidal. However, just east of Havana Harbor, there was a ten-mile stretch of ocean bottom gently sloping up from blue water to sandy beach. It was the favorite summer bathing spot for thousands of people living in and around greater Havana. It would be a difficult job of navigation to land in the night at any pre-assigned spot without the pinpoint aid of a global positioning system, a handheld satellite receiver not much bigger than a pack of cigarettes. A person with a nautical chart who knew the difference between longitude and latitude could learn to use a GPS in an hour and be able to follow the arrow on the display window to within thirty yards of a programmed coordinate.

The time and place had been sent to Frankie Alvarez seven days prior to the landing. Prior to that, Frankie had sent a list of favorable sites to the Florida contact.

Julio knew if he and the other passengers were caught, it would mean being sent back home. But if they caught Frankie with the GPS, he would be fingered as the ringleader and would do jail time.

"They'll put me so far down in a dungeon you'll have to pipe light to me," he occasionally quipped.

Frankie was not a patriot sending his fellow Cubans to freedom; he was in it for the money. Along with the Florida express boat, Frankie was into cigars, girls, and used clothes. It was black market tomatoes and garlic that had brought him in contact with Julio.

The dark sea was gently lapping on the sand as Julio and the passengers sat quietly and listened.

Then they heard the slow chugging of the Russian-made patrol boat as it prowled close to shore without running lights. The old Griffin was invisible as it moved through the darkness. Julio could smell the black smoke spewing from its single rusty stack into the gentle onshore breeze, but the three noisy fifty-eight-cylinder engines announced its arrival from as far away as two miles. Julio knew the cigarette boat was also out there listening, with its engines off, bobbing in the calm sea.

The driver of the escape boat carefully monitored his sophisticated radar screen located down low in the tiny cockpit. He kept his head down and studied the green blip on the screen as the big Cuban vessel moved along at eight knots, just a mile inside of his position. A sudden change in course would signify his detection on the patrol boat's antiquated radar system. If that happened, Joe Bob Fontain, the 40-year-old Cajun on his twenty-fifth trip to Cuba, would abort the mission, start the two 550-horsepower Mercury Crusader engines, and split for Florida. In three hours, he would be tied up at his dock fifteen miles north of Key West.

The speedboat sat motionless for another thirty minutes until the radar screen showed that the patrol boat was five miles away and moving steadily west. Then Joe Bob fired up his engines.

The sudden roar of the *Guagua* fractured the stillness of the night. Julio was up immediately.

Frankie gave the command. "Okay, let's go. Everybody stay together." He produced a waterproof dive light and began flashing the bright halogen beam seaward.

Julio held his brother's hand in the darkness and followed Frankie's light into the water. When they were waist deep, they gathered together and listened as Frankie gave boarding instructions.

"Manuel! You go aboard first and help pull the others up. Julio, you're last after you help push the others in."

Only seconds passed before the powerful speedboat was upon them. The driver pulled the throttles back, and the boat dropped its nose and settled gently into the sea next to the huddled group. Manuel scampered onto the boat and began hauling people aboard, while Julio's strong arms pushed the bodies over the gunwale and into the wet leather seats like seals sliding out of a pool.

Five minutes after the fleeing Cubans had left their hiding place on the beach and waded into the water, all were aboard and hanging on as the driver hit the throttles. The red boat reared and screamed out of the quiet waters into the night.

Julio was in the leather seat on the right side of the boat and clung to the security bar as he held his brother's arm. He watched the pilot, who kept his head down and studied the lighted screen on the instrument panel as the shiny, streamlined thirty-eight-foot-long Tiger sped toward Florida.

CHAPTER
17

"You gotta be shittin' me, Maverick. What do you mean *the guy disappeared?* You gave my twelve thousand five hundred bucks to some Cuban guy, and he's gone?"

Maverick stood looking at Dan with a blank stare. "Jesus, I'm sorry, Dan. I've been rehearsing this speech for three days ever since I went to his workplace. They told me that my guy Julio hadn't shown up for work for three days." Maverick hung his head and barely got the words out. "I went to his house, and his mother told me he was gone." He took a breath and blew it out slowly before slumping onto the settee. "You got any rum?"

"Fuck the rum, Maverick. Where for Christ's sake did he go? Can we find him before he spends the money?"

"Yeah, we can find him – if we go to Miami and wander around Little Havana for a month. He took the fuckin' cigarette boat to Florida, Dan. He used the money to buy two spots on the boat for him and his brother. Even if we did find him, the money's gone."

Now Dan reached for the bottle of Havana Club *Anejo*, poured two half glasses of seven-year-old, and slid one over to his partner. "Great. Just fucking great. First we can't find enough cigars on the street, then we give some guy a sack of money and he disappears. Excuse me very fucking much, but I'm beginning to lose faith in your surefire scheme to cash in on the cigar trade."

Dan was staring at the dark rum in the glass and feeling like a boxer who had suddenly found himself on the canvass, wondering, *Where am I? What happened? And why is this guy shining a little flashlight in my eyes?* But there was no opponent jumping around the ring holding up his arms. There was just this commando wearing war surplus fatigues with a stars and stripes bandana covering his head sitting across from him drinking the last of his rum.

"Fuck it, Maverick. That's it. I should have been smart enough not to get involved in your dumbass idea. I've had enough of your get-rich-quick schemes."

Maverick sat calmly and took his medicine. He held up his hands palms out, as if to soothe his partner's wounds, and said, "Take it easy, Dan. I know how you feel, but all is not lost. We can still make a deal—"

Dan broke in, "You are not making any more deals with my money."

"I didn't say that," Maverick said quietly. "I know a guy that will front the entire buy and deliver the cigars. You won't have to do a thing until I have the cigars safely aboard your boat, then it's off to Florida just like before."

"I suppose he's going to do all this just because he's a nice guy."

"No. He works on a percentage. He delivers the cigars to us and takes a third off the top. You have nothing to lose."

A voice inside Dan's head said, *Walk away, Dan Fletcher. Say, "Thanks, but no thanks."* Instead, he found himself saying, "Okay. Maybe. Who is the guy? I want to meet him."

"Not a problem, Dan. He's over at the yacht club right now. Let's go over."

When Maverick and Dan arrived at the clubhouse, it was empty except for one person at the bar nursing a tall glass of beer. It took a moment for Dan to comprehend that he was looking at a human being. The figure seated on the tiny stool resembled a marshmallow in shorts with two short, fat, bowling pin legs hanging halfway to the floor. A bushy mass of uncombed blond hair adorned a cantaloupe-shaped head.

"Hey, Patch," Maverick said. "I want you to meet someone."

As the mass swung around on the stool, Dan looked at what appeared to be a human reject.

The lumpy man was dressed like a tramp and needed a shave, and the aroma coming from his direction indicated that he did not enjoy showering.

"This is Dan Fletcher. He owns *Pass Line*. Dan, meet Patch Fister."

Patch managed to get his short legs under him as he eased his five-foot body to the floor. A barely understandable "Haroo, nife who mee you," came from thin lips that did nothing to shield a half set of crooked, brown-stained teeth. A thin flesh-colored stick-on bandage covered a hole where an eye had once been. It fluttered as he spoke.

Dan made a note of his sorry appearance. *My God*, he thought. *Another one. Were do these people come from? Is this a marina, or a gathering place for former circus freaks?*

Dan reached out and shook the man's greasy hand as he mumbled a feeble, "How do you do?"

Doubts about the new partner-to-be flooded his head. *It's so simple*, he told himself. *Throw in the towel with these misfits, eat the lost money, and leave this marina. Get Lily, stuff her under one of the bunks, and sail the fuck out of here.*

Instead, he found himself agreeing to Maverick's deal to take the cigars to Florida. Patch would front the money for one third of the sale. If all went as planned, there would be plenty of profit to go around.

Dan left the clubhouse alone and walked back to the boat, wondering who Patch really was. For all he knew, he might be CIA or DEA in disguise.

•

Some disguise. "That guy is one sorry son of a bitch," he chuckled. "He could be the inspiration for the joke about the doctor who took one look at the newborn baby and slapped the mother." Dan was laughing to himself now. "Or the other one about the doctor who took one look at the baby, tried to push him back in, and said, 'My God, this one's not done yet.'"

Dan arrived at his boat with tears in his eyes. He chastised himself for making fun of an unfortunate fellow human, then laughed again as he muttered, "There's a guy who forgot to show up for the start of the human race."

He sat in the cockpit trying to analyze his situation. What was it that was tempting him? Was it the thrill of stepping over the line that separated law-abiding men from criminals? Was it the money? Was it Lily? Dan had spent many nights agonizing over Lily. He wanted her like he had never wanted any other woman.

He had no problem with changing his plans and forgetting the South Pacific. Why go there if he had already found the native girl? His dream of a palm-tree-lined bay was still a reality. He and Lily could live happily on some other island in the Caribbean. There had to be plenty of nice bungalows on beaches near a city with modern day conveniences, but that would require more money. His monthly budget did not include living ashore in a house. However, he reasoned, a few trips to Florida with cigars would add several hundred thousand tax-free dollars to his net worth.

Dan wanted to know more about Maverick's pal and the new partner, so he spent a few evenings asking other sailors in the marina what they knew about Patch Fister. It didn't take long to uncover the story.

His real name was Myron Fister, and he was about seventy years old, born in Chicago. It was rumored he was worth more than a few million, which he had earned by buying junk steel from Canada then selling it to the U.S. during the Vietnam War. Later, he made a bundle on the contract to demolish the former World's Fair site in New Orleans. He was paid well to haul away materials that he sold for a good price in the junk market. He often boasted that he sold eight hundred toilets for thirty dollars apiece without even removing them from the site. He sold everything from that demolition job except the dust.

Now in Cuba, he bought his food from bargain markets, sometimes traveling all the way across Havana to save a few pesos on a sack of potatoes or a crate of oranges. "It's not the money," he would say. "It's the deal. I like making deals."

Patch lived on a horrid, decaying houseboat tied up in Canal Number Four, far from the classy yachts.

Every two months the boaters in the marina were required to leave the country and get a new tourist card on return. The cheapest way to do it was to take the afternoon plane from Havana to Nassau, clear customs, and re-board the same plane back to Cuba.

Whenever Patch needed a new visa, he would fill his suitcase with twenty pounds of crabmeat and take it to the Bahamas. A contact at the airport would purchase the cargo and pay Patch a $3.50-per-pound profit. Patch would also carry a box of Cuban cigars that he would sell to the same source. He had it figured to the dollar. The profit on the cigars and the crabmeat would equal the two hundred and seventy-nine dollars it cost him for the plane ticket, the tourist permit, airport taxes, and cab fares.

He had earned his nickname fifteen years earlier when he lost his left eye in a bizarre accident. As the story went, Patch was stealing another Coke from a vending machine when the accident happened. By flipping off the cap of a Coke while it was still in the vertical rack, Patch could tilt the machine and fill a cup without inserting a quarter. During his last petty Coke theft, he lost his footing and damn near lost his life when the heavy machine fell on him.

One of the bottles broke, tearing out one eye and punching a hole in his palate. He covered the hideous cavity with a giant skin-colored Band Aid that fluttered when he spoke. The patch, pushing out and caving in with each breath, distracted listeners from understanding the mumbled words that came out of his almost toothless mouth. The members of the marina community that came in contact with Patch never mentioned it and politely tried to ignore the undulating eye cover.

One night at the yacht club's Christmas party, after too many rum and Cokes, Maverick blurted out, "I can't help it, Patch. When you talk, I'm glued to that goddamned Band Aid puffing in and out. Where does the air come from? I always thought there was a brain back there. Jesus, man, why don't you get a parrot for your shoulder and a black leather patch for that eye? Get some character, for Christ's sake. Be somebody!"

"You don't like my patch, Maverick?" Patch growled. "Well, excuse me!" The words came out, "exchusch me." Then he added, "Atch too fuckin' bad."

Patch slowly reached up to the bridge of his nose and, with his thumb and forefinger, ripped off the patch with one quick move. The grotesque empty socket seemed to go all the way back into the center of his skull. He spoke one word as he stared at Maverick with his good eye. "Better?"

Patch was so put out by Maverick's insult he spent the rest of the night without his eye patch, hanging around the buffet table and greeting the ladies as they approached. "Goo' eefening. Ruvry pary, isn' it?"

Patch had been pissed off at Maverick since the incident at the Christmas party, but once they began talking a cigar deal, all was forgotten.

CHAPTER
18

Julio gripped the handrails of the speedboat as the pilot flew the sleek craft over the water at fifty miles an hour, the boat sometimes rising completely out of the water as it clipped the tops of the rolling swells. The shiny, slick fiberglass hull seemed to ride across the white caps on nothing more than the two seventeen-inch propellers turned by two screaming gas engines at five thousand revolutions per minute.

Julio watched Joe Bob as he gripped the wheel and studied the dark shapes of the oncoming swells.

The open cabin of the Tiger had two seats in front and three in the rear. Three passengers stood behind the front seats holding on for dear life, knowing if they were thrown out, the boat would have little chance of recovering them in the dark night.

Julio had given up his seat next to the pilot and strapped an elderly woman into the plush white padded chair. He and Manuel now had positions behind the front seat. They were forty miles from Key West when Joe Bob eased the throttles back.

The passengers were suddenly afraid. "Why are we slowing down? Is there something wrong?"

"Relax," Joe Bob announced. "We're entering the shipping lanes, the area where we're most likely to encounter the U.S. Coast Guard."

He scanned the night with his binoculars and studied the running lights of a ship in the distance. "Two white lights with a red light under the aft light indicate a large ship." A few moments later he added, "A freighter, moving east to west, about three miles dead ahead."

Joe Bob hit the throttle and set a course that would take them about a mile aft of the ship. Joe Bob's radar screen did not indicate any other marine traffic in the usually busy straits.

Julio noticed that the boat seemed to stop bucking and leveled itself into a smoother ride.

Joe Bob settled back in the seat and announced, "We're out of the Gulf Stream now and making good time. It'll be daybreak soon, light enough to get you all into shallow water at Rum Key, where you can wade ashore. Once on dry land, you can make your way to the nearest authorities and turn your-

•

selves in. If you can get your feet on dry land, you'll be legally entered into the United States."

Julio smiled. If everything went well, he and Manuel would be walking the streets of Miami before noon the next day. If they were caught before reaching land, Julio was not sure what would happen to them.

It was starting to get light as Joe Bob moved the boat along in the shallow water at a smooth twenty knots, a speed that would not draw attention from shore. He had timed their arrival so that they would be at the Key West outer channel marker at daybreak, just in time to mingle with the fishing fleet as it left the harbor. He kept a close eye on the GPS and carefully followed the arrow to his programmed waypoint.

Julio was in high spirits and wanted to scream out loud as he took in the city skyline just a few miles off.

Forty-five minutes later, they passed the last checkpoint at Nine Foot Shoal. The sun was peeking above the sea as the driver made the left turn toward the white sandy beach they could just make out two miles away.

Joe Bob smiled and said, "There you are, just up ahead. Everybody get ready. I'll get you within a couple hundred meters of the beach, then I'll give the order for you all to get off and wade ashore. It's only about three or four feet deep, so your heads will be above water. Nobody goes off the boat before I give the order."

The boat had just made the turn when it suddenly slowed then stopped.

"Not now," Julio said. "Please, God. We are almost there."

Joe Bob instantly crawled out of the cockpit and made his way back across the slippery deck to the transom. When he looked down, he saw two lines trailing behind the boat.

The sun was up now, and a red cigarette boat sitting in the Hawk Channel two miles off Saddle Bunch Key loaded with Cubans would bring the Coast Guard down on them before they could say, "Fidel Castro."

"What is it, Captain?" Julio said as he tried to keep the fear out of his voice.

"We've picked up the lines of a lobster trap. I need to go in the water and cut the ropes free from the prop."

The Cubans said nothing. They just looked at the shore that seemed close enough to reach out and touch.

Joe Bob went off the rear transom and took a couple of deep breaths before ducking under the water.

Julio spoke to his brother. "If we have to, we make for that beach, Manuel. We can almost swim to it now."

Joe Bob came up behind the boat and took several big breaths before going under again.

Julio heard the sickening sound of another boat. It wasn't the dull hum of a slow moving ship. It was the high-pitched whine of a fast-moving outboard.

Joe Bob was out of the water in a flash and back in the cockpit, where he brought the engines back to life.

The boat launched itself toward the beach as Joe Bob shouted, "Okay, everybody, listen. That outboard headed this way looks like a Coast Guard inflatable out of Sugarloaf Key. I'm going to get you in as close as I can. When I say jump, you jump and get away from the boat. You should be in shallow water. Go like hell for the shore. Get those feet on the sand."

The orange Zodiac came ripping out of the sound and headed for the cigarette boat. It was pushed by twin fifty horsepower Johnson outboards whining at top speed, and its captain set a course that would intercept the speedboat before it could reach shallow water.

Joe Bob barely won the race. He pulled the throttles back and yelled, "Jump!"

The voice from the amplified speakers broke the air as the Zodiac driver threw his craft into neutral. "Stay where you are. This is the United States Coast Guard. Prepare to be boarded."

The Cubans were frozen with fear as the patrol boat almost coasted into the escape craft. They looked at Joe Bob.

"Jump, goddamn it! Get into the water. *Jump!*"

Julio grabbed his brother's hand as he went off the boat and pulled Manuel into the water. He had come too far to give up.

There were seven Cubans and only four sailors in the inflatable. They couldn't catch them all. Julio and Manuel were followed by the other five, who hit the water and began half swimming and half running in slow motion over the coral bottom toward the beach, which was only one hundred and fifty yards away.

The Coast Guard sailor spun the Zodiac around while his three crewmembers kneeled on the tubes of the inflatable, ready to grab the fleeing illegal immigrants.

Julio and Manuel were making good headway to the beach when the old woman began screaming, "Oh God, I'm drowning! I can't swim! Help me, God, please help me!"

She was only in water up to her chin, and if she stood up, her feet would have been on the bottom, but it was the poor woman's first time in water over her waist.

Julio was ahead of the pack when he heard her cries. He yelled to his brother, "Go to the beach, Manuel. Don't look back, and don't stop."

He turned and moved back toward the woman, who had stopped yelling and was now choking and spitting water. He reached her at the same time as the Zodiac.

Two pair of hands grabbed the woman and pulled her over into the patrol boat.

Julio could see his brother, who was now in waist-deep water and moving toward land.

Two hands came down and tried to grab his shirt.

He dove under the boat and came up on the other side. "Over here," he yelled.

The Zodiac crew moved to the other side of the boat just in time to see him duck under again, only to reappear on the other side. *"Aquí, amigos."*

"Get hold of him, sailor. The others are getting away."

This time Julio went under the boat and let his flotation hold him up against the bottom.

"Where'd he go?" The Zodiac crew ran from side to side, but there was no Julio.

He had always been able to hold his breath longer than anyone in school because of his barrel chest and big lung capacity. He knew that every second he stayed under the boat his brother and the others had a better chance of making it to the beach. When he had been against the bottom for a half minute, he began pounding on the floatation tubes.

"He's under the boat."

The Zodiac captain couldn't put the boat into gear for fear the prop blades would cut the prisoner to pieces. "Wait him out. He'll have to come up soon. That son of a bitch is costing us the capture of five Cubans."

He was right. Manuel and the others had made it to shore. Manuel was jumping up and down at the water's edge, hoping his brother could evade capture. Several of the residents from nearby houses, witnessing the entire scene, came into the water to help the swimmers, while another man grabbed one of the young Cubans and tried to throw him back, yelling to the patrol boat, "Over here. Here's one over here."

Julio's lungs were bursting as he began swimming away from the Zodiac. When he finally poked his head up for a much-needed breath, he saw he had swam in the wrong direction, away from the beach.

It did not make much difference. The Zodiac crew was not about to let him get away. After a short chase, the Coast Guard crew eased up to him and pulled him aboard. Julio lay exhausted on the bottom of the boat with the frightened woman, but he was smiling. The last thing he saw as he was being pulled over the orange inflated tube was his brother standing safely on American soil.

Thirty minutes later, the Zodiac pulled up to the small dock that housed the Coast Guard post that was used specifically for preventing Cubans from landing in the U.S. The new operation consisted of the one inflatable boat and a rotating crew of one officer and three enlisted men on duty twenty-four hours a day.

The Zodiac captain stood proudly at the helm while the crew jumped onto the dock and tied the mooring lines. He had landed his first big prize: two Cubans trying to sneak into the United States.

Julio whispered to the woman, "He'll probably hang us by our heels like two marlins in a fishing tournament."

Julio and the woman were handcuffed and led to the small office on the pier. The woman was Maria Talmar, the fifty-year-old mother of a Cuban baseball player who had defected to the United States after the 1996 Olympics.

They were transported in an enclosed van with a steel mesh screen separating the driver from the prisoners, who sat on wooden benches. Julio and Maria were the sole occupants in the back of the van.

It was the woman who spoke first. "What do you think they will do with us?"

Julio was in deep thought. He had heard many stories. Just a week ago, Cuban television had aired the movie *Cool Hand Luke* with Paul Newman. It was about a man who cut down a few parking meters and was sentenced to hard labor on a chain gang. They beat him senseless several times, and in the end they shot him to death in cold blood. After the movie, a panel of communist students discussed the atrocities of the American prison system.

If Paul Newman was killed for cutting parking meters, Julio wondered, what would happen to someone who tried to sneak into the country? Would he be given anything lesser than the chain gang?

He refused to say that to the frightened woman. "I don't know, but do not worry. The Americans are nice people. I'm sure we will be dealt with fairly." He did not believe it.

It was less than a thirty-minute ride before the van stopped. They were taken into another building, where they sat in two chairs next to a door that seemed to lead out to a boat dock.

Another sailor came in and took off the handcuffs. He spoke good Spanish in a soft voice. "You are going for a little ride on our patrol cruiser. Please come with me."

They followed him out into the bright sun where the 155-foot Coast Guard cutter was moored.

Once they were on board, they were told by the sailor to go in to the shower and wash. There were two doors marked men and women. Inside, Julio took off his clothes and stepped into one of the four shower stalls and turned on the water. "*Dios mio*, the water is hot." He lathered from head to toe with the big bar of sweet-smelling soap, rinsed off, and started again. He had never bathed in such a shower. The water came at him with the pressure of a fire hose as he thought, *Go ahead and shoot me if you have to. Just let me spend another ten minutes in this shower.*

After his third lather, he rinsed off and stood with his head down while the water beat down on the back of his neck another five minutes. Finally, he turned off the water and pulled back the curtain. A giant white fluffy towel hung on the peg, and he noticed that his clothes were gone. A bright orange jumpsuit, socks, and a pair of new sneakers sat in their place. He dried, dressed, and went out to where the sailor and Maria were waiting. She too was dressed in an orange jumpsuit.

Another sailor, most likely an officer, came in. He was dressed in white pants and a white shirt with gold epaulettes. He also spoke Spanish. "Welcome to the United States Coast Guard cutter, *Freedom*. I am Captain Rodriguez. In one hour we will be going to sea to patrol the Florida Straits looking for other Cubans trying to cross to the U.S. When we have picked up enough, we will be returning all of you to Cuba. Meanwhile, you are guests of the United States Coast Guard. Seaman Franks will show you to your quarters." He smiled and left the room.

Julio was elated. They had to go back to Cuba, but that was better than being shot or taken to the chain gang like Paul Newman.

Things got even better when Seaman Franks showed them their quarters, each of which was fully equipped with a television, a VCR, and thirty of the latest American movies dubbed in Spanish. "Are you hungry?" Franks asked.

Julio had been too excited then too scared to be hungry. Now, after taking a hot shower, putting on new clothes, and finding an awaiting bed with clean sheets, he was famished.

When Seaman Franks led them to the mess room, Julio's eyes popped out at the sight of a table loaded with ham, cheese, fresh bread, crisp lettuce, fresh fruit, and strawberries next to a five-gallon container of vanilla ice cream. A big stainless urn of hot coffee surrounded by white porcelain cups sat at another smaller table. "Help yourselves. This buffet is open twenty-four hours a day. Dinner is served in the adjoining state room at seven o'clock."

Julio was in shock. Less than five hours ago he had been swimming for his life, afraid of being captured and enduring hours of painful interrogation, maybe even put before a firing squad, or at the least being sent to the road gang like Paul Newman. Now he was wondering how he could just stay on this boat. Maybe he could apply for a job cleaning the kitchen or preparing vegetables. He was good with vegetables. He would talk to the captain about it later. Right now he wanted to fill his stomach and crawl into that lovely bed. He had never felt so clean and alive as he did at that moment.

Julio never did talk to the captain about working on the boat. Seaman Franks explained to him that there were set regulations in the Coast Guard and staying aboard would not be possible.

It took two weeks for the patrol boat to intercept twelve more Cubans making their way to the United States. They were all picked up at sea and taken back to the U.S. Naval base at *Guantanamo*, then turned over to the Cuban authorities.

It was Julio's first offence, and he was released after being questioned about the identity of his Cuban accomplices. Julio lied. He told them that he had stolen a small outboard and had made it halfway across before being picked up, and that he had done it entirely on his own.

After three days of questioning, he was released and told to return home to Havana. He was relieved to know he was not going to jail, but he also realized there would be no more lucrative jobs like the ones at the produce center or the rum factory. He was blackballed from any of the decent jobs the Cuban government had. As he sat in the bus station in Santiago de Cuba, he smiled at the lie he had told them about stealing a boat and trying to escape on his own, because that was what he was going to do next time. He began planning his next escape, but next time he would find his own boat and rebuild an old outboard engine part by part. Next time, he would do it on his own.

CHAPTER
19

Dan was humming as he emerged from the shower. He couldn't remember being so content. Lily had shown up earlier and asked if they could do something that evening. They had been carrying on a casual affair for a month now that included going to the city to look for out-of-the-way restaurants. They'd been to Chinatown for Chop Suey, found a Mexican restaurant and eaten spicy enchiladas, and tried hot Arabic food on the patio of an old refurbished brick building while belly dancers whirled to the music of flutes and bells. Their favorite discovery was a small restaurant inside the tall iron fence of the old Russian consulate complex where they ate lunch at least once a week. Dan usually ordered the stuffed grape leaves. Lily favored the Borsch. At lunch earlier that week, Lily had reached across the table and taken Dan's hand. She looked into his eyes and began to speak, but stopped short after saying his name.

"What, *mi amor*?" He waited.

She smiled and let his hand go. "Nothing, Dan. It's just that I am so happy."

He heard Lily rapping on the hull and went topside.

She was standing alongside the boat wearing a white satin full-length dress that showed every curve on her body. Her hair was done up in a bun that accented her long, thin neck. In the moonlight she was stunning. This was a pleasant departure from her casual dress, which usually consisted of jeans and a simple blouse.

"I have a taxi waiting."

Dan dashed below and grabbed a light jacket to cover his open-neck sport shirt and bounded up the companionway. He could hardly wait to take another look at what awaited him.

He gave the driver directions to a classy eatery he heard about on the eastern bank of the harbor.

That night turned out to be another magical evening. They dined by candlelight at a small outdoor Spanish restaurant overlooking Havana Harbor and the lights of the city. Lily was radiant, and Dan toyed with the idea of asking her exactly how she felt about him. Was she by any chance moving toward that romantic involvement she so carefully guarded against?

Dan had found that he was falling deeper into a no-return spiral of commitment. He needed to hear something from Lily to give him a reason for sticking around a communist country hardly a stone's throw from the beginning of his great adventure.

He reached across the table and placed his hand on hers. "Lily, you know I think the world of you." He paused, and she smiled. "You know I have to go to Florida next week, and I was just wondering if there was anything you wanted to say to me."

"Of course, Dan. Have a safe trip." Then she leaned across the table and whispered, "Bring me back some perfume."

The romantic moment was over. Dan laughed. "Of course, my love. Nothing but the best. How about Chanel No. 5?"

He waved at the waiter. *"La cuenta, por favor."*

Dan made his way down the companionway and reached back to take Lily's hand as she negotiated the steep steps.

Once inside, Lily turned on the tape deck and inserted a tape of Sinatra favorites. She had not spoken much in the taxi, and Dan wondered if there was something bothering her. He rummaged around in the refrigerator and found two cold Cokes. "How about a *cubalibre?*"

Lily moved from the stereo into the galley and took the Cokes from Dan's hands and set them on the counter. "We've had enough to drink."

She pulled his head down to her lips and kissed him gently before saying, "Let's go to bed."

She stepped back and held his eyes with hers as she reached up and slipped off her shoulder straps. The silk dress slid silently to the floor. She stood half naked before him for a moment, then turned and moved toward the forward compartment.

Dan's temples pounded, and he felt his stiffness trying to explode from his pants. He took her shoulders and guided her to the V-berth. He kissed the nape of her neck and turned her toward him, easing her back onto the bunk. They locked eyes as he reached down for her last piece of clothing. She raised her hips slightly as he slipped her panties off.

Dan almost lost his breath as he gazed down on a perfect body bathed in the orange light of a dim 12-volt lamp. He didn't have to spread her legs. They opened automatically as he slipped his arms under her knees and bent his head down to take her vagina in his lips. Dan smiled as he looked up and saw she had the pillow over her face.

Her back was arched, and she was pushing her pelvis up into him as she pumped her hips in a frantic rhythm. She came quickly, abandoning the pillow and pulling his head into her. She made soft whimpering sounds before freezing her movements and settling back on the bunk. "Wow!" she said as she looked up at him.

He was still fully dressed. He unbuttoned his pants without taking his eyes off her and slipped off his Levis. He peeled off his alligator shirt and entered her moist cavity. His orgasm was almost instantaneous, but she was ready and came again with him.

It was noon when he awoke. He was alone and lay wondering when she had left. He reached down for his pants and fumbled through his pockets until he found his money clip. There was nothing missing. He smiled.

He buried his head into the pillow next to him and breathed in the scent of her perfume. God, she was lovely. She was gone again, but this time it was different. For the first time, she had given herself.

He stumbled toward the galley and flipped on CNN before starting the process of making coffee. He finished grinding the Cuban beans and was pouring the hot water into the French press when he felt the boat lurch and heard the shuffling of hard-soled shoes on the deck above him.

The hatch slid open and Lily poked her head in. "Good morning, my love."

She climbed down two steps before reaching back for a plastic bag. Once in the cabin, she took out a fresh papaya, a half dozen limes, a loaf of French bread, and a small jar of guava jelly. "I was hoping you wanted to see me again, so I brought breakfast," she joked.

She set the bag down and presented her lips. She wore no makeup and looked as stunning as she had the night before.

Dan kissed her and noticed she had changed clothes. She wore a pink tank top, white shorts, and hard-soled sandals. He also noticed he was still in his boxer shorts.

She looked down and smiled at his erection. "I guess breakfast can wait." She took his hand and led him to the V-berth.

This time their lovemaking was less hurried and tenderer. After mutual orgasms, they lay in each other's arms, bathed in sweat.

With Lily wrapped around him, Dan was lying on his back staring up at the bulkhead. *This must be what they mean by being madly in love,* he thought. *I think I just might have found my island and the native girl. She is finally mine.*

He rolled over on his side facing her, kissed her closed eyes, and whispered, "I'm in love with you, Lily."

She opened her eyes as though she had been hit in the face, but did not move away. "Please don't say that, Dan." Her voice was almost pleading. "I can't say that to you. I love my mother, my family. I have never loved a man, not like my family. Last night and this morning were wonderful. I hadn't planned on this. Damn you, Dan Fletcher. You're ruining my life." She kissed his lips. "Just don't talk about love."

He let the subject drop, but it did not prevent him from analyzing her attitude toward the forbidden four-letter word.

Here beside him was a complicated woman who had taken over his mind, ravished his body, and become his narcotic. Her sign was Gemini, which probably explained her personality: mysterious, feminine, charming, witty. She seemed to find romance enjoyable, but any commitment to love was a barrier to her main goal in life.

CHAPTER
20

It took four days to load *Pass Line* with five hundred boxes of prime Cuban tobacco. Maverick and Patch hand-carried the contraband on board in laundry bags fifty at a time, making sure each bag went on the boat at intervals to avoid suspicion. Maverick had driven a hard bargain with Patch and insisted on popular brands and sizes that he knew would bring top dollar in the States. Dan's boat now carried seventy boxes of Cohiba Esplendidos, fifty boxes of Robustos, one hundred boxes of Romeo and Julieta Churchills, fifty more Churchills in aluminum tubes, fifty boxes of Hoyo de Monterrey double coronas, a hundred boxes of Monte Cristo A, and eighty boxes of Partagas Lonsdales.

With a price of four hundred dollars a box, Dan's cargo was now worth two hundred grand. Patch's share would be a third for fronting the buy. Dan and Maverick would divide the remaining $134,000 after subtracting expenses and Dan's original $12,500 that Julio had taken.

The day before Dan's planned departure, he went to see Graham Wellington. He found him in his usual position: sitting in the cockpit, cigar in hand, surveying the passing foot traffic.

Dan sat down and dropped several rolled-up charts on the table. "You know, Graham, I have to make a tip to Florida and make landfall at a specific point. I'm not bad with navigation, but with your experience, you could be a big help going over the plan and maybe double-checking my numbers."

"Sure, Dan, I'd be glad to give you a hand. Too bad there aren't more sailors like you. Christ, every guy who buys a boat seems to be an expert the next day even though he's never seen the outside of the breakwater." He took two draws on his cigar, thought a moment, and added, "What is it about the male species that he can't say, 'Hey, I don't know shit about this. Will you give me a hand?' Any guy would bust his ass trying to help."

"I never thought of it that way."

"Bullshit, Fletcher."

Dan smiled and shrugged like a kid caught with his hand in the cookie jar.

"You are the only guy in the marina who gets all the help he needs simply by claiming to know absolutely nothing about it. Somewhere along the way, you figured it out. Maybe by accident, I don't know. I've seen you get people to help you do everything from scrape the bottom of your boat to fixing your stopped-up head."

Dan looked at Graham, knowing the old timer had a point. "If you're talking about getting what you need by making the other guy right, you're right. I don't make a conscious effort at it. I'm not conning people. I learned a long time ago that it was better to come clean right off the bat and admit I don't know, instead of faking it."

Graham was tidying up his cockpit table. There was never an article on that boat that was not in its place. "Don't get me wrong, Dan. It's a nice trait," he said as he lifted the tabletop and took out several pencils and a pair of dividers. He lowered the lid and carefully placed the pencils in a neat row as he continued talking. "People like showing off their knowledge. The difference is that one way leads to an argument, and the other way leads to someone helping out. I know I have more experience than you with sailing and navigating, but if you had come to me for help pretending to know everything, I'd have told you to go fuck yourself. Who wants to help somebody who knows it all?"

"That gets us back to my trip. I brought the charts over. Can we take a look?"

"Only if you agree that I know everything." Before Dan could answer, he added, "About everything."

"Agreed," Dan said. "I also brought over a half bottle of Havana Club. Stained charts have more character."

"That they do, my boy. That they do."

A half-bottle later, Graham summarized the proposed trip, while Dan listened without interrupting.

"You're going to hit your waypoint almost two miles south of Pickle Reef. Make sure you're not asleep here." He pointed to the mark they had made on the chart. "You should try and get there about two in the afternoon. The light will be good, and you'll be able to see the reefs. But just in case, follow the GPS to the second waypoint, seven point seven miles to the marina. I happen to know this place."

Graham knew almost every port and marina from West Palm Beach to Panama.

"Cheat a little to the north side of the indicated course, and watch your drift. Molasses Reef is a good mile and a half to your north. You can relax when you get to twenty-five degrees north, as long as you're on course.

"From there to the marina entrance, your shallow water is eight feet or more. It may look too shallow, but you'll have a minimum of six feet, and that's only one rock. You draw less than five feet, so even if you don't see the rock, you'll be okay. You might get a little nervous, though.

"The total distance is one hundred ninety miles on a course of zero-two-one. If you get any wind from the south quadrant, you'll have a reach all the way, but I think the best you can expect is wind out of the east. If you can maintain a five-knot average, you'll get to the reef at six a.m."

"Sounds good. I think I can handle it."

"Yeah, you probably can, but a lot of things can happen out there. It would be better if you took someone along."

"I can't, Graham. I have to go solo."

"Okay. I'm sure you've got your reasons. But I might as well go ahead and give you the rest of the information that I think you'll be needing."

"What's that?"

"I've been around the marina for a long time, and not too much goes by without me getting a good idea of what it is. I know you're seeing a lot of Maverick." He gave Dan a serious look. "I might tell you to be careful, but you're a big boy. It's none of my business, but I can smell a cigar deal going down before the boxes are loaded into the boat."

Dan sat motionless, saying nothing.

"This is obviously your first run at transporting contraband. And I would like to give you a little advice."

"It's a little late for that. I'm already into the deal for twelve-five."

"I'm not talking about the righteousness of smuggling. I just want to give you a little insight on how to avoid getting caught."

"Fire away," Dan said.

"First of all, get your boat ready topside. No bicycles, gas cans, cruising gear, or junk on deck. Your boat must look like you just came in from Miami on a short day-sail."

"Sounds good. I'm planning on leaving day after tomorrow. I already notified the marina."

"Don't forget to give yourself plenty of time to clear customs and the *Guardia*." He paused. "And Dan, you know you are legally allowed to take out only two boxes of cigars, right?"

Dan raised an eyebrow. "Yeah, I know. Maverick has worked out something with Eduardo at customs. He'll be working that day, and Rafael will be working at the *Guardia*. I guess the good old graft system works anywhere."

"Don't take it lightly. You can't count on these guys. They have been known to clear boats out with hundreds of boxes of cigars then call the U.S. Coast Guard. Be careful."

The following morning, Dan was up early securing everything inside the boat that could possibly move in the event he hit bad weather.

Maverick showed up at the boat lugging a big sail bag. "What have you got, Maverick? More cigars?"

Maverick threw the heavy canvas sack on the deck. "No, Danny boy, it's a new mainsail."

"A new main? What's wrong with mine? It's practically new."

"It's a surprise, Dan. Trust me on this one. Come on. We'll have it on in no time."

Forty minutes later, the substitute sail was ready to be hoisted. Dan winched the halyard, and Maverick stood on the grass thirty yards away to get a better look as the 365-square-foot dirty white sail rose to the top of the mast.

"Beautiful," Maverick said. "Come out here, Dan, and take a look at my creation."

Fletcher stepped off the boat onto the quay and looked up at the addition. "What the hell is that?"

"It's a *preventor*, Dan." Maverick was grinning from ear to ear. "It will prevent the U.S. Coast Guard from boarding you between here and Florida. Guaranteed to work. Nobody is going to fuck with a man doing the Lord's work."

Flying above *Pass Line* and flopping gently in the breeze was a weathered sail with a sign on it in all capital letters that read *SAILING SOLO AROUND THE WORLD FOR JESUS.*

CHAPTER
21

Dan Fletcher sprawled on the leeward side of the cockpit with his back resting against a cushion. His right hand had a light grip on the wheel as he watched the compass and kept the forty-foot sloop on a heading of 021 degrees. He enjoyed this part of sailing, when he was alone on the sea. There was a moderate breeze out of the east, and the boat was making a steady six knots as it hissed through the blue water toward Key Largo under a cloudless sky. He was living the dream.

He was jolted out of that dream when he realized he was going the wrong way. He was supposed to be going south, deep into the Caribbean, or west through the Panama Canal. Instead, he was going north, back to the United States with five hundred boxes of illegal Cuban cigars. No big deal, Maverick had told him. Just a walk in the park. And if he got caught, it would just be a slap on the wrist.

If that were the case, why wasn't everybody running cigars? Was he risking his freedom on the word of Maverick? He knew this was not the time to be having second thoughts, but he was starting to feel like a drug smuggler making his way to the United States with a ton of pot.

What if he was caught, and they decided to make an example out of him? What if they put him away for the rest of his good years in a place with bars and a guy named Big Bubba as his roommate? And why was it always a big black guy with a ten-inch dick named Big Bubba? Why couldn't it be a little white guy with thick glasses who was always reading?

Maybe that was what kept the majority of people honest: the threat of Big Bubba. The authorities couldn't maintain law and order if they simply said, "Be honest, don't steal, and don't kill anybody, or you will go live in a dormitory and lie around for years with an interesting roommate, reading, watching TV, and lifting weights."

No. It was always, "Don't fuck up in life, or you'll end up in a dungeon with Big Bubba."

He had known several guys who had done time for selling drugs. According to them, it hadn't been that bad. They had lived in clean barracks in a minimum-security federal correction facility with everything except an eighteen-hole golf course. One guy spent three years as a tennis instructor.

Another guy had done hard time as a lifeguard at the pool. They even referred to the place as Club Fed.

On the other hand, he thought, that was what they would tell you. Who was going to come out of prison and tell his buddies the real story? "It was bad, man, real bad. My cellmate Bubba bent me over the bunk every night for three years after the lights went out. Now I got an asshole big enough to drive a truck through."

Dan snapped himself out of it, switched on the autopilot, then stumbled below to make some coffee. The autopilot used a lot of 12-volt amps, and even though the wind generator was whining, he knew that an hour was max without starting the auxiliary to charge the batteries.

He had plenty of fuel to run the engine, but he hated the noise. He knew he would have to spend much of the night listening to that thing chug and spew noxious fumes into the fresh salt air while he watched for the lights of ships between catnaps.

Clearing out of the marina had been just like Maverick predicted. The customs inspector checked his departure papers that had the hundred-dollar bill attached and went through the normal questions as he checked off the list of items that the boat had brought into Cuba.

The *Guardia's* inspection was just as easy. Rafael went through the motions of rummaging around while pretending to look for who-knows-what. Dan was amazed at how little room it actually took to stuff five hundred boxes of cigars into the sloop that Maverick had painstakingly converted. The refrigerator held fifty boxes, the holding tank eighty boxes, and Maverick had figured a way to stuff eighty-five boxes into the two water tanks and reseal the tops. His best idea was putting one hundred boxes inside the inflatable life raft container that rode on deck. The remaining boxes had been strategically placed in two bunk mattresses, the oven, and the bilge.

Every ten minutes or so, Dan would stand and check the horizon. He had come dangerously close to hitting a container on his way to Cuba. He had only spotted the sailor's nightmare as his boat passed the metal box floating a mere thirty yards away.

It was five in the afternoon when he heard the helicopter. He felt his stomach churn as he watched the big bird circle the boat. He could plainly see a Coast Guard crewman sitting in the open doorway tapping his fist on his ear. Dan picked up his handheld radio, tuned it to channel 16, and began living the smuggler's nightmare when he heard, "Sailing vessel in the vicinity of Coast Guard helicopter, please reply."

Dan's heart was pounding as he spoke into the radio. "Coast Guard helicopter, this is the vessel *Pass Line*, over."

"Good afternoon, Captain. Please give the name of your vessel, number of persons aboard, their nationalities, and the name of your last port, over."

He could barely get the words out of his dry mouth. "This is sailboat *Pass Line*, one person aboard, U.S. citizen." He paused. There was no sense trying to change the name of his last port. They might have tracked him by satellite all the way from Cuba. "Last port, Marina Hemingway, Havana." He could feel Big Bubba's hands on his shoulders.

"Roger, *Pass Line*. Maintain your present course, slow your speed, and prepare to be boarded. Do you have any firearms aboard?"

"Negative on the firearms. *Pass Line* is slowing to three knots."

Maverick wanted him to take one of his guns, but Dan had refused. With constant patrolling by the Cubans and the U.S. Coast Guard, there was zero pirate activity between Havana and Key West.

He eased the Genoa and the main. The boat settled down to a steady three knots.

Dan felt hollow as he watched the helicopter head west. He could now see the smoke from the mother ship steaming toward him.

Did he have time to throw the cigars overboard? No, better to go to jail than face Maverick and Patch and tell them he had chucked two hundred grand worth of cigars over the side.

Maverick had been very specific when asked about the chances of being spotted by a patrol boat. "Hey, it happens all the time, Dan. If you are spotted, they may send a Zodiac with some guys carrying machine guns. The officer in charge will be very bright and ask you where you're going. The answer is Bimini, the Bahamas.

"The course you set from Havana will be toward Bimini. Even if they see a few boxes of cigars, it's not against U.S. law to be taking cigars to the Bahamas. Don't panic. They're looking for illegal aliens and drugs. They'll look below and take a dusting from your clothes and several places in the cabin to analyze. Just play it cool, and don't volunteer any information before they ask for it."

It sounded simple back there in the marina. But now, sitting in the cockpit as the big patrol boat closed toward his little, vulnerable, slow-moving sailboat, he could feel the handcuffs and the shackles as he imagined himself being led into the courtroom.

"Just act natural, Fletcher," he said to himself. "If they see you sweat, they might take the boat apart."

He sat helplessly, wondering if they would tear the boat apart or just let some German shepherd run around sniffing for drugs. Did they have a cigar-sniffing dog? He doubted it. How could any dog be smart enough to tell the difference between a Cuban cigar and a pack of Marlboros?

He could make out the ship on the horizon coming his way and estimated that it would take at least fifteen minutes for it to arrive. He would use the time to make a pot of coffee. *Maybe if I offer them a good cup of Cuban coffee,* he thought, *they'll go away.*

The big cruiser pulled alongside and stayed several hundred yards off. From nowhere, an orange Zodiac appeared. The inflatable launch was loaded with a full six-man assault team armed with automatic weapons.

When it pulled alongside, a heavyset sailor in the bow yelled above the wind, "Captain, do you have any firearms aboard?"

"No, sir."

"Is there any other crew members below?"

"No, sir."

"All right. Prepare to be boarded."

A line from the inflatable came whistling through the air and landed in his arms. Dan secured the line and gave a hand to the first sailor. Two others came aboard, and one of them untied the line and set the Zodiac free. The inflatable moved thirty yards away and maintained the speed of the sloop. Three armed sailors, ready with weapons, kept a close eye on their shipmates now on *Pass Line*.

Dan recognized the bars on the sailor who had done the talking. "Good afternoon, Lieutenant. What can I do for you?" There was no quiver in his voice.

"I'm Lieutenant Randolph. May I see your boat documents and passport, please? My chief can take the helm." He was all business as he added, "Can we go below?"

"Sure, Lieutenant. Follow me."

One of the assault team members took the wheel, and with the officer and one sailor right behind him, Dan slid the hatch open and went down the companionway on rubber legs. He lifted the lid on the chart table and pulled out the envelope containing the ship's papers and his passport.

The officer sat down and scribbled the information on a small pad he took from a waterproof pocket in his black jacket. "Do you have any drugs aboard?" The question came out of nowhere.

"No, sir."

The lieutenant scribbled on his notepad as he casually made his way through the boat. He looked into the head, the V-berth, and the two after-berths, then lifted the floorboards and checked the bilge.

Dan sat at the table and watched the sailor pull out a small battery-operated instrument that made short sucking sounds when he placed it on the upholstery. They were obviously collecting samples that would be analyzed later on the mother ship with sophisticated equipment. The last sample was taken from Dan's pockets after he was asked to empty their contents on the table.

So far it was a very casual search, not the kind he had heard about where they literally took the boat apart. He was trying to relax and act casual, but when the seaman lifted the lid on the refrigerator, Dan felt the blood drain from his face.

"Lieutenant." The crewman held up a box of Esplendidos.

The officer walked to the refrigerator and looked down inside.

Fletcher turned white. It was over. He was going to jail.

The lieutenant was turning the box over in his hands. "Cohiba Esplendidos. Great cigar. You smoke much?"

"Yeah, quite a bit. I'm trying to cut down, though."

Dan made a quick decision. If they found the rest of the hidden cigars, he was going to say that he had a bad tobacco habit. The cigars were for his personal consumption, and he intended to smoke the five hundred boxes himself.

Dan concentrated on keeping his voice level. "You smoke cigars, Lieutenant?"

"No, but the captain does. He'd kill for a box of these."

Dan was on his feet. "Hey, take a box. I've got a year's supply. Hell, take two."

"Thanks, Captain." He handed the boxes to the seaman. "We're out of Norfolk on maneuvers. Won't be back in port for another four weeks. He'll appreciate it." He looked over at his crewman. "You done here?"

The sailor nodded and closed the lid on the refrigerator.

"Have a nice trip."

They appeared to be moving in slow motion as they made their way up the steps and out onto the deck.

By the time Fletcher's noodle legs took him on deck, the Zodiac was alongside. He took the helm and watched the boarding party climb back into the inflatable.

The lieutenant pointed up to the mainsail and said, "Nice touch – the Jesus thing." He smiled and added, "But I don't think it'll help you."

Moments later, the boarding party was heading back toward the big ship with the orange stripe on the bow.

Nice touch with the Jesus thing. Great. Now he was a marked man, a smuggler with a big sign that announced, "Remember me, the Jesus boat." Dan wished Maverick were there so he could stuff the whole mainsail up his ass. He'd change it as soon as he got to port.

He was still shaking two hours later when the cutter finally broke off and headed away from *Pass Line*. His guess was that it had taken that long to analyze the sniffer results and run a check on him and his boat.

It had been four hours since he had first heard the dreaded radio transmission from the helicopter. He hadn't even noticed that it had gotten dark. He started the auxiliary, adjusted the autopilot, and began looking for the lights of freighters.

The night seemed heavy as he inhaled the moist gulf air and settled himself in the cockpit with a hot cup of coffee. As the boat skimmed along at a respectable 6.2 knots, Dan began wondering what the hell he was doing.

The Coast Guard had rattled him, no question about it. He came to the realization that he was not cut out to be a crook, even if it was only cigars, as Maverick had put it. He had never committed a crime, never been arrested. The closest he had come to stealing was when he had worked at Bernard's Saddle Club during his early days in Vegas.

Three months into his new line of work in the gambling industry, he had been called into the front office and asked to take a lie detector test. It was optional, they told him, but all employees at Bernard's agreed to take the test. In other words, you didn't have to, but if you didn't, you would not work there anymore.

It was a simple test to find out if he was stealing or working with someone who might be stealing from the club. It was an awful experience. Just the thought of being wired for truth made him sweat bullets. The questions ranged from his name, address, and his mother's name to "Have you ever been arrested?"

His heart skipped a beat when he answered, "No." It was the truth, but he was sure his racing pulse indicated a lie.

The test lasted twenty-five agonizing minutes. The last question was a simple one: "Ever find a coin on the floor and put it in your pocket?"

He answered, "Yes."

In the eyes of the Vegas gaming business, one lousy quarter, picked up off the carpet, had made him a thief.

After the test results were analyzed, Benny Bernard himself, the two-fisted, gun-toting, ex-Texas mobster who was reported to have shot four Las Vegas men who were plotting to kidnap his son, called in Fletcher. His victims were found in the desert sitting back-to-back with their hands tied and a single bullet hole in the back of each head.

When asked, "Did you shoot those guys, Benny?" he had answered, "Goddamn right. They were going to kidnap my son. What would you do?" Then he smiled.

No one knew for sure if Benny did it, but the Las Vegas police didn't look too hard for the shooter and soon dropped the case. Bernard was a legend in Las Vegas: a fair man, well liked, and feared.

Fletcher was sweating in the air-conditioned room as he sat in front of his boss. He could feel streams of water running down his rib cage.

Benny's baldhead was barely visible above the papers as he read the test results. Occasionally, he stopped and lowered the papers, carefully studied the scared young man in front of him, then returned to the telltale results that could see into a man's soul.

After what seemed like an eternity, Bernard tossed the papers recklessly onto the desk as though he never wanted to see them again. He looked at Dan and said; "I see where you kept change off the floor at least once." He did not wait for Fletcher to respond. "Company policy calls for you to put any coins back into a machine. Money on the floor belongs to the establishment."

Dan figured he was going to lose his job. Instead, Bernard leaned back in his chair, studied Dan for a few more moments, and said, "Any theft, no matter how small, is grounds for dismissal, but I like you, Dan. You answered truthfully, and I doubt that you will make that mistake again. How'd you like to go to dealers' school?"

Dan was taken by surprise.

Bernard continued, "No salary, but we'll pay for the school. It's an eleven-week course. If you pass, you'll have a good job here."

It was a fast turn of events. One minute he was being fired as a two-bit thief, and a moment later he was being offered a position in the Las Vegas gaming community.

That was thirty years ago, and he had never stolen as much as a nickel or done a dishonest thing since. So what was he doing heading to Florida with a boatload of contraband? He was supposed to be going the other direction, to the South Seas. He knew the answer: Lily. He had enough money to pursue the original dream, but Gene Tierney had come into his life at the first stop. Lily had spent her young life living in a shack. Living on a tiny boat or even in a grass hut on an isolated beach would not appeal to her. She needed the promise of a more comfortable life if he was going to win her heart.

To have this woman, he would need more money, and a few more cigar runs would double his bank account. He and Lily would not be rich, but they would live in comfort on some other island in the Caribbean.

CHAPTER
22

*P*ass *Line* moved slowly between the two rock jetties as Dan entered the quiet marina on Key Largo. He glanced down at the drawing and carefully followed the instructions written by Maverick. He made a tight right turn and fifty meters later turned left into the first canal.

He was barely making headway as he eased the boat past yachts moored to private docks that fronted sprawling lawns and luxury homes. He spotted Martinez's dock near the end of the long waterway. There were no boats moored at the last two houses, and the wind was dead calm, allowing an easy docking maneuver.

He could feel the effects of being up all night and reminded himself to be sharp. He didn't want to make a hard landing that might bring neighbors out wondering who the new guy in the neighborhood was. He swung the bow in, slipped the Perkins into reverse, and added a little throttle to stop the boat just as it nudged the dock. Dan stepped off and secured one of his spring lines to a dock cleat, then pulled the stern in and secured the boat. Everything seemed normal. He smiled as he remembered the one about the guy who fell off a sixty-story building. People on each floor heard him yell as he went by, "So far, so good."

It was a hot southern Florida day, and there was no movement in the quiet marina. Martinez's two-story white house was a short walk from the dock across a freshly mowed lawn that ended at a shaded porch.

He checked his notes again to make sure he was at the right house. Martinez should be waiting for him, and after a quick exchange of cash for the cigars, he would be out of there.

There was no welcoming committee, so Dan made his way up to the porch. He banged his knuckles on the thin wood frame and rattled the screen door. After a minute, he opened the door and made his way across the wood porch to a partially open glass door that led into the main house.

He pushed the door farther into the room, rapped his knuckles again, and yelled, "Hey, Martinez. Anybody home?"

There was no answer, but the odor that came from within gave him a feeling that things were less than okay. He moved into the room that was crowded with 1950's tropical style furniture. Martinez was sitting in a high-back wicker chair with his back to him. His head was forward against his chest. The back of his skull was missing from a bullet that must have entered his forehead.

Dan felt his knees go weak – but not from the sight of death. He had never even met the man. He was terrified because of the situation he had suddenly found himself in.

He sat down in the chair opposite the dead man and used all the strength he could summon to relax and evaluate the situation. He had been taught in the Navy to evaluate the situation first, no matter what, and not to react until he had carefully studied the options.

He had sailed into the marina and up to Martinez's dock in broad daylight. Somebody in the marina would have noticed and most likely made a mental note of the boat's name.

If he called the police, they would open a drug-related investigation and call in the Feds, who would search the boat. From the looks of the body, Martinez had been dead for some time. There were hundreds of flies swarming around the dried wound in his head, meaning no one had heard the shot. It was doubtful that the police were on their way at that moment unless the killer was watching and had called the police when he saw Dan arrive.

He did not like the idea of fleeing the scene of a murder, but to stick around and let them find the cigars did not appeal to him either.

Another option was to call the police, say he had been lost in the marina, and had stopped to ask directions. Shit on that. It would not take Perry Mason to blow holes in that story. He was at a dead end canal with just one way out, and he had stopped to ask directions?

Another option was to come clean and take his chances with the cigars and hope Maverick was right about first offenders getting off with a slap on the wrist.

He tried to think. "Take the biggest problem and isolate it," he thought. He stole another look at what he assumed was Martinez. It could be someone else, but it made little difference. The guy was dead, and Dan was obviously the first guy to arrive at the murder scene.

On the good side, if he and the boat were identified, the time of death would show he had not arrived until after the murder. Still, the best plan would be to get as far away from the murder scene as fast as he could and get rid of the cigars. Once he had dumped the contraband, he would be willing to answer any questions the police might ask.

Dan went into the kitchen, grabbed a dishtowel, and carefully backtracked out of the house, removing any possible fingerprints. He went out the back door and walked calmly back to the dock.

He had already set the bow free and stepped into the cockpit when he saw a note resting on the cushion. Someone had left a message while he was in the house:

> If you want to get rid of the cigars, leave the area now. Go
> to Miami Yacht Harbor. Slip No. 58 is reserved for you.

Dan moved the boat away from the dock and made a slow 180-degree turn as quietly as possible. Resisting the urge to push the throttle full forward, he idled quietly out of the marina and plotted a course to the outer reef. He put up the main for stability and maintained five knots as he motored into a light breeze out of the east.

He was tempted to turn south, dump his cargo, and head for Havana, but he couldn't imagine telling Patch and Maverick he had chickened out at the last minute. There was also his original $12,500 at stake. He figured if someone had wanted to kill him, he would still be in Key Largo sitting next to Martinez, feeding the flies.

He reached Mosquito Banks thirty minutes later. There were no police boats in hot pursuit, so he turned north and took up a heading of 034 and engaged the autopilot.

As the sun disappeared behind Florida, he settled back on the cushions and went over his plan. He had no intention of sailing his boat into Miami Yacht Harbor and into the hands of the guys who had put the hole in Martinez's head. He wasn't very experienced at this sort of thing, but he wasn't stupid, either.

After brewing a fresh pot of coffee in the galley, he filled the thermos and returned to the cockpit. It was thirty-seven miles to his destination, and he wanted to make the turn into the Biscayne Channel in sunlight. He eased the sails and slowed the boat down to a steady three knots.

It was seven-thirty in the morning when he hit the Biscayne marker, and two hours later he was tied up at a transient slip at Dinner Key Marina in Miami's classy South Beach suburb. He told the dock master he was just in from Ft. Lauderdale. He gave a phony address and paid for a week's dockage in advance.

It was a typical Florida day: bright and sunny, with a few puffy clouds. A moist wind rattled the stays of the boats as they made pinging music against the masts.

He turned on the air conditioner and grabbed a towel and his shaving kit. He was physically and emotionally exhausted, and he needed sleep. But he needed to clean up first. He made his way down the dock to the showers, where a look in the mirror revealed a tired, sunburned face framed by a head of uncombed, dirty hair. After shaving, he spent a good twenty minutes letting the hot water beat down on the back of his neck while he considered his options.

If the deal with Martinez's killers didn't work out, he'd call Maverick and tell him to come to Miami and sell the fucking cigars himself. Once back in Cuba, he would forget Maverick and cigars. Smuggling obviously did not agree with him. He'd made only one trip and had already barely escaped from being arrested by the Coast Guard. And now he was mixed up in a murder.

Back on the boat, he crashed in the aft bunk and fell dead to the world.

He slept hard for seven hours and woke up groggy at four in the afternoon. He had a quick cup of coffee then called a cab that took him to Bucky's Rent-a-Car, where he rented an old minivan for thirty dollars a day, including insurance.

He drove the minivan back to the boat and began taking the cigars out of their hiding places. He put as many as he could into a sail bag and stuffed a blanket around them to give the appearance of a sail instead of a bunch of boxes. On the way past the office, he poked his head in and asked where he could get a sail repaired.

"A block down on your left. Janie's. Can't miss it."

He knew he couldn't be too careful at this point. There were informers at every marina in Florida ready to share rewards given by the DEA for tips on drug smugglers. If they threw out a net for the big fish, they might catch a little guy with cigars.

Dan put the bag in the minivan and walked back to the boat. He tidied up the deck before making another trip to the van. By six o'clock he had all the cigars in the van. He checked his road map and left the marina.

Three days after leaving Martinez's place in Key Largo, he walked into the Miami Yacht Harbor office and approached the youngster behind the counter.

"Hi, I was supposed to arrive a few days ago, and my friends made a reservation for me. The boat's name is *Pass Line*. Unfortunately, I had a little trouble and had to put the boat in the yard for repairs. If my friends ask for me, I'm staying at the Marriott Biscayne. The name is Smith, Carl Smith."

The mousy kid wearing a white shirt with a nautical emblem hardly looked up, but he did make a note on a piece of paper and mumbled, "Yeah, *Pass Line*, Marriott, Smith. Got it."

Dan made his way to the parking lot and studied the area before getting into the van. Was he being watched? What if they thought he had the cigars in the van? Would they be bold enough to jump out and blast him in broad daylight? What if there was someone hiding in the back of his van? He carefully opened the door and peered into the space behind the driver's seat. It was as empty as the feeling in his stomach.

Dan paid cash for the room at the hotel, made his way across the lobby, and took the elevator to the sixth floor. The hallway was empty. He slid the plastic key card into the slot and breathed a sigh of relief as he entered the safety of his room.

He turned on the TV and sprawled on the king-sized bed, wondering if he was going to get out of this thing alive. He had the cigars safely stored. They obviously wanted them. They were killers, but they hadn't killed Martinez for cigars, or they would have waited for Dan to deliver the cargo. Something in the puzzle was missing.

He didn't realize he'd fallen asleep until he felt a nudge on his foot. He was instantly awake. The barrel of a semiautomatic was pointed in his direction.

"Please do not make any quick moves, Mr. Fletcher." The voice was quiet, without an accent.

"Who are you?"

"We are friends. We know who you are, and we have guns. Do not do anything foolish."

Still dressed in his shorts, Dan sat on the edge of the bed and studied the two intruders. The one doing the talking was in his late thirties, five-foot-six, and skinny – about one hundred and twenty. He had a lean face, with a pencil-thin mustache and greasy black hair combed straight back. When he placed the oversized semiautomatic on the table, Dan noticed the missing index finger on his right hand. It didn't seem to hamper his ability to hold the weapon.

The little guy took a seat at the small table across the room. The other one stood at the doorway, blocking any exit. He was slightly taller, but much heavier – a mulatto with a round face accented by a wide nose and flared nostrils. He had light brown skin and big, fat hands. One of the hands held another semiautomatic. They both wore white short-sleeved shirts, brown slacks, and black pointed-toe shoes.

"Please, relax," Pencil-thin spoke softly through thin lips as his fat-faced partner watched. "Perhaps you would like to be a good host and offer a drink." He motioned toward Dan's full bottle of rum on the table. "I see you like Havana Club. It was originally Bacardi, you know, until that dictator Castro nationalized the company."

•

So they're Cubans, Dan thought. *I should have known.* He got up from the bed, sat down at the table across from Pencil-thin, and slid the bottle over. "Help yourself."

He wondered if he was going to end up like Martinez. "Look," he said, "I don't know who you are, and I don't want to know. If it's the cigars you want, I have them, and they are for sale." His voice was firm. What he really wanted to say was, "Put the guns away and take the cigars. I won't say anything. Swear to God. I'll set sail for Cuba, and you'll never see me or hear about me again."

Pencil-thin poured himself a half tumbler of rum and lit a Marlboro. He ignored his companion, who stood motionless at the door.

"My name is Alfonso."

Dan nodded and wondered how they knew his name and how they had managed to waltz into his room while he was asleep.

"I'll be straight with you, Mr. Fletcher. I'm in the cigar business, just like Martinez used to be." He paused, took a mouthful of rum, and let it trickle down his throat.

Dan waited. *He's probably wondering just how much he should tell me about his business.*

Alfonso took another sip and set the glass down. He looked into Dan's eyes and said, "I didn't kill Martinez. His competitors did."

"You were a friend of Martinez?"

"No, not a friend. I was a competitor," he said, "when he was just in the cigar business."

"What do you mean?"

"Come now, Mr. Fletcher. Do you really think Maverick and Patch loaded you up with nothing but cigars?"

They knew about Maverick and Patch.

"Your friends in Cuba are just like the late Mr. Martinez. They are not satisfied with making a few hundred thousand dollars dealing in Cuban to-bacco." The long ash on his cigarette was making its way down to the yellow stains on his fingers.

Dan's fear was moving toward anger. "You seem to know more about what's going on than I do. I'm a fast learner, Alfonso. Go ahead and tell me what I don't know about my cargo."

"What you don't know, Mr. Fletcher, is that the biggest value of your cargo is not tobacco." He stared into Dan's eyes to record the reaction, "It's cocaine."

Dan exhaled slowly, slumped in his chair, and mumbled mostly to himself, "Why did I know you were going to say that?" *So Maverick and Patch set me up as a mule. The cigars were a cover.*

As the wheels started turning in his head, Dan was troubled by one detail in particular. "I was stopped by the Coast Guard. Why didn't they find the coke?"

"Your friends Patch and Maverick dipped the bags of cocaine into melted paraffin before putting them in the boxes. Also, if you check the individual aluminum tubes of Romeo and Julieta Churchills, you won't find cigars. The tubes are not only good for preserving tobacco; they make excellent containers for two ounces of cocaine.

Thank God the ones I gave the Coast Guard lieutenant were not the tubes.

Alfonso let the idea sink in before continuing, "Martinez did well in the cigar trade, but he was greedy. When he moved into drugs, he began competing with the wrong crowd." He paused and studied Dan, who was staring at the table. "He offended the big guys. And those guys do not mess around. He went overboard when he started making big money with the drug trade."

"What do you mean by overboard?" Dan asked.

"You know, flashy car, expensive suits, jewelry – the works. He was always flashing a big roll. He was a neon sign that said, 'Drugs: Bought and Sold Here.' He attracted the DEA in a way the guys who control drugs in the Keys didn't like. It wasn't like they didn't warn him. They gave him plenty of chances. We were not surprised when he went down."

Dan was thinking about what he was going to do to Maverick and that one-eyed derelict Patch when he got back to Cuba. He snapped out of it when he took another look at the weapons pointed at him. "What are your plans for me, Alfonso?"

"That depends on you, Mr. Fletcher. If you have no objections, we'd like to buy your cargo."

"I thought you said you guys were not into coke."

"I'm not, but Ramon is." He made a slight motion with his head toward the figure at the door.

Dan looked at Fat-face and asked, "May I assume Ramon represents the people who were not happy with Martinez?"

Alfonso didn't answer. "We are prepared to pay you a fair price for the cigars and the cocaine."

Dan tried to relax. He moved his chair back, crossed a leg, and tried to think. His contact had gotten his head blown off. *These guys could have killed me back in Key Largo and taken the stuff for nothing. Now they're offering me my freedom and a piece of the action. Where is the hitch? Is this the part where I take a hard line and negotiate the price? Or should I say, "Take the fuckin' stuff. Give me the twelve-five I have invested, and I'll be out of your life forever?"*

Instead, he found himself saying, "Look, Al, under the circumstances, why don't you just keep that gun on me and start pulling my fingernails out until

I tell you where the stuff is. Then you could do me in like Martinez, or simply tell me to go fuck myself."

Alfonso did not appear offended. "The guns are for our protection, not to harm you. I am a law-abiding citizen – an importer, you might say. Cigars don't hurt people like drugs. They're not even as bad as cigarettes. They just happen to be made in Cuba. I don't want to kill, rob, or even cheat anyone. Furthermore, I would like you to bring me more cigars on a regular basis. As far as the coke is concerned, it's a one-time deal with Ramon. We really do not work together."

Dan looked over at Ramon. He hadn't moved and did not make eye contact. Dan was sure his picture was next to the word *goon* in the dictionary.

Pencil-thin continued, "You took a big chance getting the goods this far. It would be a shame if you were not compensated in some form for your efforts."

Dan didn't want to believe it. "Let me get this straight. You want to give me something like a finders fee for the cocaine, buy my cigars, and order more?"

"That's right, Mr. Fletcher. I'm not a gangster. I'm a businessman who deals in tobacco. Without sailors like you, I would be out of business. As far as the deal with your so-called partners in Cuba, I don't want to have anything to do with them, and if I were you, I wouldn't either. As far as we are concerned, you found Martinez dead, left the scene, and dumped the cargo on your way back to Cuba."

Dan sat up. A ton of shit had just been lifted from his shoulders. "What did you have in mind for the cigars and the rest of the stuff?" He tried not to seem too anxious.

Alfonso didn't hesitate. "Two hundred a box for the cigars from me and another four thousand a box from Ramon for the coke."

The figure had obviously been pre-determined, and Dan was in no position to negotiate. The only bargaining chip he had was the location of the boxes.

Alfonso went on. "It's less than the going rate, but in this case, we think it's fair."

Dan didn't have to calculate the numbers. He reached his hand across the table and said, "It's fine with me."

Al shook his hand. "Good. We'll even unload the boat for you. Where is it?"

Dan's antenna went up. "The location of the boat is not important. I have the cargo in a safe place. Here's the way we do it." Dan suddenly found himself in charge. "I'll make a list of all the stuff: the total boxes of cigars and the boxes of coke. You call me here tomorrow morning, and I'll give you the numbers based on your prices."

Al stared back expressionless.

"I'll give you a meeting place," Dan went on. "You bring the money, and I tell you the location of the goods. Ramon stays with me until you check the stuff out, then when he gets the call from you, I walk away."

Alfonso thought a few moments then looked at Fat-face, who gave a slight nod.

"Okay, Dan. I appreciate your concerns. We can do it your way." He drained the glass of rum, put the gun in his belt, and moved toward the door. "I'll call you tomorrow."

When they were gone, Dan started shaking. He took a long drink from the bottle and lay down on the bed. He knew he was not out of the woods yet. First, he had to find some scales to weigh the coke then make sure he was not followed to the storage room. After that, he would decide on a busy place to make the transaction. It also might be a good idea to have someone with him to discourage Fat-face from giving him the Martinez treatment and walking out with the money. After that, he would have to get out of Florida without being followed, robbed, or killed.

Dan pulled up to the USA Storage gate and punched *2345* on the gate box. The big metal bars ground open, and Dan carefully drove into the facility where he had rented space two days before. An eerie feeling came over him as the gate closed behind him. If he had been followed, he was done for. They could be watching.

Rule One, he thought. *Don't underestimate the enemy.* If they had followed him, they would wait until he parked next to the room before going in. The only ace he held in this game was that he was the only who knew which room the cigars were in.

He had driven in circles after leaving the hotel to make sure he was not being followed. He had noticed a black SUV behind him after several turns, but eventually it had disappeared. If he had been followed, he would be a sitting duck locked in the storage area. He looked around. There was no one in the area or lights from other cars.

He moved the van forward a few yards to clear the gate and parked. He grabbed his scales and a notepad and walked into the nearest isle of garages. When he was at the far end, he turned the corner and glanced back. He saw no one following. He passed two more alleys of storage rooms, turned left, and hurried to his unit. He quickly dialed *7777* on the combination lock and rolled the noisy steel door up. Once inside, he rolled it back down. It was pitch black. He sat and listened.

He waited for ten minutes. Hearing no movement outside, he switched on the flashlight and turned his attention to the pile of cigar boxes sitting on the concrete floor, the same pile that had nearly cost him a prison term and still might cost him his life if he was not careful. Pencil-thin and Fat-face weren't fucking around. They were harmless in the hotel, but he still had what they wanted, and once he turned the cocaine and the cigars over, there was no telling what those two gangsters might do.

Dan separated the boxes of aluminum tubes and the twenty-five Partagas boxes that were supposed to contain the packages of coke and made a detailed list of the cigars. He weighed each of the cocaine boxes after checking the contents then weighed the aluminum tubes on the letter scale he'd purchased. *A little over two ounces each – just what they said.*

Dan heard the sound of a car and froze. He turned off the light and listened in darkness. A car slowly drove by.

He knew he was trapped, and if they had followed him, they could simply roll up the door and make like the Saint Valentine's Day Massacre with machine guns blazing.

He sat in the black sweatbox for twenty minutes. All he could hear was his heart pounding in his ears.

Then the car passed by again. He moved silently by feel and pressed his ear to the cool metal door. He sucked in air and slowly exhaled. He heard the faint sound of the front gate roll open and close moments later.

His hands were shaking as he continued with the inventory. Free diving sixty feet in murky black water and looking for a steel plate on the bottom during UDT training was nothing compared to this.

He finished the inventory, left the scales, and quietly closed the door. His heart was racing as he backtracked the way he had come and climbed into the van.

Thirty minutes later, he was back in the hotel, where he collapsed on his bed and fell into a deep sleep.

Dan awoke at eight o'clock and managed to wash down a plate of ham and eggs with a pot of coffee from room service before the phone rang at nine-thirty.

It was Alfonso.

"Okay, Al, here are the numbers. I've got four hundred and twenty-three boxes of good cigars." He went down the list: Cohibas, Romeo and Julietas, Monte Cristo A's, and Hoyo de Montereys. "And I've got another fifty boxes of aluminum tubes with two ounces of coke in each tube. There are twenty-five Partagas boxes of coke sealed in paraffin, a kilo each."

He gave Alfonso time to write it down, then gave him the totals. "That comes to eighty-four thousand, six hundred for the cigars and another three hundred thousand for the coke. Call it an even three-eighty-four.

He was ready for the next question and answered, "Captain Jack's Seafood Restaurant. One o'clock."

He hung up the phone and dialed the number on the card. A sleepy voice answered.

"Helen, this is Dan, the guy who called last night, remember? The deal is still on. Five hundred dollars to have lunch with me. No extras, okay? Meet me at Captain Jack's Seafood Restaurant in Miami Beach at twelve o'clock. I'll be wearing a red baseball cap that says *Mighty Mouse*. Wear beach clothes, and don't be late."

He put down the receiver and went over the entire plan one more time.

He had not swallowed that good-guy shit Alfonso had dished out yesterday, and he sure as hell was not going to be trusting guys like his silent partner Ramon. He knew he was playing hardball with the big boys, and he did not want to give Fat-face the opportunity to blow his head off as soon as they took possession of his cargo.

It was now ten o'clock. He had just enough time to check out of the hotel and position himself at the restaurant before meeting his hired hooker at noon.

She arrived twenty minutes late. His first instinct was to hide his Mighty Mouse hat and pretend he was someone else. She was a real package. Her idea of beach clothes was one for the books. She was dressed in a black halter-top that barely covered a plastic pair of 44DD's. Her belly button was pierced with a gold ring, and the miniskirt almost concealed two cheeks that sat atop long spindly legs encased in black fishnet pantyhose. Long stringy red hair framed a thin face that was caked with paint and mascara. A crooked Roman nose ended too close to a wide mouth. And a pair of red come-fuck-me-pumps rounded out the attire. From a distance, she looked exotic. Close up, she was hideous.

She introduced herself, and Dan led her to the table he had reserved in the back of the restaurant near a hallway that led to the men's room and the rear exit. He handed her five one-hundred-dollar bills and said, "I don't know anybody in town, and I need you here to witness a business deal. Whatever you do, don't talk. Just sit here and pretend to enjoy your meal. We'll be here for about an hour and a half after my friends arrive."

Helen stuffed the bills into her cleavage, shrugged, and said, "Easiest five hundred I ever made. You paying for lunch, too?"

"Sure, Helen, eat up. It's on the house."

By the time Alfonso and Ramon appeared at one o'clock sharp, Helen was well into her second Tom Collins. They were wearing the same outfits with the black pointy-toed shoes. Alfonso was carrying a light brown attaché case.

Dan introduced Helen as an old friend. She smiled and dove into the bowl of clam chowder the waiter had just delivered.

Alfonso was all smiles as he and Fat-face sat down. He slid the briefcase he was carrying over next to Dan.

Dan waited until Alfonso ordered a drink, then excused himself and took the case into the men's room. Ramon followed and waited in the narrow hallway next to the door.

Dan locked himself in a stall and opened the briefcase. It contained thirty-eight packs of hundreds with bank bands indicating ten thousand to a pack, plus a smaller wad with a rubber band that contained another four thousand. He selected one bill from each pack and checked for counterfeits. With his experience in Las Vegas, no one was going to pass bogus bills onto him. Everything seemed in order. Was it possible Al and Fat-face were actually playing it straight with him? He closed the case and returned to the table with Ramon following.

Alfonso was smiling when he got back to the table. "Everything okay, Mr. Fletcher?"

"Looks good to me," Dan said as he reached into his pocket and produced a folded slip of paper that he slid across the table.

"It's USA Storage over on Highway 1, number D-11. Here's the address and the combination for the gate and the room lock. The phone number of this place is there, too. Ask for Alden. He's the bartender, and he knows you'll be calling."

Alfonso handed Dan a business card and said, "It's been a pleasure. Here's how to get in touch with me." He turned and made his way out of the restaurant.

Dan suddenly realized he was famished. He had been too nervous to think about his stomach, but now there was nothing he could do but wait. He squeezed the attaché case between his feet under the table and ordered a fish burger with iced tea.

Helen was starting on her second pound of a double order of boiled shrimp. Ramon sat there with his normal bland expression.

He must be some sort of robot, Dan thought. *The guy doesn't drink, smoke, or eat. He just sits there with that never-changing look on that fat face.*

Dan had no doubt that Ramon had shot Martinez, and he was sure that if something went wrong, he'd be next. And maybe nothing had to go wrong.

Ramon had probably killed for a lot less than Dan was holding in the attaché case under the table.

It was an hour and fifteen minutes before the waitress came to the table and said the bartender had a call for a Ramon.

This is the turning point, Dan thought to himself. *They have the cargo, and I have the money.* He was tempted to take the briefcase and run for the exit. Instead, he sat there and waited for Ramon to return. *He won't shoot me here with all these witnesses.*

Ramon's expressionless face gave nothing away when he returned to the table. He looked at Dan for a moment before turning and walking out.

Dan breathed a sigh of relief. "Thanks, Helen. You were great."

He threw enough on the table to pay the bill, took the briefcase, and walked quickly down the hall past the men's room and out the backdoor into the narrow alley. The van was parked almost two blocks away. Once in the van and safely out of the parking lot, he'd be halfway home.

Just before he was out of the alley and onto the busy side street, he saw Fat-face step around the corner into the alley and casually took a position leaning against the building.

Dan suddenly felt lightheaded. He had made the big mistake of underestimating the enemy. Ramon must have been watching the front door when he arrived at the restaurant. He knew Dan would go out the backdoor, and he knew which way he would turn once in the alley.

Dan thought quickly about his options. He didn't like the idea of turning and running. That could mean taking a shot in the back or being stopped by a cop. He would have a hard time explaining the case full of money.

He made his decision and continued walking with a big grin on his face, like he had guessed Ramon would be there and was resigned to giving up the money.

Ramon made the mistake of taking Dan for a pushover. He was now the one who was underestimating the enemy.

As Dan approached, he held out the briefcase with his left hand and said, "I guess you are looking for this."

Ramon's expression did not change. Neither did his relaxed position against the wall.

Dan took advantage of the man's next mistake. Ramon made no move toward the gun under his left armpit as he reached for the case.

Dan dropped the case just before it reached Fat-face's outstretched right hand. He then moved forward with his weight behind the punch as Fat-face bent over to pick up the case.

The perfect Sunday punch caught Ramon on the jaw, and he landed face-down on the concrete. Dan picked up the money and hurried ut of the alley. Tires screeched as he almost ran in front of a Mustang convertible.

A horn blared, and one of the four girls in the car yelled, "Watch it, mister! There's death and destruction out there!" He could hear them laughing as they drove off.

He reached the parking lot and looked back. There was no sign of Fat-face. The ache in his wrist proved he had hit him hard. He scanned the lot for his van. *Shit, where is it?* He started to panic. It was like a bad dream. He had a rental car and could not remember anything about it other than it was light colored. He reached into his pocket and fumbled for the car keys as he wandered into the mass of parked cars. *Jesus Christ, Fletcher. It's an old fucking van.* There seemed to be a thousand cars. He had driven in, circled the first island of cars, and parked close to the exit. *There it is – over there.*

He ran up and jumped into the driver's side that he had purposely left open. Not remembering where he parked had been a stupid mistake, and it had cost him time he really did not have.

He put on the white Panama hat and sunglasses he had left on the seat and threw his red baseball cap in the back as he glanced out the rear window. Fat-face was standing a block down the street looking around and rubbing his jaw. Dan eased out of the lot and made a left turn away from his adversary. He was close to pulling this thing off, but he was not there yet. It was now a game of cat and mouse, and Dan was the mouse.

He drove the rent-a-car into the Radisson Hotel parking lot, grabbed the money and his overnight bag, and entered a side door. He made his way down the corridor and into the lobby. At the front desk, he took a room in his own name and paid for three nights in advance. If someone followed him, they would assume they had three days to make a hit, but Dan had no intention of sticking around. He took the elevator to his room and transferred the money from the attaché case into his overnight bag. He was taking no chances. The case could contain a homing device. He left the case in the room and walked down six flights of stairs to the basement.

Minutes later, he was out onto 16th street, where he hailed a cab. "Airport. American Airlines, please."

He noticed that the driver picked up the mike and said, "Thirty-seven. Airport. American Airlines." He wondered if it was for his tracker's benefit.

When they arrived, he moved quickly into the terminal, turned left, walked a hundred yards down the terminal, then exited back out onto the sidewalk, where he took a position behind the United Airlines curbside baggage check-in.

His suspicions were confirmed moments later. The sight of Fat-face getting out of the cab sent a chill up his spine. He moved fast and took the escalator down to the arrival area, where he jumped into the first bus he saw. He looked back but did not see Ramon.

The driver seemed confused when Dan asked, "Where is this bus going?"

Twenty minutes later, he was sitting in an Alamo rent-a-car and studying the buses arriving from the airport. He watched for an hour before driving to Coconut Grove, where he stashed the car and walked two blocks to the marina.

CHAPTER
23

Dan sipped a cup of hot coffee and checked the GPS. He was eight miles off Key West, making six knots. His next stop would be Hemingway Marina, eighty-seven nautical miles to the south.

He'd left Dinner Key in the middle of the night, backtracked across Biscayne Bay, then sailed through the channel past the outer reef into deep water. Only after he had turned south and set a course for Cuba did he finally start to relax.

It had been one hell of an adventure. He had come dangerously close to being arrested for trafficking during a Coast Guard inspection, had run from a murder scene, sold drugs to thugs, carried almost four hundred thousand dollars around Miami in a briefcase, and sucker-punched a goon who was trying to take it from him. Now the meeting with Maverick and Patch was coming up.

The more he thought about those two, the more he realized he had been a real sap. He'd been set up from the get-go. A thousand bars in Havana, and Maverick had just happened to come into the one he was sitting in and just happened to notice him. "You by any chance a sailor? Have I got a deal for you."

He wondered if that guy Julio had really taken his twelve-five, or if that had been a made-up story. He was pretty sure Patch had been in on it from the beginning and was probably the guy who had put the cocaine into the tubes. He had been taken by a couple of hustlers.

He smiled and said out loud to the stars, "There's one born every minute," before adding under his breath, "You can't cheat an honest man."

After all, he thought, it was greed that had gotten him into the deal to begin with, and it was greed that had gotten him to turn his boat north after leaving Martinez's murder, only to find himself in a situation that had almost cost him his life. He could have dumped the cigars and would have never met Alfonso and Fat-face. But that was over. Now he had to decide just how he was going to handle his partners when he got back.

Pass Line sailed on through the tropical night as Dan Fletcher pondered his life. He thought about Lily and how his life now revolved around her. He had never done well with women. Sure, he got plenty of sex. That was always easy. But he had only had one long relationship, and that had been with his ex-wife Nancy.

She had been good for him at the time. He was a guy with a gambling habit, making good money but going nowhere. They were married in one of those Las Vegas chapels where the ceremony took a full nine minutes, complete with a tape recording of *Here Comes the Bride*. Nancy talked him into Gamblers Anonymous, and with both of them working, the family bank account grew.

After four years of marriage and being free from gambling, his life was moving in the right direction. As a pit boss at the Hilton, he was making more money than most of his buddies who had a college education. Nancy was dealing twenty-one, and together their bank balance was moving up at a steady rate.

He remembered the day the bubble burst. He had returned home after his night shift and found the note on the kitchen table. Nancy was gone. She was sorry, but she just had to get out. She didn't take much, just her clothes and half of the bank account. He later found out through one of Nancy's friends that she had left town with the tennis pro at the Hilton. Evidently it had been going on for some time.

He had wondered how long it would take the tennis pro to go through Nancy's savings before dumping her for a younger Bambi. "Shit," he remembered saying, "she doesn't even play tennis."

At the time, he had been glad that he at least had his car, his clothes, and his job. And Nancy had been nice enough to leave his part of the savings. Besides, he had never really been in love with Nancy, not like he thought love should be: knee-deep in unconditional, nonjudgmental pleasure. Nancy had been right for him at the time. She had the right job and made good money, and the relationship was convenient. And she had been instrumental in getting him off gambling. But the relationship had always lacked that head-over-heels, complete surrender he felt must be out there somewhere. Like the love he felt for Lily.

He had grown to like the Cuban people, whose friendly attitude he admired. Cubans seemed to bear no grudges against foreigners. *How is it*, he thought, *that after forty years of being treated so badly by their closest neighbor, they still hold Americans in high esteem?*

Dan checked the sails and eased the main as he sailed on a broad reach toward Cuba. His thoughts drifted back to his relationship with Lily.

Maybe he should think about getting her out of Cuba. It wasn't impossible. He had already eliminated the option of taking her to live with him in the U.S., and sailing out of the marina with her hidden in the boat was also a foolish thought. One option would be to get her to Grenada and meet her with the boat. Cubans did not need visas to fly to Grenada.

He wondered if Lily would ever get back on a boat after the fiasco with Manny during the Christmas regatta. He would have to promise her that once they made it to their destination, he would get rid of the boat. With the money he had just picked up in Florida, he and Lily could enjoy life in a nice palm-thatched villa next to a tropical lagoon. But first he would have to talk Lily into it. The big question was: did she love him? Was her refusal to discuss that four-letter word just some hang-up, or was Dan not the man for her? He decided it was time to find out. When he got back, he would propose marriage and promise her an easy life in a free country.

Dan sailed through the night, filled with enthusiasm and new hope.

CHAPTER
24

At the Macumba discotheque, Lily waited in line to pay her fifteen-dollar cover charge. This was to be a special night, she thought confidently as she looked around at all the fancy dresses and latest fashions on the women. Her friends had told her that many rich Italians spent their evenings here at Cuba's newest and most elegant nightclub. This was where her best friend had met her Italian husband-to-be just two weeks ago.

Tonight, Lily was determined that she would find her special man. She knew exactly what she wanted. And Lily always got what she wanted.

After she paid her charge and checked her bag, she stepped into the entryway and smoothed her long black dress with both hands. It was a movement she had practiced many times at home, performed as gracefully as a ballerina assuming the fifth position.

Her hands began together, with her fingertips touching and placed on her concaved tummy. In a moment that seemed like three minutes to a man watching, her palms swept back, pulling the fabric so slightly. Her hands made a slight rotation at the pelvic bone and traveled down back across her buttocks. At the same instant, she gave a slight head fake and lifted the lock of ink-black hair from her left eyebrow. The movements of the hands, the head, and the hair lasted but a moment. To the eye of an admiring male, it was an image fast frozen in his mind.

She moved from the entryway down the steps and into the nightclub. Pierre La Cont had spent ten million dollars of his syndicate's money refurbishing a twenty-acre estate and turning it into Havana's most elegant nightclub. Patrons dined at ten o'clock in the high-ceiling restaurant. Afterward, they made their way into the adjoining poolside cabaret that contained four bars, two dance floors, and an elevated stage where skimpily clad dancers performed the cabaret's midnight extravaganza – all included in the fifty-dollar price of a mediocre dinner.

The doors at the south entrance opened at 11:00 p.m. to admit the long line of well-dressed couples and a score of single females clad in the latest fashions, complete with stiletto-thin spiked heels. Cuban beauties like Lily appeared at night, like vampires waiting until dark to emerge from their lairs. Hours earlier, they might be sitting on the porch in jeans and T-shirts, chatting with family and friends. But by nightfall these disco creatures, thousands of them, emerged and headed for the Havana nightlife with one thing in mind: having fun. The more hopeful among them might aim slightly higher, hoping to find a man – any man – except a worthless, penniless Cuban man, who would take the money they earned and give them a few knocks in the process. But it was different for Lily that late night in February. She was looking for her dream man.

Lily took a seat at the poolside bar that was decorated with potted plants and palm trees. Underwater lights illuminated the clear water. Opposing fountains crossed their backlit streams through the thick tropical night.

She reached into her small purse and pulled out a pack of Marlboros. A lighter appeared out of nowhere. Lily leaned forward and, without glancing upward, moved her cigarette into the flame. She sucked the first drag deep into her lungs before raising her eyes to look at the man holding the lighter.

She exhaled, eyes fixed on his. "Gracias."

"Carlo," he said. "Carlo Pontelli."

She studied his handsome face and guessed he was Italian. He had deep-set brown eyes, a full head of brown wavy hair, and was sporting a bushy but well trimmed mustache. A three ounce gold bar dangled from a heavy gold chain. Two smaller chains completed the jewelry ensemble that hung in front of a jet-black T-shirt. No doubt about it: Carlo was a hunk. His wide shoulders and well-defined bulging biceps stretched his tight short-sleeved T-shirt to the limit before it plunged into his belted beige slacks. *Here's a perfect body*, she thought, *all wrapped in light brown, fat-free skin*. He was not tall – about five-nine. He had a thin waist and straight white teeth that he was not afraid to show. He obviously had a body that was personally selected by God. But a sculptured body like that didn't come without regimented training, she thought.

Lily's close scrutiny failed to find flaws in this man. He looked her straight in the eye as he spoke fluent Spanish, albeit with a romantic Italian accent. When she spoke, his eyes darted from her lips to her eyes, to her hair, and back to her eyes, as though he was admiring her beauty while transfixed by her every word. It was apparent that she was as enamored with him as he was with her.

Six hours later, Lily was nestled in Carlo's arms as they lay in bed. They had left the disco early and hurried to the apartment he'd rented in a private house on a side street not far from the luxurious five-star Melia Cohiba Hotel.

After a lovemaking session overflowing with passion and hard sex, Lily was certain she had found the man she had been looking for.

She compared her new love to Dan. Dan was easygoing and a different personality than Carlo. She loved Dan, but where would she be when Dan was eighty years old, or perhaps dead? She would be an old, childless woman living alone. No man would want a forty-year-old when thousands of young women were available. Besides, Dan was an American with no desire to return to his country. Carlo was young and beautiful. He would take her to Italy.

"Carlo." She nudged him gently. "What kind of work do you do? Do you have a good job?"

"Sporting goods, my love. I do well enough to live comfortably."

Well enough for two, she figured. *He dresses well, and the gold around his neck must be worth five or six thousand dollars.* Carlo was the man she'd been looking for. He was perfect.

Later, as he slept, Lily slid back the sheet and made her way down to his manhood that was now lying limp across his leg. She took his spent penis into her mouth and felt him respond.

Carlo groaned and gyrated his pelvis as Lily's other hand went to work gently caressing his scrotum. He said nothing. It was good sex. He took without giving and seemed to be concentrating on his own pleasure.

The only sounds in the room were the soft whirling of the ceiling fan and the slurping of Lily's mouth as she increased the rhythm. She was careful not to let her hands forget their job and become too powerful in their soft, circular movements. Her wet mouth, teeth covered by curved lips, made its way up and down until she felt his thigh muscles flex and his legs go stiff as he came.

She crawled up into Carlo's arms and looked into his face. He was staring at the ceiling with a look of amazement. She whispered into his ear, "I hope you enjoyed that."

Carlo said in a soft monotone, "No man should go through life without having that done to him, just like that."

After that, she thought to herself, *he will marry me and take me out of this godforsaken country to Italy. No man could ever forget a blow job like that.*

It was a whirlwind romance. Carlo was attentive and generous. He possessed great staying power, not only in bed but also life in general. He could dance at the disco until five in the morning, not like Dan, who insisted on a 2:00 a.m. curfew.

"Come on, Lily," Dan always said. "Let's go home. Why waste a perfectly good tomorrow?"

Carlo seemed to relish the nightlife, but he never missed his four-hour workout session the next day at the nearby gym in the Kohly Hotel. Lily usually slept until one o'clock in the afternoon after another night at the disco. Carlo bought her fine clothes at Mango and the Benetton shop in the Comodoro Mall. He bought her high heels, silk lingerie that tore apart during sex, cosmetics, sunglasses, and even a stylish man-sized Swatch wristwatch. Lily also enjoyed helping herself to cash from Carlo's stash, which she easily found in a leather pouch attached by Velcro to the backside of the bottom drawer of the bathroom linen chest. She only took a few tens and some twenties. Once she took a hundred dollar bill. If he noticed, he never mentioned it.

Thirty days into the romance, Carlo said, "Lily, I know we have only known each other for a month, but I'm a man who knows what he wants." He took her hand and brought it to his lips. "I want to marry you."

Lily had been hoping for this, but when Carlo made the proposal, she hesitated – not the coy hesitation that would have shown she was taken by surprise; there was something else. Carlo was young and handsome. He obviously had money and was definitely a good lover. And yet, it was too perfect. They'd never had a disagreement, let alone an argument – nothing like the fights she was used to getting into with Dan about the smallest things. The last thirty days had been like watching someone else play her part in the story of Cinderella. It was as if she was sitting in some quiet place watching two lives.

Then she heard herself saying, "Oh, Carlo, of course I'll marry you."

"That's great, my love," he said ecstatically. "As you know, my tourist permit will expire in two days, and I am scheduled to go back to Rome tomorrow. I'll leave you some money so you can get a passport, and I'll arrange a one-month visa for you in Rome. I'll wire you some money for a plane ticket. I have some connections at the Italian consulate, and the whole process will take less than two months."

Lily was on cloud nine. She was going to get out of Cuba.

"We'll get the necessary marriage papers from the Cuban embassy in Rome, then return to Cuba together and get married. After the ceremony, you can apply for a permanent resident visa to Italy."

For the first time in her life, Lily could plan for the future. She would come back and visit her family whenever she wished, at least every six months. She would be sure to visit at least every eleven months so she could keep her Cuban citizenship and her right to buy food with her ration card. Big deal.

The plan was all spelled out. It was perfect. But if it was so perfect, why was she lying in bed next to her future husband staring out the tiny barred window unable to sleep? As she lay there listening to Carlo's steady breathing, she had doubts. What was it? It wasn't her, and it was not Carlo. No, it was something about the two of them together. She had spent a month with this man, the man she was going to marry, the man she was going to leave her family and Cuba for, the man who would raise her children. If there was something missing, it could not be important. But still, there was that nagging feeling in her stomach. Was it because her mother did not approve of this man?

Lily recalled the encounter two weeks earlier when she and Carlo had come across her mother by chance in a small coffee bar in Havana during one of their shopping sprees.

Her mother had sat at the table trying to size up her daughter's suitor. "Tell me about yourself, Carlo."

He leaned forward and placed his elbows on the table, a move that bulged his shoulder muscles and flexed his biceps. "I'm thirty-three, and I spend a minimum of four hours a day, six days a week in the gym pumping iron, climbing Stairmasters, and trying to wear out every body-building machine in a variety of health centers. I also import and sell apparatuses for people to work out in their homes."

Lily remembered being so proud of Carlo. But when he went to the bar for more coffee, her mother cautioned her, saying, "Lily, what are you doing with this man?"

"Mama, he's rich. He's Italian. And he's beautiful."

Alma answered stiffly, "Big muscles do not make a man beautiful. All he can talk about is his body. He is a cold man with the soul of the devil." Then she added casually, "And what about Dan?"

Lily remembered that day now. Could it just be that her mother did not like Carlo? That she liked Dan? Mama would change her opinion when Lily started sending money home. She drifted off, thinking of Italy, fine clothes, elegant restaurants, theaters, the opera, cinemas, television – and shoes. Italy had the best shoes. She would own a hundred pairs.

She watched Carlo pack in the morning. They didn't speak. When the taxi arrived to take him to the airport, Lily walked him to the car. They kissed briefly, and Carlo climbed into the backseat, rolled down the window, gave her one of his Pepsodent smiles, and said, "See you in Rome."

The taxi sped out of sight, and Lily began walking toward the *Malecon*, clutching her bag with the five hundred dollars Carlo had given her to pay for exit papers. Carlo would send more when Lily faxed him a copy of her passport.

While she waited on the side of Havana's most picturesque street for a private taxi to come by, she watched local fishermen dangle baited hooks from long cane poles hoping for some pan-sized perch to supplement the family's daily rations of rice and beans. With a little luck, one might land a big *Pargo* that he could sell to a restaurant and earn enough to buy a quart of milk for his children at the dollar store, where a person could buy almost anything.

.

Lily hated the Cuban system, where everyone earned seven dollars a month – paid in Cuban pesos – to work for the Bearded One. The pesos and a ration card bought a kilo of rice, a few soft buns, some bread, a kilo of beans, and maybe a liter of cooking oil that was rarely seen on the shelves. She knew there were people starving to death in America, where everybody seemed to have so much. She had even heard of homeless people in America who lived on the street. The Castro government publicized the poverty in the U.S., pointing out how everyone in Cuba had a place to live and nobody was starving to death. It left out the part about everyone being hungry, about life in Cuba being a form of shared misery.

"It is no wonder," Lily said to herself as she watched the fishermen, "why young girls at the age of sixteen take to the streets and the discos looking for a tourist to help them escape this island of hypocrisy."

Lily thought of the food she could buy for her family with the five hundred dollars Carlo had given her. She'd already spent the two hundred she had lifted from his stash on meat, chicken, oil, and milk for her family. But no, she would use the money for its intended purpose. As soon as she was married and living in Italy, she would send money home on a regular basis. There would be enough for her mother to buy lots of chickens, pork tenderloin, and even lettuce, tomatoes, onions, and potatoes. There would be enough to buy oil and vinegar so Alma could make big salads with dressing. There would even be enough for a big two-kilo beef roast every Sunday to put in the pressure cooker with potatoes and carrots. Alma, her sisters, her brother-in-law, and her precious nieces would live a good life with good food and never be hungry again – as soon as she was in Italy with Carlo.

She flagged an oncoming car. She could spot an illegal taxi from a block away. It screeched to a stop, and Lily got in. "*Baracoa, por favor.*" She wanted to go home and tell her family the big news.

CHAPTER
25

Maverick didn't bother banging on the hull to announce his arrival. He boldly climbed aboard the dirty houseboat and hit his head once again on the hanging board that read *Rat's Nest*. Only Patch Fister would give a boat a name like that, he thought.

He opened the door to the salon and yelled, "Hey, Patch, wake up. Fletcher's back."

Patch stumbled out of the room where he slept. To call it a stateroom would be an insult to the boating industry. The forward part of the square wooden structure was filled with ropes, anchors, rusty chain, and a variety of wrinkled clothes. A large bed made of old two-by-fours rested in the far corner.

Maverick did a double take as he realized his partner was not wearing the flesh-colored bandage over his left eye. He'd seen it before but was still repulsed by the sight of the ugly, hollow cavity.

"Did you talk to him? What happened in Florida?"

Maverick threw a dirty pair of pants off one of the chairs and sat down. "No, I didn't see him yet. Rafael from customs called and said he came into the marina about an hour ago. He should be finished with the paperwork and arriving at his mooring in thirty minutes or so. Get some clothes on and we'll meet him, and for Christ's sake, put something over that hole in your head."

"Gee, sorry'f I ruined your breffast," Patch mumbled as he walked to the sink and looked into the mirror. "Funny, it doesn't bovver me." He tore off the backing of a giant Band Aid and stuck it over the remains of the eye socket.

Maverick studied the grain of the wood tabletop until Patch sat down and said, "Better?"

"Yeah, you know how I am about that. Without the patch, you look like half a cadaver. Anyway, Dan is back and hopefully with some money, but I have been having a problem getting hold of Martinez. His phone rings, but he never answers."

Patch had a serious look as he scratched a three-day stubble on his face and slipped in his false teeth. "Maybe he's out of town." Patch's voice had a slight edge to it.

"It ain't right that he's out of town now. If he made the deal with Fletcher, he's holding a lot of our money for the coke that he would not have given Dan, and he usually makes contact right after a transaction."

Patch said nothing. Maverick fidgeted with a food-encrusted spoon until he realized what it was, then added, "Dan's been gone for more than two weeks. Martinez should have called."

"Forget Martinez for now," Patch said. "Let's get over to Dan's slip and give him a hero's welcome. We'll divide up the cash from the cigar sale, tell him what a great job he's done, and set him up for another run after he's rested up for a few weeks. Then we can get hold of Martinez and get him to send our share of the drug money."

Dan left the customs dock, motored slowly through the turning basin, and made a right turn into the first canal. He knew Patch and Maverick, his pals, would be there to greet him. He had gone over his plan a hundred times on the three-day sail from Miami. He had also used the time to cool his anger. Patch and Maverick had set him up to take the fall if anything went wrong. The boxes full of cocaine could have landed him in prison for a long time. He doubted that the judge would have been sympathetic. "Look, your Honor, I didn't know anything about the drugs. I'm just a simple cigar smuggler." He decided to play dumb about the drugs.

If Patch and Maverick knew about Martinez being dead and about the deal he had made with Fat-face and Pencil-thin, he would cross that bridge when he came to it. He was not about to share one nickel of the drug money. After all, he was the patsy who had taken all the risks.

Pass Line drifted into the dock, and Maverick grabbed the bow line. Patch caught the stern line as Dan shut down the engine.

"Welcome home," Maverick said after securing the line on the iron cleat. "Have a nice sail?"

Fletcher looked for a sign, something in his voice, or a look from Patch – anything that would signal that they knew.

"Yeah, great trip. Good wind and good seas. Come on aboard and have a beer."

Once below, Maverick couldn't contain himself. "Well, how'd it go? Everything okay?"

They don't know. Dan turned on the air conditioner, opened three beers, and handed two over to Patch and Maverick before answering. "I've got bad news and good news," he said as he took a seat at the table. The words hung in the air as the two partners waited. "The bad news is that your friend Martinez is dead."

Maverick leaned forward. "Dead? How?"

Dan shook his head and said, "Someone shot him. I followed your instruction and found him in the house. I got the hell out of there before anyone showed up."

Maverick and Patch almost said it at the same time: "What happened to the cigars?"

Dan sat back, took a swig of beer, and smiled as he studied his partners. "That's the good news. When I got back to the boat, I found a note in the cockpit with a name and number on it and a short message that read, 'We'll buy the cigars.'"

"Then what?" Patch said as he gave Maverick a look.

Dan was smiling big now, like he had run into a bad situation but managed to save the company from total destruction. "Well, under the circumstances, I figured I better get rid of the cigars as soon as possible. I was sure someone saw me enter the marina, and I knew it wouldn't be long before I was brought into a murder investigation."

"What did you do?"

"I got out of there and sailed to Miami, where I called the guy who left the note. I was a little disappointed at the price he offered for the cargo, but I was in no position to argue, and he knew it."

Maverick had a sick look on his face and barely got the words out. "How much did we get?"

Dan pulled out a piece of paper with the numbers on it. "Okay, here we go. I settled for two hundred a box."

Patch groaned.

"Hey, it isn't *that* bad," Dan said in a happy tone. "I managed to get our money back and show a profit. It's not much, but it's better than it would have been if I had left Martinez's place and dumped the boxes in the ocean, which, I might add, was my first thought."

Patch had his head on the table, obviously thinking about the cocaine going for two hundred a box. Maverick just stared at Dan with his mouth open.

Dan continued reading off the paper. "The total came to one hundred thousand dollars. Patch, you get a third off the top for buying the cigars. That's thirty-three thousand, three hundred and thirty-three. I take my twelve thousand, five hundred off the sixty-six thousand, six hundred and sixty-seven that's left – you know, the money your friend Julio got away with."

He looked at Maverick, who still had a dumb expression on his face, then returned to the paper. "I take eight hundred dollars for trip expenses, then you and me, Maverick, split the rest."

Dan kept the cheerful tone in his voice and said, "Let's see. Maverick, that makes your share twenty-six thousand, six hundred and eighty-three dollars.

Not so good, but not so bad, either. We'll do better next time. I have the guy's phone number in Miami, and he's waiting for another batch of cigars"

Before Patch and Maverick could reply, he added, "For a better price, of course."

Dan bubbled over with enthusiasm, all the while feeling petrified that he would be found out. He got up and went to a hatch in the bilge, opened it, and brought out a bag that contained the one hundred thousand dollars. He spread the money on the table and carefully counted out each share. The other bag containing two hundred eight-four thousand dollars was well hidden under five hundred pounds of iron in the chain locker.

After giving patch and Maverick their shares, Dan said, "Well, gentlemen, that's it. Now if you don't mind, I'm bushed. I was up all night trying to dodge tankers in the straits. I'm going to get some sleep, then I'm going to go over to Baracoa and find Lily."

Dan watched through the porthole as Maverick and Patch slowly walked down the quay in animated conversation. He wondered what they were saying and guessed they were trying to figure a way to get in touch with the guy Dan had sold the cigars to in order to find out if he had found the cocaine.

Dan smiled. Lot of good that would do, even if the name and number he gave them existed. He laid down in the V-berth and relaxed for the first time in two weeks. "Maybe good guys do finish first," he said to himself as he closed his eyes and fell into a deep sleep.

CHAPTER

26

Lily slid the hatch back, poked her head in, and yelled, "*Hola, mi amor.*"

Dan was into his second cup of coffee and watching the eight o'clock CNN news. "Hey, how are you? Uh, sorry, I forgot your name. Lily! Yeah, that's it. How have you been, Lily?"

She came down the stairs, walked over, and gave him a kiss. "Don't be funny, honey. I've been in Santiago with my family. It was wonderful. We went to the beach and danced at a different disco every night. I missed you." She gave him a mischievous smile, raised her eyebrows, and asked, "And where have you been, my love? You said you'd be gone on a short sailing trip to Florida. That was weeks ago."

"I was detained." He felt it was better that Lily knows nothing about the cigars.

She walked over to the refrigerator and pulled out a Coke. "Come on, honey. If I didn't know better, I'd say you went back to the States to see another woman." She said the words slowly as she took too long to unscrew the cap on the Coke.

She put the bottle to her lips while keeping her eyes on Dan. She reached behind her head and undid the clasp that held the long locks that came tumbling down over her shoulders. She sucked on the neck of the bottle for a moment without taking her eyes off Dan, then set the Coke down and began unbuttoning her jeans.

Dan took short panting breaths as he tore off his clothes and met her naked body with his in the forward bunk. The sex was swift, compassionate, and complete.

When it was over, they laid quietly together, tangled and sweating.

"I love you, Lily," Dan said. He was sorry as soon as he said it.

She said nothing but put her two fingers over his lips and slowly shook her head, as if to say, "Don't say that, Dan."

He had wanted to propose marriage but thought twice about it when she made the subtle rejection. This was not the time. He was willing to wait a little longer to spring his plan to leave Cuba with her and live in luxury. Enjoying his company and having fun would eventually overshadow any doubts she might have.

.

Dan was optimistic about finding the ultimate relationship with this woman. He wanted the perfect love triangle with three equal sides: physical, emotional, and spiritual. Maybe he would find the perfect moment to propose, but not yet.

Over the next few weeks, Lily would go from hot to cold. One moment she would be tender and loving, the next she would simply disappear for a week.

That night they went out and watched the Cuban National Ballet perform Swan Lake at the elegant national theater in Old Havana. Afterward, they had a late night dinner at the French restaurant on the top floor of the Rivera Hotel.

The perfect evening culminated with tender sex in the cockpit of the boat. She sat on him facing away as he caressed her breasts. The silver spotlight of a full moon ran across the Gulf of Mexico and highlighted their naked bodies grinding slowly against each other. They stayed like that, watching the tropical sky long after their orgasms. When Dan awoke the following morning, Lily was gone again. There was no note.

CHAPTER
27

Dan sat in the salon having his morning coffee and reading a novel when Lenny rapped and opened the hatch.

"Hey, Dan," Lenny said. "Can I come aboard? I have to talk with you."

"Sure, Lenny. You know you don't have to ask."

Lenny sat down and put his hands on his knees and began rubbing his legs. He sat there, saying nothing, and rocked back and forth, obviously in deep thought. Dan waited.

"I have a problem with a girl."

How do I do it? Dan thought. *I got crazy Manny on one side of me and love-sick Lenny on the other. I feel like changing my name to Dan Landers.*

"Remember that little thing I was with a couple of months ago at Rumbos – Ella?"

"Yeah, kind of."

"I figured she was the one. She's new in town, just in from Holguin. She didn't even ask for a dollar for rice, and she was great in the sack. Just how wrong can a man be when it comes to women?"

This sounded serious. Dan sat the novel down, put his feet on the floor, and leaned forward to listen.

"When I finally took her back to her aunt's place, her uncle, who turned out to be a captain in the secret police, greeted me like a long lost son. They served me coffee and fresh fruit, then a big breakfast before I came back to the marina. I had been looking for this girl ever since I came to Cuba, and I finally found her. Then she stopped me one night just as we were about to make love and said, 'Leonardo, will you give me money?' 'Sure,' I told her. 'I said I would help you. What do you need money for? Food?'

"You know what she said, Dan?" He didn't wait for Dan to answer. "She said, 'Well, it's not for anything special. I just thought forty dollars – you know, for making love.'

"I couldn't believe it. I asked her, 'What are you, a *Puta* now, charging for sex?' She just shrugged her shoulders and said, 'Sure. All the other girls at Rumbos get paid something. I want a little, too.' You ever hear shit like that from a nice girl, Dan?"

Dan smiled, "Well, it is Cuba, Lenny."

"Well, even so. I treated her good, then she starts asking for cash. Okay, I can handle that, and I worked out the money thing. I agreed to give her ten dollars a week – four times what the captain makes at the police station."

Dan sensed that Lenny hadn't gotten to the real problem but was building up to it. "Ten Dollars a week seems fair, Lenny." Dan knew that to be a lie. Forty dollars a month would not buy shoes, let alone some pork chops.

"Then I came up with a brilliant idea. You know, Dan, I don't have a lot of money. They don't call me *Tacaño* for nothing. I live on a small pension, and I've been thinking, if I found the right woman, I could sell my boat and save the four hundred a month dockage fees and live in a small house with my girl. I thought Ella might be that girl." He looked at Dan.

Dan didn't speak. He was thinking, *I have my own problems. I'm all mixed up over a woman who can't say the love word and I have this guy coming to me for advice?"*

Lenny was wringing his hands and looking down at the deck, obviously reliving a terrible experience. "Anyway, I was looking at the house where Ella lives, and I saw an opportunity. There are two rooms: one for Ella and one for the aunt and uncle. Her brother sleeps on the sofa. I figured, why get another house? I could fix up Ella's room, and we could stay there. The money we'd save could be used for food and other expenses. The family loved the idea, so I bought some paint, a new mattress, and a fan for the ceiling."

Dan was hoping his neighbor would get to the point so he could get back to his novel.

"I spent a week drilling into that fucking concrete ceiling. I even put in lead sleeves and put the fan up with stainless steel bolts and lock washers so we'd never have to worry about the thing falling on our heads. I worked a whole week, painting furniture and really fixing up the place. That was nothing. Installing that goddamn fan was real work."

Dan had never seen such hatred in the eyes of this quiet Canadian. He sat back, sensing there was more to come. It was not time to interrupt.

"So I go over there this morning, and you know what?" Lenny's eyes burned with fire. "The fucking fan was gone, taken from the ceiling, bolts and all. And there was Ella, with the aunt and uncle standing in the living room looking at me with blank expressions on their faces. When I said, 'Excuse me, where is the fan?' Ella and the aunt looked away. But the fucking uncle, he looked me in the eye, shrugged his shoulders, and said, 'I sold it.'"

Dan wanted to laugh, but he had his own problems with Lily.

Lenny took a deep breath and slowly exhaled, as if he was blowing the whole affair out of his system. He relaxed and said, "It's over. First she wanted me to pay for sex, then she let her uncle steal the fan." There was a pause before he added, "Besides, I found out she has been working as a hooker two nights a week at the Jazz Club in Havana."

Lenny went on for fifteen minutes and poured out the whole story.

Dan couldn't believe it. The more Lenny talked, the more pissed off Dan became. How on God's earth could a guy like Lenny, who prowled the nights pretending to be Mr. Cool, be so stupid when he fell in love – which was way too often.

"The worst thing is," Lenny said, "she sleeps with her brother. He sleeps in the front room for the time I'm there." He was looking at the ceiling with a puzzled expression. "But I think he sleeps in the same bed with her the rest of the time. I think she even has sex with him. I found some condom wrappers in the ashtray alongside the bed. Geez, Dan. She's fucking her brother. I give her twenty-five dollars a week now. You'd think she could live a decent life."

Lenny finished and looked at Dan. There were tears in his red eyes. "What am I going to do?"

Dan said nothing. He got up and went to the head before returning with one of Lily's compact mirrors. "Here, take a look at yourself, Lenny." He handed him the mirror. "You ever seen anyone as stupid as what's looking back at you? First of all, it's not her brother she's fucking. It's her lover, maybe even her husband. You are nothing more than a couple of fucks every weekend, and you're paying about ten bucks a pop for it."

Lenny tried to speak, but Dan kept on. "You actually think a hundred a month buys you a monogamous relationship in Cuba? Dream on, my man."

Lenny's mouth was open, trying to get in a word. "But ... but ... she sleeps in the same bed with her brother."

He wasn't listening. The shock treatment wasn't working. Dan tried another approach by softening his speech. "Lenny, Lenny, Lenny. This is Cuba. It's not like New York, Toronto, or any other place in the world. Sex here isn't a dirty four-letter word spelled *f-u-c-k* and written on alley walls. Sex to Cubans is like having coffee. You ever see *c-o-f-f-e-e* written on a bathroom wall in the States? Ever heard of a woman in Cuba being raped? It would be like some crazy guy in Chicago dragging some young pretty thing into a dark alley and pouring coffee down her throat. It just doesn't happen. There is no rape in Cuba because sex is free and plentiful. Your girlfriend isn't doing anything wrong by fucking her 'brother.'" He held up his fingers and made the four-fingered quote sign to emphasize the last word. "No more than her boyfriend thinks she is doing something bad by having sex with you when you show up. Believe me, they're counting your hundred a month together."

He was tough on Lenny, he thought, tougher than he should have been. *It hurts to have a guy tell you that the girl you love is spreading her legs for another guy.* But he had to set him straight. "That, my friend Lenny, is Cuba. Go home. Go back to Poland, Toronto, or Saskatoon or wherever the fuck you come from. You'll never be happy in Cuba, not even for a couple of nights a month with your girlfriend, with or without her 'brother.'"

They were harsh words, and Dan didn't like himself for coming down so hard on his neighbor. He half expected his guest to take a swing at him.

Instead, Lenny stood and said, "Sorry, Dan, I shouldn't have come. I hear your words, but I get the feeling you're not talking to me. Thanks anyway, Dan. We'll talk later."

He went up and out of the companionway, closing the hatch behind him.

It was not like Dan to launch into a lecture like the one he'd given Lenny. Lenny was right. He had been talking to himself. Lily was missing again, and it was tearing him apart. He picked up the mirror. "It's you, Fletcher. If you can't take it, get the fuck out of Cuba, for Christ's sake. You're in love with Lily, and she treats you like some lovesick tourist. You're on a one-way street. You're nuts about her, and she sees you as nothing more than a ticket to good times."

Dan tossed the mirror aside and downed the remainder of Lenny's rum. He put his fist on the table and rested his forehead on it as he recalled one of his favorite movie scenes. Cyrano de Bergerac had just delivered his declaration of independence from the power and corruption of royalty and ministers with his famous no-thank-you speech, seemingly venting his rage at those excesses. But hidden behind that speech was his rage at his hopeless love for Roxanne. His friend La Bret had patiently listened to Cyrano's dissertation, then quietly said, "Yes, tell that to all the world, then to me softly, that she loves you not."

Dan put a CD into the stereo. He poured himself a shot of rum and sat back down at the dinette as Jose Carreras launched into *Vesti la giubba* from *Pagliacci*. "Laugh, clown, laugh," Dan said. It seemed all too appropriate for the situation. Lenny was not the only man in the marina that night with a woman problem.

CHAPTER

28

Dan ground the Cuban beans for a count of fifteen seconds before putting them into the French press. After pouring in the boiling water, he stirred the dark brown mixture just so and waited exactly four minutes before slowly pressing the plunger down into the steel-banded glass container. The stainless reusable filter pushed the grounds to the bottom, and four perfect cups of coffee were ready.

He seldom had to share the brew with other sailors that came by in the morning. They usually declined the strong Fletcher mud, but always accepted the croissants. Dan kept a good supply that he bought fresh each morning at the French bakery not far from the marina.

He buttered a croissant and balanced it on the coffee as he made his way up into the cockpit. He always sat on the southeast side of the boat in the mornings and let the early sun warm his back.

He was into his second cup when Lily appeared out of nowhere. She stepped onto the boat and kissed him on the cheek. "How are you, man?"

"Don't give me that how-are-you crap. Last week I gave you eighty dollars to buy a new dress at Mango. Remember? It was so we could go to the Tropicana and see the special midnight show of Van-Van. Remember? Where the hell have you been?"

"I'm sorry, Dan." She had tears in her eyes. "My mother's sister in Holguin died that day, and I took my mother and the whole family to Oriente on the bus. My mother and her sisters are very close. I thought she might die of grief. I just returned last night." She lowered her eyes and said, "I'll pay you back the eighty dollars."

He softened. "You could have called."

"I wanted to call you. But I couldn't. We were in the country. There was no phone. My mother cried all the time, and every day we went to the grave."

If she had any guilt from being with Carlo for a month, becoming engaged, and planning a trip to Italy to meet the Italian family, Lily didn't show it. She jumped right back into her sweet, lovable self as if nothing had happened.

Dan saw the tears and melted. "Okay, Lily. That's okay."

It wasn't the first time she'd disappeared during the time he'd known her. She always had a good excuse, some better than others. A one- or two-night no-show called for something a little less dramatic than a death in the family. Former excuses included, "I fell asleep at Odalia's house. She was supposed to wake me in an hour, but she didn't wake up until morning." "I was stopped by the police and spent the night in jail because I didn't have my identification." "My mother had chest pains, and I took her to the hospital."

The one Dan remembered as the most creative was, "My brother was arrested for having beef bones." Cattle belonged to the State, so all beef was considered stolen. One bone made a person a rustler.

It had taken two hundred dollars to get her brother out of jail – if he really was in jail. He wasn't sure she even had a brother.

Dan always bought the story, but never really believed it.

Like all *chicas*, Lily was good at lying. It came with the growing-up process. Almost everyone in Cuba watched a soap opera four times a week on TV. The Cuban *telenovelas* featured continuing situations of lying, cheating, and sleeping with everyone's wife, husband, sister, brother, aunt, or uncle. There was constant deceit and trickery. The problem was, other than long speeches by Castro, the *telenovela* was the only thing on television. Young people grew up relating the daily soap opera to real life. When a young person was fed a constant diet of deception, adultery, manipulation, and human conflict, it became reality.

Later that week, Dan and Lily walked down to the local Italian restaurant called Pizza Nova. It was an outdoor place on Canal Number Four, with an adjoining air-conditioned bar and poolroom. It was a good place to light up a fat Cuban cigar, order a pizza, and shoot a game of billiards.

Dan and Lily went there frequently. On this night, they were engaged in Lily's favorite game: Chicago. Dan won the game by double-banking the fifteen-ball into the side pocket. It was a good shot, and Dan went into his Jackie Gleason impersonation, "Aaand awaaay we go."

Lily had never heard of Jackie Gleason, but she went into hysterics over Dan strutting around the table with a stupid look on his face and flapping his arms like a chicken.

Suddenly she knew what had been bothering her. Carlo never laughed. In the month she had spent with him, she could not remember one time when either of them had had a good laugh. When she was with Dan, she laughed a lot. It was what she'd missed in her relationship with Carlo.

Lily loved Dan in a special way. But he had told her he would never take her to America. He was going around the world on his sailboat, a scenario that did not appeal to Lily. She wanted to live in Italy.

Lily began spending more time visiting her sick mother in Baracoa. She told Dan she had to be home everyday between noon and two o'clock to take

Alma to the hospital. Actually, Lily needed to be close to the neighborhood telephone located two doors down and across the street in Mattie's house.

Carlo had begun by calling three times a week to say hello and check on her progress with her passport. Later, he called once a week, but she never knew when that would be. More than once, Lily received a call on the boat from her sister. "Carlo called. I told him you were at your girlfriend's house. He said he'd call back in an hour."

"Dan, I have to go see my mother. I'll be back in two hours. Give me ten dollars for the taxi."

It had taken several months to get all the papers necessary for Lily's thirty-day trip to Italy. Carlo had wired money to the local bank, and Lily had purchased her ticket for Sunday.

She spent Saturday night in Dan's arms. Dan was surprised to see Lily up before him and making coffee in the galley the next morning. She poured him a cup through the little strainer, sat down across from him, and looked over the table at him with sad eyes.

It was then that Dan noticed her packed bag sitting next to the companionway. He looked at Lily and saw the tears begin to flow. "What is it, *mi amor?*" he finally asked.

"Dan, I want to tell you something." She paused and looked down at her hands, her bangs hanging over her eyes. She began picking at her fingernails before stammering on.

"Today I am leaving for Italy. There is this man. He sent me money for the ticket. I have all the papers. If his family likes me, we are returning next month to Cuba to get married. I'm going to live in Italy."

Dan had known this day might come, yet it hit him hard right in the stomach.

They sat in silence. Lily was finished. She had no more to say. Telling the truth was much harder than she had imagined.

Dan broke the silence. "Do you love him?"

"I don't know."

"Does he love you?"

"I think so."

"How old is he?"

"Thirty-three."

"Great. Just fucking great. A young Italian. Probably a handsome stud with a lot of bushy hair and a mustache – and a big dick."

"Come on, Dan. Please."

It could be worse, he thought. *Jesus, what if she had said he was an eighty-year-old owner of an Italian car company?*

•

144

Since being with Lily, he had harbored the fear that some young stud would come along and take her from him. More than once he had prepared himself for this. He knew it was over. He reached across the table and took her hand. He made a feeble attempt to go down like a man, but his emotions betrayed him as his voice quivered softly. "Lily, look at me."

She raised her head and revealed red eyes.

"Lily, I understand. We've had fun together. Nothing lasts forever. I hope you'll be very happy. You'll love Italy." He took a deep breath and added, "I'll take you to the airport."

"No, Dan, all my family will be there. They like you. I told them you left me. Your presence would be awkward. Besides, I have to go home for the rest of my things." There was a long pause as she looked into his sad eyes. "Give me eighty dollars for a new suitcase, honey. I don't want to get off the plane in Rome carrying an old sack of clothes."

CHAPTER
29

Lily's Alitalia flight landed at Rome's Leonardo Da Vinci International Airport at six in the evening. The flight from Havana to Spain had taken one night, and there was a six-hour layover before boarding the connection in Madrid. Sleep was out of the question. She was free from Cuba for one month, and if she had her way, she would be awake for the entire thirty days.

She claimed her new suitcase and made her way through immigration and customs. Italian came easy for her, and she had studied during the months it took her to get the papers for the trip out of Cuba. She wanted to be prepared for Carlo's family and make a good first impression.

Lily came through the automatic doors that separated customs from the throngs of waiting families. She cut a striking figure, even after the long flight across the Atlantic. She wore a two-piece brown suede suit and medium high heels. Her long hair hung loosely down her back, and with the exception of eyeliner, she wore no makeup.

Carlo rushed to her, took her in his arms, and kissed her. "Welcome to Italy."

He was paler than she remembered, and she was surprised to find Carlo alone. Where was the family?

"Grazie, Carlo," she said.

They drove the crowded maze of narrow streets in his Alpha Romeo.

"The car is too small for the family," he told her. "You'll meet everybody later."

Carlo lived in the fourth floor of a modern high-rise building. Lily tried not to show her disappointment with the sterile two-bedroom apartment decorated with glass and chrome furniture. Modern art hung on the white walls. It struck Lily as being rather cold. It was new, but her old family house in Baracoa had more warmth. Carlo's place was void of soul. She would change that after they were married. Now was not the time to start complaining about the way a bachelor lived.

One bedroom had a large bed. The other contained a bench that sprouted iron bars that Carlo called his Bowflex workout system. One wall contained a nine-foot-wide floor-to-ceiling mirror.

"Even in bad weather when going to the gym is a problem, I can still get a good workout right here," he explained. "I sometimes prefer my home system to the crowded bodybuilding center. Too many businessmen who snicker at guys like me who admire our bodies." He struck a pose. "At home I can flex in front of the mirror and even apply a light oil to accent the muscles."

Lily kept from smiling as she realized just how vain this man really was.

When the apartment tour was over, Carlo took Lily by the hand and led her into the bedroom, where he began peeling off his tight black T-shirt.

Lily was a little taken back by his sudden presumptuous manner. When he reached for her, she pulled back and said, "Please, Carlo. I need a shower. It's been a long trip. Pour us a glass of wine while I clean up, my love."

Lily was flattered to be desired, but cleanliness before sex was Cuba's only religious commandment. It had also been months since she'd seen him. He was almost like a stranger – not that it had mattered much that first night she met him at Macumba.

The first three weeks went by quickly, but Lily found herself longing for the warm, moist air of Cuba. She missed watching the puffy white clouds move from the hills to the sea and craved the smell of damp air after an evening thunderstorm.

Rome was beautiful. The elegant buildings were old, but well cared for. They reminded her of old Havana, except the structures in Rome were not falling apart. She loved the fountains and the pigeons, thousands of pigeons. *If they had pigeons in Havana*, she thought, *the people would not be so hungry*. The Italians were well fed. They didn't have to kill the pigeons.

Carlo took her to the museums. Interesting, but a little tiring after the first three or four thousand paintings and statues. She could only compare Italy with one other country: Cuba. She loved her country, and someday Castro and his regime would be a passing slice of history. Cuba was her home, and after three weeks she wondered how she was going to mold her feelings to accept her future husband's homeland.

Another day, and Rome's sky was like a veil of brown gauze that covered the sun. It was as if one of God's angels was pissed off at the Pope and had thrown down a gray net to cover the Vatican but missed and hit the whole city. The angel, she surmised, must have been upset with the pope for outlawing two of the world's most liberating inventions: the condom and the pill.

For all she knew, the angel had thrown the net over the whole country. She would not be able to tell on this trip. Carlo had been as generous with his time as he could, but with his daily trips to the gym and the hours he spent selling his "sports stuff," as he called it, there was little time to see the countryside.

"Next time, my love," he promised. "After we're married and come back, we'll take a vacation. We can drive into the country. We'll go to Venice. You'll love Venice. And we can even travel through the hillside vineyards and see the Alps."

Lily refrained from showing her disappointment at being limited to Rome for a month. The thing that bothered her the most was the weather. It had been cloudy and drizzly for much of her visit. She was told that it was usually warm and sunny. She also did not let her feelings show when it came to eating with Carlo's family. She wanted to get to know the family, but every night was a little too much. His fat mother, fat father, and his two older single fat sisters had forced enough pasta down her throat to last a lifetime.

It was no wonder Italians were fat, she thought. Adding up all the meals she had taken at the Pontelli flat, she estimated that Carlo's family had shoveled enough ravioli, spaghetti, and linguini down their throats to feed Lily's whole family in Cuba for a year. Actually, she thought, her family would never eat that much pasta, even if they had it. They'd die of starvation before slurping down all that slippery shit. Lily longed for just one meal of greasy pork or boiled chicken with rice and beans, something she could sink her teeth into. Food she could chew, not something that raced down to her stomach as soon as she sucked it through her lips.

Lily sat in the "Chrome Dome," her name for Carlo's apartment, applying another coat of polish to her nails and going over the last few weeks. It had not been the trip to fairyland she had envisioned. Everything seemed cold. The food, the weather, Carlo's apartment, and even his family seemed cold. There was not the warmth she expected to see among them. Carlo never kissed his mother or his sisters, and a simple businesslike handshake was the only contact he had with his father. Carlo never introduced her to his friends, and she spent a lot of time alone in the apartment waiting. Even Carlo's libido had lessened. In Cuba, he'd wanted sex twice a day. Here in Rome, it was only three times a week, and at times even that seem labored. Perhaps it was her. Maybe she had not disguised her disappointments and dislikes well enough. Maybe Carlo's lack of *amor* could be explained by the drab weather, or his work schedule, or worse, maybe he was tiring of her.

She had heard stories of young Cuban girls being swept off their feet by gold-chained Italians who took them to Italy and later turned them out into the street as prostitutes. "It is time," they were told, "to start contributing some income to this relationship by going out and doing what you Cuban girls do best."

Lily had no fears that Carlo might send her out as a hooker after they were married, but there was still that haunting question. Did she really love this guy? Did he love her? In the time they had been together, he'd never taken her in his arms and simply said, "I love you."

Dan had asked her, "Do you really love this guy, or do you just love where he lives?" He had pounded his fist on the table and said, "Damn it, Lily, I want the best for you, but be sure you're not marrying this guy just because he lives in Italy. Life leads us to think about greener pastures just over the hill. So go ahead and take a look, but please, for your own sake, think about it and make sure this is something you really want to do."

Now, alone in the apartment, Lily was having second thoughts. "About what?" she said aloud. She closed her eyes and let her mind wander, looking for something to quell her apprehensions. She thought about how different Carlo was from Dan Fletcher. Carlo had great passion, but they spent most of their time alone. Dan always had people around. His pals in the marina were always dropping by the boat with their Cuban girlfriends. They'd all sit around drinking rum and puffing on black market cigars, with Dan going on at a mile-a-minute in English that was too fast for her to understand. Sometimes, they'd all go to Rumbos, get a bottle of rum and a six-pack of Coke, and talk well into the night. Other nights, they would go out to a Paladar and eat greasy pork and French fries, or eat pizza during a knock-down-drag-out game of 8-ball.

With Carlo, they were usually alone. Even the other people who lived in his building never acknowledged him. After living in that apartment for two years, he'd made no friends. Dan had lots of friends, and they always had fun. There was always lots of laughter.

Maybe the passion in her relationship with Carlo had fogged her brain. Carlo was so serious. His family was serious. They never joked. Life without laughs. Where was the fun? Carlo's idea of fun was watching his oiled muscles ripple in the mirror.

Lily snapped out of her thoughts when she heard the apartment door open. Carlo came in with a big smile, grabbed her, and kissed her hard. She could feel his stiffness pressed against her thigh, and she knew she was in for one of their afternoon love sessions.

She reached down, unbuttoned his pants, and slid her slender fingers inside his shorts. "Hmmm, what's this?"

In rapid succession, she pulled his pants and shorts down to his ankles, grabbed his swollen cock, and pulled him into the bedroom. Carlo stumbled like a chain gang prisoner trying to keep up. When she got him to the bed, she turned him around and pushed him down onto his back. He lay there in a comical position, with his T-shirt on and his pants and shorts down to his shoes.

"You are my prisoner, darling. You must do as I say and not move."

Lily lowered her lips to within a fraction of an inch of his erection and began subduing it with rapid flicks of her tongue. Just as he was about to explode, she slid her panties off with her free hand, and in one swift movement she was straddling him. She rocked back and forth a grand total of six times before she saw his eyes roll back. She tightened her stomach muscles and began coming just as she felt his warm juices flowing inside her.

Carlo dozed as Lily showered then slipped into a pair of jeans. She selected a bright orange sweater from her growing collection of Italian clothes, then put on a pair of brown flats before waking the physically satisfied Carlo.

He took her to a small neighborhood outdoor café with red and white-checkered tablecloths and multicolored Cinzano umbrellas. The tables were separated from the sidewalk by a row of blooming planters. It was a cool clear day, and the sun was out for one of its rare visits to the city. It was beautiful, and just a short walk from the apartment. Why hadn't they come here before? She wondered. All those lonely days by herself in the apartment she could have come here. She was pleased to find a menu that had something besides pasta. She ordered chicken fricassee with a side of fries.

"Hold the pasta," she said as the waiter left the table.

Carlo smiled. He knew Lily was not fond of Italian food when it came to pasta, but he failed to commend her for tolerating Mama's cooking. Besides, he had something to talk to her about.

She sensed a serious tone at the table as they sipped Chianti in silence.

Finally, he reached across the table and took both of her hands in his. "Lily," he said, "everything is in order for your flight back to Cuba on Friday. I called this morning and confirmed your reservation. I hope you have had a good time." He paused. "I know it has been trying at times – you know, Mama's cooking." He smiled and continued, "But I hope you still want to marry me."

Lily had been giving this moment a lot of thought. Sure, there were some problems with Carlo and his lifestyle, but she was confident she could loosen up his serious demeanor. As for the food thing, once she got into her own kitchen, she could begin eating a more tasty diet. And she would not let herself forget that this was her dream: a life outside of a police state. It was what she wanted. She could send money to her family and make life easier for them. Even visit them every New Year with presents.

"Of course I still want to marry you, Carlo."

Carlo smiled and sat back in his chair. "I was hoping you hadn't changed your mind. I've arranged for your medical checkup at nine a.m. tomorrow."

Lily laughed. "Checkup? I'm as healthy as a horse, and honey, if I do have some disease like syphilis or AIDS, then so do you." She teased him now. "Carlo, baby, it's you who should get the checkup. You can't fuck for more than thirty minutes anymore." Carlo was not amused. "Come on, Carlo, loosen up. I'm just joking. Of course I'll take the exam, and if they find an inoperable brain tumor, I'll leave you my entire wardrobe and you can give it to your next girlfriend."

Carlo made a feeble attempt at laughing.

God, she thought. *He is uptight. I'll have to get started soon to loosen him up.*

Lily sat at the desk in the doctor's office. Carlo was in the chair beside her. Doctor Renaldo Medina was studying the sheet of paper in front of him, the results of Lily's examination taken earlier that day.

He looked up and smiled. "Well, Miss Lopez, you are one healthy woman. You should live to be a hundred."

Lily relaxed and gave Carlo the I-told-you-so look.

"However," Dr. Medina said, "There is a slight problem with your eyes."

"My eyes?" Lily was stunned. "My eyes are perfect. Aren't they?"

Dr. Medina smiled. "I shouldn't alarm you, Miss Lopez. Yes, they are perfect, as far as seeing goes. That is for now. But the ophthalmologist who examined you found a defect in the retina of both eyes called anti-conjectural optic dysfunction." He had trouble pronouncing the diagnosis. "That's the bad news. The good news is that a simple, painless laser operation will correct the problem. It's in the early stages. Our specialist tells me you will most likely never have to worry about it again."

Lily suddenly felt ill.

Dr. Medina continued, "I understand you are scheduled to leave the country on Friday. I would suggest you postpone your trip for just a couple of days. You'll need to be bandaged for forty-eight hours."

"That's impossible," cried Lily. "My Cuban papers will not allow me an extension, even for a day. Why can't I wait and have it done in Cuba?"

The doctor answered in a soft, sympathetic voice. "Unfortunately, there is no such treatment in Cuba. Perhaps if you could get to the United States – they have the same treatment system there."

Carlo interrupted, "The United States is out, Doctor. What if Lily waited a few months until we are married and she gets a permanent visa to Italy?"

"That is possible, but anti-conjectural optic dysfunction progresses quickly. We have no way of telling how long it has been there. You could wait. But you would be taking a chance with perfectly good eyes."

Carlo interrupted. "Wait a minute. You say there will be no pain?"

"Well, very little," replied Medina. "More like an uncomfortable irritation. A few pain pills will take care of that."

"Fine," Carlo said. "We do the laser treatment and go back to Cuba with the bandages on. I'll be with you, Lily, all the way. And in two days, we'll have the bandages removed in Cuba. How about it, Doc?"

"Well, the bandages are only on to keep the light out. The mild discomfort will be taken care of with the pain pills. It will be a little awkward, but as long as you are with her all the way, it should be a simple solution."

Lily panicked. "Carlo, I can't get off the plane in Cuba and meet my family with my head in bandages. My mother will have a heart attack."

"I understand, *mi amor*, but how about this? We call your family and tell them your flight has been delayed for two days. When we get to Havana, we'll go straight to a hotel until the bandages come off then show up at your house as a surprise with all the presents."

Lily's life was suddenly becoming complicated. She had left Cuba as a twenty-year-old girl in perfect health. Now she would be returning as a sightless invalid, probably five kilos heavier with all that pasta.

"Ah, the hell with it," she said. "Let's do it and get it over with."

She wanted one last assurance from the doctor. "Are you absolutely one hundred percent sure there is no chance my eyes will be less than perfect?"

Dr. Medina leaned across his desk, smiled, and reassured her. "Trust me, my dear. Your eyes will be perfect."

CHAPTER
30

Lily and Carlo's plane landed at Jose Marti Airport in Havana just after one in the afternoon. The flight from Rome was easier than Lily had anticipated. Other than the short stop in Madrid to change planes, Lily had not been inconvenienced. The mild pain pills Dr. Medina prescribed kept her in a semi-euphoric state, and she slept most of the way.

A wheelchair was waiting for her as she and Carlo deplaned. She could only imagine how she looked. When she felt her head with her hands, it seemed as though she carried a giant basketball on her shoulders. There was a little more pain than Dr. Medina had predicted, probably from the tight bandage of white gauze that wound from the bridge of her nose up and around her head. The bandage secured two lumps of cotton that pressed hard against her tightly closed eyes. She had tried to open her eyelids once, but the bandages were too tight. Dr. Medina had given specific instructions to keep the bandage tight for three days and try not to move her eyelids. The bandages would come off tomorrow evening.

Lily imagined what it would be like to be permanently blind. If she had the choice of a physical handicap, she thought, she would take the loss of a limb or being deaf and mute over the loss of her sight.

Lily and Carlo were led to the front of the line and quickly passed through immigration. She sat in silence in her darkness as Carlo waited for their baggage and the big duffel bag stuffed with the presents for the family. She was sorry that they were not going to meet her, but in her condition, looking like the victim of an auto accident, it would be easier if she and Carlo just appeared at the house in Baracoa the day after tomorrow before everyone left for the airport. They told the family their arrival had been rescheduled.

She was more excited to be home than she had anticipated, and as she sat waiting, she thought about her future, about leaving Cuba. Everyone assumed that Cubans wanted to leave their homeland and live in the United States, or Italy, or anywhere but Cuba. It was true that life under Castro was hard, but life was also hard in Rome, based on what she had seen. Driving was nerve-wracking, even as a passenger. Everyone worked eight hours a day, paid high rent for glass-and-chrome-furnished apartments like Carlo's, and spent much less time visiting each other than people did in Cuba. She never saw any of the tenants in Carlo's building talking to each other. They passed

•

quietly in the halls and the lobby without so much as a *Bon giorno*, unaware of the other's presence, as if they had more important things on their minds than being friendly.

Cubans were always aware of each other, always willing to help someone. Cubans were all in it together. There was a common bond. It was like everyone was standing in shit up to their chins, she thought, with the big boss walking around high and dry carrying a paddle. *Get a little out of line, try to stand a little higher, and the big guy pushes your head down to the level of the others. Then he makes a small wave with his paddle that splashes into your mouth. That's life in Cuba. Meanwhile, we try not to make waves, and wait. Wait for the Bearded One to go away and stop refilling the shit pit.* That could be what kept Cubans together: waiting for the change. Meanwhile, everyone sang, danced, and laughed with each other.

There was a hollow feeling in her chest as she realized that after she and Carlo were married and she had moved to Rome, she would thereafter be returning as a tourist.

Carlo finally retrieved the luggage. "Are you sure you got the duffel bag?" she asked.

"Yes, my dear. It's all here. I have a porter with a cart."

Outside the terminal, Carlo offloaded the bags, paid the porter, and sat Lily down on one suitcase. "Don't move, Lily. Keep two hands on the bags. I'll get us a cab."

An hour later, she heard a friendly voice. "Excuse me, *chica*. I am a security policeman, and you have been here for quite a while. Is there something I can do for you?"

"I'm waiting for my fiancé," she told him. "He went to find a taxi."

The policeman spoke in a concerned tone. "There are fifty taxis waiting. I don't think he was looking for a taxi. Are you Cuban?"

"Yes, I am." Lily was now on the verge of panicking. "Maybe there's been an accident. Can you see if there was an accident, please?"

"I have been no more than fifty meters away for quite a while, miss. I could not help noticing you when you came out with the young man. I'm afraid he left you. I saw him get into a taxi and drive away."

Lily was dumbstruck. "I don't understand. He's my fiancé."

"I'm sorry. Look, I can get you into a taxi. Tell me where you want to go, and I'll have the driver take you. Will there be someone there to meet you?"

She was numb with disbelief, but managed to mumble the directions. "Baracoa, 204 Second Avenue."

The policeman flagged a cab and helped load the baggage. Lily sat in the backseat, wondering what could have possibly gone so wrong as the taxi rumbled down the street.

Lily's mother was frantic. "What happened? Where is Carlo?"

Lily spoke softly as though she was resigned to the fact that Carlo was gone for good. "There must have been an accident, Mama. Call the police again." She refrained from mentioning the part where the policeman said he saw Carlo leave the airport in another taxi.

The next day, after no word from Carlo, Lily gave up any hope that he would appear with an explanation.

Lily's mother made one last comment before the subject of Carlo Pontelli was dropped. "I never liked that man. He was a devil."

Lily was ready to forget Carlo, but the first and most important thing was to get the bandages off so she could see again. Stumbling around the house for two days had been a nightmare in itself. "Mama, it's time to take off the bandages. Come in and please help me."

The gauze seemed to be ten miles long as Alma kept unwinding. Finally, she reached up and took out the two cotton balls from Lily's eyes.

Lily's sister heard the scream come from the bedroom and rushed in to find her mother on the floor.

Lily was sitting on the bed holding her hands over her eyes, or what should have been her eyes. When she lowered her hands, Darma didn't see her sister. She saw a head of black hair and a face with two hollow cavities where Lily's beautiful eyes had once been.

When they finished unpacking Lily's bags a few hours later, they found an envelope containing a thousand dollars and a one-line note that simply read, *Lily, I'm sorry. Carlo.*

They found Lily's body hanging from a water pipe in her bedroom three days later. A smooth Italian leather belt encircled her small neck. A barely legible note was on the bed. It read, *Please forgive me.* A sealed envelope lay beside the note addressed to Dan.

More than a hundred people attended Lily's funeral. Dan stood off to one side, leaning against a leafless tree while they lowered the casket into the ground. Lily's mother, her body draped over the casket and shaking with uncontrollable sobs, refused to let her daughter go. Had no one restrained her, she would have followed her child into the grave and been covered with earth to die – and stop the pain.

CHAPTER
31

After four days alone in the boat, most of them spent numbed by alcohol in an effort to drown his pain, Dan was jolted to consciousness by a constant banging on the cabin.

The hatch slid open, and Graham poked his head through the opening. "I'm coming aboard, Dan."

"You're already aboard," Dan said as he rolled out of the bunk and put his feet on the floor. "Come on down."

"God, this place smells like a waterfront dive on Monday morning." He softened when he saw Dan's condition. "You look like hell." Graham sat down on the settee. "I heard about Lily. A real tragedy."

Dan sat down at the dinette and began rubbing his temples with his fingers.

Graham could see he was in more emotional pain than the physical discomfort of a simple hangover. "We were a little worried about you, Dan. How about I make us some coffee?"

"Sure," Dan said without moving. His mind was numb as he looked up at Graham and tried to think of what to say. One part of him wanted to recede back into the stupor he'd been in; another part wanted to get on with his life. It was the third part that troubled him the most. It was the part that wanted the nightmare to go away, to have it be the way it was – when Lily was alive.

Graham put on some water and searched the fridge until he came up with a box of cold mango juice. He poured a glass and handed it to Dan. "Anything we can do for you?"

Dan drained the glass and set it on the table. He ran his hands through his hair and answered. "Thanks, Graham, but don't get the wrong idea. I'm not going to do anything foolish like drink myself to death. I'm all right, really. I just felt like doing some thinking and tying one on. I haven't lost track of time or anything. It's been four days since Lily's funeral. Three days since I read her letter." He pointed to the crumpled pages lying on the table. "Go ahead. Read it."

Dan picked up the scribbled notes and handed them to Graham as he got up and made his way to the coffee water on the stove. "It's tough to read." He swallowed hard. "She always had such beautiful handwriting." Dan's voice trailed off as he began grinding coffee beans.

Graham picked up the letter and began reading the barely legible scribbling.

Dear Dan,

I am so sorry. I know you are the one person in this world who will understand what I am about to do. I wanted to be the one who would always be there to take care of my family. I cannot go on as I am, a burden on them. Remember when you told me about Pinocchio and how he went to the place with all the candy he could eat … and he turned into a donkey? You cautioned me about always looking for a place better than where you are. You are so wise, and it is too late to listen to you.

I have something to say that I never told you. I love you. I never said that to anyone except my family. You once told me that there were different kinds of love. Family love, love of friends, and love for a lover. You said someday I would discover the other kind of love. I guess I discovered the love of a lover when I was with Carlo, but it was not Carlo I found myself in love with. I was beginning to see through his youth and physical beauty. I had doubts about marrying Carlo. I kept thinking about seeing you again and telling you of my apprehensions. On the plane I thought, Dan will talk me out of it. He loves me. He'll tell me about Pinocchio again. And now it's too late.

You know me so well. You know I could never allow you to take care of me, a blind person. I love you too much to let you try. With all my heart, and all my love – a little too late.

Lily

Dan was staring at the whistling kettle. Tears were streaming down his face as he turned the letter over in his mind. He turned off the fire and poured the hot water into the French press and over the ground coffee. He cleared his throat and gave Graham a few moments to digest the words before he looked up and spoke.

"You know, Graham, I've discovered something over the last four days. There is a stronger emotion than love. It's hate. I'm through loving. Not forever, I hope, but as long as it takes to get rid of the hate."

As he listened, Graham saw a look of madness in Dan's eyes he had not seen before. The next line brought a chill to his spine.

"I'll get rid of the hate as soon as I take my revenge."

•

157

CHAPTER
32

D an finished tidying up the cabin and washing down the deck. It was a nice cool day, with a slight breeze out of the north, and he whistled as he worked. There were fresh flowers on the cockpit table, along with the morning coffee and a few croissant crumbs. He had spent several days pondering the course of action he knew he had to take to avenge Lily's horrible death and had come to some rather drastic conclusions.

He settled onto one of the cushions, poured the dregs of the coffee into a dirty cup, and dialed Big Mac's number.

Mac MacDonald was one of Dan's favorite drinking buddies. He was also a former CIA agent who had run off with five million of Uncle Sam's dollars and had been living in Cuba for twenty years.

"Mac, it's Dan. Yeah, I'm okay. Listen, I need your help. Could you meet me? No, not here. How about the Pain de Paris? Thirty minutes? Fine, I'll see you there."

Dan was in maximum thought process as he pulled up and switched off the ignition of the black Yamaha Virago. He flicked out the kickstand of the 535cc motorcycle with his heel as he instinctively reached down with his left hand and removed the key from the lock. He'd bought the slick motorcycle from a guy who had brought it over on his boat and run out of money by spending too much time in the discos chasing women. It was a dangerous mode of transportation on the Havana streets, but it beat the hell out of a bicycle.

He eased the motorcycle onto the stand and made a mental note to wash it down and polish the chrome. As he swung his leg over the leather seat, he caught himself saying out loud, "I'll wash you this afternoon, my pretty thing."

Jesus, now I've started talking to a motorcycle. Get a grip, Dan. He smiled and entered the bakery.

Big Mac was sitting at one of the small round marble tables drinking a can of Bucanero. Mac was hard to miss. His bald head and clean-shaven face glowed red most of the time, partly from the booze and partly from the hot sun beating down on skin that was never meant for the tropics.

Dan approached and said, "Little early for beer, isn't it, Mac?"

The big Sydney Greenstreet look-alike smiled and said, "I have made a personal commitment not to touch a drop of rum before noon."

Mac was in Cuba at the invitation of Fidel Castro himself. He must have felt safe in his present situation, because he talked freely about stealing five million dollars from the CIA's covert account and starting his own business selling arms and explosives to any country agreeing to the price. "What the hell," he had said. "If the Agency can do it, why can't I?"

When things in the Middle East heated up and the arms business became too dangerous, Mac looked up Castro and received an offer he couldn't refuse. "Work for me for five years," Fidel said, "and I'll give you protection from your CIA and a resident visa in Cuba."

The waitress brought Dan's normal order of coffee and six freshly baked croissants, still hot.

Mac stuffed one of the croissants into his mouth and sent the rest of his beer in after it, then waved to the little waitress and held up the empty can. "*Otro vez, por favor.*"

She came to the table almost instantly. When Mac talked, everybody listened. He had a deep growl that boomed out of two hundred and sixty pounds of flesh crammed into a five-foot, nine-inch frame.

Big Mac was never seen out of his normal dress of white pleated pants, a white open-neck long-sleeved shirt, and a Panama hat – a getup right out of the Alec Guinness film, *Our Man in Havana.* He posed as an import-export entrepreneur but never seemed to be working on any deals.

He had been on the CIA's hit list until a few years ago when the Agency, fearing a Mac-tells-all book, called a truce and sent two agents to Cuba to talk with him. "You promise not to write a book, and we'll stop trying to kill you."

"I took the deal," Mac had said. "I had no intention of writing a book anyway."

Mac drove a new Mercedes and lived with his young Cuban wife Yudani in a sprawling Spanish-style mansion just off Fifth Avenue. He loved to tell the story about how they had met.

"I was taking in the floor show at the Tropicana and had been watching this cute little dancer in the chorus. When the show was over, she passed my table, and I stopped her and said, 'Tell me, chica, how much do you earn as a showgirl in Cuba's most famous night club?'

"'Four hundred pesos each month, *Señor.*'

"'Fine,' I said. 'That's about twenty dollars. I'll give you a hundred dollars a week if you come live with me.'

"She took off her two-foot-high Carmen Miranda fake fruit hat, set it on the table, and said, 'Let's go.'"

Mac wondered why Dan had called for the morning meeting. They usually met at Papa's in the evenings. He watched Dan sip his coffee and munch on a French bun before saying, "I was sorry to hear about Lily."

Dan held up the palm of his hand, indicating he was not there for sympathy. "Thanks, Mac. But I'm over that, at least the self-pity part of it." He waited until the waitress had refilled his coffee and left the table before going on. "You're wondering what's so important that I called you this early."

Mac nodded but said nothing.

"I need you, Mac. You're the only one who can help me."

There was a serious tone in Dan's voice, and a demeanor Mac had not seen before. "Okay, Dan. What do you want me to do?"

Dan leaned forward, lowered his voice, and looked around to make sure no one overheard. "I want you to help me kill someone."

Mac was taken aback. Here was Dan Fletcher, the happy-go-lucky last of the romantics who had never done anything shady in his life other than sell a few Cuban cigars to rich Americans, and his eyes had the look of murder. Mac had seen it before when he had been with the Agency. He remembered the electric charge that had gone through his body every time he had been ordered to compromise someone. Mac had never actually pulled the trigger. He had been too high up in the chain of command. But he had masterminded complicated hits, like the remote transmitter that had taken out the PLO ambassador as his limo drove over a manhole cover in Beirut.

"Look, Dan." He put both palms out. His body language said no. "That was a long time ago. I don't do that kind of stuff any more. It was my work. I was with the Agency and under the supposed flag of justice." His own words sounded like a bad movie script, but he kept going. "It was justified – at least in the eyes of people much higher than I was. But that was then, and this is now. I'm not a killer. I won't get involved. This conversation never even took place."

Mac was getting nervous and glancing around the room. He gulped down the rest of the beer and looked Dan in the eye. He spoke in a forced whisper. "I can't – and I won't – help you. I live a good life here. I'm lucky I got out of the Agency alive. Sorry, Dan. If you want to take out some competitive cigar smuggler or some Cuban who ripped you off, you'll have to do it without me. The answer is *no*, and I don't want to hear any more about it."

Fletcher was not fazed. "I understand, Mac, but I just need a little information. And before you say no again, I want to tell you the circumstances surrounding Lily's death."

Dan talked for twenty minutes about his relationship with Lily and about how she had told him she was going off with a guy named Carlo to Italy. He finished with the scene of Lily's mother when she unwrapped the bandages from Lily's sightless face.

Mac listened intently, showing no emotion. When Dan finished, Mac drained the last of his third beer and set the can down on the table. His expression did not change, but his voice did. "I know just how we're gonna kill the son of a bitch."

CHAPTER

33

Dan Fletcher arrived in Zurich on the first of August, the beginning of the crowded holiday season. It had taken Mac and Dan almost six weeks to come up with a suitable plan and assemble the materials to find and kill Carlo. It had taken another tedious two weeks to complete Big Mac's crash course in clandestine travel – and the psychology of killing.

The first step, passport control, had been carefully rehearsed. After claiming his bags, he passed through customs by selecting the green, nothing-to-declare exit lane. It was Dan's first tense moment, but Mac had assured him that Swiss customs would not be interested in anything that appeared to be for personal use. The satellite telephone and the laptop computer were normal businessmen's communication aids of the twenty-first century.

Outside the terminal, Dan climbed into a taxi and handed the driver a slip of paper with the address, *37 Hoffstrasse*.

"Here for the holidays?" The driver spoke perfect English.

"No, business. I'll be here for just a short time." Dan was trying to keep as low a profile as possible.

"Too bad. You should really take some time to see the Alps. The mountain villages are beautiful this time of year."

"Yes, I'm sure. Maybe another time."

The taxi pulled up in front of a tan four-story stucco building that displayed a small bronze plaque with the number *37* inscribed on it.

Dan got out and poked his head into the front seat window. "Mind waiting? I shouldn't be too long." He had jotted down the number of the driver's I.D. hanging in the backseat to feel confident about leaving his bags in the trunk.

"Not a problem." The cab driver turned up the music on the radio and settled back in the seat. "Take as long as you want. I'll be right here."

There was a small set of steps and a single glass entry door that led to a small lobby. He studied the faded list of businesses until he found Schenk Export on the fourth floor, number 417. There was no elevator. He made his way up the stairs, wondering what kind of a place it was. There were no sounds coming from any of the rooms as he passed each floor, and he saw no workers or clients. On the fourth floor he found the door with *Schenk Export* painted on the opaque glass. *Please come in* was written in English beneath it.

•

Inside he found a straight-nosed, thin-faced middle-aged woman wearing tiny oval glasses. She looked up from her computer and without smiling said, "*Gutten tag.*"

Well, finally a word of German, Dan thought, sensing the coolness in her voice. *You could put this dame on What's My Line, and without asking a single question, the panel would guess, "Swiss secretary."*

Dan got right to it. "I have come to see Herr Joseph Schenk."

"Junior or Senior?" she countered in English and looked at him with a blank expression, waiting.

I guess it's going to be twenty questions now, thought Dan. He hadn't been prepared for this. His first test in a clandestine conspiracy, and he was stumped. He made a rapid calculation. It had been thirty years since Mac had worked over here. If this guy had been a friend of his, it had to be the old man.

"That would be Senior, I believe." He handed her a card. "My name is James Carter."

Mac had given him names that were easy to spell and hard to forget. He liked movie stars or old U.S. presidents. "When things get tight, forgetting the name you are going by could be a deadly mistake," he had cautioned.

She took the card and walked to the glass door that led to the inner office. She knocked twice and went in. Dan noticed the nameplate on her desk. Frau Prim. He smiled to himself. *I know her sister, Proper.*

She reappeared moments later. Holding the door open, she said, "Herr Schenk will see you now."

The office was small but well kept. Schenk was standing behind an antique oak desk that supported neatly arranged piles of papers. A picture window framed a lovely lake in the background.

He did not offer his hand. "I am Joseph Schenk. Please sit down."

Dan took the only chair in front of the desk as Herr Schenk sat down and looked at the card Mac had made for him. It read *James Carter, President, Amalgamated Pyrotechnics and Storm Door Company.* Dan thought it a ridiculous cover, but Mac had made just one card. It was for Herr Schenk only.

Schenk was about seventy, with gray sideburns that framed a round baldhead. A tight white shirt caused the veins in his neck to bulge and the skin to hang over the starched collar. His coat was hanging on the back of the chair.

Dan felt underdressed in his blue T-shirt, khaki pants, and matching windbreaker. He waited as the old man studied the business card.

Finally, Joseph Schenk looked up and said, "Just what can I do for you, Mr. Carter? I suppose your friends call you Jimmy."

Dan detected a slight smile on the stuffy man's face. Perhaps he *did* have a sense of humor. Dan spoke the rehearsed words. "I have been referred to you by an acquaintance you should remember, Mr. Jack Wayne. I believe you and he worked on an export project known as K-100. It's been a while. The year was 1971."

Schenk did not react. "That's a long time ago, Mr. Carter. Give John my regards." He emphasized the name *John,* as the curl on his mouth became a momentary smile before he returned to business. "But tell Mr. Wayne that his memory is slipping. The project he was referring to was K-151. Not K-100. What do you need?"

He had come to the right place. Herr Schenk caught the K-100 error. He had the right man.

Dan took out the envelope from the inside pocket of his jacket and handed it across the table. It contained three sets of passport photos, ten thousand dollars in cash, and a detailed list of instructions from Mac.

The export broker took the sealed envelope and slid it into the top drawer of the desk without looking at it. "I'll see what I can do. Come back tomorrow at ten in the morning."

Dan left the inner office, nodded to Prim and Proper, and made his way down to the waiting cab. "Okay, now take me to a nice hotel."

The driver said, "No problem. The Zurich Hilton is just a few blocks over."

At the hotel, he paid for the cab and entered the swinging doors to the lobby. He waited several moments until the cab had driven off, then exited the front door and hailed another taxi.

"Take me to the Lorenzo Hotel, please."

He checked into the ancient establishment under his own name and took a room on the second floor. *So far so good,* he thought, but he knew this was the easy part. Rome would be something else.

Once in the room, he was surprised at the $195 accommodations. He'd seen better rooms at Motel 6 for $16.95 plus $2.00 for the TV key. At these rates, he'd be out of cash soon. He began to worry that the treasure plan of Mac's might not pan out. If the buried money map didn't turn up a good supply of cash, the whole operation would be a bust.

He left his things in the room and went down and out onto the street. He'd noticed a sidewalk café a block away on his way to the hotel earlier. He bought a copy of the *London Herald,* sat down at a small table, and ordered *Wienerschnitzl* and a glass of chilled white wine. It was the first time since leaving Havana he had felt relaxed. An hour later, he crashed on one of the single beds in his room.

He was wide-awake, staring at the ceiling at four in the morning. "Damn that jetlag." He got out of bed and took a look at the lighted city through the small double-hung window that hadn't been opened in years. He figured it would take a hammer and chisel to get through the layers of paint that glued the wood frames to the sill. He hated hotels, especially old European hotels that charged sky-high prices.

Dan rated hotels by the quality of the shower. Consistently hot water that came out in a powerful, even stream rated a ten in his book. The number went down as the water got colder and the calcium buildup in the showerhead sent an uneven spray everywhere but on his body. The worst was the lukewarm model that suddenly sent a ten second scalding stream onto his back.

The shower in the Lorenzo called for a special rating. There was no shower curtain, and the showerhead was at the end of a flexible tube. It took one hand to hold the telephone-shaped nozzle and the other hand to wash while he was on his knees in the tub. The drain was so slow that Dan noticed a ring-around-the-penis dirt line when he got out. The Zurich Lorenzo finished first on his list of the worst showers. The giant fluffy towel he used to dry off had probably cost five times that of a good shower curtain and a wall-mounted showerhead. He would have gladly dabbed himself dry with toilet paper if he could have traded the towel for a top-rated shower.

After the morning bathing ordeal, he dressed in jeans, running shoes, and a yellow golf shirt that sported a little alligator on the front pocket. He would have killed for a good cup of coffee, but hotel restaurants never opened before 7:00 a.m., and there was no such thing as an all-night Denny's anywhere in Europe.

He was downstairs at precisely seven o'clock and the first to be seated in the restaurant that resembled an Egyptian tomb. The ceiling was twice the height of the width of the room. Thirty tables covered by white tablecloths sat on a cold tile floor. He slipped a starched napkin from its silver ring and placed it on his lap. When the waiter arrived, he ordered a full pot of coffee and said he would wait until the coffee came before ordering breakfast. Europeans had coffee after their meals, but he needed his caffeine now. If he ordered everything up front, he knew he'd sit there for twenty minutes and get the whole mess at once.

When the coffee arrived, he ordered two boiled eggs in a glass, ham, and toast. Satisfied he'd beaten the European breakfast system, he took his first sip of coffee and mumbled one of his favorite lines from an old Bogart movie: "Don't mess with Fred C. Dobbs."

He returned to his room after breakfast, spread a European roadmap out on his bed, and began going over his travel plans. The first stop after renting a car would be the 110-kilometer marker just over Brenner Pass. With luck, the concrete post would still be in place. Big Mac had given him six different markers along his intended route. The locations had come from a small black book in Mac's safe in his house in Cuba.

When he produced the book, Mac said, "Dan, my boy, here is one of the CIA's best-kept secrets. The European kilometer-marker book."

Dan was not impressed. "Wouldn't a simple road map do?"

Mac ignored the sarcasm. "This book is so secret that it's the only one in existence. Don't ask me where I got it. That's an even bigger secret. Just call it my retirement pay for service to my country."

Dan wanted to ask if the five million counted for anything, but he knew Mac was building up to something. "Okay, I give up. So what's it for?"

"It's for the money we'll need to implement our plan. I know you're willing to use some of your savings, and that will get us started, but we'll need plenty more to take care of what you're going to do on the Italian front." Mac was playing war games again and loving every minute. "Some years ago, the Agency buried suitcases, hundreds of them, under kilometer markers all over Europe. Each case contained a radio, clothes, and a hundred thousand dollars in various currencies."

He patted the small volume on the table. "This book is the only known record of the markers that have buried luggage. We'll go over your travel route and select some locations. With any luck, you'll dig up a good one and be able to use the cash in Rome."

Dan always wondered what Mac did on his short trips to Europe. He was never gone for more than a few days, and he always traveled light. Now he knew how light: a change of underwear, a flashlight, and a shovel. He assumed that the five million Mac had slipped out of the Agency's bank in New York would have been enough to retire on. But maybe living in Cuba offered little opportunity to invest the money. Besides, the way Mac lived; he needed plenty just to cover his bar bill.

Ten o'clock finally came around, and Dan found himself back at 37 Hoffstrasse with a small carry bag. Inside the office, Frau Prim-and-Proper gave no sign that she remembered him from the day before. She hardly looked up from her computer when he walked in and said good morning.

"Herr Schenk is out for the day."

His heart skipped a beat before she added, "He left this for you."

She handed him a carefully wrapped bundle from under her desk and went on typing.

Dan accepted the package and placed it in his carry bag.

He was on his way out the door when Frau Prim stopped him with a loud voice, "Mr. Carter!" She then spoke softly, "Give Big Mac my regards." A broad, toothy smile crossed her face. "Tell him if he doesn't stop in the next time he's in Switzerland, I'll cut his balls off." The smile was gone as fast as it had appeared, and Frau *not-so-Prim and-Proper* returned to her chores.

Dan closed the door and began walking down the hall to the stairs, shaking his head as he said to no one, "Never judge a book by its cover."

In his hotel room, he opened the package and carefully inspected the contents: two passports, one for James Carter and another in the name of Frank David Roosevelt (F.D.R.: another president, and easy to remember); two drivers licenses; luggage tags; and credit cards, even though he planned to pay cash for everything. The passports showed Vancouver as the places of issue. He inserted the Carter passport into the special pocket that had been sewn into his left pant leg just above the ankle. The F.D.R. model he put in his pants pocket sewn into the lower part of his right leg. "Left is Carter. Right is Roosevelt." Remembering which was which could be crucial later on. He was now a Canadian with two passports in the names of U.S. presidents.

"Keep it light," Mac had said. "It's easier to remember things that are funny."

He opened a pack of business cards that read, *James 'Jimmy' Carter. Traveling editor. Body World Magazine. 666 Avenue of the Americas. NY, NY. 90028. Mailto: bodyworld@aol.com.* All e-mails would end up at Mac's computer in Cuba.

He would be Jimmy Carter until he left Rome. F.D.R. would be used on the Prague-Madrid leg. From there, he would become Dan Fletcher again for the return trip to Havana.

The last item he took out of the bag was wrapped in white oilcloth. He carefully unfolded the 9mm SIG-Sauer semiautomatic and checked the magazine. Nine shells, none in the chamber. There were no extra bullets. Mac had told him during his indoctrination, "If you need more than nine bullets, you'll have problems you won't be able to solve with a gun." He added the items to his suitcase that contained the special equipment Mac had given him.

After leaving the hotel, he took a cab to the airport and rented a Fiat sports coupe from Avis. Using the James Carter Visa card as collateral, he paid cash for a thirty-day rental and left a substantial damage deposit. He asked for a map of Switzerland, Austria, and France and made arrangements to drop the car off in Cannes. He had no intention of going there, but he was trying to cover as many tracks as possible. No sense raising a red flag like an overdue rental car. It was hard for Dan to imagine himself as a fugitive murderer. The thought of hiding in Cuba as a wanted killer did not appeal to him, but it would be harder living at all knowing that Carlo was out there hustling pretty young women for body parts. If Mac's plan worked, Jimmy Carter and F.D.R. would disappear forever, relegated to history books as former presidents.

•

Once on the road, Dan stopped at a small town and purchased a pick, a shovel, and a good flashlight from a hardware store. He had brought a head-lamp with him but wanted the strong flashlight as a backup. Tourists did not walk around wearing headlamps.

Six hours later, he stopped for dinner in the old part of Innsbruck, an historic Austrian city surrounded by freeways and modern buildings. He ordered the Tyrolean special, *knoedl* soup, veal, and boiled potatoes. After washing the meal down with a glass of local white wine, he paid the bill and left.

Once Innsbruck was in his rearview mirror, he drove over the Brenner Pass into Italy. He passed a sign sixty miles later that read, *Wolkenstein-Val Gardena – 60 km.* An arrow pointed to the left. He was getting close to his first stop. He continued on the four-lane highway for a few more miles until he saw the 105km marker. He slowed down three miles later as the 110km concrete post came into view. It was sitting innocently alone in the Italian countryside with nothing in the vicinity to prevent him from doing a little digging so long as he shielded his work with the Fiat.

He kept going until he found a service center and pulled in to get gas. It was ten o'clock, but there was still a lot of traffic, so he decided to hang out in the restaurant and wait until there were fewer cars on the road. He was not hungry, but he ordered a salad and French fries and managed to kill an hour.

He paid the bill, left the restaurant, and crawled into the Fiat. He lowered the seat, leaned back, and closed his eyes. He was surprised when he awoke out of a dead sleep at twelve-thirty. The intense pace had taken its toll. He made a mental note to slow down and make sure he got his rest. Mac had cautioned, "It's easy to get careless when you're tired."

He pulled out of the service station and headed back in the direction he had come until he passed the 110km marker. He made a U-turn across the grassy divider and moments later pulled up next to the marker, turning off the headlights. It was dark and quiet. He maneuvered the coupe so that the passenger door would shield him from oncoming traffic on the other side of the divider. He had jockeyed the car so the back end was hiding the marker from cars approaching on his side.

He quickly opened the trunk, found the jack, and slid it under the frame on the right rear side. A couple of turns raised the car so it looked like he was changing the rear tire. It was a good cover as long as some good Samaritan didn't stop to offer a hand. When the car was in position, he took out the pick and started on the marker. The soil was softer than he had anticipated. The pick sank to the hilt on the first swing. He went to the shovel, and before long, he had dug a three-foot-square hole, a foot deep, behind the marker.

He stopped working and leaned on the shovel. The evening was cool, but he had built up a good sweat. Suddenly, he felt stupid. What the hell was he doing in the Italian countryside digging for CIA treasure? Did he really believe he would suddenly hit the box like in the movies? What if there was no money at any of the kilometer markers? He didn't have enough cash to complete the complicated killing plan, and Mac had made it crystal clear: "If it doesn't go according to plan, don't start improvising. Forget it and come home. There is no sense in spending the rest of your life in prison because of a botched murder plot."

When the little hole had grown into a big pit three feet deep and he still had yet to strike pay dirt, Dan began chipping away at the side of the pit that was under the concrete footing that held the marker. When his shovel hit the side of some kind of box, he wasn't sure he should be happy or disappointed. "Shit! The fucking case is not buried behind the marker; it's *underneath* the marker. But," he said with a smile, "there is a suitcase, and there just might be money in it. Fuck this digging shit."

He climbed out of the pit and lowered the car off the jack. He then moved the Fiat so the rear bumper was within a few feet of the cement pillar. He took the snow chains out of the small canvass sack in the trunk and slipped one end over the marker and the other end around the bumper. He got behind the wheel and put the coupe into gear. The chain tightened, and the tires began spinning in the dirt. Coupling the other chain with the first one was still no help. It was too far from the pavement, and the tires just spewed out gravel.

He realized he was out on a limb. *Shit! What if someone drives by and sees this fiasco? I'm in a rented Fiat trying to pull down an Italian road marker in front of a freshly dug hole.*

"What the hell," he mumbled. "Let's do it!"

He moved the car around to face the marker. There were now eight feet of slack in the two snow chains. Dan revved up the engine to 5000rpm, slammed the gearshift into reverse, and popped the clutch.

When it was over, the snow chains, the marker, and the foundation were lying in a heap on the shoulder of the highway. Half the bumper of the Fiat was now dangling straight out in front of the sports car. Dan looked both ways, praying there was no traffic.

He ran back to the hole and looked down to see the plastic suitcase sitting there like someone had just put it down. He grabbed the handle, and with one yank he pulled the case from its grave. With his momentum carrying him toward the car, he threw the dirty thing into the trunk, jumped in the drivers seat, and took off, leaving the marker, the pile of dirt, the tools, and the chains on the highway.

He could feel the beads of sweat running down his ribs as he drove through the night, trying to put some distance between himself and the vandalized Italian roadside.

After driving for thirty minutes with his eyes fixed on the rearview mirror expecting to see flashing blue lights chasing down the highway mauler, he turned off onto a quiet side road and parked. He leaned back and took a deep breath before chuckling. "No, Officer, I don't know anything about a kilometer marker back there. The bumper? I hadn't noticed. It must have been bent like that when I rented the car."

When he had calmed down, he took the flashlight then opened the trunk. He was somewhat surprised that the case was still there, as if it was some living monster that had been released from captivity.

He examined the relic. It was a plastic Samsonite two-suiter, the 1960s businessmen's travel luggage and the best on the market at the time.

"Okay, baby, show me da money." He easily unsnapped the two latches, as though the suitcase was still sitting on the floor of the luggage shop, and instinctively jumped back as he threw the lid open. *It could be a bomb or a poisonous snake coiled and ready to strike.* He'd seen too many movies. The open suitcase just sat there and looked at him without malice. He went closer. The flashlight revealed some musty clothes. Underneath was a radio wrapped in oilcloth. The money was neatly arranged on the bottom, with bank bands around the small bundles.

He exhaled and said, "Jesus Christ, there it is."

Until this moment, Dan had been giving it a fifty-fifty chance that a box even existed, another fifty percent chance of it containing money – and a real long shot that it was a lot of money. He'd been wrong. It was sitting in front of him, illuminated by the dim light. He couldn't tell how much, but there was plenty. He put the money into the leather carry bag and dumped the suitcase with the rest of the contents into the high grass, along with his work gloves, and the headlamp.

As he sped off toward Bolzano, he couldn't help wondering just how much of the U.S. taxpayer's money was buried and long forgotten under the world's highway markers. How many other black books had been lost or stolen? And what the hell were they for? Any spy from any country could simply walk into a bank and get funds transferred in a minute. Digging up suitcases in the dirt seemed like something out of a Captain Kidd pirate story, not something from the age of sophisticated electronics and jet travel. On the other hand, he was happy the Agency cash was now in his hands. The plan to find and do away with that asshole Carlo was still on track.

He was amazed at how easy it had been to find the marker and the suitcase, and for the first time, he actually believed Mac's bizarre plan might work.

Before finding the money, he had harbored fears that that his co-conspirator was nothing more than another bullshitting ex-patriot living a boring life in exile and vicariously living a *Mad Magazine* "Spy vs. Spy" fantasy, that this whole adventure might just be Mac's way of going back and reliving the old days. But even if part of that was true, Mac had put a lot of time and effort into the Carlo plan and must have had a certain amount of confidence that Dan could hold up his end.

Dan remembered the enthusiasm Mac had showed as he explained each part of the satellite phone equipment, the computer, the gun, the drugs, and most of all, the last part – the actual killing of Carlo.

Mac had been very serious. "Look, Dan, I know your background – Navy UDT and all that – but you have never been in a situation like the one you're going to be in when you come to the moment where you have to pull the trigger."

"I hate that cocksucker—"

"I know," Mac interrupted, "I know. But believe me, I have taught courses in this stuff. No matter how much hate you might have, the power of life or death changes things. It's no different than some macho hunter climbing around in the mountains year after year, only to freeze up when he finally gets the trophy deer in his sights. They call it Buck Fever, and the deer hunter is not holding a human life in his hands." He let his words sink in.

Dan broke the silence. "Have you ever killed a man, Mac?"

"No. My job was not pulling the trigger, but I did plan assassinations for the Agency. It's not something I talk about."

"I didn't think our CIA ever killed people."

The conversation was getting too serious for Mac. "Just like a true American, Danny Boy. The KGB does it, the Mossad does it, and the PLO does it. We even pay big bucks to see Double-O-Seven do it in the movies, but the Stars and Stripes' spy agency? They'd *never* kill anybody. Get real, Dan. It's the same the world over."

Mac paused, then said, "I know. I was one of the bad guys. But let's get to the business at hand. My question is, can you do it? If not, let's stop this whole thing now. It'll be a big waste of time and money if you do find Carlo and simply punch him around a bit until he cries and you feel so bad about hurting him you apologize. Then he goes off and keeps doing what he's been doing to other young girls."

While Mac was talking, Dan visualized pulling the trigger of the gun that was against Carlo's forehead. It was a vivid image, but after the gun went off, the picture in his mind froze.

"What about it, Dan? Do you have any reservations about going through with the plan? Can you see it? Can you visualize death by your hand?"

Dan was confused. "I see myself pulling the trigger, and that's enough."

"No, it isn't, damn it. You have to see his head snap back. You have to visualize the blood and brain matter exploding from the back of his skull. If you can't see it now, you'll have a problem with that final moment. Prepare yourself, Dan. Think about Lily. Think about Carlo gouging out those beautiful eyes."

Mac's painful reminder had done the job. The freeze frame was gone. He had a clear picture of the look of disbelief in Carlo's eyes as his head exploded and his brains splattered against the wall.

Dan arrived in Bolzano early in the morning and booked a room at the first small bed and breakfast he came to on the outskirts of town. It was a small two-story concrete building with a restaurant on the main floor and rooms above. He presented his James Carter passport and paid for one night.

The desk clerk looked confused. He looked at the passport and compared the photo to Dan's face several times, then he glanced out the glass doors at the Fiat parked outside.

Dan could only imagine what the clerk thought. Here was a dirt-covered American driving an Italian sports car with the bumper dangling three feet in front of the vehicle.

Dan shrugged his shoulders, turned his palms up, and said, "Car trouble." The clerk smiled and handed him the key to Room 12.

Dan locked the door behind him and sat his bags on the bed. He opened the one with the money and counted the bills. It came to seventy-five thousand in U.S. dollars, mostly hundreds, with several thousand in tens and twenties.

He went into the bathroom, and one look in the mirror told him why the clerk had looked at him so strangely. He was a real mess.

He filled the old bathtub and eased his body into the surprisingly hot water. As he lay submerged with just his nose above the water, he wondered where the other twenty-five thousand had gone. There was supposed to be a hundred thousand in the case. *That's easy*, he figured. The guy that had originally planted the money took the other twenty-five. Short every bag twenty-five grand, plunk it into a Swiss account, and retire with a little extra in his pension fund. Bury enough two-suiters and retire. The planter probably ended up sitting on some beach in St. Tropez drinking one of those tropical cocktails with an umbrella in it.

"What line of work were you in, Mr. Jones?"

"Luggage. Samsonite luggage."

Then he wondered what kept the guy from taking the whole amount. The CIA originally planted the untraceable money during the Cold War to be used by foreign agents in the event the Soviets took over Europe. What were the chances of a spy filing a report that said, "Hey, I dug up a suitcase in Europe at the location you gave me, and there was no money in it?" Besides, if there was only one book and Mac had it, who was going to find out?

He came out of his daydream and opened his eyes to see the brown water he was soaking in. Suitcase digging was dirty work. He pulled the plug and rinsed off with the telephone-shaped showerhead.

He wondered what some archeologist was going to say a thousand years from now. He imagined some little guy in a pith helmet after digging up a bathtub saying, "My God, look at this, Maynard. An ancient bathtub. Man used it to bathe in his own filth, and here's a showerhead he used to wash away the dirt he bathed in. I wonder why he did not just start with a clean shower like modern man?"

He dried off with a giant fluffy towel as he moved into the bedroom. He took the stacks of money off the bed and flopped down, wondering just how rich Mac was if he really held the only copy of that little black book. *To hell with smuggling cigars,* he thought, *just give me a few pages of that little black book.*

He fell asleep and dreamed about his own warehouse filled with suitcases once owned by the CIA.

Dan allowed himself a full night's sleep. He awoke at 11:00 a.m. and managed to get a decent cup of espresso and a couple of boiled eggs in the café downstairs before hitting the road.

He checked his map and estimated four hours to Rome. He changed his estimate to three hours when he found it difficult to keep it under eighty miles an hour in the slow lane of the *Autostrada*. The normal traffic in the left lane was whizzing by at one hundred and twenty.

As he sped toward Rome, he focused on the chore ahead of him. So far, the plan was progressing like clockwork: the meeting with Schenk, the passports, and the money. He found himself thinking once again about the actual act of putting the gun to Carlo's head and pulling the trigger. If he hesitated at that moment, he would think about Lily and her lifeless body hanging by the leather Italian belt. At the thought of Lily, he felt tears welling up and he instinctively pressed down on the accelerator, as if getting there a little faster would make the impossible task of locating the bastard easier. When he found him, he could do it. He would shoot Carlo and enjoy it. There would be two shots – the first one into his balls.

CHAPTER
34

Dan stood on twelfth floor of the Excelsior Hotel admiring the skyline of Rome. The spacious penthouse was five hundred a night, but the location would make it easier to set up his satellite phone. Mac had been specific about which hotel to book, and Dan had made the reservation from Zurich. From his position, he could look down at the roof of the U.S. embassy and see the direction the communication antennas were facing.

He put out the do-not-disturb sign and double-locked the door before unpacking the photo equipment Mac had prepared. The bulky 35mm Nikon would act as his cover while he pretended to be taking pictures for his publication. The photos he would send to Mac in Cuba he would take with the remote pocket-sized digital model that could store sixty color shots on a 96MB chip. The little camera was connected to a tiny fiber-optic lens concealed in the Yankees logo on his baseball cap.

After plugging in the voltage transformer, he took out the Magellan satellite phone and connected the data cable to the Toshiba laptop computer. He turned on the phone and entered the six-digit security code. He pressed the *seek-satellite* button and took the aerial to the steel table sitting on the patio. He eyeballed the big parabolic dishes down on the roof of the U.S. embassy and turned his antennae toward the southern sky. He adjusted the vertical and horizontal plane until he heard the low tone from the sat-phone change to a high whine. He was amazed by the ease of making contact. *ET phone home*, he thought as he went inside and pressed the *okay* button. A minute went by, and the message on the sat-phone read, *Dial 00, the country code, and the telephone number.* He was in business. He dialed the number of the sat-phone in Cuba, and after a few moments he heard Mac's voice.

"Hello."

"Hello yourself. How's the reception?"

"Five by five," came the reply. "Everything okay?"

"Fine. I checked my bank account, and it looks like I'll have plenty of money to enjoy the vacation. I'm going to hang up and send you a picture of Rome. Call me back and let me know how it looks."

Dan broke the connection. He knew Mac would be pleased with the report of finding the money. He took the little digital camera out onto the balcony, aimed his cap, and took a shot of Rome from twelve stories up. He connected the camera to the computer with a small cable and followed the instructions taped to the bottom of the keyboard. When the photo appeared on the screen, he was impressed with the quality. "Let's see how it looks on the other end," he said as he typed Mac's electronic address. They had agreed on *killem@hotmail.com.*

He double-clicked on the *send* window, and the first of what would be many digital photos from Italy was on its way to Cuba.

A quarter of an hour later, the sat-phone rang. It was Mac. "Good photo, Dan. Clear as a bell."

"That's great, Mac. But it took twelve minutes to send. It might end up taking hours sending you the pictures."

"Don't worry, my boy. There can't be that many brown-haired Italians in Rome with bushy mustaches."

"Very funny. Is Lily's mother all set up for a look-see when we start sending?"

"Affirmative, but to speed things up, I bought a good four-color printer. I'll make hard copies first before taking them to her in Baracoa. It'll make things easier. I don't want her sitting around waiting twelve minutes for each mug shot; it might impair her ability to make a positive identification if we get lucky with the Needle." Needle was their code name for the one in the haystack named Carlo.

Dan hung up and imagined Lily's mother rocking back and forth, her eyes staring straight ahead and her hands in her lap wringing a handkerchief. She had been like that every time he had stopped at the house with Mac. Through watery eyes she had told them of this Italian, this Carlo person. She described his appearance and his manner. She said there was something about him she hadn't liked, but she did not know what it was. She said he had never come to the house and had seemed nervous when she ran into him and Lily in the café in Havana. He wore three gold chains, one holding a gold bar. He had a fancy gold Rolex and muscles that bulged from beneath a black T-shirt. Would she recognize this Carlo? "The monster that killed my Lily?" she asked. "Oh yes. I see him every time I close my eyes, as if someone glued his face to the insides of my eyelids. Show me a picture of this Carlo. I will know him."

Dan and Mac had stopped short of expressing any sort of desire for revenge, and Lily's mother had asked no questions. But her eyes could not hide her feelings. If Dan could find Carlo in Italy, he would kill the man.

Dan caught a taxi and went over his plan as the driver careened like a pinball around fountains and statues from one piazza to another.

He arrived at his first stop and paid the driver with a shaky hand. This would be the first test of his new identity as a magazine writer-photographer for a muscle magazine, and he was nervous.

He walked up to the front desk of Prizzi's Gym, presented his business card to the pretty dark-haired woman behind the counter, and said, "Good Morning. Do you speak English?"

She looked at his card and said, "Yes, a little. What can I do for you" – she glanced back at the card – "Mr. Carter?"

He estimated her to be about forty, though she had the body of a teenager. The wrinkles around her mouth and the bony wrists were the only signs that betrayed her age. She wore a black leotard with a green silk scarf tied around her twenty-five-inch waist. He translated her nametag: *Annette, Manager.*

She smiled and waited. Dan's once-over had not gone unnoticed.

"I'm with *Body World* magazine." He spoke up with confidence in his voice. "It's a new publication. Our head office is in New York, and we're looking for well defined bodies to be featured in our first edition." He smiled and continued his well-rehearsed speech. "My job is to find subjects in Europe. I've already sent back photographs of potential candidates from Spain, Germany, and France. I'd like to know if there is a possibility of interviewing candidates here in your gym?"

Annette was expressionless as she listened intently. When she was sure he had finished, she said, "I am very sorry." She spoke in slow motion compared to Dan's rapid-fire delivery. "I do not understand. Could you please speak a little slower?"

Dan was embarrassed. He was trying so hard to get through his first attempt at establishing a false identity that he was failing to communicate. "*Scusi, Signora.*" He made a feeble attempt at Italian before going into broken English. "My name – Carter. I work for magazine. I want take pictures of men with muscles." He held up both arms and flexed.

She was now wearing a toothy smile. "Not that slow, Jimmy." She had been studying his card while he was talking. They both laughed when she added, "I think I get the picture."

"No, Annette, *I* get the picture." He tapped the Nikon he was wearing around his neck as they both laughed again.

Under different circumstances, he would have found out more about Annette. She had a sparkle in her eye, and she was not wearing a wedding band. But Jimmy Carter had to keep a low profile. There was no way he could spend an evening with a lady as lovely as Annette without revealing too many details about his life that might lead authorities to him later.

She said in her best businesslike voice, "If you leave a number, I will give you a call if I see someone who is interested." She leaned both elbows on the counter, rested her face on both hands, and in a very un-businesslike voice said, "You are not looking for a woman, are you?" She waited a long moment before adding, "You know, for the magazine?"

In an equally businesslike voice he answered, "No, it's a men's magazine." That was a dumb statement, he thought. "I would really like to just come and go in the gym and look over the men working out. If I find someone who I think might be a candidate, we can arrange for an interview."

Dan wanted to make a move on this muscular but still quite feminine woman, but he knew it would be no good. Lily was dead, and until he finished the last chapter with Carlo, he couldn't imagine himself with another woman.

She smiled and put the card in the drawer without taking her eyes off his. "Feel free to come … and go … as you please."

She handed him a key and a towel. "It's on the house."

Dan made his way into the locker room and found the steel locker that matched his key number. He hung the Nikon on the hook and changed into the workout sweats he had brought in the gym bag. He inserted the remote camera into the sewn pocket on the inside of his baggy shirt and adjusted the baseball cap that held the tiny remote lens. He closed the locker and made his way out into the gym.

The big room had an array of modern machines designed to pump up every muscle on the human body. In addition, there were four stationary bicycles, four treadmills, and a free-weights area set aside from the other apparatuses. There was a speed bag in the far corner, and a boxer danced around a body bag that hung from a hefty chain. Floor-to-ceiling mirrors lined the walls. With the exception of the boxing stuff, it was no different than the thousands of physical fitness establishments found the world over.

It was quiet in the gym. He had not expected many bodies working out early on Monday morning, but it was a good test run to gain confidence in himself and his fabricated story. He stopped briefly, aimed the bill of his cap at the face of a bulky guy doing bench presses, and took two test shots he would send to Mac from the penthouse later that night.

The miniature lens Mac had installed in Dan's baseball cap was aimed by centering the white dot painted on the underside of the bill on the subject. Pressing with his thumb the ring on his left index finger actuated the shutter. With a little practice, he would be able to snap digital photos while talking to potential candidates for the magazine.

With the exception of Annette's tight body, Dan found little of interest at Prizzi's, but he felt good about the practice run.

Five weeks passed without taking one picture of what Dan would call a good suspect. He had prowled Rome's thirteen fitness centers that boasted a total of more than fifteen hundred members, but he saw no young muscle-bound Italian with bushy hair and a mustache. The haystack was getting bigger. Most of the gyms had agreed to his requests. A few originally suggested that they ask their members first then call him.

"That may take too much time, and I wouldn't want the subjects to be self-conscious," he had said. "How about I just wander around the gym and talk to a few of the members? You can back me up by saying we are doing some publicity photos. Then, if I make a candid selection, we can explain the details and schedule a simple photo shoot in private." Dan did not believe for one moment that someone whose job it was to steal body parts would show up for a prearranged photo shoot. If he were going to get a shot of Carlo, it would have to be a candid photo taken with the cap camera.

Dan lay in the massive bed in the master bedroom and stared at the high ceiling. He wondered why anybody in their right mind would pay five hundred dollars a night to sleep there. He rated the shower a seven. Hot water, good spray, and separate enclosed glass shower stall – it had a few pluses. But low water pressure was inevitable on the twelfth floor.

He thought about how far he was from the life he had grown accustomed. He longed for the warm breeze coming in off the gulf, the salsa music, Papa's Disco, and *cubalibres* by the pool at El Viejo El Mar Hotel. He fell asleep thinking about Lily, her throaty laugh, the way she moved on the dance floor – those beautiful green eyes.

Guiseppi knocked at preciously 7:00 a.m. and, without waiting, used his key to enter the suite. He wheeled the breakfast cart into the room and out onto the veranda. The boy who could not have been more than thirteen placed the silver-dome-covered plates on the table and quietly left the room.

Dan's daily breakfast order was strong black coffee served in a silver pot, two four-minute boiled eggs, orange juice, two slices of toast, and a copy of the *London Herald*.

He made sure to put away the sat-phone and the computer each night after transmitting to Mac. The communications system was locked in a suitcase in the closet, along with the SIG semiautomatic and the rest of the special equipment.

He arrived at Club Mario later that morning, the fourteenth fitness club on his list. He had stopped by the day before and laid out his story. He told the kid at the desk he would be back in the morning.

He was issued a key and towel compliments of the club. He changed into his sweats and carried his Nikon into the weight room.

Two middle-aged hard-bodied men were the only occupants in a single room typical of what he'd seen in the other gyms. There were a variety of benches, some angled, each with a Christmas tree of weights alongside. Both weightlifters were working out on a prone press bench in front of a mirrored wall. They wore sturdy leather belts, leather gloves without fingers, and tight spandex shorts. The one laying on the bench was grunting and blowing air like a steam engine with each upward push. The second lifter stood spread-legged over his partner's forehead, ready to grab the heavy barbell and assist with the last two reps. Dan saw no reason to take candid shots of these two. They were both balding, and even with a full head of hair; they were too old and bulky to fit Carlo's description. But to maintain his cover, he held up the Nikon, smiled, and motioned to the weightlifters, "It's okay?"

"*Si.*"

Dan snapped off two shots from the empty camera and said, "*Grazie.*"

He heard a polite "*Prego*" as he turned and walked into the larger adjoining room filled with nautilus equipment. He thought he might as well work the muscles a little while waiting for Carlo to hopefully appear.

Dan set the Nikon down on a bench and took a seat on the stomach machine. He selected one hundred and forty pounds and began scrunching the padded roll bar across his chest and down to his knees. He closed his eyes, concentrated on his stomach muscles, and exhaled slowly on the way down. After thirty reps, he could feel a slight burning in his abdomen. He continued to forty.

For years his test for checking body fat had been to tighten up his chest and stomach muscles and jump up and down in front of a mirror, grading his condition by how much the fat jiggled. That morning in the hotel, the test had revealed only a slight ripple.

He had looked into the mirror and joked to himself, "Your muscles don't look any better, Fletcher, but your fat looks much harder." He flexed and added, "Maybe a slight improvement in muscle tone, but a long way to go for a washboard."

He had begun his workout sessions with three sets of fifteen reps at one hundred pounds. He was now up to four sets of forty reps at one hundred and forty pounds and looked forward to his daily exercises.

But the result of the physical activity was a hollow victory. He was getting into shape but getting nowhere finding Carlo, or whoever he was. Maybe the guy didn't even live in Rome. Maybe he was on another eye search at this very moment. Was he bedding some unsuspecting young girl, gazing into the eyes of another victim? The thought sickened him.

•

He rested with his arms hanging over the leather-covered foam roller and thought how foolish the whole thing was. He was wandering around looking for a brown-haired man with a mustache – an Italian in Rome, for Christ's sake. He felt so stupid. For the first time since he had left Cuba, he began thinking it was a lost cause. It all suddenly seemed so Hollywood-ish: Mac vicariously reliving his old days as a spy, the clandestine passports, state-of-the-art killing weapons, digging up old suitcases, and this stupid fucking cap camera. Maybe it was time to throw in the towel. He sat like that for a long time with his eyes closed and his chin digging into the leather, feeling lower than he could remember in a long time. *There has to be a cut-off point,* he told himself. One week more, and he'd give it up. It was a gallant effort, but the odds were just too overwhelming.

When he lifted his head and opened his eyes, he focused on a piece of equipment on the far side of the crowded room that stood out from the typical Nautilus workout apparatus. His heart began racing at the sight of it. He'd seen it advertised many times on television. It was a Bowflex.

Carlo had told Lily's mother that he sold sporting goods, and he maintained his muscles by using his own home gym, which used bow-like metal bars. Maybe the gym had bought one from Carlo. Dan wiped the sweat from the machine he'd been using and made his way back to the front desk.

The young boy smiled as he approached. "Are you having a good workout, Mr. Carter?"

"Yes, thank you."

"And you saw Mr. Lochentis and Mr. Lamont pumping iron? They have very good bodies, no?" He smiled with tight lips.

"Yes, I took a few pictures while they were working out. Tell me," he said as he glanced at the young boy's nametag, "Toni, the Bowflex machine you have in the gym – I've seen them advertised on TV in the States, but I've never seen one in a professional gym. Is it a good system?"

"Oh, I guess it is okay, but we have many better machines that focus more precisely on different muscles groups." Then he added with a smile and a shrug of his shoulders, "The boss, *Signore* Mario, he sells them. We keep that one as a display."

Dan felt a shortness of breath. "I'd like to meet this Mario. Does he come in often?"

"*Signore* Mario is away on a business trip. He returns next week."

"I'd like to talk to him. How will I recognize *Signore* Mario?"

"Oh, *Signore*, he is a beautiful man. He works out all the time." His eyes gave away a more than casual admiration. "But I do not think you will want to take his picture for your magazine."

"Really? Why don't you think he'd be a candidate?"

"He has a perfect body, and he is very handsome, but he does not have the really big muscles you want. I have seen the magazines: *Mr. America, Mr. Universe.* Those bodies are incredible." He leaned forward and spoke in a lower voice. "Between you and me, *Signore* Carter, *Signore* Mario is very well muscled from the waist up, but his legs are not in the same class with his upper body."

Dan made the rounds for the next six days, looking for candidates at the other weightlifting centers. He saw some of Rome's most beautiful bodies and took a few pictures. None came close to Carlo's description. Even though he felt he was just going through the motions, he sent transmissions of digital photos every night. Every morning he received a negative response from Mac. He refrained from telling Mac about the Bowflex.

The week passed slowly. The owner of Mario's would be back tomorrow, and for the first time since Dan had been in Rome, he was excited. It was a long shot, but Mario's Bowflex machine was the only one he'd seen in any of the gyms in Rome. Mario could turn out to be Carlo. He reminded himself not to appear too anxious, or ask too many question. He would have to wait until Mac had the photos anyway.

If Mario was not Carlo, he would know who sold the Bowflex to the gym. Carlo had told Lily's mother that he had one in his apartment and had gone into detail about the bow system. If Carlo was not the Bowflex distributor, he was a user.

Dan had transmitted more than fifty different shots of brown-haired bodybuilders from the thirteen gyms he had visited in Rome. Lily's mother had failed to recognize any of them. He had taken into account the possibility of Carlo changing his appearance, or at least shaving the mustache and coloring his hair. Carlo could be worried about being identified.

Dan and Mac had discussed the possibility that Carlo had pulled off his ugly theft more than once and could change his appearance to prevent anyone from wandering around the city and spotting him. That was probably the reason the son of a bitch took both eyes. It eliminated the victim's opportunity of returning to the scene of the crime and leading authorities to the doctor's office or Carlo's apartment. And he most likely picked Third World countries like Cuba for his evil scheme because it would be more difficult for family members to leave the country and track him down.

Dan had played with the computer and added mustaches and curly brown hair to some of the pictures he had sent in case Carlo had changed his looks. But there was still not one hint of recognition from Lily's mother.

He awoke to the 7:00 a.m. knock on the door, and Guiseppi wheeled the breakfast cart into the suite's sitting room. *"Bon giorno, Signore."*

Dan was thinking how much he enjoyed the first-class European treatment.

Guiseppi pulled back the drapes that covered the twelve-foot-high floor-to-ceiling glass balcony doors to let in the early light of an overcast sky. "Another cloudy day, *Signore* Carter," Guiseppi said as he lifted the silver covers from Dan's daily breakfast. He refrained from watching Dan, who was taking a look at Rome's skyline. Dan liked the Italian hotel system, in which bellmen were paid to service hotel clients, not to observe them.

Even though Guiseppi came with the cart at seven o'clock sharp seven days a week, Dan hardly ever made eye contact with the frail youth. Dan did not appreciate bellmen who chatted nonstop from the time they entered the elevator to the time the tip was expected. They asked about length of stay, where he was from, what he planned to visit, yadda, yadda, yadda. He just wanted to eat in peace.

Dan's usual breakfast of coffee and boiled eggs had been replaced this morning by fresh-squeezed orange juice, eggs Florentine, mixed fruit salad, toasted onion bagels with cream cheese and jelly, and the pot of coffee that he insisted be brewed fresh and put on the cart last. He was getting used to the high life – and gaining weight, but not because of the food; his workouts in the gym were building muscle.

The thought of the gym jolted him back to reality and the reason he was in Rome. He was here to kill a man, an act that, if he should succeed, would change him forever. Should he bungle the task, the fallout would be even more profound. If he were caught after completing the act, it would mean spending the rest of his life in prison.

Dan had begun every morning in Rome with the thought that that day would be the day he would find his quarry. But today was the first day he actually had reason to believe he had a suspect. This Mario guy could be his man. He had carefully pried out a description of Mario from the desk clerk, who had been more than willing to give details about his boss's wonderful body. When Dan had pressed Toni for more details about Mario's looks, he noticed the kid's eyes light up in admiration; the kid was obviously gaga over his boss.

What's a sweet kid without a muscle to his name doing working at a gym? Dan wondered. He was hardly the kind of poster boy one would want as the first point of contact at a muscle-building establishment. Better that, he thought, than having him in the shower room handing out towels. It didn't fit, unless Mario was a switch-hitter. Gay, perhaps?

Dan entered Mario's gym at nine-thirty and was met by the smiling Toni, who was anxious to tell Jimmy Carter that Mario was indeed back from his trip and very anxious to meet him. Fear suddenly ran through Dan. What if Mario was Carlo? What if he had seen Dan's picture, maybe in Lily's purse? Maybe he had even seen him in Cuba. If so, the plan was not going to work unless he simply lay in wait and blew Carlo's head off with the SIG on the streets of Rome.

Dan was led into the small office behind the front desk. "Mario will be in soon. Coffee, *Signore* Carter?"

"Sure, Toni."

The kid magically produced a tiny cup of espresso, smiled a little too prettily with too much eye contact, and set it down.

The one thing Dan had never gotten use to was drinking his coffee out of something that resembled a shot glass. Italians served espresso in a thimble-sized cup. The black fluid barely coated his mouth and throat, and by the time the eyedropper-sized swallow made it down to his stomach, there was little to provide the necessary caffeine fix he had spent a half century getting accustomed to. Dan longed for a coffee shop where he could pay a buck and get continuous refills from an attractive waitress while he read the morning paper.

"Is *Signore* Mario married?" Dan asked.

A frown crossed the kid's face. "He has a fiancée, but it won't last. It never does." Toni's eyes gave away some inner secret. Did Toni believe he was the reason Mario's engagements didn't last?

"He's been engaged before?"

"Oh yes, the last one, Lily, a few months ago"

Dan's knees buckled. He steadied himself on the counter.

Toni went on, "She was very beautiful, but it didn't last. They never do." He said it almost under his breath.

Toni had turned to place a folded towel under the counter and did not notice the blood drain from Dan's face.

Dan was now positive he had found Carlo, and he realized he was going to live the rest of his life knowing he had taken another man's life. In the eyes of the law, revenge or not, he would be a murderer. If caught, he would go to prison. He did not let the idea of the death penalty enter his thoughts, but he could not prevent his imagination from putting him on the hangman's platform.

The door opened, and a handsome, curly-haired Italian man wearing a tight black T-shirt came in and said, "Hello. I'm Mario."

Dan stood and offered his hand. "Jimmy Carter, *Body World* magazine."

"Yes, I know. Toni has told me all about you and your mission."

He gave Dan a firm but not overpowering handshake. He had straight white teeth, curly brown hair, and a bushy, well-trimmed mustache.

Dan had trouble keeping his composure. He could feel his hands begin to tremble. The man in front of him was exactly what Dan had imagined Carlo would look like, everything from the full head of hair to the gold chains around his neck. He was one good-looking hunk of a man. It was no wonder Lily had fallen for the guy.

He could hear Mac talking. *"Take it easy, Dan. Don't fuck up here. You want this to be the guy. Don't make this a rush to judgment and take a chance on killing an innocent person."*

He had a hard time delivering his lines. "Well, if you're amenable, I'd like to take a few photos for the guys back in New York, and I might add, I think you have the qualifications of a serious candidate for our Mr. Italy spread. Do you mind if we go out in the gym and take a look at the rest of you, after you pump up of course?" Dan was sure that Mario had arrived early and had already spent an hour in the weight room.

"Sure, but one thing: I'd like the photos to show me using a specific apparatus. I'm sure you are familiar with the Bowflex?" Dan's heart stopped. "I am the Italian distributor, you know."

"Not a problem, Mario." Dan almost caught himself saying *Carlo. Don't panic now, Fletcher. Take it slow.* He had felt a rush of blood to his face when Mario mentioned the Bowflex. "They advertise them in the United States on television. Is it a popular apparatus here in Italy?"

"Not really, at least not yet. One problem we have here is that we have small houses and apartments with many people in the same house. There is not a lot of room for people to dedicate an area for the system at home."

They were standing next to the machine as Mario began explaining the weird-looking contraption, hooking and un-hooking different metal bars that bent like bows when the person pulled various cables.

"It combines cardiovascular with strength training. There are sixty different exercises that will reshape a man like you." He looked Dan up and down and added, "in just six weeks."

There was no stopping Mario. "A twenty-minute workout burns fat and reshapes your body faster than free weight training." He reached over and pulled down one of the metal bars. "Ten power rods, five on each side, provide from ten to two hundred and forty pounds of resistance."

"How many have you sold, Mario?"

"Twenty-two systems here in Rome, and about another two hundred in the rest of the county. It is something new, but I think it will catch on. There is a growing interest. If I had the funds, a little TV advertising would give sales a kick."

By now Mario had stripped down to a tank top and a pair of spandex shorts that stopped just above the knee.

Dan couldn't help wondering how much he had under the bulge in his crotch. Was it a big dick that had appealed to Lily? Was this guy a stud? It was hard to tell. Mario's dick was more than a fleeting thought, and he caught himself staring before returning to business.

What Dan found interesting was the gold chain that held a sizable gold bar. He was anxious to take some pictures and get the hell out of there before he made a slip and called him Carlo. He could hardly wait to send photos of this guy to Mac.

Mario was working up a sweat but carefully dried off as he warmed up. Dan noticed that he had a light coating of oil, which he had obviously applied earlier that morning. No doubt he had been in the gym long before Dan had arrived, preparing for his future role as *Body World's* pick of an Italian body.

Mario flexed, posed, and smiled for Dan's motor drive Nikon, which contained no film. The digital micro camera in his pocket snapped off twenty-four candid shots through the cap lens while Mario rested between sets.

"You realize, of course, that I am not the photographer who will shoot the photos for the spread in the magazine in the event you are selected. These negatives will be sent to the New York office, but in my opinion, you have a good chance."

Dan had the bait out. Now he had to set the hook. "Look, why don't I have this roll developed here in Rome?" He was putting the plan in motion, but he still needed Mac to give him a positive identification from Lily's mother. "Then I can leave a set of prints so you can use them in your brochure, or whatever."

Mario's eyes widened, "You'd give me the magazine's photos for my personal use?"

Dan wondered if he was suspicious. "Sure, until you sign a release and a contract, you legally own the use of these shots. Adam West, our staff photographer, would be the one doing the spread." Dan was sure to remember the Batman actor's name should Mario ask him at a later time who'd be doing the shoot. "I'll give you a call when I see the photos. Maybe we can get together for dinner."

Mario smiled. "Sure, why not. It would be a pleasure."

Dan gave his biggest grin and thought, *The pleasure's going to be all mine, you son of a bitch. If you are who I think you are, you are a dead man.*

Then he heard Mac's words, "Confirm the Bowflex in his apartment, Dan. Be one hundred percent positive."

Dan tried a little fishing. "From the looks of you, Mario, that Bowflex does a good job."

Mario's eyes did not leave the reflection in the mirror as he flexed his trapezoids.

Dan set the hook. "Do you have one at home?"

"Sure, I use the Bowflex on days I don't want to come in. For the average guy, it's the best home system on the market."

Bingo. Dan did not react to the statement, but his gut churned at the mention of the Bowflex in his apartment. Mario had just added a major piece to the puzzle.

Toni was folding towels behind the front desk as Dan and Mario approached.

Dan couldn't help thinking the kid was working in the wrong place. With his physique, Toni would fit in better as a receptionist in a sleazy massage parlor.

Toni glanced at Dan then Mario. "So did it go well?"

"It went fine, Toni." Mario reached over and picked out a business card from the holder and wrote down a number on the back. "This is my home number. Give me a call. I'd love to see the photos." He gave Dan a masculine handshake and a feminine smile.

"I'll be in touch," Dan said.

His legs felt weak as he made his way down the short flight of stairs, and his head was spinning as he walked out into the warm summer sun. He needed to think.

He found an open-air café and took a seat at a small table next to a colorful array of potted flowers. He ordered a double Bacardi without ice. The waiter seemed unconcerned about serving rum so early in the morning and quickly returned with the drink.

Dan noticed his hand shaking as he slowly brought the glass to his lips, then felt the soothing effect of the warm liquid as it trickled down his throat. Mario was Carlo. No doubt about it. Everything fit: the description, the gold chains, the Bowflex in his apartment, even Toni mentioning that Mario's last fiancée was named Lily.

Big Mac's parting words came back at him again. "Be one hundred percent sure, Dan. If you are wrong and you find out later, it will have a lasting effect on your future state of mind. Don't take a chance. Let Lily's mother make the identification, then use the sodium Pentothal."

There were two more things to do: get a positive identification from the photo and get some sort of confession with the truth serum. *Fuck it*, he thought. *The truth serum shit is a long shot. If Mac comes back with a positive on the photo, it'll be enough. I'm going to kill that muscle-bound prick and love doing it.*

He paid the bill and took a cab back to the penthouse to check the photos and make his transmission to Mac.

•

186

CHAPTER
35

Big Mac drove along Fifth Avenue on his way to Baracoa with another set of pictures for Lily's mother. Dan had been gone for more than a month, and Mac was allowing doubts to creep into his mind. Had Carlo changed his identity? How could the man remain in the same city where he had committed the crime? Was it a one-time thing Carlo had done for a family member – or a lover? Why both eyes?

Then he answered his own questions. They had taken both eyes and severed the optic nerves so a cornea transplant would not restore sight, thus preventing the victim from identifying the criminals. It was not a one-time crime. If it were, how would he get doctors to go along? It had to be a conspiracy. There had to be others involved, and they would still be in Rome. They wouldn't be moving from city to city.

Mac contemplated the latest set of photos Dan had sent the night before. There were twelve, all of the same guy in various poses. *Interesting*, he thought. Dan usually sent five or six different subjects and in one candid pose. The new subject had the usual bushy brown hair and mustache, but the bench this guy was sitting on heightened Mac's interest. It was a Bowflex home gym. And he wore a heavy gold chain that held a sizable gold bar. Carlo had worn gold chains in Cuba, but so did every other Italian tourist who came to the island. Mac couldn't help being excited but cautioned himself on making a decision based on a hope-so emotion. He reminded himself to act nonchalant when he showed the photos to Lily's mother.

He parked the Mercedes sedan in front of Alma Lopez's house and extracted his big frame from the vehicle. The neighborhood was full of kids, each of whom hardly gave the big car a second glance. Mac had made many trips to Lily's house in the past weeks with photographs sent by Dan and printed on Mac's computer. The latest was just another pretty face. He knew Dan had purposely left out any additional information on this one, except his name, Mario.

As Mac approached the house, he could feel his excitement rising. He felt something in his bones about this new guy.

He dreaded entering the house in Baracoa. The closed-entry door that usually stood open displayed a black ribbon that was now faded into a dull

•

gray by the morning sun. The stained, cracked plaster walls of the sixty-year-old home seemed more depressing even than the creaking of Alma's rocking chair or the closed windows that added to the gloomy atmosphere.

Mac rapped several times.

Lily's sister Darma slowly opened the heavy door. *"Buenos dias, Señor Mac."*

"Buenos dias, Darma. Como esta su madre?"

"Ella signe igual … querrias café?"

"Si, gracias."

The family had nothing, but every visitor was offered coffee. It would be insulting to decline. He had called earlier to the only home on the block with a telephone and passed the message that he would be coming by at 10: 00 a.m.

Darma led Mac into the dark parlor, where Alma sat rocking in the chair. It seemed to Mac that she had not moved from the chair since Lily's funeral. She rocked slowly, hardly taking notice of Mac's arrival.

"Buenos dias, Señora."

Alma did not speak, but nodded as Darma placed the coffee on the small table and took a seat next to her mother.

Mac took a sip of the coffee and said, *"Gracias."* Then he waited a few moments before asking, "Is your mother all right to look at more pictures?"

"I am afraid she will never be all right. For her, there is no escaping the pain. When she's awake, she sees Lily's smiling face. Nights are more difficult. In her dreams, she sees Lily" – Darma dropped her head and barely got the words out – "hanging from the pipe. Then she says she sees the face of the devil. Carlo's face."

Alma's face was drawn tight. She had aged ten years in the last three months.

He sat opposite the woman, old in demeanor, young in years. She looked up slowly at Mac. Her eyes pleaded to his, as if he was her only salvation, the only one who could provide the closure she needed.

Each time Mac had come to the house with photos, her spirits had seemed to lift until she carefully scrutinized the pictures. Time and time again, she had said, "No, he's not the man."

Mac opened the big envelope, set it on the coffee table, and said in a soft monotone, "I have more photographs, *Señora.*"

Señora Lopez had shown little emotion in the past while shuffling through Dan's pictures of Italian faces. Mac wondered if she would be able to identify Carlo even if Dan was lucky enough to snap a shot of the right guy,

Darma was adamant. "My mother will know," she had said with conviction time and again.

Mac took the twelve 8x10s out of the manila envelope and handed her the first glossy. It was an excellent reproduction, considering it had come from the satellite telephone.

Mac's enthusiasm dropped when Alma's face displayed no sign of recognition. She looked at the photo for a moment and extended her hand toward Mac for the next one without looking up. He handed her another glossy. She repeated the process without emotion. When all twelve photos were in her hands, she slowly looked up from the stack at Mac.

Her eyes were black with hatred, and she spoke slowly. "This is Carlo. He is the one who killed my Lily."

He didn't have to ask if she was sure. Mac had experienced these types of identifications in the past. Alma's eyes told him everything he needed to know.

Mac gathered the photos, inserted them into the envelope, and left the house.

On the way back to his home, he found it difficult to keep from speeding. He had to call Dan, then he would burn the photos and the negatives. The computer, the sat-phone, and the printer would also be destroyed. Some guy in Canada would complain about his satellite phone bill and insist that he had never made or accepted calls from Italy. After Mac's confirmation call to Dan, all traces of the communication system would be destroyed. An acid bath would take care of a computer's hard drive.

CHAPTER
36

Mac's call came in at 6:00 p.m. It was short and to the point.

"You did it, Dan. Your last transmission was positive. You got your man. It's your show now. Be careful."

Dan sat in the chair after hanging up the phone. His entire body was tingling. He gulped in short breaths of air and held his hand out in front of his face. His fingers were shaking badly. The search was over. Until now, his time had been consumed with finding his man. Mac's short transmission had changed everything. From here on out, he would have to change modes from search to destroy.

Dan took a long drink directly from the rum bottle to settle his nerves and set to work. He brought in the satellite antennae from the veranda and took the phone and computer into the bathroom. His heart was racing. Until now, it had been research. From this moment on, he had to think like a criminal and cover his tracks.

He took out a screwdriver and began disassembling the computer. He removed the hard drive and immersed it in a plastic developing tray that contained a solution of hydrochloric acid strong enough to destroy the memory of everything that went on in Rome. Mac had told him of cases back in his Agency days when information had been retrieved from computers burned to a crisp in fires and from hard drives found on the bottom of the ocean.

Mac's bottle of acid was guaranteed to destroy all the evidence that would tie the computer or the sat-phone to calls to Cuba.

He gave the hard drive an extra thirty minutes in the solution before bathing the sat-phone. He had already smashed the innards, but a little acid wouldn't hurt. The last step was to destroy the memory chips of all the digital photos. Last to go was the cap camera itself. Everything was wiped clean of fingerprints, and he put on a set of rubber gloves before packaging the remaining parts into the suitcase that he would later throw off a bridge. Then he carried the case down to the underground garage and placed it into the trunk of the Fiat that had been repaired back to its original condition. He looked around to make sure he was alone before taking a small case out of the trunk and working on the passenger seat of the Fiat.

An hour later, the hypodermic needle was in place. He tested it several times before he was sure it would do the job Mac had designed it for. One sharp bump and the passenger would feel a slight prick of a bad seat spring. The tiny injection of the seashell poison would render the recipient paralyzed in one-hour. If it went as planned, Dan would have Mario, AKA Carlo, in his penthouse, where they would have a little chat.

Mac McDonald was one of the world's only possessors of the seashell toxin. The Agency had come across the solution in a rare experiment that had taken one hundred tons of clamshells to produce one small vial of toxin. When Mac had made his unscheduled departure from the Agency, he had taken the vial with him. Its contents, dropped into a reservoir, would wipe out an entire city. A small amount injected into a human body would cause death within seven days, with no sign of the toxin. There was no known antidote, because it was an unknown poison. Dan knew he would not have seven days to watch Carlo die, and he wanted to talk to him first.

The plan was to inject a diluted solution of the toxin and render Carlo helpless but conscious. There were things he wanted to know, and a second injection of sodium Pentothal would get the answers. A confession from Carlo would eliminate any last reservation Dan might have about killing him. Dan wanted a clear conscience when he put the SIG to Carlo's head and pulled the trigger. If something happened that caused doubts about Mario being Carlo, he would use the knockout drops and get the hell out of Italy. If that happened, he would have to give up the search for Carlo. There would be no second chance.

Dan placed a call to the gym the next morning and arranged a meeting. He would pick up Mario at the club at 6:00 p.m., go to the penthouse to look at the new shots and have a drink, then talk about the details of the contract.

He spent the rest of the day driving various routes from the gym to the hotel. Finding the right street with the right bump would be essential.

The first day Dan had tried driving in Rome, he had become hopelessly lost and had found that asking directions was even more confusing. He had finally paid a cab driver to let him follow the taxi back to his hotel. He paid extra to have the guy go at half speed. After that, he took a lot of taxis, using the car late at night to slowly learn the streets and the flow of traffic.

He knew the city fairly well now but needed to locate a street with a bump that would bounce Mario down on the needle that protruded from just under the leather. He found two that he felt would do the job. One was a pothole that made quite a jolt and was maybe a little too severe. The second place was better, a pipe excavation where the asphalt had not been replaced. Dan circled the block several times until he was satisfied with the speed the Fiat would have to be going to get the right jolt in the seat. Too fast, and the suspension would absorb the shock. Twenty kilometers an hour would be just right.

It was 10:30 in the morning, and Dan circled the block several times before finding a parking place a block from the gym. He was a few minutes early. He leaned back in the seat and took a series of deep breaths, then closed his eyes and shortened his breathing until he was in a tranquil state of mind. Then he went over every detail of the plan. He wondered why he should not simply invite Mario to the penthouse, pull out the SIG, and say, "Stick 'em up!" What then? Just kill him? No, he needed to subdue him. Carlo had to be conscious. He would stick to Mac's original plan of injecting ten CCs of sodium Pentothal directly into a vein. He needed all the answers before he could have closure on Lily's death. Mac's plan was specific. Paralyze, interrogate, and confirm – before pulling the trigger.

Mario was behind the desk talking to Toni when Dan entered. "Hi, Mario, Toni."

Mario waved, and Toni smiled and said, "Hello, Mr. Carter. Mario tells me you are recommending him to your office for the magazine's choice for Italy."

"Yes, I saw the proofs. They're drying on the line in my makeshift darkroom. We're going to have a look right now. They are only black and white but good enough for my first report. I shot a roll of color that the magazine insists on being processed in the States when I get back, which will be the day after tomorrow. Thanks to Mario's good looks and a well defined body, my work here is finished."

Mario's chest puffed a little and he smiled at Toni, who had his eyes on his boss. Mario closed the office door behind him and locked it. "I won't be back tonight to close up, Toni. See you tomorrow."

He lifted the heavy leaf in the counter and gently laid the varnished slab of mahogany back into place as he had done so many times before. He had a way of lowering the leaf that accentuated his triceps, which bulged under the tight sleeves of his shirt.

"Good night, Mario," they heard Toni say behind them before they exited the framed glass door and descended the stairs.

"I'm just around the corner," Dan said to Mario as they walked toward the Fiat.

So far, it was all going according to the plan, but the next forty-five minutes were going to be crucial. Dan found it difficult to stay calm. He knew he was not dealing with an exact science. Mac said the serum in the seat needle was more lethal than anthrax. What if the clam shit killed Mario right in the car? He'd be driving around Rome with a dead guy next to him. Just how accurate was the measurement that was supposed to paralyze him? Suddenly, he wanted to take off running, leave Rome, and forget the whole thing. He was not cut out for this shit. But the thought of failure was not something he could fathom.

He went over the plan again. He would have somewhere between thirty minutes to an hour after the pinprick before Mario would feel the effects of the paralyzing drug – plenty of time to get him up into the penthouse. From there, things would be easier.

Suddenly, a voice came out of nowhere. "Antonio! Antonio!"

A short girl about twenty years old rushed up and threw her arms around Mario.

Mario turned pale and gave her an affectionate kiss. He seemed confused and at a loss for words. "Anna, what are you doing here – so far from the apartment?"

"I was tired of sitting alone in the apartment, so I decided to take a walk. That was three hours ago. I got lost. I'm so lucky to have found you here."

She looked at Dan with a beautiful pair of hazel eyes and said, "Hello, I'm Anna." She extended her hand. "Antonio's fiancée. We are going to be married."

Dan took her hand and simply said, "James Carter," as he gave Mario a look.

Mario shrugged and said, "Antonio is my middle name."

Dan would call him Antonio in the presence of Anna. He didn't want to muddy the waters at this point, and he didn't want Mario fishing for explanations. Let him play his game.

He wondered if Anna was really his bride to be, or just another victim. "You are Italian?" he asked.

"Heavens, no. I am Brazilian. Antonio says no one will ever take me for an Italian the way I talk. You are American, yes?"

"Yes, from New York, and I don't think anyone will take me for an Italian, either."

She laughed. A wide smile displayed a set of straight white teeth.

Anna's sudden appearance seemed to bother Mario. "Anna, Mr. Carter and I have to tend to some business. We'll drop you at the apartment. I'll be along shortly."

Anna pleaded as she tugged on his arm. "Oh, Antonio, please let me go with you, wherever you are going. It's so lonely in the flat. I'll be quiet as a mouse. I won't be in the way. Please?"

"Okay, Anna, why don't you come along? I don't mind, and I'm sure Dan doesn't mind, do you?"

Dan had not planned on a third party, but with what was about to transpire, how could he leave this unsuspecting victim alone in Mario's apartment?

"I guess it will be okay." The words came out before he remembered about the seat.

Dan led the way to the car, evaluating the sudden change in plans. "I'm afraid it's going to be a little crowded, Anna. Maybe it would be best if you did take a taxi back to your apartment. Antonio won't be long."

"Nonsense, I can sit on Antonio's lap." She leaned her head against his shoulder as they walked. "We've been closer than that." She smiled and looked up at Mario with raised eyebrows.

Dan opened the passenger door and watched as Mario got in and Anna climbed in after him, playfully bouncing her butt on his lap. "Plenty of room, see?"

"Ouch! Jesus, Carter, what did you rent? Move up, Anna."

Dan could see Mario shift his weight to get away from the needle that had pricked his right cheek and sent the toxin into his system, and his mind started to race. How much time did he have now? If he took the direct route back to the hotel and bypassed the bump, how long would it be before Mario began feeling the effects of the poison? He had given himself an extra thirty minutes from the bump, but now he would have to change the route and head directly to the hotel, which was a good forty minutes in traffic. If Mario passed out now, or died, Anna would be a witness and he'd be swinging from the gallows within a year.

Why had he let Mac talk him into the clam stuff? There had to be other poisons that were safer. *That's a good one*, he thought. *A safe poison.* God, he was making jokes. He was losing it. He wanted to speed up and get to the hotel fast, but there was no way to go faster than the traffic ahead of him on the narrow streets. His nervousness showed.

"Take it easy, Carter," Mario said as he pecked Anna's cheek. "Don't let Rome's traffic get to you. Just go with the flow."

Dan's well-thought-out plan had suddenly changed. Now he needed to avoid bumps that might poke the needle up through the seat and prompt its discovery by Mario. He hoped Anna didn't get too playful and resume bouncing her ass on Mario's crotch.

The entire plan, the whole time in Rome, would be wasted if Mario suddenly became paralyzed before entering the penthouse. They would call for an ambulance, and Dan would have to get the hell out of the country. If he could just get Mario to the penthouse, he didn't really care if the guy died. But getting a confession as a result of the sodium Pentothal would put the ribbon on the already tied package. He had to get Mario into the penthouse. Instinctively, he put his foot down on the accelerator.

By the time they had reached the hotel, Mario was uncomfortable and moving around in the seat. "Move onto my other leg, Anna. My foot is going to sleep."

Damn, the stuff is starting to work already. Dan made the turn into the underground garage and squealed into his parking space. He tried to act nonchalant. "Well, here we are – safe and sound."

Mario had trouble getting out of the car. "Not any too soon. My whole leg is numb."

The elevator ride from the basement took forever. It seemed to stop at every floor. When they finally arrived at the penthouse, Dan moved quickly to the door, key already in hand.

Once inside, he felt relieved. "Welcome to the Excelsior. Can I get you a drink?"

"I'll take a gin and tonic if you have it," Anna said as she opened the double doors and stepped out onto the veranda.

Mario was walking around shaking his legs between steps. "A rum and Coke for me, Jimmy."

"With lemon? That would make it a *cubalibre*, wouldn't it?"

"Exactly." Mario had taken a seat on the sofa and was now rubbing the tops of his thighs with the palms of both hands.

"Ever been to Cuba, Antonio?"

"Yes, once. Lovely place. Can't say much for Castro, but the Cuban people are very friendly."

Dan mixed the drinks behind the bar. His hands shook at the mention of Cuba as he poured Coke over ice for himself. He was not sure what effect the alcohol would have on the poison now working its way through Mario's body, so he poured his drink with just a half shot of rum. He made Anna's drink with a double shot of Gilbeys and splashed it with quinine water.

Anna came in and took a seat next to Mario, who was leaning back on the sofa with a pained expression on his face.

"Something is wrong." Mario's voice was strained. "It feels like there are a thousand needles all over my body."

"Must be the altitude, Antonio," Dan joked. "When was the last time you were twelve floors up?" *Just a little longer,* he thought.

"No," Mario said. "My legs are completely numb, and my arms are falling asleep." His voice was softer now, almost a whisper. "My God, I can't move."

"Maybe I should get a doctor." Anna moved toward the phone on the bar. "I'll call the desk."

"No!" Dan said sharply.

Anna stopped and, with a startled expression on her face, turned to Dan.

Dan moved swiftly past her and reached behind the bar for the SIG semiautomatic.

"Don't move, Anna." He pointed the gun at her, and the ominous silencer emphasized the seriousness of the situation. "I don't want to kill you."

Anna stopped short of the telephone and stared at the gun. "What do you want with us? We have no money."

Mario was frozen. His eyes stared in disbelief.

"Please, Anna," Dan pleaded. "Sit in that chair. I'll explain everything. But first, you have to help me. He threw her a roll of gray duct tape. "Tape your legs around the chair."

Anna didn't move. "I don't understand. I'm just a poor girl from Brazil. If it's sex you want, you don't need a rope. I'll cooperate. Just don't hurt us."

"Just sit in the chair and tape your ankles. I promise to explain everything." His words were soft and reassuring. "Please, Anna."

Once Anna had bound her feet around the chair, he lowered the gun and moved behind her. "Now give me your hands." He secured her wrists behind the chair and took a deep breath and exhaled.

Dan looked at Mario. He was awake and wide-eyed, but unable to move.

Dan put the SIG back on the bar and knelt down in front of the terrified girl. He spoke softly. "Anna. Do not be afraid. I guarantee—"

Anna's lips were trembling.

"I guarantee that you have nothing to fear from me. I will not hurt you. I work for the government," he lied, hoping it would calm Anna. "Now listen. I have reason to believe that Antonio is not who he says he is, and I intend to prove it. Just be quiet and listen, okay?"

Anna nodded and Dan set to work. He left the room and came back with a small case that he opened and set beside Mario. This was the difficult part. He had never injected a needle into a person before. He had heard of people dying if the injection had air in it, which caused a bubble to go to the heart. Thank God for Mac's practice sessions. At the time, Dan had thought that sticking hypodermic needles under the skin of oranges was overdoing the training program.

Mario was starting to panic. His breathing was short and rapid. "What are you doing to me?" he rasped in a small voice.

Dan didn't answer. He wound the surgical tubing around Mario's bicep and tied it. The vein on the inside of his arm popped up, and Dan carefully picked up the syringe and removed the plastic protective cap from the needle. Then he pointed the needle up and pressed the plunger to remove any air.

"Are you going to kill me?"

"Maybe, but first we are just going to have a little chat, Antonio, or Mario, or should I call you Carlo? It is *Carlo*, isn't it? I'm going to record everything you say on this tape machine for the police. Then I'm going to give you a present from Lily."

Mario stiffened.

"You remember Lily, don't you, Carlo? She killed herself. She wouldn't go through life as a blind person. She hung herself, Carlo." Dan's eyes watered, and for a moment he forgot his mission of retribution.

"I don't know what you are talking about." Mario's voice was pleading. "You have me mixed up with someone else."

Anna began talking. "Please, that's enough. Let us go now. Antonio needs a doctor."

Dan paid no attention to her as he slipped the needle into the bulging blue vein. He emptied the syringe and dabbed the wound with cotton soaked in alcohol. *Don't die on me yet, pal.*

"That's just a little something to relax you, kind of a truth serum, Carlo, and the truth will either set you free" – he paused and looked into Mario's eyes – "or it will kill you."

"You promised you would not hurt us," Anna protested.

"Feel good now, Carlo?"

"Yes, I feel fine." His words were soft and clear.

Dan switched on the recorder and got right into it. "How much did they pay you for Lily's eyes?"

Carlo answered quickly, quietly. "Twenty-five thousand dollars."

"Plus expenses?"

"Yes, plus expenses."

"Plus all the free fucking you could get, right?" He couldn't help adding that.

"Yeah, something like that."

Anna sat helpless and watched in disbelief. The look of panic on her face had softened to an expression of interest.

"Who did the operation? Who took out the eyes?"

"Dr. Franz Stuben."

"Is that his real name?"

"I think so. He also goes by the name of Medina, Renaldo Medina."

"Where is this Dr. Stuben-Medina located? The address, Carlo."

"49 Via Romano, Room 416."

"How many are involved in the eye scheme?"

"I don't know. I just deliver the girls."

"Girls? How many girls have you delivered, Carlo?"

"Eleven."

Dan's heart sank at the thought of those girls – taking off the bandages, the horror of the families looking into the empty sockets. Eleven victims. He glanced at Anna. Tears were streaming down her face.

"Why both eyes? Why not just one?"

Carlo was in a sitting position with his head back against the sofa cushion. He spoke in a monotone voice, without hesitation. "So they could never identify anyone. They could never return to the doctor's office."

"Why the entire eye? Why not just the corneas?" Dan knew the answer, but he wanted it on the tape.

"Same reason. A cornea could be transplanted. There would be witnesses. By severing the optic nerve, there was no chance of future reprisals."

"One last question." Dan looked at Anna as he spoke. "Were you going to deliver Anna to the eye doctor?"

"Yes."

Anna was now sobbing.

Dan added one more question. "Did you have any feelings for Lily? Did you love her?"

"No. I don't get emotionally involved."

"You are a lowlife cocksucker, Carlo."

He didn't respond.

Dan wanted to get the SIG and blow the fucker's head off right there, but not in front of Anna. *Anna!* What was he going to do with Anna? He had not planned on a witness. She could identify him.

Anna realized the position she was in as she sat tied in the chair and watched Dan walk to the bar. "Please don't kill him," she blurted out.

He poured a half glass of rum and took a gulp. "You still have feelings for that piece of shit after what you just heard? He was going to cut out your eyes, Anna."

"I know, but killing him will make you just like him. Let the police take care of it. Please, Mr. Carter."

"Anna, I'm sorry you got mixed up in this. I have no reason to harm you, but I can't leave you here to be interrogated by the police."

Carlo was still on the couch. Saliva dribbled from the side of his mouth as he waited for Dan to decide his fate.

Dan sat at the bar looking at Carlo and Anna. He needed to improvise a new plan. He couldn't leave Carlo to continue his evil deeds, and he couldn't leave Anna behind, even if she promised to take the tape he'd made to the police. Carlo would turn the whole thing around, and he would have trouble getting out of Europe without being arrested. Staying and going to the police would be insane.

Dan ran another scenario through his mind and made a quick decision. Maybe with a few minor changes, he could work it out.

"Anna, if you cooperate with me, I'll see that you get safely back to Brazil."

Anna was studying him. "I won't be part of a murder. I can't."

Dan walked to Anna and untied her hands.

She was rubbing her wrists when he returned from the bar with a strong gin and tonic and handed it to her. *This must be a real nightmare for her,* he thought as he watched her raise the glass to her lips with shaking hands. "Do you have your passport with you?"

"Yes, I always carry my passport."

"Okay, look. If I promise not to kill him, will you come with me and cooperate?"

"I hate him," she said as she took a hard look at the feeble body on the couch. "He is a monster and should go to prison. If you promise not to kill him, I'll go with you and do whatever you want – but you must promise."

"Okay, untie your feet and help me get him onto the bed."

Dan and Anna dragged Carlo into the master bedroom and managed to get him onto the bed. He was in a semiconscious state, lying on his back and staring at the ceiling. Dan was not sure how long the poison would be effective, so he tied Carlo's hands and feet securely and taped his mouth.

He took Anna by the hand and led her out of the room but purposely left the door to the bedroom half open so Carlo could hear the conversation.

"First, I'll explain who I am, Anna. I am a paid assassin hired by the family of one of lover boy's victims, but your presence here changes things. I'm not going to kill him, but I am going to leave the tape recording for the authorities, along with a note. If you are a good girl, I'll put you back on a plane to Brazil, and I will return to Israel." He spoke loud enough for Mario to hear, hoping he would remember enough to tell the authorities where to look for him. It was a long shot, but better than nothing. And if they ever did locate Anna, all she could tell them was that he was a hired killer from the Middle East.

Dan took the medical case back into the bedroom. He kept Anna close by in case she made a run for it. He took out another syringe and filled it from another small bottle.

"What are you doing? You promised."

"I'm not killing him. This is a little more sodium Pentothal. He should sleep for another twenty-four hours, and by that time, we'll be long gone."

He emptied the syringe into Carlo's vein and threw the remnants into the bag. He watched as Carlo's eyes fluttered and closed. Then he slipped on a pair of black driving gloves and began wiping down the parts of the apartment that he had touched since he had cleaned his prints that morning.

"You should do the same, Anna. I can't be sure what kind of crime you've committed under Italian law, but tying up someone and just carrying them from one room to another constitutes kidnapping in the States. When you leave with me, you become an accomplice. Let's not leave any evidence behind."

The last thing he cleaned was the bar, the glasses, and the doorknobs.

When he was satisfied all fingerprints had been wiped clean, he took a handkerchief and picked up the phone.

The front desk answered immediately. "Good evening, Mr. Carter. How can I help you?"

"I'll be driving out to the country tonight and won't be back until the day after tomorrow. I have things here in the penthouse that I do not want disturbed. Please ask the maid not to come in."

"No problem, Mr. Carter. Have a nice trip."

The hotel would have no problem with its best guest leaving for a few days. Dan had paid his hotel bill that morning and left a deposit to cover charges for another week.

Before leaving, Dan took a look back into the room for a last check before facing Anna. "From here on out, we are going to be moving fast. I have to be able to trust you."

She nodded without saying anything.

They left the room and took the elevator to the underground garage. Dan put his two bags into the trunk and started the car.

Anna seemed calmer now. "You said he wouldn't die, that you would not kill him. That injection you gave him – it was just for sleeping, wasn't it?" She searched his eyes for the truth.

Dan didn't answer. He sat with both hands on the wheel and listened to the Fiat idle. Why hadn't he just put the SIG against Carlo's temple and pulled the trigger? Was it because of the sudden appearance of Anna, or was it that he just didn't have it in him to take a man's life, even Carlo's? His only direction for the last four months had been to find and kill Carlo. Now he could not go through with it. What was Mac going to say when he told him that he had left the son of a bitch sleeping like a baby with nothing but a tape recording left for the police, who might not even find it? When someone did find Carlo and turned him loose, he'd get to that tape first and destroy it. He thought about taking Anna back, tying her up, and killing Carlo.

Anna was waiting for an answer.

"No. He won't die from the injection. Wait here," he said as he turned off the car. "I need to get that tape."

He took out the keys and headed for the elevator. When the door closed, he pushed the penthouse button.

Anna was sitting patiently when Dan returned fifteen minutes later. He opened the trunk and tossed in a plastic trash bag. He did not look at Anna as he got in and started the car. Neither spoke as he drove out of the garage and into the Rome traffic.

He stopped the Fiat two hours later on a long bridge that spanned a slow-moving river and threw the suitcases over the railing. The last thing to go was the small plastic bag. He watched as it faded into the blackness.

A half-hour later while the Fiat was cruising along in the right lane at eighty miles an hour, Dan spoke to his passenger, who was looking straight ahead at the highway through the headlights, obviously in deep thought. "My name's Frank Roosevelt. Forget you ever knew a Jim Carter."

"You went back, didn't you?" she blurted out. "You went back and killed him."

"No, Anna. I did go back. But I did not kill him. I should have, but I didn't have the guts. I'll call the police in the morning and tell them there is a killer in the penthouse and I am sending a tape recording that explains everything."

They both let the subject drop.

At the airport in Prague, Dan purchased a ticket to Rio for Anna and slipped an envelope containing $5,000 of Mac's money into a flight bag.

He handed the bag to her and took her hand. "You are a lovely girl, Anna. I'm sorry you had to get mixed up in all this."

She looked up at Dan with a pained expression. "You must have loved her very much."

When he didn't answer, she put her arms around him. "Will I ever see you again, Frank – maybe in Rio?"

Dan looked into her hazel eyes and said, "I don't think so, Anna. You are a lovely girl, but—"

"I know. I would always remind you of Rome, of Mario – and her." She paused then said, "Thank you, Frank – or whoever you are. You saved my life. God bless you. I hope you find peace."

She turned and walked down the narrow corridor to begin the long flight back to Brazil.

Dan studied the layer of clouds as they slowly drifted by under the 747. He was finally at peace for the first time in months, drained of the hatred that had consumed his thoughts since Lily's death.

•

He had called the police from Madrid and given them the details, making sure they understood about the tape he had posted and the details of Carlo's eye-stealing scheme.

Dan leaned back in the seat and closed his eyes. He replayed the scenario again in his mind. *They must have found him sleeping soundly in the hotel room and taken him to a hospital, he thought.*

He envisioned Carlo waking up in a hospital bed and slowly becoming aware of the pounding in his head as he tried to focus the eyes that were not there. It would be like his lids were frozen shut. The harder he would try to open them, the more pain he would feel. Then Carlo would slowly begin to remember the events that had taken place in the last twenty-four hours. The hotel! The penthouse! Carter! He was still alive, but he could not open his eyes. He would reach up with his hands to pull his eyelids apart and gasp as his fingers found the empty sockets. "Oh God – *no!*"

Carlo would be in shock after realizing his eyes were gone, but the real screaming would begin when he suddenly became aware of the second pain in his body.

Dan smiled.

He would reach down for his manhood and find nothing but space. His eyes and his virility – gone – thrown off a bridge in a plastic sack somewhere north of Rome.

CHAPTER
37

Dan spun the four tumblers on the lock to 7-7-7-7. *What other combination would a former gambler choose?* he thought. The nine-dollar lock clicked open and freed the five-dollar Chinese bicycle that was chained to the palm tree.

He climbed on, wrestled with the loose handlebars, and swore at the pedals that kept slipping sprockets.

The chrome Yamaha was long gone: another casualty after Castro had thrown his latest turd into the punchbowl by closing the loophole that allowed foreigners to ride motorcycles owned by foreign medical students. The federal police had confiscated the Yamaha, and he had been forced to buy the piece of crap he was riding for one hundred and fifty dollars. It was the same bicycle Cubans could buy for five dollars if they could prove they had one of Fidel's pitiful government jobs.

By the time he had made it the half-mile to Papa's, he was seriously considering throwing the thing into the canal. It didn't matter. He was thinking about leaving Cuba as soon as he pulled the boat and painted the bottom. *Pass Line* had been sitting in the marina's polluted water and growing barnacles since returning from his Florida trip.

It had been two months since he had returned from Italy, and he had settled back into marina life. The episode with Carlo was a distant memory, as if someone else had tracked down the Italian and cut off his genitals.

He thought a lot about Lily and caught himself more than once thinking he saw her on the street.

It might be time to move on, he realized, but somehow the wind had been blown out of his sails. He lacked the desire to continue the long voyage he had originally begun. Maybe he'd stick around a while longer.

Graham, Lester, and Lenny were sitting with three other mariners at the bar when Dan walked in. The sailors who had gathered in Papa's were chuckling over something as Dan approached.

"Hey, what's going on?" Dan asked.

"Hi Dan," Graham said. "It's Manny. He's got problems again."

Dan wondered what kind of new trouble the marina's walking calamity could possible get into. "He can't be in trouble again; he's done it all."

203

"Up until now, we thought so, too," said Graham. "But he got busted again. He tried to leave the marina three days ago with a load of lobster he was going to sell in the Bahamas. That was bad enough. But when they found the lobster, they took a closer look and found Manny's girlfriend hiding under piles of rope in the *lazerette*."

"What happened?"

"They sent the girl back to her parents and impounded Manny's boat. He probably won't go to jail, but he'll lose his boat if he can't come up with the fine. He's under house arrest and can't leave the marina. Even you can't help him this time, Dan."

"Why does that make me feel relieved?" Dan said as he sat down and ordered a beer. "How does he do it? That guy attracts trouble like a magnet attracts pig iron."

The waitress brought Dan's bottle of Hautey and sauntered back to the bar.

Graham studied Dan and said, "What's up, Dan? You didn't even take in that nice-looking backside swinging its way back to the bar. New gal. Name's Luana. You sick or something?"

Dan smiled and tried to recover. "No, just a little bored. I've been thinking about heading out, but my heart isn't in it. I feel like that guy in the song that never got off the train in Boston, except I'm stuck in Hemingway Marina."

He awoke with a start from the tapping on the boat's cabin. He checked his watch. It was 2:00 a.m. "Shit," he mumbled. "Some fucking custodian thinks I got a girl in here."

Fletcher slid the hatch back, tossed the mosquito netting aside, and poked his head out. "*Que Pasa? No chicas aqui.*"

"Quiet, Dan. It's me, Mac. I'm coming aboard."

Mac heaved his heavy frame over the lifelines of the forty-foot sloop and made his way down the companionway. He was talking before he hit the deck.

"Sorry, Dan, I couldn't call. The phones are tapped, and they're listening to everything. You gotta get out of here. Out of Cuba."

"Why? What happened? Is there a war on?"

"Yeah. Looks like you started a war with some guys in Miami. There's an assassin squad on the island. You ever heard of a couple of guys named Alfonso and Ramon?"

"Yeah, Pencil-thin and Fat-face. I had a run-in with them during a cigar deal last year."

"Well, it looks like you crossed the wrong guys. They're well connected with the big guys here, and at eight o'clock this morning the secret police are coming to take you away. They're calling it a drug smuggling sweep. It's not a good scenario, Dan. Once you're arrested, it isn't like the States. The guys you pissed off want you out of the picture. Permanently.

"I got some friends in the big office, and they got hold of me. They know you're a friend of mine. I thought I'd better get over here and tell you. I figure you've got less than an hour to slip out of the marina. Hopefully you can sneak by the *Guardia Frontera* and clear the twelve-mile limit before daybreak. If you stay here, you'll either be prosecuted as a smuggler or your buddies from Florida will put a bullet in you."

Dan sat and listened to Big Mac spill it all out. He was thinking fast. The idea of leaving the marina at three in the morning without a clearance did not appeal to him, but the idea of taking up residence in a dungeon or getting his head blown off had less appeal.

"Thanks, Mac. I'm out of here. You'd better get back home. You going to be okay after coming here to warn me?"

Dan knew Mac had been connected at a high level with the Cuban government since his defection from the CIA. Still, he knew that Mac had taken a big chance warning him. If he were remembered entering the marina, he would have some explaining to do when Dan and his sloop were discovered missing at daybreak.

"Yeah, I'll be okay. You'd better get going." Mac reached out and took Dan's hand. "Good luck, Fletcher. See you in the movies." He ran up the stairs and disappeared into the darkness, moving gracefully for a big man.

Dan noticed that the security lights were off. He moved out from under the bimini and looked around the marina. All the lights were off – another of the regular power outages. If it lasted for another two hours, he could use the darkness to get out to sea undetected.

His mind raced as he went through his normal departure checklist. He had to forget warming up the auxiliary engine; the only way out would be under sail. There was a light breeze out of the east, and it would be a run down the canal and through the turning basin, then a hard right after he passed the customs dock. Hopefully the night watch would be snoozing. A boat under sail on a dark night might make it out.

It took thirty minutes to take in the electrical cord and the water hose, stow the fenders, and set the jib sheets. No time to stow the dinghy. He'd tow it behind.

As he was casting off the last dock line, a form sprinted from the shadows and jumped onto the bow.

"What the hell?"

"Dan! It's me: Manny. I'm going with you. I heard the news, and I got problems too. They're making a big sweep, and you're not the only one in trouble. Everyone who's ever taken a box of cigars out of here is on the list. Take me with you, Dan. My boat makes too much noise, and you know I can't sail out of here by myself anyway. Please!"

It was no use arguing. Although Manny was considered bad luck, it might be better having him than not.

The marina was dark and quiet as Dan and Manny moved silently down the one-hundred-foot wide canal, making a knot and a half on just the jib. A sliver of moon made visibility difficult, but they could make out the white hulls of the tied up boats.

Dan searched the darkness for any movement or even a flashlight. Everything was still.

It was normal to move from tie-up to the *Guardia* dock while waiting departure papers. Even with a 3:00 a.m. start; no one would suspect that a boat would make a run for it without the *Guardia's* approval. They cleared the canal, angled across the turning basin, and slipped past the immigration dock.

As they turned the corner, Manny was ready with the jib sheet.

"Keep it off the winch, Manny," Dan whispered. "Trim it by hand."

The sleeping guards would certainly hear the ratchet sound of the winch. They were no more than two hundred feet from the barracks.

The only sound was the lapping of the sea against the hull as the boat picked up speed on the new heading. He would like to have had the main up, but the added speed would make little difference if the military started shooting.

Dan checked the GPS and centered the small image of the boat on the screen. He had set the marina entry buoy as a waypoint; now all he had to do was follow the electronic course through the narrow channel and out to sea.

Manny crept back from the bow where he had been keeping watch and slipped into the cockpit. "I think there's a boat in the channel. Something white dead ahead."

Dan stood on the seat to get a better look over the dodger. He could just make out a white shape where there should have been water.

"Shit," Dan whispered. "You're right, Manny. It looks like the patrol boat is blocking the channel.

"Let's go back, Dan. We've done nothing wrong so far. We're still in the marina."

"Listen, Manny," Dan spoke in a quiet but affirmative voice. "We're not going back. It's got to be the patrol boat, and it looks like it's moored sideways between the markers. The channel is about a hundred feet wide, and that boat's only about thirty feet long. We'll slip around the stern. I doubt there's anybody aboard. Here, take the helm and maintain this course."

Dan scrambled below and moments later came back up carrying a small plastic case. He took the helm and said, "Open this and load the flare gun."

"Flare gun – you crazy? The last thing we need is light."

"Shut up, Manny. Just get ready with the flare gun and do exactly as I say."

They were closing on the white shape, and Dan could now make out the patrol boat and the red entry buoy behind it. He pulled Manny close. "When we're abeam of the patrol boat, fire a flare into the cabin. If you can get off two shots, do it."

"Jesus Christ, Dan, you're gonna get us killed."

"Goddamn it, Manny, we've got no time to argue. Just get ready."

Suddenly the marina was bathed in light.

"Fuck! What a time for Fidel's electric company to wake up. Get ready, Manny."

The floodlights that normally lit the channel suddenly became search-lights. The loud speaker broke the silence. "Vessel in the channel! You must stop and turn around. I repeat: you must stop and turn around. You must go back to the customs dock at once."

Manny was lying in the cockpit, yelling, "Give it up, Dan. Go back."

Dan aimed the boat between the patrol boat and the channel marker. It would be a tight squeeze, but there was room. He glanced toward the dock and saw men in uniforms running toward the old cannon that sat next to the green channel marker on the end of the dock a mere hundred feet away. If they started shooting, *Pass Line* would be hard to miss.

Manny had climbed down the companionway and was lying flat on the floor with his arms over his head, as if his bony limbs were going to protect his skull from .50 caliber machine gun slugs.

With Dan's only crewmember out of commission, he reached for the flare gun as the bow of the sloop passed aft of the patrol boat.

He had just gotten the flare shot off as the keel of the sloop hit the sub-merged stern line running between the marker pole and the patrol boat. It was not a sudden stop – more like running into a giant rubber band. When the sloop stopped, the wind in the headsail blew the bow to port. Dan's stern came to rest next to the stern of the patrol boat. *Pass Line* sat crossways in the channel, with the keel hung up on the mooring line and the wind holding the bow against the channel marker. The stern was firmly wedged against the Cuban gunboat.

Machine gun fire kicked up about the same time the flare started burning in the cabin of the patrol boat.

·

"Manny, get up here!" Dan reached down and hit the starter switch to the auxiliary engine. "Take this knife and see if you can cut that line we're hung up on."

Manny didn't move. He was still lying on the cabin floor with his hands over his head.

The gunfire stopped. The patrol boat was covering the sloop, and the *Guardia* could not get a good look at what was going on behind their own patrol boat that was now in flames. Dan reloaded, aimed the pistol, and lofted another magnesium flare in the direction of the customs house. The flare settled onto the palm-thatched roof, which began to burn.

The new fire and confusion onshore gave him time to run forward. He fished the mooring line up with the boat hook and cut *Pass Line* free just as a shot from the cannon hit the bow. The explosion blew him backwards against the boom, but he managed to throw both arms over the furled sail to steady him. He climbed back into the cockpit, slammed the throttle forward, and yelled, "Manny, where the hell are you? I need your help. We've been hit."

The explosion had jarred Manny into action. He climbed halfway out of the cabin and poked his head up with fear in his eyes. "There's a hole in the bow just below the waterline. The boat is taking on water. Give it up, Dan."

Dan revved the Perkins diesel up to 4000rpm, and the sloop began pulling away from the burning patrol boat.

"What are you doing, Dan? We're going to die. Give it up, for Christ's sake. Prison's better then death. Where the hell are we going?"

"Out to sea, Manny. With luck, we can make it past the twelve-mile limit before they catch up with us."

"Twelve miles?"

They were now clear of the burning patrol boat and moving broadside along the dock that was no more than a hundred feet away. Dan was expecting another cannon shot that would blow them out of the water, but it didn't come. Then he saw the remains of the ancient gun that was now out of commission. "Too many old beer cans stuffed in the barrel," he chuckled.

Dan concentrated on keeping the boat headed toward the friendly white glow of the light on top of the entry buoy.

"We just might make it, Manny. They don't have another boat, and even if they send one from Havana, we have a good chance of making it into international waters. See if you can stuff something into that hole down there."

"Fuck you, Dan. You can go die at sea without me. I'm swimming to Santa Fe. They don't know who I am. I'll walk back to my boat."

Manny dove into the channel before he had the words out of his mouth and began stroking the three hundred yards to the other side of the marina. In the confusion, the Coast Guard probably would not notice him, and even if they did, he would be back on dry land and back to his boat before they went looking.

Dan had no time to worry about Manny. He pressed the autopilot button to keep him on the course to the outer buoy and went below. There were already two inches of water in the cabin. He grabbed some pillows and began stuffing them into the two-foot hole the cannon had blown in the fiberglass hull just above the waterline. He managed to slow the flow of water, but some of the damage was under the V-berth, and there was no way to get to it easily from inside the boat. Even with the pillows held in place with the mop handle and two boat hooks, he could still see the water rising, slower than before, but it was now just a matter of time. He figured he had three hours, six tops, until the boat foundered.

He went topside and checked his position. He had passed the entrance buoy and was holding a three-hundred-degree heading. He could see the patrol boat behind him and the *Guardia* shack that were now fully engulfed in flames. He knew that there was no fire department in the marina, so the fires would keep them busy for a while. A chilling thought crossed his mind. *If they catch me before I get to the twelve-mile limit, I'm fucked. I'll be in one of their dungeons for life.*

Dan headed into the wind and went forward to raise the mainsail. He then went back to the cockpit, trimmed the Genoa, and changed course to 030 degrees. He throttled the engine back to 2,800rpm and read the GPS, which indicated the boat was still moving well at four and a half knots.

After checking to make sure he was showing no navigation lights, Dan went to work on the leak. He switched the bilge pumps from auto to manual. Then he pulled the whale-gusher handle from the *lazarette* and inserted it into the fitting in the cockpit. He moved the handle up and down for a few seconds before the water began flowing up out of the bilge and into the Florida Straits.

An hour had passed, and he was still free. He went below and checked the cabin. The water level was at about the same depth. The pumps were taking out the same amount that was coming in through the hole in the bow. Even with the tiring whale-gusher effort, it would not be long before he would have to abandon ship. He had to get out of Cuban waters before taking to the dinghy. He went topside and continued pumping.

Three hours later, he noticed the ground speed on the GPS had fallen to three knots. After checking longitude and latitude, he made his position at thirteen miles off the coast of Cuba in international waters.

·

After exhausting himself on the whale gusher for another four hours, the bow of the boat finally broke off. It was time to abandon ship. He had three gallons of water in the cockpit, along with the flight bag that contained the money. He might die adrift, but he would be damned if he was going to let the money that he had almost been killed for twice go down with the boat.

The bow was underwater and the mast was awash before he had climbed into the dinghy and set himself adrift.

Pass Line settled slowly at first, then seemed to hurry toward the bottom, as if the boat finally realized there was no hope. There was no splashing or big sucking action when she slipped beneath the surface, just a few bubbles. Then it was quiet.

CHAPTER
38

Dan lifted his head up from the floor of the dinghy and studied the horizon. *Nothin' but water.* His mouth was parched, and the sun had cooked every piece of exposed flesh bright red. He had been drifting for three days.

The wind had changed and was now blowing out of the east against the current, most likely keeping him in the same spot. With these conditions, he knew the best he could hope for was an easterly drift of one knot. He thought about the thousands of Cuban rafters that had thrown themselves into the same ninety miles of water and had hoped for the best.

He looked at the calm sea. Maybe there was a windsurfer floating by, sitting on his board waiting for more wind. He imagined himself sailing his board, hanging in the harness, feet in the foot straps with the wind blowing his hair back. Those were some good days in Baja. He vividly remembered skipping along outside the reef at Cabo Pulmo, knowing there would be another of Zeke's fish fries on the beach that night. Zeke was the world's best fisherman. His daily catch had fed the entire beach community of windsurfers. *A fried fish would taste pretty good right now,* he thought. *Hell, a raw fish would be okay.* He was no fool. He knew his situation was serious. His chances of drifting to land before dying of exposure and thirst were small. The chance of being spotted by a passing freighter was less than nil. He knew those ships never kept a visual watch, and the little dinghy wouldn't make much of a blip on radar. There was nothing to do but drift and wait. He passed the time trying to imagine the scene after he had left Carlo in the hotel in Rome. His cracked lips broke into a smile when he thought again about Carlo waking up.

How many times had Dan imagined the scene? How long had he been floating? It wasn't hot anymore. The sun seemed to be losing its heat. He felt cold.

When he looked up, she was there, sitting on the bow of the dinghy, as beautiful as she had ever been.

"Hi, Dan."

"Hi, Lily."

They drifted together for hours, talking and laughing about the times they'd had together.

Lily suddenly jerked her head around and looked to the horizon then back to Dan, who was still lying on the bottom of the dinghy. "Get up, honey, there is a boat coming."

He could not move.

Lily spoke again. This time she raised her voice. "Dan! Damn it, Dan! You've got to get up and signal the boat!"

Then he heard it. The sound was faint, but it was definitely the hum of an outboard motor. He picked up the white T-shirt tied onto the end of the oar and poked it skyward. He was too weak to stand on the slippery floor, but he made it to his knees and began waving the white flag back and forth.

"The flare gun, Dan. Send up some smoke. Use the flare gun, Dan."

He reached for the canvass bag on the floor of the dinghy and fumbled for the metal flare gun. He held the pistol over his head with both hands and fired the white smoking projectile into the air.

It seemed like forever, but the sound of the motor seemed to be coming closer. "I hear it, Lily." Dan looked to the bow, but she was gone.

He could make it out clearly now. A small white skiff was headed his way, with one man aboard waving with one hand and bailing furiously with the other. The boat was sitting low in the water and barely making headway.

The boat finally pulled alongside the dinghy, and Dan threw a line to a dark-skinned man in the little skiff.

He was about forty, wearing dirty white shorts, a light blue shirt, a baseball cap, and dark sunglasses. "*Hola*, my name is Julio. You by chance need a good outboard?"

Dan extended a hand with newfound energy. "Hi, friend, Dan Fletcher's the name. You by any chance need a good boat?"

The man laughed. "Sure. My motor, your boat. I'm going to Florida. I know the way. I've been there before. Good you fired the smoke."

They worked for a half-hour, bailing out the boat long enough to change the outboard from the sinking wooden skiff to the transom of the inflatable. Other than the rotted boat, Dan's new friend was well equipped. Julio had five gallons of water, ham, cheese, and some crackers, along with three cans of gasoline.

Dan's dinghy skipped along at a steady four knots, pushed by Julio's ancient nine-horsepower outboard as they motored toward the United States.

Julio thought about the chances of being caught. If they did catch him again, he'd try it again. He knew he could never be happy back on Fidel's island selling vegetables and black-market cigars.

Even though Dan Fletcher's luck had held and it appeared that he had been rescued, he felt empty inside. His companion might be going forward to a new and exciting life, but he was going backward to Florida, his starting point.

When *Son of Fury* was over, Tyrone Power just selected a new script and started a new film. But Dan's only movie was over, and it didn't have a happy ending. Instead of living on a tropical island with his lovely native girl, his closing scene was nothing more than a sad memory of lost love.

The steady hum of the outboard continued into the night as Dan and Julio stared into the darkness, looking for the lights of Key West.

AUTHOR'S NOTES

Marina Hemingway is based on personal experiences and information gathered while living aboard my sailboat in Cuba's Hemingway Marina between 1997 and 2002.

The names have been changed, but Graham, Lenny, Maverick, Manny, and Patch are real people. So is Big Mac, who continues dodging the CIA and wishes he really did own that kilometer-marker suitcase book.

Dan Fletcher's character is taken from several sailors, including a mental picture of the man I wish I were.

Lily's character is partly fiction, partly based on women I knew in Havana.

Dan's cigar smuggling trip to Florida is taken from the stories that circulated around the marina during my five-year stay in Cuba. It was common knowledge that private yachts left the marina on a regular basis loaded with Cuban cigars bound for Florida.

Julio was an acquaintance who motored his small skiff to within a few miles of Florida before the U.S. Coast Guard returned him to Cuba. Two Cubans did sail their Windsurfers to freedom, and the anecdote about driving the Buick to Strom Thurmond's beach house in Florida is based on a true story.

The character of Carlo and the Rome search is fiction, but the stealing of Lily's eyes is sadly based on a true incident.

The yacht race is based on the events of the Hemingway Christmas regatta of 1997, in which I had the misfortune of crewing aboard the yacht Fantasea.

The description of Hemingway Marina is mostly authentic. The dock master and marina workers attempted to make the facility a mariner's haven, but communist-appointed supervisors and Castro's KGB-style security forces thwarted their efforts.

Cuba, as though it were a company store, is owned and managed by Fidel Castro. When he eventually leaves the planet and the U.S.A. ends its ineffective embargo, Marina Hemingway will most likely take its place in the boating world as one of the Caribbean's most desirable yachting destinations.

ABOUT THE AUTHOR

Dick Barrymore is a master storyteller and internationally acclaimed lecturer and producer of ski adventure films.

He was born in Los Angeles, CA. After a short semester at Los Angeles City College and a four-year tour in the U.S. Air Force as a survival instructor, he worked with the U.S. Forest Service and the Los Angeles City Fire Department.

Barrymore left to pursue a career as a skiing cinematographer. He enjoyed success and notoriety as an award-winning ski filmmaker between 1960 and 1990, producing more than fifty films, including sixteen theatrical releases and a television series.

In 1997, Barrymore wrote his autobiography titled Breaking Even, published by Pictorial Histories Publishing Company. He was inducted into the United States Ski Hall of Fame in 2000.

Between 1997 and 2002, Barrymore lived on his sailboat in Cuba's Hemingway Marina, gathering material for his novel.

Barrymore is an active skier, surfer, and tennis player. He now lives with his wife in Cabo Pulmo, a small village in Baja, California. He can be reached via rdbmore@yahoo.com and www.dickbarrymore.com.

ISBN 141203756-5